THE
WALKING
DEAD

Other Books in the Walking Dead Series

ROBERT KIRKMAN'S

THE WALKING DEAD

SEARCH AND DESTROY

JAY BONANSINGA

PAN BOOKS

First published 2015 by Thomas Dunne Books
an imprint of St. Martin's Press

First published in the UK 2016 by Pan Books
an imprint of Pan Macmillan
20 New Wharf Road, London N1 9RR
Associated companies throughout the world
www.panmacmillan.com

ISBN 978-1-4472-7578-7

1 3 5 7 9 8 6 4 2

A cip catalogue record for this book is available from the British Library.

Printed and bound by CPI Group (UK) Ltd, Croydon, CR0 4YY

Visit **www.panmacmillan.com** to read more about all our books
and to buy them. You will also find features, author interviews and
news of any author events, and you can sign up for e-newsletters
so that you're always first to hear about our new releases.

Dedicated to All the Missing Children

ACKNOWLEDGMENTS

Special thanks to the Progenitor of All Things *Walking Dead*, the Great Mister Robert Kirkman; also love and gratitude to Brendan Deneen for tailoring the suit; Nicole Sohl for commandeering the ship; Justin Velella for extra-special events; and Susannah Noel for brilliant copy editing. Also a *grande gracias* to the poet warrior, Master Sergeant Alan Baker, for cleaning up my gun gaffs (and more); Andy Cohen, my manager extraordinaire; the staff and volunteers of The Walker Stalker Con, super-fans all; and Sean Mackiewicz for incredible ideas. Also major shout-outs to David Alpert, Shawn Kirkham, Mike McCarthy, Matt Candler, Dan Murray, Ming Chen, Melissa Hutchison, Dixon Martin, Lew Temple, John and Linda Campbell, Jeff Siegel, Spence Siegel, and my amazing sons, Joey and Bill Bonansinga. The biggest thank you of all shall be saved for last: I owe everything I write, everything I am, and everything I dream, to the love of my life, the brilliant and beautiful Jill M. Norton.

PART 1

Stone Soup

Rescue those who are being taken away to death;
hold back those who are stumbling to the slaughter.

—Proverbs 24:11–12

ONE

On that sweltering Indian-summer morning, not a single person working the rails has any clue as to what is transpiring at that very moment in the small survival settlement once known as Woodbury, Georgia. The restoration of the railroad between the village of Woodbury and the outer suburbs of Atlanta has consumed these people—occupying every daylight hour for nearly twelve months now—and today is no exception. They are closing in on the midway point of the project. In a little less than a year, they have cleared nearly twenty miles of track, and have laid down a sturdy barrier of split-rail and chicken wire on either flank in order to keep the line clear of roamers, stray feral animals, and any other obstruction that might blow, seep, grow, or creep across the tracks.

Now, oblivious to the catastrophe unfolding right then in her home community, the crew's de facto leader, Lilly Caul, pauses in her post-hole digging and wipes the sweat from her brow.

She glances reflexively up at the ashen sky. The air, buzzing with the drone of insects, is redolent with the fecund stench of fallow, neglected farm fields. The muffled clang of sledgehammers—spikes going into ancient railroad ties—provides a syncopated drumbeat to the thudding diggers. In the middle distance, Lilly sees the tall woman from Haralson—the one who goes by the name of Ash—patrolling the edge of the worksite, a Bushmaster AR-15 on her hip. Ostensibly, she's keeping watch for any stray walkers who might be drawn to the construction clamor, but on a deeper level, she's on hyperalert today. Something doesn't feel right. Nobody can articulate it but everybody senses it.

Lilly peels off her soiled work gloves and flexes her sore hands. The Georgia sun hammers down on the back of her slender, reddened neck where her auburn hair is pulled up in a haphazard French braid. Her hazel eyes, buried in the fine crow's-feet of her skin, scan the area, surveying the other workers' progress along the fence line. Although still a few years shy of forty, Lilly Caul has developed the worry lines and wrinkles of a much older woman. Her narrow, youthful face has darkened over the four hard years of plague life. Her boundless energy has flagged in recent months, and the perpetual slump of her shoulders has given her a middle-aged air, despite her trademark hipster attire of tattered Indie-rock T-shirt, ripped skinnies, broken-down motorcycle boots, and countless rawhide bracelets and necklaces.

Now she notices a few errant walkers a hundred yards to the west, dragging through the trees—Ash notices them as well—nothing to worry about at this point but still something on which to keep tabs. Lilly regards the other members of her crew spaced at regular intervals along the rails, slamming post-hole diggers into the stubborn ground cover of kudzu and ironweed. She sees some familiar faces, some unfamiliar, some she just met days ago. She sees Norma Sutters and Miles Littleton, inseparable since they joined the Woodbury clan over a year ago. She sees Tommy Dupree, the boy now fourteen going on thirty, hardened by the pandemic, a prodigy with firearms and edged weapons. She sees Jinx Tyrell, the loner from the North who proved herself to be a walker-killing machine. Jinx moved into Woodbury a few months ago after being recruited by Lilly. The town needs new citizens in order to flourish, and Lilly is exceedingly thankful to have these badasses on her side of the playing field.

Interspersed among Lilly's extended family are the leaders of the other villages that dot the ramshackle countryside between Woodbury and Atlanta. These are good, trustworthy people such as Ash from Haralson, and Mike Bell from Gordonburg, and a number of others who have joined Lilly's crew out of common interests, common dreams, and common fears. Some of them are still a bit skeptical of the grand mission to connect the survivor towns with the great city to the north via this rough-and-tumble rail line, but many have joined the cause purely out of a belief in Lilly Caul. Lilly has that effect on people—a sort of osmosis of hope—and the longer these people work on this project, the more they buy into it. They see it now as both an admirable attempt to control an environment that is out of control as well as an attempt to recapture a lost civilization.

Lilly is about to put her gloves back on and get back to her digging when she sees the man named Bell about a quarter mile away, coming around a bend from the north at a fast canter on his swaybacked horse. The thirty-something leader of the small survivor group hunkered down in the little village once known as Gordonburg, Georgia, is a diminutive man with a mop of sandy hair that now bounces and flags in the wind as he approaches the work crew. Some of the others—Tommy, Norma, Miles—glance up from their work, ever protective of their friend and leader.

Lilly hops the guardrail and walks out onto the gravel apron as the man approaches through the haze on his mangy strawberry roan.

"Got another one in our path," he calls out. The horse is a twitchy animal, thick in the neck, probably a cross-breed with a trace of draft horse in its blood. Bell rides with the awkward, bouncy clumsiness of the self-taught. He yanks back on the reins and staggers to a stop on the gravel, raising a small whirlwind of dust.

Lilly braces the horse by grabbing the bridle and steadying its wildly nodding head. Dirty foam drips from its mouth, its coat damp with sweat. "Another *what*?" She looks up at Bell. "Walker? Wreck? Unicorn . . . *what*?"

"Big old trestle," Bell says, sliding off the horse and hitting the ground hard with a grunt. A former IT guy from Birmingham, his boyish face sunburned and slathered with freckles, he wears homemade chaps stitched from tent canvas. He fancies himself a country boy but the way he wrestles with the horse and speaks only with the faintest trace of drawl screams city. "About a half mile north of here," he says, jerking his thumb. "The land ditches, and the tracks go right across this rickety span for about fifty yards."

"So what's the prognosis?"

"You mean with the trestle? Hard to tell, the thing's pretty furry."

"Did you take a closer look? Maybe ride across it, test it or whatever?"

He shakes his head. "I'm sorry, Lilly, I just thought you'd want to know about it right away."

She rubs her eyes and ponders. It's been a while—months, actually—since they've encountered a trestle. And the last one was only a few yards long. She starts to say something when the horse rears suddenly—spooked by either a noise or an odor undetectable by humans. Lilly girds the animal, gently strokes its withers. "Ssshhh," she utters softly to the creature, rubbing it along its tangled mane. "It's okay, buddy, chill out."

The animal has a goat-like scent, musky from its sweaty spoor and filth-encrusted fetlocks. Its eyes are rimmed in red from its labors. The fact is, this broken-down roan—and its species as a whole—has become as valuable to survivors now as they were in the nineteenth century to those attempting to tame the West. Cars and trucks that are still operational are getting more and more rare every day—even the supplies of cooking oil for the biodiesel are dwindling. People who have had even a rudimentary knowledge in horse breeding in their prior lives are now becoming highly sought after and respected as wise elders who are expected to teach and pass on their knowledge. Lilly has even recruited a few to live in Woodbury.

In recent months, many of the rusted-out carcasses of cars have been sliced in half and made into makeshift buggies and contraptions to be hitched to horses and teams of horses. In the years since the outbreak, the pavement has weathered and deteriorated beyond repair. The remaining strips of weedy, crumbling, impassable pathways are the bane of survivors' existence. Hence the need for a safe, dependable, and fast transportation system.

"He's been like this all day." Bell nods deferentially at his horse. "Spooked by something out there. And it ain't walkers, neither."

"How do you know it isn't walkers? Maybe a swarm coming or something?"

"We passed a bunch of 'em this morning, and the things didn't even faze him." He strokes the animal and whispers to it: "Did they, Gypsy? Did they?" Bell looks at Lilly. "There's something else on the wind today, Lilly. Can't put my finger on it." He sighs and looks away like a shy schoolboy. "I'm sorry I didn't check the trestle for stability—that was pretty goddamn stupid of me."

"Don't sweat it, Bell." Lilly gives him a smile. "I think the old saying goes, 'We'll cross that bridge when we come to it'?"

Bell chuckles a little too loudly, holds her glance a little too long. Some of the others pause in their work and glance up at the twosome. Tommy leans on his shovel and smirks. It's basically an open secret that Bell has a desperate crush on Lilly. But it's also not something Lilly wants to perpetuate. Taking care of the Dupree kids is all she can handle in her personal life at the moment. Plus, she's still grieving the loss of just about every person she ever loved. She's not ready to dive into a relationship yet. But that doesn't mean she doesn't think about Bell sometimes, usually at night, when the wind whispers through the gutters and the loneliness presses down on her. She thinks about running her fingers through Bell's gloriously thick ginger-colored hair. She thinks about feeling the downy touch of his breath on her collarbone. . . .

Lilly shakes off the wistful ruminations and pulls an old Westclox turnip watch from her hip pocket. Attached to a tarnished fob, the watch once belonged to the late Bob Stookey, Lilly's best friend and mentor, a man who died heroically a little over a year ago trying, among other things, to save the children of Woodbury. Perhaps this is why Lilly has all but adopted the town's orphans. Lilly still mourns her lost pregnancy, the spark that could have been Josh Hamilton's child, miscarried in the tumult of the governor's regime. Maybe that's why her ersatz motherhood now feels almost like part and parcel of survival itself—an innate piece of her future as well as the future of the human race.

She looks down at the yellowed face of the watch and sees that it's edging toward lunchtime.

She has no idea that her town has been under attack now for nearly an hour.

When Lilly was a little girl, her widower father, Everett Caul, once told her the story "Stone Soup." A well-loved folk tale with myriad versions existing in many different cultures, the story tells of three wandering strangers who are starving when they come upon a small village. One of the strangers hits on an idea. He finds a pot in the town trash heap and gathers some stones and collects some water from a nearby creek. Then he builds a fire and starts cooking the pebbles. The villagers get curious. "I'm making stone soup," he tells them when asked what the hell he's doing, "and you're welcome to have some when it's finished." One by one, the residents begin to pitch in. "I've got some carrots from my garden," offers one. "We've got a chicken," says another. And soon, the stone soup is a bubbling caldron of savory goodness with vegetables and meats and herbs from the various homes.

Perhaps the memory of Everett Caul's beloved bedtime story lay in the back of Lilly's mind when she decided to connect the small survivor towns in her area with the big city to the north via the defunct railroad.

She had first thought of the idea last year, after meeting with the leaders of the five principal communities. Initially, the purpose of the meeting—which took place in Woodbury's venerable old courthouse building—was to share resources, information, and goodwill with the other towns in Central Georgia. But when the leaders of the five communities began to vent about their supplies dwindling and travel becoming so dangerous and the feeling of being so isolated out in the rural wastelands, Lilly decided to take action. She didn't tell anybody her plan at first. She merely began to clear and repair the old petrified rails of the West Central Georgia Chessie Seaboard line that runs up through Haralson, Senoia, and Union City.

She started small, a few hours a day, with Tommy Dupree, a pickax, a shovel, and a rake. It was slow going at first—a few hundred feet a day in the blistering sun—with the walkers continually being drawn to the noise. She and the boy had to repel countless dead in those early days. But walkers were the least of their problems. It was the land that gave them the most grief.

Nobody is certain of the causes, but the postplague ecosystem has changed over the last four years. Opportunistic weeds and wild grasses have taken over to the point of choking culverts, clogging creek beds, and virtually carpeting roads. Kudzu vines have multiplied in such profusion that entire billboards and barns and trees and telephone poles have been literally covered in riotous tendrils. The green rot has turned everything furry with vegetation, including the countless human remains still lying in gullies and trenches. The world has grown hair, and the worst of it seems to have seized up the iron rails of the Chessie Seaboard line in stubborn braids of flora as thick as cables.

For weeks, Lilly and the boy chipped away at the unforgiving vines, sweating in the sun, moving a hand-car northward over cleared sections with laborious slowness. But the noisy work—not unlike the bubbling pot tended by the strangers in the "Stone Soup" story—attracted curious glances, folks peering over the walls of survivor towns along the way. People began coming out and pitching in. Before long, Lilly had more help than she ever anticipated. Some folks volunteered tools and construction equipment such as augers, hand mowers, and scythes. Others brought along maps of derelict rail lines found in public libraries, hand-cranked two-way radios for communication and reconnaissance purposes, and weapons for security. There seemed to be a general fascination with Lilly's quixotic mission to clear a rail all the way to Atlanta. In fact, this fascination spurred an unintended development that surprised even Lilly.

By the second month of the project, people started seeing Lilly's foolhardy undertaking as a harbinger of a new era, perhaps even a bellwether of a new postplague regional government. And nobody could think of a better person to be the leader of this new regime than Lilly Caul. At the outset of the third month, a vote was taken in the Woodbury courthouse, and Lilly was unanimously voted the town figurehead—much to her chagrin. She didn't fancy herself a politician, or a leader, or—God forbid—a *governor*. At best, she considered herself middle management.

"In case anybody's interested," a voice behind Lilly says as she digs in her pack for her meager lunch, "we just crossed the twenty-five-mile marker."

The voice comes from Ash. She carries herself with the pronounced swagger of a jock, all bowlegged and muscle-bound. Today she has a Vietnam-era canvas bandolier of twenty-round magazines canted across her Hank Williams Jr. tank top and a do-rag bandanna around her coal-black hair, all of which belies her aristocratic former life in the wealthy enclaves of the Northeast. She ambles up with a half-eaten can of Spam in one hand and a wrinkled map in the other. "This seat taken?" She points to an unoccupied stump.

"Take a load off," Lilly says without even looking up, digging in her canvas rucksack for the stale dried fruit and beef jerky that she's been rationing for weeks. She sits on a mossy boulder as she pulls out her delicacies. Lately, only edibles with long shelf lives—raisins, canned goods, dried meats, soup mixes—are all that's available in Woodbury. The gardens have been harvested to the nubs, and it's been a while since any wild game or fish have drifted within killing range. Woodbury needs to expand its farming capabilities, and for months now Lilly has been tilling the earth around the periphery of town.

"So let's do the math." Ash puts the map in her back pocket, sits down next to Lilly, spoons another gob of Spam into her mouth, and savors the processed meat as though it were foie gras. "We've been at it since last June. At this rate—what? We hit the city by next summer?"

Lilly looks at her. "Is that good or bad?"

Ash grins. "I grew up in Buffalo, where construction lasts longer than most marriages."

"So I guess we're doing okay."

"Better than okay." Ash glances over her shoulder at the others scattered along the site. They are currently devouring their lunches, some sitting on the rails, some of them in the shade of enormous, twisted, ancient live oaks. "I'm just wondering if we can keep up the pace."

"You don't think we can?"

Ash shrugs. "Some of the folks have been complaining about the time spent away from their people."

Lilly nods and glances out at the jungle of kudzu twining and weaving over the land. "I'm thinking we can take another break this fall when the rainy months roll in. It'll give us a chance to—"

"Excuse me if I sound like a broken record," another voice chimes in from behind Ash, interrupting and drawing Lilly's attention away from the dense jungle of vegetation to the east. She sees the gangly, knob-kneed man in the fedora and khaki shorts loping toward them from the ring of horses. "But is there a reason nobody has a clue as to what our fuel situation is?"

Lilly sighs. "Take a breath, Cooper. Eat some lunch, get that blood sugar back up."

"This is no joke, Lilly." The rawboned man stands before her with his hands on his hips as though waiting for a report. He has a Colt Single Action Army .45 holstered on a Sam Browne belt around his waist and a coil of climbing rope on the opposite hip. He juts his prominent chin as he speaks, affecting an air of rakish adventurer. "I've been through this too many times."

Lilly looks at him. "Been through *what*? Was there another plague that I missed?"

"You know what I mean. I just came from the depot in Senoia, and they still haven't found any fuel up there. Lilly, I'm telling you, I've seen too many projects fall by the wayside because of fuel issues. If you remember, I was involved in designing—"

"I know, you've told us that one before, more than once, we got it memorized, your 'firm designed more than a dozen of the biggest skyscrapers in Atlanta.'"

Cooper sniffs, his prominent Adam's apple bouncing with frustration. "I'm just saying . . . we can't do a damn thing without fuel. Without fuel, we're just cleaning up metal rails that go nowhere."

"Cooper—"

"Back in '79, when OPEC goosed the oil prices and Iran shut down their fields, we had to completely write off three buildings on Peachtree. Just left their foundations like dinosaurs in the tar pits."

"Okay, listen—"

Another voice rings out behind Ash. "Hey, Indiana Jones! Give it a rest!"

All heads turn toward Jinx, the young drifter whom Lilly took in earlier this year. A volatile, brilliant, bipolar mess of a person, Jinx wears a black leather vest, myriad tattoos, multiple knives sheathed on her belt, and round steampunk-style sunglasses. She approaches at a fast clip, her hands balled into fists.

Cooper Steeves backs away as if giving quarter to a rabid animal.

Jinx gets in his face, her body as tense and coiled as a watch spring. "What is this compulsion of yours to bust this woman's balls every fucking day?"

Lilly stands and waves Jinx back. "It's okay, sweetie, I got this."

"Back off, Jinx. We're just having a conversation here." Cooper Steeves's bluster thinly veils his fear of the young woman. "You're way out of line."

By this point, Miles and Tommy have sprung to their feet behind Ash with cautious expressions knitting their faces. Over the past year, probably more due to the heat than the stress of being out in the open, there have been horrendous arguments and even a few fistfights along the train line. Everybody has their guard up now. Even Norma Sutters—the zaftig, Zen-like former choir leader—now cautiously moves her plump right hand to the grip of her .44.

"Everybody dial it down!" Lilly raises her hands and speaks tersely, firmly. "Jinx, back off. Cooper, listen to me. You're raising legitimate issues. But the truth is, we're making progress on cooking up more biodiesel, and we got that one engine in Woodbury we've already converted. Beyond that, we've got the horse-drawn flatcars and a few handcars to get us where we need to go until we get more engines running. Okay? You happy?"

Cooper Steeves looks down at the dirt, letting out a frustrated sigh.

"Okay, everybody! Listen up!" Lilly gazes out beyond the group around her to the rest of the crew. She squints up at the flinty sky, then back at her people. "Let's finish up with lunch and get another hundred yards cleared and fenced off before we knock off for the day."

By four o'clock that afternoon, a thin layer of clouds has rolled in and stalled over Central Georgia, turning the afternoon gray and blustery. The breeze carries the smell of rust and decay. The daylight diffuses to a pasty glow behind the hilltops to the west. Exhausted, sweaty, the back of her neck prickling with inexplicable nervous tension, Lilly calls an end to the workday when she finally sees Bell's offending trestle in the middle distance ahead of them. The rails follow the span across a densely forested gulley like the bulwark of a Gothic drawbridge, an ancient broken-down span of mildew-black timbers tangled in vines and wild ivy, crying out for repair and reinforcement—a massive undertaking that Lilly is more than willing to put off until tomorrow.

She decides to ride home alongside Tommy Dupree in one of the makeshift horse-drawn carriages—a burned-out shell of a former SUV, the engine, front wheels, and quarter panels removed to accommodate a pair of draft horses tied to the jutting stubs of its frame. Tommy has rigged a system of elaborate reins and slipknots to the team, and between the snorting and clopping of the animals, and the creaking and squeaking of the jury-rigged cab, the whole thing makes quite a racket as they wend their way down the dirt access road that descends into the tobacco fields to the south.

They travel mostly single file, Tommy's carriage in the lead, followed by the rest of the work crew, some on horseback, some in similar hodgepodge conveyances.

When they reach Highway 85, some of the team splits off from the group to return to their communities to the north and east. Bell, Cooper, and others proffer nods as they turn westward and vanish into the haze of the dying afternoon. Ash gives Lilly a wave as she leads a half dozen of her fellow residents of Haralson around the petrified remains of an overturned Greyhound bus lying across the northbound lanes of the highway. The years have blanched and covered the wreckage with such thick vegetation that it looks as though the earth itself is in the process of reclaiming the bus's metal shell. Lilly looks at her fob watch. It's already after five. She would prefer to make it home before nightfall.

They don't see signs of the attack until they reach the covered bridge at Elkins Creek.

"Wait—hold on—what the fuck?" Lilly has moved to the edge of the cab's bench seat, and now leans forward, peering up at the tarnished pewter sky over Woodbury about a mile and a half away. "What the hell is—?"

"Hold on!" Tommy snaps the reins and leads the carriage through the darkness of the covered bridge. "What *was* that, Lilly? Was that *smoke*?"

The gloomy shadows swallow them for a moment as the horses labor to pull the buggy through the malodorous enclosure, the noise bouncing off weathered planks. When they come out the other side, Jinx has already zoomed past them and spurred her horse up an adjacent hill.

Lilly's heart begins to race. "Jinx, can you see it? Is that smoke?"

At the crest of the hill, Jinx yanks her horse to an awkward halt and reaches for her binoculars. She peers through the lenses, then goes perfectly still. Fifty feet below her, Tommy Dupree brings the carriage to a rattling stop on the access road.

Lilly can hear the others pulling up behind her. Miles Littleton's voice: "What's going on?"

Lilly hollers up at the young woman on the horse. "Jinx, what *is* it?"

Jinx has gone as stiff as a mannequin as she peers through the binoculars. In the distance, a column of smoke as black as India ink spirals up from the center of town.

TWO

They approach from the northeast, the horse-cart rumbling over petrified rails as it crosses the switchyard. The air crackles and reeks with the odors of burning timber and cordite. Walker bodies litter the vacant lot near the train yard, the adjacent barricade punctured with necklaces of bullet holes. Inside the wall, several buildings exude thin spires of smoke from either fires or sustained volleys of gunfire. Lilly pushes back the urge to charge into the fray with guns blazing—she needs to assess the situation first, gauge what they're up against. For the last ten minutes, she has been trying unsuccessfully to raise David Stern on the hand-cranked two-way, and now the radio silence reverberates in her brain.

She sees a car with its windshield shattered, its driver's door gaping near the corner of Dogwood and Main, indigo smoke billowing up into the winds from a nearby section of the barricade that's been knocked down. Lilly's heart chugs faster as she takes it all in—the smoldering fires inside the wall, the bullet-riddled panels, the shattered windows, and the tire tracks and debris strewn across the vacant lot between Jones Mill and Whitehouse Parkway. Those circular tracks and the innumerable pieces of shredded cardboard and broken glass hadn't been there earlier that day when the construction team departed town.

Lilly checks her pistol. The Ruger SR22 has been by her side since the early days of the plague. A former resident of Woodbury named

Martinez found six in a Walmart once, and he gave Lilly two of them. From the beginning, the best thing about the weapon has been the abundance of compatible ammo: .22 long rifle bullets were sold in most sporting goods stores across the South for less than five cents per round, and Lilly had usually managed to scavenge cartons on shelves or in lockers or desk drawers wherever she went. There always seemed to be leftover boxes of American Eagle or Remington hollow points lying around. But that was *then*, and now is now, and lately the larder has been bare. Lilly is down to her last hundred CCI copper-plated rounds, so she's using them judiciously, trying not to waste them on walkers when an edged or blunt weapon will do just as well.

"Let's ditch the carts and horses, go in on foot," she orders Tommy, who snaps the reins and guides the team around the north corner of town. He pulls up next to a small grove of palmettos, yanks the horses to a stop, and climbs out of the carriage to tie the reins to a branch. Lilly throws a glance over her shoulder and sees Jinx and Miles coming up fast on their horses, Norma on her carriage, raising dust devils in the noxious wind. They awkwardly tug their animals to a stop, dismount, and check their weapons. Lilly clicks the Ruger's release and pulls the magazine, checking the rounds. The mag is full, ten rounds ready to rock. "It looks like whatever happened here already happened."

The grave tone in her voice—an unintentional doom-laden air that speaks more of exhaustion than of terror—gets Tommy's attention.

"Who would do this?" Tommy's voice comes from the depths of his gorge, thick with anguish and horror, as he gazes out across a derelict red-brick post office with boarded windows and ancient, faded signboards of smiling postal carriers and freshly scrubbed families overjoyed to be receiving parcels from their aunt Edna. "Why the fuck would anybody—?"

"Focus, Tommy." Lilly points off at the dense thicket of trees to the south. "We'll go in through the south gate . . . if the fucking gate is still there." She glances over her shoulder at the others. "Keep your eyes open for hostiles. Stay low, keep quiet, and watch your backgrounds." Nods all around. "Okay, let's do it."

A tide of emotion rises in Lilly as she turns and leads them past the Piggly Wiggly toward the gate. The silence presses down on them. No sign of David or Barbara yet, no sounds of any residents inside the barrier. No walkers in sight. *Where the fuck is everybody?* Electric adrenaline jolts down Lilly's spine, the urge to storm the town so strong it nearly takes her breath away. She thinks of the Dupree kids in there somewhere, the Sterns, Harold and Mama May and Clint Sturbridge. But she bites down on the compulsion to charge inside. Right now, the immediate priority is threat assessment. They need to investigate quietly, quickly, and see what they're up against.

For a moment, Lilly finds her gaze being drawn to the woods beyond the supermarket parking lot. She can see dozens of walker remains along the edge of the forest, still bound in a thick blue haze of gun smoke.

In the back of her mind, the forensic details accumulate, painting a picture of the attack. Whoever invaded the town probably came from the northeast, taking out the undead stragglers that populated these woods this morning. And from the looks of the carnage—most of the creatures are dispatched with single head shots, neatly lined up along the periphery of the pines—Lilly starts to deduce that the assailants were very organized, very skilled. *To what end, though? Why spend the resources and energy on such a costly venture as attacking a town?*

She stuffs the panic back down her throat as they scuttle across Folk Avenue and approach the gate. Over the last year, Woodbury has grown more and more self-sustainable—another long-term goal of Lilly's—both outside the wall and within its confines. These small single-story homes along Folk have been retrofitted with makeshift solar panels, huge tanks of filtered pond water for showering and laundry purposes, and massive compost areas in the backyards for fertilizer. A few months ago, David Stern began collecting horse droppings for the compost heaps in an effort to put every last shred of their natural resources to good use.

Lilly pauses outside the gate and speaks quickly, whispering loud enough to be heard above the wind. "Stay together, eyes wide open, no talking unless absolutely necessary, and conserve your ammo. You run into a walker, use a blade. And don't wander. I don't want anybody getting ambushed."

Tommy swallows hard. "What if it's a trap?"

Lilly looks down, draws back the Ruger's slide, peeks in the chamber, and confirms that there's a round ready to go. Then she makes sure that the safety is disengaged and finally glances up at Tommy. "If it's a trap, we fight our way out of it."

With a nod, she grips her gun with both hands and leads them through the gap.

For the first couple years of the plague, survivors learned a hard truth about each other: while the walking dead certainly pose major challenges for people, the sad truth is, the real dangers come from the living. For a while, the world of the living evolved into a crucible of tribal conflicts, barbarism, opportunistic crimes, and territorial pissing matches. But lately, it seems that instances of survivor-on-survivor violence have become more and more rare. Unprovoked attacks are far less frequent now. It's almost as though survivors have grown leery of the cost of conflict—too time-consuming, disruptive, and just plain illogical. Egos have been sublimated by the imminence of extinction. Energy is better spent on the defensive now. All of which is why Lilly and her crew are so mystified by the aftermath of this inexplicable attack. Even more confounding is what they find lying on the ground at the base of the courthouse steps.

"Hold up!" Lilly hisses at the others, jerks a hand up, and then waves everybody against the wall of an adjacent alley, which faces the wooded square in front of the quaint little building.

With its chipped white paint, decorative columns, and copper-colored capitol dome, the Roman-style courthouse has been around for over a hundred years, and since the outbreak it's served as a sort of community nerve center for the town. The various regimes that have been in power here—including the tyrannical Philip Blake—have used the building for ceremonial meetings, debriefings, planning sessions, and the storage of common resources. To this day, the council of the five villages meets in the building's back room. But now, the double doors at the top of the steps stand wide open, stray pieces of paper and trash blowing around inside the front hall. The place looks ransacked. But that's not what's bothering Lilly right now. In the eerie silence that grips the town—the fires almost completely dwindled, the pockets of blue haze dissipating, the assailants apparently long gone—what's bothering Lilly more than anything else is the fact that they have yet to see any of their people.

Until now.

"Lord have mercy," the strangled voice of Norma Sutters rings out behind Lilly. "Is that Harold? Lilly, is that *Harold*?!"

"Norma, keep it together!" Lilly shoots a glance at the others. "Everybody, keep it together and stay put for a second!"

Fifty yards away, the body of an elderly African American lies in a motionless heap, soaking in a pool of its own blood. Miles Littleton moves closer to Norma and puts an arm around her. "It's okay, sis."

"Let go!" Norma lets out a snort of agony as she wriggles out of his arms. "That's Harold!"

"Keep it together, goddamn it!" Lilly keeps her pistol at "low ready"—in front and to the side just below her peripheral vision, as Bob taught her—as she quickly surveys the general vicinity around the crumpled body at the bottom of the stone steps. Despite the disturbing silence, and the barren, empty wind blowing through the heart of town, the strange tableau feels like a trap to Lilly.

She gazes from rooftop to rooftop, from the sun-bleached water tower to the old-fashioned white-washed gazebo at the northwest corner of the square. No sign of snipers. No indication of anybody lying in wait. Even the stray walkers who have apparently wandered in through the open gates have been destroyed quickly and efficiently by the unknown assailants, many of the ragged remains still lying along the town's parkways and gutters. Now the village sits quietly, as sleepy and bucolic as it must have been back in 1820 when it first sprouted from the red Georgia clay as a tiny railroad burg.

"LET GO OF ME!"

Norma Sutters breaks free from Miles Littleton's grasp. The portly woman races across the street corner.

"NORMA!" Lilly hurries after her, the others following. Norma reaches the courthouse lawn and nearly trips on the curb as she hops up and dashes across the grass. Still gripping her .44 Bulldog in one hand, she hurtles toward the crumpled body on the cobblestones. Lilly and the others chase after her, their gazes scanning the periphery.

"Lord-Lord-Lord-Lord." The words come out of the former choir director from some deep well of emotion that perhaps she wasn't even aware she had for this older man as she flops down on the stones where he lies. She feels his neck for a pulse and realizes he's been dead for a while—maybe hours—the cause of death apparently three large-caliber bullet wounds in his chest. But from the way his hands are curled into claws, and the way the expression on his dark-skinned, deeply lined face is frozen into a furrowed look of anguish, it's clear he died a difficult death, locked in a mortal struggle. The man's blood soaks Norma's skirt as she pulls his limp form into an embrace, stroking the back of his salt-and-pepper head. Norma softly weeps. *"Lord-Lord-Lord-Lord-Lord-Lord-Lord-Lord-Lord-Lord-Lord-Lord Lord-Lord-Lord. . . . "*

Lilly arrives and keeps a respectful distance. The others approach behind her, keeping their weapons at the ready in case a sniper's bullet happens to interrupt. Norma sobs, rocking the corpse of the man with whom she had been falling in love. Tears streak the ashy skin of her plump face. Lilly looks away. Then she notices something that may or may not be important.

Blood tracks streak the pavers behind Harold Staubach's body. Evidently, the man crawled quite a way before hemorrhaging the rest of his lifeblood and dying. What was he trying to elude? Or was he trying to chase after something in his death throes? Lilly looks up at the open doors and the scraps of litter skittering on the breeze across the front corridor floor. She thinks about it, then turns and scans the rest of the town.

The revelation hits her like an ice pick between the eyes. She turns to Miles and Jinx. "Okay, listen to me very carefully. I want you two to go check the Sterns' place, then check the station house. Right now. Tommy and I will go check the speedway. We'll meet up back here in ten minutes. Watch your blind spots. DO IT NOW!"

For the briefest instant, Jinx and Miles share an awkward glance. Then Miles turns and looks at Lilly. "What are we looking for?"

Lilly has already started out in a dead run toward the intersection north of the square. She howls over her shoulder as she goes: "The kids! Gotta find the kids!"

Decades earlier, long before anyone would have even *conceived* of a dead person reanimating and consuming the flesh of the living, somebody got the brilliant idea that the one thing the town of Woodbury sorely needed was stock car racing. More than a new playing field for the high school, more than a revamped medical clinic, more than anything . . . Woodbury needed a speedway. A pair of local businessmen spearheaded the fund-raising efforts throughout the winter of 1971 and the spring of 1972. Using the time-honored carrots of job creation, tourism, and economic development, the steering committee raised an amount just shy of $500,000—enough to break ground and pour the foundation for the massive complex, which would include underground service bays, seating for seventy-five hundred fans, a press box, and state-of-the-art (for its day) infield pits. The remainder of the funds were raised the following year, and on July 1, 1974, the Woodbury Veterans Speedway opened its turnstiles for business.

Had the racetrack been built in any other part of the world, it would have been shunned and seen by many as an affront to the agrarian charm of the farmland. But this was the South, and country folks around here appreciated the finer points of NASCAR like no-where else. The smell of hot rubber and smoking tar, the whine of thousands of cubic inches of Detroit combustion filling the air, the glint of hot Georgia sunlight off Metalflake bonnets shooting past the stands in a beautiful blur, the snap of the neck as your guy edged into the lead for the final lap around the oval—it was all part of the fabric of the southern genome, as organically a part of those people's lives as the sky for sparrows. And over the last quarter of the twentieth century, Woodbury became a marquee venue for the Southeastern United States Short Track Racing Association.

It was only in the early millennium that the Woodbury Veterans Speedway began to decline—rising fuel costs, the proliferation of electronic entertainment, recession, and the expense of upkeep brought the heyday of racing in Woodbury to a close. By the time the plague broke out, the massive complex on the west side of town—with its flying-saucer-shaped stands, labyrinth of underground service bays, and upper decks the size of an aircraft carrier—had become more and more of a curiosity, more and more of a white elephant. For years, it had been used for storage, the parking of school buses, an occasional country music festival, and the rampant growing of weeds and kudzu that eventually wound and spiraled around the upper stanchions like Byzantine serpents in some Boschian nightmare triptych of the nine circles of hell.

When Philip Blake (aka the Governor) burrowed into power here a couple of years ago like some kind of satanic weevil—turning the town into a third-world dictatorship—the speedway became a symbol of all that was unholy about these apocalyptic times. The Governor transformed the semicircle of bleachers, the massive portals, the oval banked asphalt, and the vast, seared infield of dead grass and oil-spotted cement pits into a gladiatorial arena worthy of the Roman circuses. In kill-or-be-killed spectacles, ringed with clusters of captive walkers chained and drooling and clawing at the combatants, the Governor's thugs would compete for the right to live or die for their beloved emperor. The theory—according to Blake—was that the bloody razzmatazz provided catharsis for the residents, kept people happy and docile and manageable. Never mind that the whole thing was faked in the best style of World Federation Wrestling. To Lilly, a longtime Woodbury denizen, there was something deeply disturbing about the events. The obscene, surreal feeling of watching the undead, chained under the metal-halide lights, performing for the crowd like organ grinder monkeys haunted Lilly's dreams, and to this day continues to taint her memories.

All of which is why she feels waves of emotion crashing up against her as she leads her team of rescuers through the chain-link gates outside the north corner of the speedway. They pause just inside the turnstiles.

Over the last ten minutes, they have stumbled upon half a dozen more bodies: Clint and Linda Sturbridge, Mama May, Rudy, and Ian. Practically every new resident of Woodbury has been murdered in cold blood . . . *but for what?* Whoever attacked the town wasn't interested in stealing any of the fuel reserves in the tanks out behind the market. They left the food pantry in the warehouse on Main Street intact. Not a single provision or supply was taken from the feed store on Jones Mill. What were these jackals after?

"Jinx and Miles, you two go around the back and check the service entrance." Lilly points off toward the massive gray mortar columns flanking the cracked pavement of the loading dock. "The rest of us will go in through the front." Lilly turns and looks at Tommy and Norma. "Safeties off, rounds in the breach, and remember—whatever we find, walkers or hostiles or whatever—don't get tunnel vision, stay off the walls, fingers off the triggers until you have a target." She gives Tommy a look. "You remember what I taught you?"

Tommy nods with a frustrated blush of anger. "I remember, Lilly. Jeez, I'm not a goddamn baby."

"No, you're not." Lilly gives the others a nod. "Let's go."

They move single file up the ramp toward the high archway of the main entrance, while Jinx and Miles shuffle around the side of the building, vanishing in the shadows of the deserted loading dock.

Wheelbarrows full of peat and potting soil stand near the portals;

shovels and hoes and huge rolls of chicken wire are stacked near the entrance. A few carriages are parked under the portico, as well as bags of oats for the horses. For the last year, Lilly has been expanding the farming activities inside the arena, and she's been using horses to pull the plows and help with the heavy work. Many of the animals are kept in the former service areas below the arena—the large rooms lining the corridors working well as makeshift stables. It's been a wet spring this year, and Lilly has been hoping and praying that the overharvested crops will regenerate quickly. Now all thoughts of farming are obliterated from her mind.

She leads Tommy and Norma through the archway over which the wind-blasted sculpture of Mercury—Roman god of speed, travel, and, ironically, guide to the underworld—stands in eternal tableau.

They are plunged into a dark, damp, moldy cement passageway. The air smells of dry rot, rat droppings, old urine, and spoor. To their left stretches the litter-strewn, blood-spattered mezzanine of deserted food stands and restrooms. To their right, the stone steps lead down to the service level underneath the stands.

Lilly communicates with hand gestures and the muzzle of her .22 as she leads the other two down the steps. It is understood—in fact, unspoken—that the children would be brought here, probably by Barbara Stern, in case of emergency. The underground service areas are akin to safe rooms or bomb shelters. Lilly takes the lead as they reach the bottom of the staircase.

A number of sensations hit them the moment they enter the passageway—the stench of horse dung and fermenting hay, the sound of dripping, the atmosphere as fecund as a greenhouse. They hear the snuffling, snorting noises of horses in their pens, some of the animals banging the walls nervously with their hooves, some of them whinnying suddenly at the scent of humans in their midst. Lilly moves with her Ruger gripped in Israeli commando position—both hands, feet shoulder width, muzzle forward, body angled—followed by the other two, both of them wide-eyed.

They reach the end of the hall and see the metal door to the safe room standing open.

Lilly's heart thuds in her chest as she peers into the room, taking in the empty space, the kindergarten chairs overturned, water cups knocked over on the low tables, the children's storybooks strewn across the floor. No blood, though, no sign of walkers. Some of the original items in the room are missing: the small toy box, some of the blankets, a crib. What the fuck? Lilly's head spins. What is going on? She turns back toward the corridor.

"What the hell, Lilly?" Tommy's eyes water with horror, both his sister and baby brother missing. "Where the hell are they?!"

"Maybe they're back at their house," Norma volunteers, knowing how unlikely that is.

Lilly shakes her head. "We passed it on the way here, it was empty."

Tommy looks around the cold, stone passageway, his lips trembling with horror. "Still haven't found David or Barbara—maybe they're with the kids."

"Yeah, maybe . . . maybe." Lilly mumbles this, trying to settle her nerves and think clearly. "Maybe we ought to go back and look in the—"

A noise, faint at first, cuts her off. She snaps her gaze toward the far end of the corridor. The others hear it too, a garbled voice that at first sounds as though it might be a walker. Gun barrels go up immediately, hammers pulled back. The noise is coming from the side tunnel up ahead, about a hundred feet away.

Lilly puts her finger to her lips. They slowly shuffle toward the intersecting tunnels, guns locked and loaded, muzzles raised and ready to blast away at the cranium of some moldering dead person. Lilly's mouth goes dry as they approach the intersection. Somewhere behind her, a horse snorts softly, nervously. Other horses stir. Lilly's hands are sweaty as she reaches the side tunnel and suddenly lurches around the corner with the Ruger's muzzle up and out front.

About thirty feet away, a middle-aged man—still clinging to

life—lies twisted on the floor at the base of the exit ramp, one arm still reaching toward the top of the incline. Dressed in a tattered silk roadie jacket, the Bob Seger Band insignia on the back punctured with blood-rimmed bullet holes, he trembles softly as he labors to get air into his lungs. His grizzled gray face presses against the floor, puffing dust with each pained breath.

Lilly lowers her weapon and rushes over to the injured man, the others close on her heels. Lilly kneels. "David," she murmurs as she gently cradles the man's head. "Can you hear me? David?!"

It takes quite a while for the man to muster enough energy to speak.

THREE

"They took Barbara. . . ."

The man on the floor coughs, swallows hard, licks his chapped lips, and takes shallow breaths. His face is pallid and glistening with sweat, his eyes bloodshot and unfocused. His expression suddenly tightens into a mask of pain. "Motherfuckers . . . came out of nowhere . . . and they took my *wife*. . . . "

Lilly turns toward Jinx, who has just arrived with Miles from an adjacent corridor. "Jinx! The infirmary at the end of the hall! Get a stretcher . . . and the first-aid kit! Tommy, help her!"

With a series of nervous nods and awkward glances, Jinx and the boy back away and then hurry around the corner.

Lilly gently raises David Stern up and then sits him against the adjacent cinder-block wall. She inspects his wounds. Two out of the three gunshots seem to have passed through the meat of his shoulder, exiting in a tuft of fabric out the back of his jacket. The third one appears to be lodged somewhere in the chest—no exit wound, not a good sign—and that's when Lilly feels the man's neck. His pulse is racing, and his flesh is hot.

He coughs. "Fucking bastards surprised us." He coughs some more. Norma and Miles come closer, kneeling next to Lilly in order to hear better, David's voice crumbling with pain and shock and rage. "Armed to the teeth . . . paramilitary is my guess . . . had some kind of grenade launcher."

Lilly looks at him. "What the fuck were they after? They didn't touch the storehouse . . . there's not a drop of fuel missing from the tanks."

A thin, delicate spattering of blood spurts across his chest as David convulses in another spasm of coughing. He finally manages to look up into Lilly's eyes. "They were after the kids, Lilly."

"*What?!*"

"They took the kids."

For the briefest instant, Lilly stares with utter incomprehension, the silence punctuating the gravity of the situation. Norma and Miles look at each other, thunderstruck, speechless. They look back at Lilly, who's now staring at the floor, shaking her head, trying to wrap her brain around it. She looks up. "They took all six of them?"

David manages a nod, coughs, and closes his eyes. "That's why they took Barbara . . . to keep them calm . . . I tried to stop them." He breathes hard through his nose. "Harold tried to hide Mercy in the courthouse . . . but they found her . . . and when Harold fought back, they took him out just like that." David snaps his bloodstained fingers. "Like he was a goddamn walker."

Lilly shakes her head, vexed, still groping for explanations. "But why—?"

"Motherfuckers were like fucking robots."

"But why go after the kids? What in God's name do they want with the children?"

David's eyes look glazed with pain. "Like fucking robots," he murmurs.

"David!" She shakes him. "Why the kids!"

"Organized . . . stone cold . . . calculated."

"GODDAMN IT LOOK AT ME!!" She slams him against the wall. "WHY TAKE THE KIDS?!"

"Lilly, stop it!" Miles reaches out and pulls Lilly back, holds her still. "Calm the fuck down!"

Lilly catches her breath, shaking her head, staring at the floor.

Jinx and Tommy return with a black satchel and a folded portable stretcher.

They set the bag down and quickly unfurl the canvas stretcher on the floor next to David. Lilly's mind swims as she glances at the shopworn black doctor's bag. It's the same bag that Bob Stookey used to carry around with him during times of crisis—a satchel once owned by a former practitioner from Atlanta named Stevens. The black bag radiates doom for Lilly. She saw that bag on a stainless-steel table next to her when she lost her own baby two years ago; the miscarriage and subsequent D and C performed by Bob became one of the great ordeals of Lilly's life. Now Jinx snaps open the bag and frantically fishes through its contents.

"I'm sorry," Lilly says to David at last. "I'm losing it." She strokes the man's shoulder. "Let's get you back to the sick bay. We'll talk later."

Jinx presses a gauze bandage down on the worst of the chest wounds, and she holds it there while Miles and Tommy carefully lift the man onto the canvas conveyance. Meanwhile, David is mumbling, "I don't have a clue, Lilly . . . why they would . . . they would . . . go to all the trouble. . . ." His voice trails off as they tape the bandage in place, secure his skinny legs with nylon straps, and tuck his arms at his sides. David Stern loses consciousness then, his head lolling to the side, his body sinking into the folds of the canvas.

There's a portion of the brain—way down in the cerebellum, in the tangled synapses of the basal ganglia—associated with the perception of time. Some neuroscientists believe that the deepest part of this area—known as the suprachiasmatic nucleus—is where the most immediate timekeeping occurs: *ultradian* time. This is where urgency is born. This is where the ticking clock starts, which tells us something is going to happen—maybe something awful—if we don't get our asses in gear and hurry the fuck up.

Lilly Caul always had a highly developed sense of ultradian time. As a child, she could sense the ticking clock as dinnertime approached, during tests at school, or when Everett was out looking for her after curfew. With almost preternatural sensitivity, she would feel the ticking time bomb in the back of her mind when a fire alarm was about to go off, or a school bell was about to ring, or a thunderstorm was about to erupt, or even the precise moment when her period was about to hit. Since the advent of the plague, she has noticed this sixth sense in the moments right before she smells a walker in the vicinity or walks into a trap. It's not a *psychic* gift. It's not magic. She just has a highly developed sensitivity to imminent change.

All of which is why she feels time ticking away that night as she hurries to secure the town.

"I got this, Lilly!" Jinx calls out from Lilly's right flank, the dusk closing in on them, the crickets starting to roar. It's already half past seven, and the two of them are approaching a single Port-o-Let unit situated out by the semitrucks on Dogwood Street. The two massive eighteen-wheelers face each other, forming a movable gate. The Port-o-Let was dragged over here by the Governor's crew two years ago to serve the men reinforcing the wall, and now a wide pool of deep-crimson arterial blood leaks out from within the toilet. Something moves inside it. "Stand back." Jinx raises her enormous, gleaming bowie knife as she prepares to yank the door open. "Here goes."

She unclasps the door handle and with one fluid motion pulls open the plastic hatch.

The walker inside the Port-o-Let convulses at the smell of humans, reaching blindly, making mucusy snarling noises. Not long ago, Clint Sturbridge was a jovial former electrician from Macon, Georgia, who had lost his ex-wife and teenage daughter to the riots that gripped the cities in the weeks right after the Turn. A big, pear-shaped man with pork chop sideburns, he had proven himself a major asset in Woodbury's recent renaissance of rebuilding and reinvention. Now he lurches toward Jinx just as the tip of her bowie slams down into the hard shell of bone above his frontal lobe, blood and fluids effervescing around the hilt.

The thing that was once a decent, hardworking man sags and collapses.

Jinx wipes the blade on the thing's pant leg, then rises. "Poor son of a bitch."

Lilly takes a closer look at the profusion of blood coating the inside of the plastic enclosure. "Looks like he got shot in the attack and bled out in here." She searches for a weapon. "The man was *fucking unarmed*."

Jinx gives a disgusted grunting noise and a nod. "At the risk of stating the obvious, I would say these are not your ordinary home invaders."

Silently, Lilly stares at the carnage, completely and hopelessly vexed.

"What if they're just bughouse crazy?" Norma Sutters muses, sitting by the side rail of David Stern's gurney in the dank, dimly lit infirmary, dabbing a cold rag on the man's forehead. Lying in a tangle of sweat-damp blankets, David wavers in and out of consciousness. An hour earlier, Norma and Tommy had managed to patch up the shoulder wounds and dig one bullet out of his left pectoral. They gave him the last of the morphine powder, and now David drifts on a cushion of narcotic haze, every few minutes mumbling some witty retort just to let everybody know that he's not only still alive but is also his old irascible self and would appreciate it if people would stop staring at the top of his skull as though it were a target.

Across the infirmary, Lilly chews the inside of her cheek as she thinks about it. "I don't know . . . I get the feeling there's a purpose here . . . even if it makes no sense to us."

"So we're thinking they come from Atlanta?" Norma Sutters has moved from David's bedside to the sink, and is now rinsing the wet rag.

"From the looks of the tracks, they're heading back that way." Lilly glances at Jinx. "Why don't you give Ash or Bell another try on the radio—I'm worried this isn't a one-stop deal—especially if these bastards are heading north."

Jinx goes over to a shelf and furiously winds the crank on a small wood-grain radio. She thumbs the Send button in the mic and says, "Ash, it's Woodbury calling, do you read?" Pause. Static crackles through the speaker. No reply. "Ash, it's Jinx in Woodbury. Do you copy?" Pause. Static. "Bell? Anybody out there? Over?"

Nothing.

"Goddamn it!" Lilly angrily shoves two spare ammo mags down into the back pocket of her jeans. "We can't just wait around for somebody to—"

She stops abruptly at the faint sound of a voice coming from across the room. David Stern, semiconscious, his head lolling on the pillow, has muttered a single word that Lilly hasn't quite registered. Norma stands up, gazing down at him. Lilly takes a few steps toward the gurney and pauses. "David, did you say something?"

"Bryce. . . ."

She takes a step closer. "Excuse me?"

David takes a deep breath, grimaces at the pain, and manages to sit up. Norma adjusts the pillow behind his back. David exhales a pained breath and says, "Bryce was a name I heard them call this guy, seemed like the honcho . . . maybe a military man."

Lilly stares. "Can you describe him?" The others have moved closer, leaning in to better hear the injured man's feeble voice. "David?" Lilly reaches down and puts a hand on David Stern's shoulder. "Did you see what he looked like?"

He nods. "Big guy . . . jarhead type . . . had a flak vest on . . . but was older . . . gray at the temples, you know? He looked like . . . a drill instructor."

Lilly processes this. She looks at David. "Did you see how many people he had with him?"

"Not sure . . . I think about a dozen, maybe less . . . younger men, military types, grunts, tightly wired."

"Do you remember what time it was when they attacked?"

David takes deep breaths as he gathers his thoughts. "It was like late morning, maybe noon?"

"Do you remember how long they were here? How long the attack lasted?"

He thinks it over. His voice gets almost dreamy as he remembers the events of the day. "They came at us hard and fast . . . like it was a strategy . . . a surprise attack . . . whatever. We held them off for a few minutes . . . I don't know how long . . . but they out-gunned us. We thought they were after the diesel in the tanks and our food supply, stuff like that . . . so Barb decided we should give it all up . . . just give it up . . . and we should all hide in the sublevels of the speedway while they helped themselves . . . she thought the kids would be safe down there. We tried to close ourselves in. Harold had to be the hero." David Stern pauses, closes his eyes, furrows his brow as a single tear leaks out of one eye and tracks down his cheek. "That little guy held them off single-handedly with a .30-30 rifle and one box of ammo from the courthouse window . . . tough little son of a bitch, I'll tell you that." David wipes his eyes. "Little did we know they just wanted the kids . . . God only knows why. I think the whole thing, from beginning to end, maybe lasted an hour, two hours at the most."

Lilly wipes her mouth. "What the fuck? None of it makes any kind of sense." She turns and paces some more. "So they got a five-hour head start on us." She looks back at David. "You said they were armed to the teeth?"

David gives her a nod.

Lilly strides back over to the bed. "Did you get a look at their resources, their ammo, their weapons—were they well equipped?"

David shrugs, swallowing back another pang of agony. "I couldn't tell how much ammo they had . . . but they were geared up like Navy SEALs, and I got the sense they were hopped up on something."

"Hopped up? Like drugs? They were on drugs?"

Another nod. "Yeah . . . it's hard to explain . . . I didn't see anything specific . . . but they were acting strange the whole time they were taking us down . . . eyes bugging out, some of them howling like goddamn rabid dogs." He pauses again to swallow a twinge of pain and measure his words. His weathered, deeply lined face tightens. "I even saw one of them get shot in the leg . . . and it didn't even faze this guy, didn't even slow him down." Another pause. David swallows hard again and looks at Lilly. "Did you find anybody?"

"What do you mean?"

"Any survivors?"

Lilly looks down and doesn't say anything at first.

David lets out an anguished breath. "Mama May Carter . . . did she . . . ?"

Lilly shakes her head.

David bites his lip. "Clint? Jack? Anybody?"

Lilly looks at the floor and says softly, "You're it, David. You're the only one."

The older man sniffs back the sorrow and looks up at the ceiling. "Not true, Lilly. I'm not the only one." He looks at Lilly then, his eyes glittering with emotion and maybe even a trace of defiance. "The kids and Barbara are gonna survive this thing as well . . . because you're gonna go and you're gonna get them back from these motherfuckers. Right?"

Lilly stares, holding his gaze, the invisible clock deep within the folds of her brain ticking.

FOUR

In the dead of night, the switchyard on the north side of Woodbury drones with crickets and sparkles with fireflies drifting through the hazy, humid mist like snow on a blank TV screen. In the dark, the dull gleam of old rails embedded in the sandy topsoil, crisscrossing the yard, resembles bones petrifying through the ages. The boarded station house where navy-blue-uniform-clad engineers and brake-men once took their coffee and received their itineraries from thriving railroad companies now sits dark except for the flicker of propane lanterns behind one of the shrouded windows.

Inside that building, Lilly and her rescue team—Jinx, Miles, and Norma—pack without speaking, loading packs and satchels with cartons of ammunition, a nylon tent, a camp stove, water bottles, flares, matches, propane lanterns, freeze-dried soup, protein powder, and practically every last weapon in Woodbury. The only firearm they choose to leave behind is the cut-down pistol-grip 12 gauge with which Lilly spent the last twelve months teaching Tommy Dupree to shoot. She considered leaving Norma to hold down the fort along with Tommy and David, but she realized immediately that she needed as many skilled adult hands on the journey as she could get. And Norma Sutters is one of those people who can easily be underestimated. Despite her zaftig figure, matronly air, and angelic singing voice, the woman is badass to the core, and Lilly needs all the help she can get.

They spend less than ten minutes inside that building, preparing to embark on what each of them knows down in their hearts is a suicide mission. Nobody says it specifically, but Lilly can see it in their eyes—the way they silently stuff the last of their supplies into their packs with somber expressions, knitting their faces as though they're about to take a final walk down a death-row corridor to the gas chamber. Norma keeps throwing nervous glances at Miles as she wraps duct tape around her plump ankles above her Reeboks—a last-ditch preventive measure to protect the extremities from the teeth of biters—while Miles compulsively clears his throat as he quickly zips his rucksack and straps his 9mm into the holster on his skinny hip.

"What the hell is eating you two?" Jinx finally asks them, standing with her arsenal of edged weapons sheathed, strapped, tucked, dangling, and tied to various parts of her S and M Goth garb.

Lilly looks up from her last-minute packing to see what's on their minds, although, deep down, she knows. She knows what they're thinking. She's thinking it herself, and she keeps pushing it from her mind.

"All right, I'll be the one to say it." Norma sets her heavy pack down on the floor, jutting out her chin with righteous indignation. She looks at Lilly. Norma's eyes soften suddenly, the sadness creeping into her expression. "Are you going after these people because you want to save them kids . . . or because you just want cold, hard vengeance?"

Lilly doesn't answer, just angrily stuffs her extra magazine into her ruck.

Norma bites her lip, choosing her words. "Lilly, listen. Nobody loves them little ones more than me, I would die for them kids. But *this* . . . what we're doing . . . I ain't sure it's the smart play here."

Lilly pushes back the anger stewing inside her. The clock ticks. She looks up. "What are you saying? Just spit it out, Norma."

Norma sighs. She glances at Miles, who looks down as though the heat of her gaze is too much to bear. She turns back to Lilly. "What I mean to say is, once upon a time you had some kinda law and order.

Somebody did something awful—they kidnapped children, murdered people like this—you called the cops."

Lilly takes a step closer to the woman. "There are no cops anymore, Norma."

"I understand that."

"*We're* the cops."

"Lilly, I ain't saying we shouldn't search for Barb and them kids."

"Then what *are* you saying exactly?" Lilly has her fists clenched and isn't even aware of it. She inches closer to the heavyset woman. "Do you want to opt out? You're welcome to stay with David and Tommy, hold down the fort. We're wasting time talking about this."

Norma wrings her hands. "All I'm asking—and it's real simple— is do you just want to get them kids back? Or do you just want to waste these kidnappers in the harshest way possible?"

Lilly's eyes flare. "Maybe a little of both—so what? That's the way it goes."

Jinx steps into the fray and puts a hand on Lilly's shoulder. "Okay, let's all take a deep breath. We're just talking here."

Norma sighs, continuing to parse her words. "Lookit . . . I'm just sayin' we're heading off on this mission in the dark of night, not one whit of an idea how we're gonna get them little ones back."

Lilly tamps down her rage, and she says very softly, "I've got a plan, Norma. Trust me. We're going to find Barbara and the kids, but only if we—"

A muffled sound from across the room interrupts, taking everybody by surprise. Miles goes for his 9mm. Lilly stands stone-still, cocking her head, trying to figure out if she heard what she *thought* she just heard.

Somebody knocking?

Jinx goes over to the door, slides the bolt, and opens it wide enough to reveal Tommy Dupree standing outside in the dark, fists clenched, face all twisted with anger. He wears a tattered leather jacket he found in the Goodwill box in the courthouse basement, along with a gun belt around his waist that's two sizes too big for him. The night shadows shift and dance behind him along the tree line of the west woods, the moonlit forest alive with movement, the breeze smelling of dead flesh long decayed into offal.

He steps into the station house and Jinx clicks the door shut behind him.

"Tommy, this is not the time." Lilly takes a step toward him.

"Don't even say it!" He breathes hard through his nose as he burns his gaze into her. "The more I think about it, the madder I get."

"What are you talking about?"

"That you would go after them without me!" He spits on the plank floor. "No fucking way!"

"Okay, first, watch your language. Second, we already talked about this."

"I changed my mind."

"Tommy, c'mon—"

"I get that David needs somebody to look after him, but *seriously*? You're gonna make me be the one, stay behind while you guys go on the rescue mission?! No way! You need me!"

"Tommy—"

"I'm coming with you!" His gaze shimmers with emotion. "That's all there is to it!"

"Really?" Lilly walks over to him, crosses her arms against her chest. "Okay . . . since when do you give the orders around here?"

He gazes up at her, his eyes welling up. His voice trembles and quavers but remains steadfast. "We're talking about my sister and brother here. You taught me how to use that shotgun yourself, you taught me how to survive in the wilderness and stuff. I'm going with you."

Lilly exhales a long sigh, the clock in her head ticking away the seconds, the minutes, the hours. At last she puts a hand on the boy's shoulder, then strokes his thatch of unruly hair. "Point taken." Lilly thinks about it for a moment. She turns and gives Norma Sutters a look. "Can you stay with David?"

Norma puts her hands on her ample hips and tilts her head with a flourish. "Honey child, you need me more than he does."

Lilly shakes her head. "Now *you're* gonna give me shit about this?"

Norma sighs. "I realize you're just trying to do the right thing. But I talked it over with David. I offered to stay with him, but he wants everybody who can draw a breath out there trying to find Barbara and the kids. He's doing fine, Lilly. He's safe behind the barricade, he's got food, water, medical supplies. It's a done deal, we're all going along. So we might as well saddle up and ride before them kidnappers get too far down the line."

They gather five of the best horses—three of them from the make-shift stables under the speedway, two from the regular team that had been working on the rails that day—and they bring them out across the switchyard under a clear night sky. The clouds from earlier in the day have evaporated, and now the heavens glitter down on the dark yard with eerie calm, a deep black canopy spangled by countless stars and a full moon as brutal and impassive as a prison searchlight. They work quickly in the trough between the main rails, leading the horses up a ramp onto a flatcar in a single-file line. All at once, without much warning, three stray walkers appear on the edge of the adjacent woods, drawn to the noise of the team. Miles takes one of them down with a shovel to the head, which makes a ghastly ringing noise before the creature collapses in a fountain of its own brain fluids. Tommy takes the other two down with a machete—a half-dozen inelegant blows to the cranium of each—sending bone flak and plumes of blood into the night air until the last of them falls.

Jinx quickly leads her massive, sturdy thoroughbred to the front of the flatcar. The horse has a head as sculpted and tapered as that of Roman statuary, a coat as shiny and chocolate brown as sealskin. Nicknamed Arrow, the animal snorts and nods as Jinx leads it into position. Arrow's bridle is linked to the horse behind it, and *that* one is linked to the one behind *it*, and so on, down the line, five deep, until Tommy and Miles hook the last animal in line to the tail of the flatcar.

Meanwhile, Lilly and Norma have climbed aboard the renovated engine, which sits fifty feet ahead of the flatcar and rises fifteen feet above the ground, a real beast with an exterior as chipped and aged as a shipwreck pulled off the bottom of the ocean. The old Genesis turbine locomotive still has the ghost of its Amtrak paint job, its front bumper retrofitted with a skid from a combine, sharpened to a razor's edge and wrapped in barbed wire—Bob Stookey's makeshift countermeasure designed to repel walkers. The rear door is missing, replaced by chain link. Before his death, Bob had been monkeying with the engine, getting it to run fairly well on biodiesel made from the fry oil of dozens of greasy spoons up and down the Highway 24 corridor. Now Lilly and Norma squeeze into the greasy, malodorous pilothouse—which is no bigger than a large restroom—and take their positions in front of the filthy control panel.

Bob had showed Lilly a few rudimentary things about operating the train, and now she frantically searches her memory for the proper sequence of ignition switches to be punched and dials to be turned and gauges to be checked and valves to be opened. After a series of aborted attempts, she manages to kick the big diesel power plant to life, and the chassis trembles, and the smoke and the low gurgle fill the night air outside the narrow window ports, the stars visible through the fractured panes of safety glass.

A moment later, the gears engage, a canopy of smoke shoots up, and the engine drags the car out of the yard and into the night.

By the time they reach Walnut Creek, Lilly has pushed the iron monster up past thirty-five miles an hour. Norma keeps a death grip on the vertical rail, tense and silent as she peers out the window at the passing wreckage of Highway 422, the blur of the treetops, and the vast ceiling of stars broken only by the twisting column of exhaust that swirls up from the engine and dissipates in the ether. Lilly gazes out the rearview mirror.

Behind them, the horses rear and convulse on the flatcar with each bump. The track is untested, cleared only months earlier, and Lilly can feel every flaw in her solar plexus, every vibration in her bones.

Next to her, Norma's voice suddenly penetrates her thoughts. "Tell me again!" the woman shouts above the wind and rumbling of the turbine. "What happens when we get to the part of the track that's unfinished?"

Lilly nods. "The plan is to use the horses from that point on."

Norma stares out the window. "Can I ask you another stupid question?"

"If you don't mind a stupid answer."

"Why not just use horses from the start?"

Lilly shrugs. "Take us twice as long to go half as far." She nods at the passing landscape. "It's tough going out there, Norma, even for four-wheelers, all the shit in our way, wrecks and swarms and God knows what else. They got a major head start on us, I'll grant you that, but we'll gain on them, believe me. We'll find them."

Norma nods, looking unconvinced.

Lilly can hear the muffled voices of Jinx and the others behind the firewall door. They're hunkering down now back there in the darkness of the passenger bay, avoiding the wind. Once a cabin featuring first-class seating for genteel business travelers, the enclosure is a squalid cell of discarded fuel cans, detritus, and spent shell casings rolling around like pinballs.

Turning back to the windshield, and the rushing blur of steel rails flowing under them, Lilly puts all thoughts of suicide missions, failure, and death out of her mind.

On most train engines built in the twentieth century, a long iron lever sprouts up from the corrugated floor in front of the control console—a greasy remnant of the days when safety regulation required that engineers manually engage the throttle at all times. "The dead man's stick" is designed to shut down the engine immediately if that manual pressure is released for any reason—especially if that reason is a sudden heart attack or aneurysm that drops the engineer to the floor.

Now Lilly turns to Norma. "Do me a favor, will ya? Take the stick for a second."

Norma reluctantly grasps the spring-loaded handle, her lips pursing with nerves. "Got it!"

Lilly finds her rucksack on the floor, digs in it for the radio and her binoculars. She pulls the items out, sets the radio on a ledge, raises the field glasses to her eyes, and peers through the windshield at the dark horizon line barely visible beyond the magnesium-white cone of light from the train's headlamp. She can see the occasional silhouette of a ragged figure emerging from the forest on either side of the train, lumbering toward the light and noise, and then brushing up against the makeshift fence, giving Lilly a momentary feeling of accomplishment. The barrier is holding for the time being. Everything seems to be in working order.

At this point, however, it's far too dark for Lilly to notice the smoke on the horizon.

The noxious corkscrew of haze curls up into the black heavens less than two miles away, rising off the treetops, unseen at first, a stain against the vast abyss of the night sky. A trace odor of burning rubber registers just for an instant in Lilly's brain but she passes it off as an unfamiliar by-product of the engine getting too hot. Or maybe the train's burning oil. They're still too far off from the smoke for Lilly to recognize the source.

They close the distance, the train maintaining a speed of forty miles an hour now, the undercarriage sounding like a drum roll announcing some imminent change in their fortunes. Lilly stares at that black stain against the sky. Orange light crackles within it, flickering up across its underbelly in veins of luminous color. Is a storm brewing?

"Can I ask another stupid question?!" Norma hollers from her spot in front of the control console. She keeps her eyes on the horizon, the stick clutched tightly in her grip.

"Sure, go ahead," Lilly replies, keeping the binoculars to her eyes, starting to see the strange storm-like pattern of darkness rising against the black sky.

Norma looks at her. "You know how to stop this thing, right?"

Lilly offers no reply as the train careers around a gentle curve, revealing a burning section of track about a quarter mile away.

In dry, western states, during droughts, the smallest, feeblest lightning strike can touch off infernos of biblical proportions. At first, as the train approaches the smoking length of track, it looks to Lilly almost like a natural phenomenon. At this distance, in the moonlight, the flaming railroad ties appear as glittering yellow plumes, almost pretty, like Chinese lanterns. The smoke chokes a dozen acres of the surrounding farmland—a microclimate of hazy pollution that makes Lilly's heart start to race.

"Keep us steady," she orders Norma, then pushes down one of the side windows, leans out into the foul-smelling wind, and peers through the binoculars at the sabotage most likely perpetrated by the kidnappers. At least a thousand feet of track roars with some kind of accelerant—lighter fluid, alcohol, gas—something to get the ancient creosote-sodden wood to go up like that. The envelope of air around the train as it approaches crackles with char and heat and menace. They are maybe a thousand feet away. At this rate, they will plunge into the fire in about twenty to thirty seconds.

Norma's voice rises an octave. "Why in the hell are we not stopping?"

Lilly looks at the portly woman, and for a fleeting instant, all the moving parts of their situation, all the variables, all the consequences of their actions, all the potential victories and utter disasters crash up against each other and seize Lilly in a momentary and inexplicable paralysis. She freezes, stricken silent for a moment. The clock in her brain stops ticking. The invisible sweep-second hand reaches high midnight. Alarms go off.

Then, over the space of a nanosecond—the time it takes a single synapse to fire in her brain—Lilly Caul remembers saying goodbye the previous morning to ten-year-old Bethany Dupree and her little elfin six-year-old brother Lucas. Bethany had been sitting up in her bed in the darkness of her room, dressed in her trademark baggy Hello Kitty sweatshirt, rubbing sleep from her eyes. Lucas was on the opposite side of the room, peering out from his tangle of blankets. A quick kiss on the little sleep-perfumed foreheads, and a hasty goodbye, and all at once, a simple gesture on Bethany's part, Lucas looking on, nodding, took Lilly completely by surprise. Bethany was clutching a corner of Lilly's shirttail and wouldn't let go. "Make sure y'all come back," the little girl softly beseeched Lilly. "Just make sure, okay?"

Lilly snaps out of her spell. "Keep it steady, Norma, stay on course."

"What?!—*what?!*"

"We're not going to stop."

"WHAT THE FUCK—?!"

"Just do what I say! Keep it on course, and don't let up on the speed!"

Norma starts to object but Lilly has already pushed her way through the rear chambers of the pilothouse, kicking open the firewall door, and lurching through the opening into the passenger enclosure.

She ducks down to avoid hitting her head on the metal lintel, and the smell of nervous tension in the form of BO and musk instantly floods her sinuses. In the light of a single battery-powered lantern, as well as the shifting shadows and shafts of moonlight coming through the windows, she can see three figures like owls on opposing sides of the passenger car. "What's going on?" Jinx wants to know, her hand reflexively going to the handle of her machete.

"Don't talk, just listen!" Lilly nods at the overhead bins. "Jinx, there's canvas—"

"Is that fire up ahead?" Tommy demands.

"LISTEN TO ME!" She points at the bins. "There's canvas tarp up there, and wool blankets. Grab as many as you can carry out to the flatcar, and use them to keep the flames off the animals."

Without a word, Jinx spins and starts digging the fabric out of the bins.

"Tommy and Miles, see those water canisters in the back? Grab them and bring them out there to put out any part of the train that catches."

Miles looks at Tommy, and Tommy glances over his shoulder at the tanks.

Lilly bellows: "RIGHT NOW! DO IT!"

The two young men spring into action. They lurch toward the rear of the enclosure, each grabbing a rusty metal canister. Meanwhile, Jinx has already procured a handful of blankets, and now she slides open the hatch, revealing the windswept flatcar and jittery horses. The smell of manure and diesel blows into the bay. Bits of trash and cinders swirl up on a slipstream of wind that bullwhips through the enclosure. The young men follow Jinx outside. One after another, they each leap across the massive coupler.

Lilly pivots and howls at Norma. *"Don't let go of that stick, Norma! The faster the better! Keep it steady and don't let go!!"*

Through the narrow opening in the firewall, Lilly catches a glimpse of an alarming panorama.

Visible through the windshield, the dancing yellow radiance looms dead ahead, growing larger and larger as they bear down on it. The flames rise off the ties, flagging in the wind, licking at the sky. The flickering light illuminates the undersides of high tree limbs on either side of the tracks. Lilly can feel the heat on her face.

The train roars toward the inferno. Ten seconds. Five, four . . . *three . . .*

And that's when Lilly—her irises contracting down to slits in the supernova—sees that the sabotage goes deeper, and the situation is far worse, than she originally thought.

. . . *two* . . .

She turns and rushes headlong toward the flatcar.

. . . *one* . . .

PART 2

Scorched Earth

And for your lifeblood I will require a reckoning: from
every beast I will require it and from man.

—Genesis 9:5–6

FIVE

The train plunges into the heart of the maelstrom, the flames and sparks leaping up and forming a radiant pipeline around the engine. The roar of the fire blends with the rumble of the turbine as glowing embers jump and swirl around the flatcar. One of the horses catches fire, and Lilly rushes across the gap to Jinx's side, helping with a wet blanket, frantically tamping out the flaming strands of mane. The horse rears up in agony, squealing and kicking out with its fore hooves, cracking the floor of the flatcar. Other voices cry out—first Tommy, then Miles—as a tidal wave of sparks streams across the rear of the car, touching off smaller fires at the weak points, the oil spots, the duffels, the planking. Crawling on their hands and knees, shuddering at the rocking motion of the speeding train, Tommy and Miles take turns slamming wet canvas down on the flames. Meanwhile, Jinx grabs a canister and splashes water on another horse that's caught fire. The noise is spectacular—the engine, the wind, the burning track, the screams, the banging of hooves, the wild whinnying of the animals—and it's also *distracting*. Lilly doesn't see the first flaming dead person until the thing has climbed onto the rear of the flatcar. Three more have hooked themselves onto the sides of the train as the engine hurtles through the tunnel of fire. The tattered human revenants pull themselves up onto the clattering conveyance, the flickering light shimmering in the centers of their milky eyes.

Later, Lilly will do a postmortem of the incident, trying to piece it all together in her mind—the *why* and *how* of it—and she will conclude that the perpetrators not only sabotaged the track by lighting it on fire, but also knocked down the adjacent fence, allowing the swarm into the track area for good measure. There's no science to their actions—they had no way of knowing for sure that Lilly would choose the train as her mode of travel, or that she would even retaliate so promptly—but there's a certain sadistic panache to these countermeasures that can't be denied. These kidnappers are nothing if not *thorough*, there's no denying that fact.

Now the dead close in from both sides of the flatcar, enrobed in sparks, throwing cinders into the wind like comet tails, their stupid arms reaching, their flesh and toxic fumes radiating off them.

Jinx is the first to fight back, her twin curved fighting blades practically materializing in her hands as she spins toward the closest one, a male in an advanced stage of decomposition, the sole of Jinx's boot catching its midsection and sending gouts of blood and sparks into the wind-wake. The creature staggers. Twin blades slash silently, making a divot in its neck that is so deep and oozes so much blood it smokes and cackles as the fluids run down its ragged, smoldering shirt. Then Jinx makes a fist, winds up, and unleashes a powerful blow to the creature's face.

The cranium detaches—still sputtering with flames, still smoldering—and bounces to the platform before rolling under one of the horses.

"*Get down!*" Lilly lets out a cry that gets everybody's attention.

She has her gun in both hands, a full magazine, when she starts squeezing off pin-point blasts, careful not to hit a horse, each shot catching the incoming dead square between the eyes. One shot practically takes a female's face clean off, leaving behind a slimy mask of gristle and marrow that shimmers in the moonlight before the wind blows the creature off the flatcar. Another blast opens the top of a flaming walker's skull, the fountain of black fluids extinguishing the sparks and flames chewing up the front of its filthy dungarees. A third shot misses a large male, going high over its head. The thing turns and lunges at Miles, each of its outstretched arms flagging flames in the wind, sending fountains of sparks up into the draft.

Through it all, in the darkness of the pilothouse, Norma Sutters keeps an iron grip on the dead man's stick. She manages to hold the train at a steady forty miles an hour—fast enough to keep the fire from immolating them and hard enough to cast aside most of the walking dead with the makeshift cow catcher. Lilly keeps catching glimpses out of the corner of her eyes of moving cadavers appearing ghost-like in the cone of light from their headlamp, only to be catapulted into the air by the barbed-wire skid. Some of them disintegrate, limbs torn asunder in great gusts of rancid tissues and old blood swirling up into the back drafts. Others go down and are sliced in two by the speeding steel wheels keening along the ancient iron. Before long, a steady stream of blood and fluids begins crashing up against the bulwark of the rumbling engine with the throb of waves hitting a rocky shore. The mist washes across the flatcar, drenching the horses, slathering all who now cling to its slimy platform with gelatinous spoor.

Lilly finishes off the last of the uninvited passengers with a well-placed blast, penetrating the forehead of a middle-aged male in ragged mechanics overalls.

The biter staggers backward for a moment, slamming into a horse. The animal rears up, its eyes bugging wide like marbles in the flickering spark-light, causing the other horses to stir and snort and bob their heads frantically, stretching the guidelines holding them in place to their breaking point. One of the animals kicks out violently with its rear haunches, ramming the terminated walker with the force of twin wrecking balls. The hooves cave in the dead man's skull and send the mutilated remains skidding off the back of the car and into windy oblivion.

Almost without anyone noticing, the train has passed over the burning section of track, and now it speeds through the cold night, spontaneously blowing out most of the remaining sections that had caught fire. Miles and Tommy slap canvas down on a few oil spots still flagging sparks, while Jinx tosses water on a horsetail still smoldering.

Literally within seconds the chaos has subsided, the horses have settled, and the train has passed over the worst of the fire, the rumbling engine still steady at forty-some miles an hour, the flatcar covered in a coating of gore. Lilly glances over her shoulder and sees the inferno receding into the distance behind them, a fireball of yellow light scraping the clouds, a dying sun shrinking back into the blackness of space and time.

For the longest moment, as the train speeds away from the fire, Lilly just stands there on the windy surface of that flatcar, bracing herself against a horse's saddle, glancing from person to person, all of them expressionless, speechless. She shoves her gun back in its holster.

The train rumbles on, passing another mile marker closer to Fulton County.

Miles and Tommy crouch by the rear of the flatcar, wedged between two horses, still breathless from the plunge through the fire. Jinx holds on to a guide rope, stricken silent, gazing back over her shoulder at the pinprick of brilliant yellow light shrinking behind them into a tiny spot deep within the void of the night.

Lilly starts to holler something into the wind when the sound of Norma's voice pierces the slipstream.

"Y'ALL OKAY BACK THERE? WHAT IN THE WIDE WORLD OF SPORTS IS GOING ON?!"

Lilly shakes her head and lets out a wry, edgy chuckle despite her adrenaline-fueled nerves. The others stare and begin to laugh. The release of tension is immediate, and it passes from person to person like a punch line. Miles lets out a hilarious stoner's guffaw, laughing so hard his tears well up and then instantly dry in the wind. Tommy giggles. Jinx begins to laugh at the absurdity of the laughter, finding it so inappropriate she can't help but join in. Soon, the four of them are all chortling at the awkwardness of the situation, the surreal quality of what they're trying to do. And this goes on for another long beat until Lilly says, "Okay everybody, let's calm down and take a deep breath."

"HEY!" Norma's voice from the pilothouse. "SOMEBODY ANSWER ME!"

"We're good, Norma!" Lilly calls out. "We're all good. You can take the speed down a notch."

As the train slows back down to around thirty miles an hour, Lilly motions for everybody to stay low and meet her in the rear of the engine.

The sudden stillness of the passenger enclosure is a shock to the system. Lilly's ears ring from the gunfire. Her gloved hands are charred. She feels her spine tingling with emotion as she closes the hatch behind them, sealing them in that airless chamber of broken-down bench seats and discarded detritus. "Stay away from the windows," she advises.

"Why?" Jinx looks out at the blur of the passing nightscape. "What are you thinking?"

"The trap, the fire—they can't be far. They knew somebody would retaliate, they knew we'd come after them. They're scorching the earth."

Miles thinks about it for a second. He sits near the rear hatch, shivering, his goateed ebony face furrowed in thought. The fabric of his hoodie is torn and burned in spots. "But how would they *ever* fucking know we'd use a train?"

"They didn't." Lilly looks at him. "My guess is, they're covering their asses."

Jinx gives her a nod. "You think they're watching us right now?"

"If so, they just got one hell of a show. Just so we're prepared for whatever."

Jinx nods, takes a breath, wipes her sweaty face. "You think they got snipers on us?"

Lilly shakes her head. "I don't know. It's doubtful—I don't think they can afford to stay in one place. But you never know."

The muffled clatter of the rails and the low snorting of the horses outside the hatch punctuate the gravity of their situation. Lilly can feel the sand in the invisible hourglass leaking out, the clock in her head ticking down. They are using the last of their biodiesel and the last of their ammunition.

Tommy sits across the aisle from Miles, holding on to his 12 gauge in a valiant effort to conceal his trembling hands. "What now, Lilly?" he asks.

"We're going to be reaching the end of the usable track pretty soon." She looks at her watch. "Sun's coming up soon, so hopefully we'll have daylight when we have to switch over to horseback. I'm thinking we—"

Norma's voice from the pilothouse cuts her off. "LILLY! GET IN HERE—WE GOT A SITUATION!"

The moment she enters the pilothouse and smells the musky odor of fear coming off Norma Sutters, Lilly can tell something is wrong. Through the windshield, she can see the familiar deep woods rising up on either side of the track, the pine barrens north of Thomaston passing in a blur. Dawn isn't far off. The sky has turned ashy black, the stars receding, and now the wind blowing in through the vents has that cool, blue smell of imminent morning.

"What's the problem, Norma?"

"You recognize this neighborhood?"

Lilly shrugs. "Yeah, sure, we got another couple miles of finished track, at least."

Norma lets out a grunt of frustration. "While y'all were having a big laugh back there, we crossed the line into Coweta County."

"So . . . ?"

Norma's voice is thick with panic. "You ain't gettin' it."

"Getting what?"

"We're gonna hit the halfway point any minute now, the place we left off yesterday."

"I understand, and we'll break out the horses when it's time."

"You still ain't gettin' it."

"Would you just tell me what you're worried about?"

Norma stares through the windshield, teeth clenched with anger. "Does Bell's bridge ring a bell?"

"Bell's bridge?"

All at once, the events of the previous day come back to Lilly, and she remembers the massive wooden trestle, and she recalls the fact that Bell had neglected to check it for load worthiness. And now it looms a few short miles dead ahead in their path. "Okay, I get it . . . I get it." Lilly gathers her thoughts. "I want to be as far north as possible before we go to the horses."

Norma shoots a glance at her. "You're kidding me! You're gonna trust that thing enough to cross it?"

Lilly takes a deep breath. "If it was going to fail, it would have collapsed a long time ago."

"I can't believe what I'm hearing."

"Look, it's not that far across, and the creek is only twenty feet or so down."

"Are you messing with me now?" Norma throws another skeptical glance. "Because I can't tell anymore, I can't tell if you're the same old Lilly or if you've blown a gasket because of all this."

Lilly glares at her, acid roiling in her empty stomach. "You signed up for this, Norma. I gave you an out, and you insisted on coming, so you better fucking get your brain wired right."

"It would be a hell of a lot easier to get with the program if you just were honest with us."

Lilly looks at her. "What the fuck are you talking about? What is *wrong* with you? I've been totally honest. I told you, like I told the others, I'm going to get those kids back. Period."

Norma's voice gets huskier, lower. "I didn't sign on for some crazy-ass suicide mission." Another rueful glance. "I know what you're doing."

"Oh really? What am I doing, Norma? You tell me! What am I *doing*?!"

Norma unleashes her full church-choir-trained voice in a single bellowing shout from deep within her lungs: "YOU'RE USING US AS BAIT!!"

It takes a moment for Lilly to realize that the others have gathered in the hatchway behind her and now look on with grim, tense expressions. Lilly feels the heat of their gazes on the back of her neck.

The rumbling silence stretches. She never asked to be the leader of this community. The role was foisted upon her. But now, deep down in some secret place inside her, she has ripped free of Woodbury's orbit and operates in some feral, lizard-brain place that she never knew existed within her. More than mere bloodlust to destroy these kidnappers, more than all the pent-up grief and rage that has been building inside her for so long now, she has taken an evolutionary step in her development, a genetic imperative: *she will save her children or die.*

She glances over her shoulder at the others, then looks back at Norma and says, "I'm sorry." In a soft, almost tender voice, she adds, "You're right." Another glance over her shoulder. "I should have explained it to all of you. We have no hope of catching up to these people unless we can ferret them out. Draw them out of the sticks by acting as bait. It's the only way we're going to save our kids."

Norma keeps her white-knuckled grip on the stick, gaze locked on the horizon ahead of them. Her dark face gleams in the predawn glow through the windshield. She looks down for a moment. "I just wish you had been straight with us."

"Lilly—" Jinx starts to say something but her words are cut off by Lilly's contrite voice.

"I wouldn't blame you all for bailing on me right now—I probably would myself if I were you. I swear to you, though . . . I will die before I let harm come to any of you. The thing of it is, this is not an exact science."

"Lilly—"

"We have one thing going for us, though, which is the fact that they've taken our children. They've taken our kids. This is how we will—"

"LILLY!"

Jinx's voice finally penetrates, and Lilly looks up to see that Jinx is pointing at the windshield.

In the middle distance, maybe two to three hundred yards away and closing, stretches the dark span of ancient timbers and rusty iron girders known as Bell's Trestle.

Norma instinctively pulls back on the throttle, the train shuddering for a moment as the engine slows. The air fills with the odor of scorched oil. Through the windshield, the encroaching dawn bruises the edges of the horizon with pale-green light, the stars gone now, the moon retracted up into the wan canvas of the sky.

"Okay, I'm asking you to trust me on this," Lilly says to Norma. "I'm going to need you to go ahead and keep it steady, not too slow, but not too fast."

Norma nods, her face glistening with flop sweat, the smell of BO heavy in the pilothouse. The others bunch into the hatchway, nervously watching.

Lilly grips the edge of the vent so tightly she tears through the palm of her glove and doesn't even notice the sharp edge of the ledge breaking her skin. Ahead of them, the trestle looms. The closer they get, the more the sunrise illuminates the massive silhouette of the bridge, the mossy side rails enrobed in mist, the early rays of sunlight filtering through the lattice. The thing looks ancient, as though it were built by Aztecs or Paleolithic men, the cross ties as black as mildew, the oxidized railing the color of pond scum. Old, brown, dead kudzu twines up through its convolutions and shades the middle of the span.

"Keep it down around twenty miles an hour," Lilly says. "Maybe twenty-five."

Norma does so as the train approaches the bridge. All gazes turn to see down below, their necks craning to glimpse the dry creek bed twenty-two feet beneath the bridge clogged with leaves and trash and dark shapes that may or may not be human remains. Walker activity has been brisk up around these parts, and the stream features a trough of rusty, stagnant water down its center that looks suspiciously like old blood.

The engine cobbles onto the bridge.

The high-pitched keening of the rails instantly dampens and changes into muffled wooden drumming noises, hollow sounding and syncopated with the throbbing of the turbine. Out of the corner of her eye, Lilly sees dust and debris falling from the timbers beneath her, sifting down through the shadows onto the leafy carpet of the creek bed. She can hear the horses stirring, the low snorting sounds of alarm filling the air. The flatcar comes next, bumping onto the bridge.

The entire structure of the trestle beneath them shifts suddenly with the full weight of the train, one side sagging and creaking like an aging sailing vessel tossed by a wave. They feel the center of gravity pitch slightly, the pilothouse leaning at a twenty-five-degree angle as the wheels lose traction for a moment. Lilly can feel the loss of purchase. The train slows to a crawl. The creaking noises rise, the pilothouse listing severely.

"PUNCH IT!" Lilly's cry gets drowned by a massive cracking noise, which pierces the air. Gravity shifts as the trestle floor begins to rupture, a weightless feeling rising in Lilly's gorge. Norma shoves the throttle forward, the steel wheels spinning in place like knives on a whetstone. A scream from the rear hatch slices through the air as the span begins to collapse, sending up a great cloud of dust in the harsh morning light.

Lilly slams her hand down on Norma's throttle hand, pinning the lever against the panel, causing the engine to scream and churn, sending waves of vibrations through the undercarriage. The engine reaches the end of the trestle, its wheels still spinning, traction nearly gone. The machine jumps the track and slides into the mud.

In that horrible instant before Lilly glances over her shoulder, the entire rear of the train shudders suddenly as though yanked backward by a massive hand. Lilly and Norma are thrown forward. Someone yells a garbled warning as Lilly looks back through the open hatch and feels a wave of cold terror travel through her midsection.

A thunderhead of dust explodes beneath the flatcar right before the entire trestle gives way.

SIX

It seems to happen in slow motion. The bridge rends in the middle and collapses into itself, wrenching apart with the speed and finality of a house of cards. The horses tumble into each other as the flatcar rips free of its coupler and slides backward at a severe angle. The rear end hits the ground first, most of the animals skidding across the pitching platform, guide ropes snapping.

The animals land in a heap, mostly on top of each other, their plunge broken by both the trash heap of the creek bed and each other's girth.

Meanwhile the flatcar has broken apart on impact, the rucksacks and duffel bags flying, giant pieces of the frame falling on either side, sending up a virtual mushroom cloud of dust. The last few shards of the platform splash into the brackish mire of the creek, followed by a shocking silence, a square acre of dust obscuring the writhing animals and wreckage in the ditch.

Twenty-two feet above the scene, coughing, waving away the dirty haze, Lilly leans out the rear of the engine. Spindly lengths of rebar, bent sections of railroad tracks, and long shards of ancient timbers overhang the miniature dust storm below. The sounds of the animals snorting, struggling, squealing in pain and confusion, all of it suddenly drifts up through the brown miasma. Lilly starts to say something when she sees the first animal dart out of the cloud.

Jinx is the first to speak. "Shit!—shit!—shit!—SHIT!"

The huge seal-brown thoroughbred is instantly recognizable, despite the fact that massive creature is now covered in dust, thorns, and oily muck from the stagnant creek. A gash is visible in the hide of her rear haunch, the wound shiny with blood and filth. The horse leaps over a logjam and gallops up the side of the muddy slope.

"ARROW! NO!" Jinx pushes her way through the crowded hatch.

Down below, in the creek bed, other horses burst out of the dust cloud, following Arrow's lead. Within moments, all five animals have staggered across the creek bed and then vaulted, one after another, up the slope. Jinx climbs over the coupler, drops herself to the ground, and then rushes headlong down the muddy slope, moving as fast as she can, her boots sinking into the soft earth.

Lilly sees this and for a brief instant is paralyzed with panic and indecision, a cold fist squeezing her guts, clenching her innards. If they lose these horses, they might as well give up. At last, Lilly turns to the others. "Norma, you and Tommy stay here and guard the supplies!" She looks at Miles. "How fast can you run?"

In this part of the world—especially after a long, brutal dry spell— the wetlands and the swampy areas of West Central Georgia get covered with a thick sediment of dead leaves, twigs, kudzu vines, moss, and windblown trash. The ground cover can mask extremely hazardous bodies of water—former ponds that have transformed due to the overgrowth of the plague years into soupy, marshy, unsteady swamps. On that morning, after galloping side by side across nearly a mile of farm fields—the animals bunched together due to herd instinct—the runaway horses cross just such a patch of swampy water. Jinx is the first to see the horses go down, and she yells something that Lilly can't quite hear. Lilly lopes along behind the younger woman, heaving and panting, drenched in sweat, her side stitched with pain. She can see what Jinx is screaming about now.

About a hundred yards in the distance, on the edge of a marshy section of land bordered by densely packed pines, the five horses abruptly sink into the earth as though running down a ramp. Their elongated heads periscope above the surface of the sinkhole, tossing and shaking the muck off themselves, throwing stringers of foam through rays of intense early-morning sunlight, trying to swim their way out of the vortex of mire pulling them down. Lilly can see the dark, ragged silhouettes of the dead emerging from the woods on either side of the marsh, meandering toward the noise and commotion of living things in trouble.

Miles rushes past Lilly, and then past Jinx, and reaches the edge of the pond within seconds. He dives in headfirst, making a phosphorescent splash of green scum, and then dog-paddles as fast as he can toward the closest horse, Jinx's big thoroughbred, who's in trouble, barely able to hold its muzzle above the surface of the sludgy water. Miles reaches the horse and manages to tread water while he lifts the majestic head above the mire.

But the suction of all the frantic movement starts to pull Miles down.

Meanwhile, Jinx approaches the scene. Slipping on the wet ground, skating to a stop along the edge of the marsh, she sees that Miles is now also in danger of drowning and she pulls her belt free. She leaps into the sinkhole feetfirst and swims toward Miles. "ARROW!" she calls to her steed. "ARROW! OVER HERE, GIRL!"

Jinx throws the end of the belt to Miles, who manages to latch on to it. The other horses gurgle and snort as they go under a second and third time. Arrow starts paddling madly toward his master, Miles holding on. Jinx tries to yank on the belt but it slips out of her hand, and she staggers backward, slipping under the surface for a second. She bursts back out of the water gasping, spitting, cursing.

Lilly sees all this from a distance as she closes in on the sinkhole, but just as she's about to leap into the water, she notices about a half dozen walkers pressing in from the east, and another five or six approaching from the west. Lilly has four rounds left in her magazine, not enough to take down all of the dead. She draws a bead on the closest walker and squeezes off a single shot. The thing jerks backward as though electrocuted, the top of its head opening, disgorging a flood of black fluid that flows down its body in runnels before the thing collapses and sinks into the marsh. She shoots another, and another, and another, things happening very quickly now, almost all at once. Faces cleaving, heads erupting, ragged forms sinking out of sight, Ruger clicking empty, Jinx screaming wet, choked cries thirty feet away, Miles bobbing in the muck, the horses wriggling and tossing heads in futile survival instinct mode, the whole scene captured in radiant slanting rays of brilliant sunlight.

At a certain point, an enormous deadfall lying nearby catches Lilly's eye, and she acts without hesitation or forethought. It takes all her strength to shove the massive log across the surface of the sinkhole. The timber splashes into the muck, nearly hitting one of the horses in the head. Miles manages to grab hold of it, as does Jinx. Miles holds on with everything he has, clutching Arrow's bridle, keeping the huge horse from sinking into oblivion. Meanwhile, another half dozen biters are approaching from the east, shambling toward the commotion with arms outstretched and mouths working and eyes reflecting the sun like tarnished coins. One by one, they tumble into the swamp, vanishing under the surface of the sinkhole.

Lilly pulls a bowie knife from her belt and dives into the mire.

Something moves beneath one of the horses, something dark and slimy and dead. The horse rears and squeals. Something below the surface latches on to it and digs into its midsection, causing the animal to let out a horrifying caterwaul of agony. In the sunlight, the iridescent surface of the marsh darkens with the horse's blood. The animal twists and writhes, its muzzle lifting to the heavens in its death throes, the blood bubbling up from its craw, choking it, taking it down into the dark rheumy silt below. The animal sinks out of sight, the bubbles spreading across the scummy surface of the marsh as dark shapes move below.

Lilly swims to the log and grabs hold, gasping for breath, her grip unsteady on the slimy timber. She tries to get air in her lungs. She starts to slide off. She drops the knife and hugs the log. The sunlight blinds her. She can barely see Jinx and Miles out of the corner of her eye, each of them clinging to the log. The stench fills Lilly's senses, an indescribable mélange of methane, rotting flesh, coppery blood, and grassy swamp gases.

Another horse shrieks in agony twenty feet away, the swamp filled with the dead, the muck turning dark crimson red with the profusion of blood now infusing the marsh, warming the pocket of water around Lilly's legs, causing Lilly to get dizzy with terror. She can barely see now. Out of ammo. No knife. Shivering. Hypothermia coming on. A dark shape moving beneath her. She can hardly breathe or see with the sun and tears in her eyes. How did this happen? The log shifts in the water, begins to sink.

Lilly can barely see the blurry shapes of Jinx and Miles holding on to the opposite end of the sinking log, gasping for breath, trying to kick at the dark moving shapes beneath them. Only three horses remain, each one hyperventilating, the sound of their breaths like heartbeats fading, slowing, dying. Lilly tries to think. Her brain has seized up. Nothing on her mind screen now but dark red covering everything, pulling down a shade over her consciousness. The log sinks below the surface. Lilly feels the clammy cold swamp water rising up over her chin and mouth and nose. Her strength gone, her mind blank, she hears a strange noise right before the surface of the marsh rises over her ears.

"HOLY FUCKING SHIT!!—HOW DID THIS HAPPEN?!"

A ghostly disembodied voice echoes in her ears as if in a dream. Lilly sinks below the surface.

"JACK! TAKE THOSE FLESH EATERS OUT WHILE I GRAB A FUCKING ROPE!!"

The voice goes all muffled, watery, and dreamy as Lilly sinks, blinking languidly and gazing through the rheumy green soup of the swamp. The thick stew of underwater weeds, floating detritus, and strands of unidentified organic tissue drifting aimlessly practically glows in the radiant ribbons of early-morning sun, which now penetrate the water. Lilly can see dead people walking across the silt directly below her like citizens traversing the alien streets of a necropolis.

All at once, a series of blasts as brilliant and sudden as lightning bolts pierces the marshy atmosphere, tracer bullets threading through the water, canting directly down toward the dead people. The blasts take each walker in a slow-motion *ballet macabre*—heads snapping forward, clouds of darker fluid pluming out, shoulders hunching as bullets exit and drill into the silt floor in little puffs of darker muck.

Somewhere in the deepest recesses of Lilly's mind, a clarion bell sounds. She kicks and flails and swims back up toward the surface with every last shred of strength she can muster, her lungs catching fire, her oxygen-starved brain turning everything around her into streaks of purple, magenta, and red-tinged neon light. She nearly doesn't make it—her body starts to shut down one nanosecond before she surfaces with an enormous, heaving gasp.

"There she is!"

Things are happening too quickly for Lilly to lock on to any one thing. A length of thick, heavy-duty rope splashes in the water only inches away from her. She grabs hold of it. Another volley of gunfire pierces the air. In her bleary vision, Lilly can see silhouettes of figures gathered along the edge of the marsh in front of her, some of them on horseback, others aiming high-powered rifles at the dead things polluting the swamp. Lilly catches glimpses of Jinx and Miles and the three surviving horses being hauled out of the water, and she hears a familiar female voice.

"Thank God we came along when we did!"

Moving with the drunken slowness of a stroke victim, Lilly winds the rope around her hand and forearm, and then feels the tug as they pull her toward dry land. She crawls with agonizing sluggishness out of the water and then collapses into a fetal position, taking great lungfuls of air. She rolls onto her back.

A woman stands over her, smiling down at her while holding an AR-15 on her hip. Tall, sinewy, hair pulled back in a tight ponytail, the woman wears a tactical vest laden with mag pouches and gear over her chambray top, and has a patrician face that brings to mind summers in Hyannisport and cocktails on the veranda. "Just about lost you there, kiddo," the woman says with a wink. "You need to be more careful—especially now."

Lilly manages to speak in a hoarse croak. "Ash? How did you—?"

The woman—Ashley Lynn Duart—interrupts with a deferential wave of her slender hand. "Plenty of time for questions, Lilly . . . but not here."

The town of Haralson—where Ash currently resides and runs things for a small, tightly knit group of twenty-two survivors—was once a sleepy little farming community on the southern edge of Coweta County. Not much more than a couple of intersecting two-lanes, a Baptist church, a coffee shop, a small grocery store, and a few modest wood-frame homes and professional buildings, the place had a pickled-in-time feel to it when Ash ended up here three years ago after escaping the walker-riddled suburbs of Atlanta. From the tin roofs of the grain elevator to the actual pickle barrels on the porch of the feed and seed store, the little hamlet looked as though it had been built by Walt Disney and art directed by Norman Rockwell. But the last few years have militarized places such as this, draining the quaint out of them, and Haralson, Georgia, is no exception. In addition to massive barricades of found materials erected around the center of town, the fifty-caliber gun placements at each corner and the proliferation of concertina wire along every fence give the place an air of martial law.

"Don't do this," Ash pleads with Lilly and her crew late that morning in the Haralson Baptist church rectory, her voice grave and low. "Go home."

The large, airy room still has its stained-glass panels from before the Turn and fake plants are arrayed along the windowsills. Book-lined walls, shaded lamps, and a large conference table in the center of the room complete the picture of preplague order, gentile society, houses of worship, and a loving God. Lilly paces, chewing her fingernails, moving with a slight limp from her misadventures on the railroad. The others sit around the room in various stages of medical dressing, bandages, and Betadine swaths. Miles sits at one end of the conference table, still shivering slightly from hypothermia, a blanket wrapped around him. Jinx sits on a sill, listening as she wipes down her blades. Norma and Tommy sit side by side at the other end of the conference table, hanging on every word Ash says.

"These are serious dudes," Ash elaborates, sitting on a padded swivel chair at the head of the room, her slender arms crossed against her flat chest. Still sporting her tac vest and tight ponytail, she's all sharp angles and lean muscle, like a fitness instructor. "They pack major heat and they have a mission—don't ask me what the hell it is—and they will kill you just as soon as look at you. Trust me on this."

Lilly stops pacing and puts her hands defiantly on her hips. "All the more reason to go after them."

"Lilly, you're not listening. They've already hit every major survivor group from here to College Park—they killed five of my people. Now Moreland doesn't answer the radio, and I'm worried that they hit Heronville as well. They're on some kind of binge, some kind of fucked-up thrill-kill binge."

Lilly thinks about it for a second. "I assume you talked to Cooper?"

Ash lets out an exasperated sigh. "Radio silence."

A thin trickle of chills passes down through Lilly's midsection, her complex relationship with the man coloring her reaction. It's no secret that Cooper Steeves's faux Indiana Jones posturing gets to most people. In fact, if Lilly took a poll among the survivors, and asked to whom they would award the prize for the Most Obnoxious Douche Bag Among the Living, Cooper Steeves would win in a landslide. But Lilly has always suspected the existence of another side to Cooper, a deeper layer of humanity lurking beneath the fedora and fake bullwhip. She has always found him amusing and handy and useful in a crisis as a devil's advocate. Sure, he's fussy and arrogant, and maybe even a little bit narcissistic, but he's also brilliant and well read and an independent thinker. Most importantly, he would never allow a transmission sent to his walkie-talkie to go unanswered—hell, if you got him drunk he would claim he *invented* the concept of walkie-talkies.

Lilly vividly recalls the day last year when Cooper Steeves introduced the idea of interconnectedness among survivor towns. He had sent a courier to Woodbury—one of his teenage charges on a swayback pony—requesting the presence of the leaders of each town along the South Central corridor. Lilly set out the next morning for Moreland. When she arrived, Cooper had gathered Ash and the others in the police station lobby for an impromptu presentation. He had a whiteboard at the front of the room and was strutting around in his bomber jacket and fedora, wielding his dry-erase marker as if it were a medieval mace. "The key to everything is *communication*," he began in his stentorian voice, as pompous and pedantic as ever. Then, with a dramatic flourish that would put an infomercial pitchman to shame, he tossed a dog-eared catalog on the end table where everybody could see it. "Introducing the key to everything . . . right under our noses."

Lilly remembers recognizing the old Hammacher Schlemmer catalog from the old days in Marietta when she and her father would receive the upscale knickknack catalog around Christmastime each year. Teenage Lilly loved to peruse the latest gadgets and gewgaws, the nose hair trimmers and heated full body massage chairs and rechargeable streaming video camera pens. But that day in the Moreland Police Department lobby, staring at that faded, water-stained catalog, she got what Cooper Steeves was talking about as soon as he turned to page 113 and pointed at the device circled in red at the bottom of the page. The Crank-Wound Rechargeable CB Radio Base with Three Portable Walkie-Talkies originally went for $199.99 (or four easy installments of $49.99 per month). "There's a Hammacher Schlemmer store in the Moreland Mall on the north side of this very town," Cooper had announced then with all the pomp and circumstance of a minister delivering the good news of the blessed savior Jesus Christ. His cleft chin had jutted with so much pride that day, Lilly thought it might pop off his face as he pontificated. "Now, I realize the place is overrun with the dead, but with the right battalion of hearty souls, we could very easily procure enough of these crank-wound radios to keep the entire network of survivor towns wired and connected for the duration." This was how Cooper Steeves usually talked, like an evangelist teaching a class, but Lilly remembers thinking at the time what a brilliant perspective it was.

Now . . . nothing but radio silence.

"They took my kids, Ash." Lilly stares at the tall woman, an unwavering gaze. Lilly's fists clench involuntarily at her side as she paces and thinks. "I don't fucking care what I have to do."

"I understand that, but what I'm saying is, we barely kept them at bay with the best fortification I know of in these parts, and we drew major casualties. You're nothing to them. No matter how motivated you are, you will *not* make a dent in these guys, you will *not* stop them."

Lilly paces some more. "I don't want to stop them, I don't need to make a dent in them." She looks at the others. "I don't want to drag anybody into a suicide mission." Her eyes well up. "I just want my kids back. That's all." She wipes a tear off her cheek. "I want my kids back."

Ash looks down, doesn't say anything, and the silence stretches for an interminable length of time as the others avoid eye contact with Lilly. The rays of sun through the stained glass give the room a strange, ethereal quality that seems to accentuate the stalemate. At last, Ash takes a deep breath and lets out a pained sigh. "I want to show you something. All of you. Follow me."

The body lies in Haralson's makeshift morgue, the holding room of a former grain elevator on Main Street. The high ceiling of cobwebbed girders and skylights combine with the corrugated tin walls to give the space an air of institutional despair, a purgatory of gurneys like a Civil War mobile hospital. Lilly stands over the last bed in a row of sheet-covered bodies, the bloodstained fabric covering the last body forming Rorshach-like patterns.

"Who am I looking at?" Lilly asks as Ash steps around to the head of the gurney. The others hang back at a respectful distance.

"He was out there in the barrens with his beloved wind machines when the kidnappers picked him off." Ash pulls the sheet away and reveals the identity of the corpse on the metal table.

"Oh, God." Lilly almost involuntary looks away. In the back, Norma gasps, and the others make anguished sighing noises. For a moment, Lilly looks as though she might vomit. Her voice crumbles around the words as she gazes back at the body. "Goddamn it."

Bell's remains are shirtless, a towel over his groin, and the body is surprisingly pristine, tranquil, and undisturbed. Although it's never spelled out, Lilly will later deduce that Ash demanded special attention be paid to this body, and to the postmortem business of destroying the brain and preparing the cadaver for burial.

Everybody loved Bell, and Bell loved his wind farm. For the last year, in fact, he had preached the gospel of wind energy to anyone who would listen. With his ragtag crew from Moreland, he had retrieved at least a dozen of the massive windmills from various rural locations across the South, dismantling them and bringing the parts back to West Central Georgia where he lovingly rebuilt them and started his own wind farm in a meadow between two tobacco fields. Not many of the windmills worked yet, but Bell was obsessed, and he was not the only one. Homemade wind farms had been cropping up all over the place in recent months. Some survivors were even working on ways to refurbish electric cars for future use with wind-generated power. Bell was a true believer, and he could often be seen wandering the meadow among the giant shifting shadows of the turning blades like a vintner proudly strolling the length of his vineyard.

Lilly loved Bell as much as anybody else—in a platonic sense, of course—and that tormented the man. He had such a raging crush on Lilly that someone once found a notebook of Bell's in which he had scribbled Lilly's name, birth date, hometown, and personal data over and over—à la the scrawl of some lovelorn high school kid—as if she and he should be going to the prom together. Now, the sight of his empty shell of a body—discarded like trash, two clean entrance wounds like tiny coins above his left nipple—tortures Lilly. His boy-ish face and his crazy mop of hair, still wiry tendrils of flaming red, call out to her. He looks like he was merely asleep.

"They just . . . killed him in cold blood?" Lilly can barely form the sentence. "For no reason? Like . . . like some game animal they were hunting?"

"Maybe . . . but I don't think so." Ash swallows and leans down to the body. She gently lifts the left arm and rotates it slightly so that Lilly can see the tiny puncture wound in the crook between fore-arm and bicep—the spot where his veins still bulge. "We found him facedown in the meadow, the windmills burning. Looked like he tried to stop them. He got hit on the head first, then dragged before they shot him execution style for reasons unknown."

"Jesus."

Ash points at the puncture wound. "We saw this when we got him back here."

Lilly leans in. Jinx and Miles move in closer to look over Lilly's shoulder at the faint ringworm of a bruise around a tiny pinprick of a hole in Bell's arm, which is rimmed in red. Lilly tries to focus her thoughts. She wipes her eyes and says, "What is it?"

Ash shrugs, lowering the arm back to the edge of the gurney. "I'm not sure, I'm no pathologist, but that looks like a needle mark."

"A needle mark? Are you saying Bell's a junkie? He did this to himself?"

Ash waves the possibility off. "No, not at all. It's too fresh."

"So you're saying *they* did this to him? These paramilitary motherfuckers, they drugged him?"

"I know it doesn't make any sense." Ash sighs. "Why drug a man you're going to waste in two seconds?"

Lilly rubs her face. She looks at Jinx. "Nothing these people do makes any sense."

Ash nods. "Agreed." She looks at Bell's remains. "But that doesn't mean they're crazy. It would be a mistake to think they're just nuts or wasted or whatever. They're dangerous as hell, Lilly."

"I think we've established that much." Lilly takes a deep breath as Ash gently puts the sheet back over Bell's upper half. Lilly sighs, rubbing her eyes. She tries to gather her thoughts, tries to think of her next move. She looks at Ash. "You mind if we stay the night? Rest up? Maybe borrow a few items?"

Ash gives her a look. "You're not going to take my advice, are you?"

Lilly looks at the others, looks at the floor. She can't think of anything else to say.

"You're going to keep going after these people until you find them or get yourselves killed." Ash crosses her arms against her chest. "Do I have that about right?"

Lilly meets her gaze but says nothing.

That night, after dinner, Lilly meets with her team in the church rectory.

"I want to make sure you all know what's in store for us north of here." She stands at the front of the meeting room, the door closed, a kerosene lantern at each end of the table illuminating the room. The genial quality of the place during daylight hours has now been transformed into an atmosphere of somber, shadow-draped secrets. The stained-glass panels are all dark and opaque, their ornate Bible scenes now looking cryptic and mysterious. The skylights glow with pale, cold moonlight, the faces of the listeners looking almost simian in the low-key light, the traumas of the day, as well as the shock of seeing Bell's remains, still hanging heavy in the air like an odor. Brows furrow in thought as Lilly elaborates. "Trust me on this. Nobody wants to go north of here if they can help it. From this point on, it's hairy as hell, and twice as dangerous."

"Go on," Norma Sutters says from her chair at the end of the table. She sits with her plump hands folded in front of her as though about to say grace before dinner. Miles sits on one side of her, Jinx on the other. Tommy stands behind them, preferring to lean against the windowsill as he listens, every few moments shooting a nervous glance outside through a gap in the boarded window.

"You've all heard rumors about the swarm rings and such," she goes on. "About an hour ago, one of Ash's scouts rode the high ridge road and saw how bad it gets as you cross into the suburbs."

The room remains silent as everybody processes. Rumors have circulated for months now that the megaherds—which normally migrate across the land with glacial slowness—have for some reason settled into inexplicable orbits around the outer burbs of the city. No one is certain why, but it seems as though the massive swarms have stalled there in this strange, inscrutable pattern, like moths circling a flame, and anybody dumb enough to try and get into Atlanta from the south is walking into a little piece of hell on earth.

"I know I've said this all along," Lilly finally chimes back in, breaking the spell of silence. "But I want to give all of you another chance to bail out."

Jinx rolls her eyes. "Do we really have to play this tired old record again?"

"This is different, Jinx. Seeing Bell in there, seeing Haralson like this . . . I have no right to force any of you to continue on this gonzo fucking mission." She looks around the room and feels her heart panging with love for these people, her inner circle, her family. What good would it do getting the children back if these folks lost their lives in the bargain? Lilly pushes the feeling of desolation back down her throat as she tries to smile at them. "There would be no shame in pulling out at this point. No guilt, no questions asked. We're going to be leaving just before dawn . . . I want you all to think it through tonight. I want you all to be sure. No pressure, no expectations. I'll be fine, whatever you decide. I'm a big girl. I'll be okay."

She turns and starts to walk out of the room, but pauses before turning the doorknob. She glances back over her shoulder at them. "Whatever you decide, just know that I will always love you guys."

She walks out.

SEVEN

Lilly would never know for sure what was said in that rectory conference room that night after she made her exit. She would always have her theories, though. Tommy and Norma probably had a heated debate on the pros and cons of continuing. Perhaps Jinx just sat there and listened silently with a disgusted look on her face. Maybe Miles suggested they take a vote—Miles Littleton, the practical car thief, the voice of reason. Lilly never would have expected Norma to continue. Jinx and Tommy were another matter altogether—definitely candidates to stay on board. But Miles was the wild card.

A former gangbanger from the mean streets of Detroit, wheelman for mob heists and freelance criminals of all stripes, the young man is the living embodiment of the Hoodlum with the Heart of Gold. From his gentle, long-lashed eyes, to his delicate little goatee, his face reflects the contradiction of his life. He's a gentle soul in a brutal environment. He wouldn't hesitate to erupt with violence if the need arose, but the fact is, he has no taste for it. All of which makes it impossible to predict what he's about to do that next morning.

The uncertainty torments Lilly that night as she settles into bed in a small bungalow next to Ash's apartment building and tries desperately to get some sleep. She'll need the rest, regardless of what her team decides. But sleep remains stubbornly elusive that night. The lonely, unfurnished bungalow—stacked to the ceiling with supplies and canned goods—tics and settles in the moonlit darkness as Lilly tosses and turns. Intermittently, she drifts off into falling dreams—falling from planes, falling from sheer cliffs, falling from bridges and buildings and precipices.

The next morning just after dawn, she meets Ash in the grassy court-yard across the street from Williams Grocery. The courtyard borders the massive gate on the north side of town, and in the predawn darkness, the silhouettes of telephone poles, road signs, the barricade, and the gleaming concertina wire curling along the top of the wall all look unreal, like construction paper cutouts in a pop-up book. The sky has that gray, dead, washed-out quality that it gets right before dawn, and the chill in the air is bracing.

For a moment, gazing around the empty yard, Lilly assumes that she'll be alone from this point on. She helps Ash retrieve the three surviving horses, and they hook the biggest, sturdiest animal, Arrow, to a retrofitted, rust-pocked old Volvo station wagon that's been chopped up, the windshield removed to allow the traces through. The rear cargo bay is filled with guns, ammo, and supplies.

Lilly is about to say something when a voice from behind her interrupts.

"Don't tell me you're gonna put me on one of them skinny little geldings."

Lilly spins and sees Jinx and Tommy walking up with their tactical vests on, their holsters jangling on their hips, and their heavy packs strapped to their shoulders. Relief courses through Lilly as she clears her throat and says, "Sorry about that, Jinx . . . gonna need Arrow's muscle. Tommy, why don't you ride with me in the buggy?"

Jinx throws her pack on the closest horse, making the animal snort and rear backward. Jinx softly whispers to the creature, patting its withers and stroking its mane. She pulls a roll of duct tape from her pack, kneels, and begins wrapping the silver tape around the horse's fetlocks. The protective measure won't save the animal from a swarm but it will ward off the bite of a single walker.

Lilly comes over, puts a hand on Jinx's shoulder, and speaks very softly: "Thank you . . . I was worried there for a second that I lost you."

"You think I'd miss all this fun?" Jinx gives her a wicked little smile.

"C'mon, Lilly," a voice says from behind her. She pivots to see Tommy thrusting his hands in his pockets, shyly looking down at the ground. "Give us a little credit."

Lilly reaches out and touches Tommy's hair. "I'll never doubt you guys again."

Footsteps crunch across gravel on the other side of the courtyard, yanking Lilly's attention over her shoulder toward the east.

"Sorry I'm late, y'all," Miles Littleton says as he approaches in his hoodie with the rucksack on one arm, his Glock holstered on a bandolier across his skinny chest. "Had to find some toilet paper. My mom used to say, 'Never go anywhere in nature without toilet paper.'"

Lilly swallows a lump in her throat, her eyes moistening with emotion. Something about the tone of Miles Littleton's voice, the sadness in his eyes, the clench of his jaw, tells her that he's not all here. He seems a little overwhelmed. But Lilly doesn't have the luxury of getting emotional right now. She breathes in the crisp predawn air, claps her hands, and says, "I've never been so happy to hear about toilet paper in my life."

Inside the shadow of his hoodie, he cocks his head warily at her. "You didn't think I'd bail on ya, did ya? What do you think I am, King Pussy?"

Lilly swallows back another surge of emotion. "C'mon, Your Highness, let's get this show on the road."

By this point, Ash has secured the big thoroughbred to the carriage, battened down the rear hatch, and checked the rear tires for road-worthiness. She looks skeptically at the makeshift carriage as the others climb in—Lilly at the reins, Tommy sitting shotgun. Jinx climbs onto one of the geldings, awkwardly snapping the reins when the horse begins complaining, snorting and backing toward the closest building. "Easy, sport," Jinx soothes in a soft voice, checking her largest machete for quick access.

Miles mounts his horse and makes sure his Glock is safety-on, loaded, and properly holstered on his bandolier. He has nearly a hundred rounds courtesy of Ash and her well-stocked arsenal.

"Thanks for everything," Lilly says through the side window of the carriage to the tall woman.

Ash nods and then says, "You're missing one, aren't you?"

Lilly shrugs. "To be honest, I don't fault her one bit. She may be the smart one."

"We'll make sure she gets back to Woodbury in one piece."

"Check on David Stern, will ya? He's a tough old dude but he got pretty banged up."

"Will do." Ash steps away, puts her hands on her hips. "I hope you get them back."

Lilly looks at her. "But you don't think we will, do you?"

"I never said that."

"You don't have to."

The sun has already broken on the horizon, the mossy light rising behind the rooftops, turning the ancient tin buildings into silhouettes. The air buzzes with birdcalls and drones with insects. Ash is formulating a response when the sound of a voice calls out behind them.

"HEY Y'ALL!"

All heads turn when the large, dark-skinned women with the do-rag over her hair comes trundling quickly around the corner of an adjacent building. She jangles and jiggles as she approaches, a brand-new machete dangling off one ample hip, an overstuffed rucksack strapped over her shoulder. "Don't leave without me!"

Norma comes up to the driver's side of the horse-cart and pauses outside Lilly's open window.

The two women make eye contact, and they hold each other's gaze for quite a long moment without saying a word. The transaction of body language and facial expressions is subtle but also powerful. The way that Norma's chin juts ever so slightly with defiance and pride, and the way that Lilly cants her head in an almost paternal I-told-you-so expression—all of it passes in a brief instant. Then Lilly cracks a big shit-eating smile, and Norma's face lights up with affection, maybe even a touch of admiration as she grins back at Lilly. The exchange is complete, no words necessary.

Lilly turns to Tommy and says, "Clear a space in the backseat for her."

They exit Haralson and head north, Lilly taking the lead in that Frankenstein's monster of a carriage, the enormous horse instantly going damp with sweat, foaming at the mouth with effort. Jinx and Miles ride along behind the buggy, on either flank, deathly silent, tense, and jerking at noises. Everybody can feel the stakes being raised, the presence of something unseen and menacing as they close in on the outskirts of the fallen city.

That morning, they pass through the southern portion of Coweta County without incident.

Around noon, they pass by the still-smoking remnants of Bell's wind farm. Off in the distance to the west, the giant windmills lie in ruins, some of them broken in half, some missing fan blades, some still smoldering. The sight of it puts a pinch in Lilly's gut, the twenty-acre farm now resembling some medieval stronghold razed by torches and flaming catapults. As they rattle pass the north corner of the complex, they realize how recently this attack must have happened when they see a low, brackish swamp still sparking and crackling in veins of light as the tangle of power cables continues to drain its residual electricity. The remains of about a dozen walkers lie mired in the crater, twitching and convulsing involuntarily with each random bolt of dying energy.

Lilly picks up the pace, snapping the reins and getting the massive thoroughbred to transition from a trot to a canter. The others spur their animals on, hurrying to keep up. For hours now, very few words have been spoken among Lilly and her team. They all sense the presence of the kidnappers, the invisible menace intensifying. They can smell dead flesh on the winds. They can feel the presence of the hordes in the way that their eyes are starting to burn, their stomachs tightening, their pulses quickening.

By midafternoon, they reach the apex of a hill and get their first glimpse of the outskirts of Fulton County off in the distance below.

Lilly instantly pulls the carriage to a stop, the others halting on either flank. Lilly's heartbeat throbs in her ears, her stomach clenching as she breathes in the rancid death-stench infusing the atmosphere. She gazes out at the evidence of what people have been warning her about now for months. The others stare in speechless shock. The low ambient hum of monsters echoing up against the sky is overwhelming as Lilly slowly scans the panorama of thousands of dead—maybe tens of thousands—milling about down in the meadows and valleys along the county line.

Like a diabolical ant farm of ragged figures, the hordes stretch for several hundred yards in either direction. From this distance, the throngs undulate and ooze like a moving black pointillist painting splashed across the plague-worn countryside. There is no progress to their movement, no shift in their position. Against her better judgment, Lilly reaches down to her knapsack, pulls out her binoculars, and peers through the lenses.

Norma's strangled voice comes from the backseat. "What now, d'ya think?"

In the telescopic field, Lilly sees the ocean of moldering faces chewing at the air with blackened teeth and eyes like old ivory. Most of the tattered clothing clinging to the dead is weathered to a gray parchment, the bodies brushing up and bumping against each other, all shapes and sizes and degrees of decomposition, standing room only for miles and miles, random particles filling the void, their cold gray hands clawing at the abyss, insatiable, driven by the unfathomable compulsions of the plague.

"I have a feeling they're waiting to see what we do," Lilly mutters, more to herself than anyone else.

"Who?" Tommy's voice is stretched as taut as a piano string. "The walkers?"

"The kidnappers."

"You think they're watching us?"

"I do."

Tommy studies her for a moment. "Wait, I know that look, you're not thinking of—"

"Fasten your seat belt!"

"No, Lilly—"

"Hold on!"

Lilly snaps the reins and the thoroughbred launches into a gallop, making the carriage lurch.

Instantly they plunge down the slope.

Jinx and Miles follow at a dead run.

Since the advent of the plague almost four years ago, survivors have pondered, ruminated, and agonized over something that has come to be known as walker behavior—as if the appellation "walker" has heralded the advent of some new genus and species (which, in a way, it *has*). Do they learn? Do they digest? Do they get filled up? Do they display only involuntary behavior? Do they poop? But the area of inquiry that has long obsessed most survivors and kept them up late at night has come to be known as "herd behavior."

To this day, nobody's quite certain why herds form, or if they have a purpose, or how long they stay intact before drifting apart like leaves on the windy surface of the sea. The only thing that's indisputable is that they're catastrophically lethal, a moving tide of destruction due to the cumulative effect of so many eating machines in one place, moving in accord with each other. Lately, though, a more subtle aspect of herd behavior has come to the attention of the sharper-eyed survivors. It seems the larger the herd becomes, the more loosely packed it is. For some reason, large open spaces begin to form amidst the densely organized throng, almost as though the sheer number is spreading the herd too thinly across the landscape.

This phenomenon has come to be known, among some survivors, as "bald spots"—and it's precisely why Lilly has currently chosen to lead her team directly into the heart of the mob. If she can navigate the bald spots with minimum contact, she just might be able to weave her team through the worst of the herd and emerge out the other side with their skins intact. But in order to do this, she has to go aggressively into the breach without hesitation.

Right now, in fact, the gravitational forces of their contraption rushing headlong down that scabrous hill behind the horse named Arrow press Lilly and Tommy into their seats. The rear tires, almost flat by now, cobble and thrum over stones and corrugations. On either side of the carriage, Miles and Jinx gallop wildly along, trying to keep up with the buggy's momentum.

Ahead of them, at the bottom of the hill, about a hundred yards away now, the outer edges of the mob shuffle along without purpose or direction. As the rattling noise of the carriage and the drumming of the horses draw nearer and nearer, the pasty gray faces begin to pivot and turn toward the commotion. Milky eyes latch onto the oncoming humans with the focus of angry drunkards.

"Keep your arms and legs inside the ride at all times!" Lilly shouts at Tommy and Norma without humor.

"FUCK!" Tommy practically shrinks inside the conveyance as they hurtle toward the leading edge of the multitudes. He fumbles for his 12 gauge.

They are already close enough to smell the fog bank of rotten meat-stench that hangs over the horde, to see the black drool on their faces, and to hear the low din of feral, guttural groaning. Fifty yards, thirty, twenty.

Lilly leans out the window and screams into the wind for the benefit of Jinx and Miles. "FOLLOW THE BALD SPOTS ALL THE WAY THROUGH!!"

She snaps the reins again and again and again, getting the animal up to its maximum speed. Fifteen yards away now . . . ten . . . five, four, three, two, *one*.

The first impact turns out to be a young female in late-stage decay, the left quarter panel of the carriage colliding with the creature with massive force. A wave of rotten blood and tissue sprays across the open prow of the carriage—the area where the hood and engine used to be—and covers Lilly and Tommy with a fine layer of reeking spoor. Tommy lets out a gasp and fires two blasts out his open window at a column of biters pressing in on them, sending blood mist plumes across the high rays of sun beating down on the meadow.

Lilly's eardrums pop and ring as she keeps the reins taut and snapping.

The thoroughbred makes a sharp turn to avoid another wall of the dead and slams into a middle-aged male in a tattered burial suit. The hardware on the horse's bridle strikes the walker's face so hard, the thing's rotting eyeballs pop out of its skull like corks, flying through the air on tails of bloody nerve bundles. Another one gets ground under the huge animal's hooves, the horse letting out high-pitched whinnies and vocalizations as it bobs and weaves through the morass of stiff-legged dead.

The horse roars as it makes another turn to the left, knocking down a half dozen lumbering cadavers before it bursts out the other side of the cluster and crosses a bald spot—almost an acre of bare ground—devoid of any walkers. Lilly takes the opportunity to peer out at her side mirror at Jinx and Miles.

The two of them charge into the clearing, their legs and horses covered with oily black matter. Each of the riders wields a long-edged weapon crusted with gore—Jinx a three-foot-long machete, Miles a tarnished Civil War sabre cribbed from a derelict museum back in Michigan—and each huffs and puffs with fatigue after slashing their way through scores of dead.

Lilly snaps the reins. The big horse gallops across the clearing, snorting and foaming. Lilly yanks on the left rein in order to steer the animal back onto a northerly path.

Nobody notices that the clearing is starting to collapse in on itself.

Another facet of the bald spot phenomenon is that the random formation of these empty cells seems to change constantly, fluidly, without warning, with the suddenness of waves rolling back out to sea. In fact, at this very instant, Lilly can tell that the closest circle of dead people—maybe fifty feet away—have already sniffed out their presence and have whirled around awkwardly, reaching for the humans in their midst. The bald spot begins to shrink. The herd presses in.

Up until this moment, Lilly hasn't registered much about the individual walkers on this journey other than blurs of menacing, reeking, slimy teeth. But now, in broad daylight, as the creatures close in on all sides of the clearing, Lilly sees a woman with half her body torn open, one side of her face dangling like a fleshy scarf, her green teeth chattering robotically as she approaches. Lilly sees another one, a male, very old, dragging toward her with a hole so big in its midsection the daylight shines through it like a portal. Another one, an older female, dressed in a filthy nurse's frock, has a four-foot length of rebar impaled between its breasts.

Lilly scans the distant horizon to get her bearings. She sees the beginnings of a forest in the middle distance, enrobed in the shadows of a vast gulley.

All at once, she notices, just beyond that forest, in the heat waves of the afternoon sky, a rusty water tower rising up with the Moreland, Georgia, town seal on it, and she realizes that Cooper Steeves and his armory lie just over that next wooded hill, and she decides instantly, without much hesitation, to make a mad dash for those trees. She yanks on one rein, and then snaps both of them as hard as she can. "THIS WAY, EVERYBODY!"

They won't learn what a terrible mistake they have just made until minutes later.

For a few frenzied moments, it seems that Lilly has made the right decision. The muscular thoroughbred barrels through the oncoming wave of the dead with the inertia of a battering ram, knocking down corpse after corpse before any of them have a chance to sink their teeth into the animal's sweaty hide. Pasty white faces snap back upon impact; bodies go down in great heaving eruptions of tissue and fluids, the hooves grinding through seething masses of organic matter. Clawlike hands grab for a passing wheel or a churning fetlock but the duct tape holds, protecting the horse's legs. The noise of it is incredible—a symphony of hissing, gasping, growling vocalizations drowned by the thunder of the hooves and the carriage wheels.

Directly behind the makeshift carriage, Jinx and Miles follow along at dead runs. The flash of their long blades in the sun forms a lethal steel blur as they slash at the waves of dead pressing in on either side, slicing a passageway through the horde, keeping their eyes on the rear of the carriage as it fishtails on the slime of human remains. Spumes of blood and bile splash up at them with each strike, looping through the air like stringers of black crepe. The odors are so strong now, it's difficult to breathe.

Ahead of them, the carriage thunders toward the crest of a hill.

Lilly frantically snaps the reins, keeping the horse at top speed, heading northward, but it's not easy to see over the horse's rear end, or over the edge of the natural plateau ahead of them, which runs along the edge of the meadow overlooking the wooded gulley. All Lilly can see now are the treetops and the sky. She has no idea how steep that slope is, or if the downgrade is free of walkers, or if the carriage can even negotiate the rocky ground of the hill beyond it.

When they finally reach the ledge, Lilly lets out a gasp as the horse careens down a forty-five-degree angle. The stray walkers clinging to the hill are catapulted into the air as the animal and carriage plummet.

Lilly pulls back on the reins with all her might in a futile attempt to slow their descent.

The fear of falling is primal (and virtually universal)—the psychological analogue to the terror of losing control. It fuels Lilly Caul's nightmares, and when it unfolds—as it's about to—in her waking life, it devastates her.

When the horse reaches the bottom of the hill, it slams into a cluster of a half dozen large, moving cadavers. Mostly decomposed, their wormy flesh hanging by threads, the enormous monsters literally burst apart upon impact like the pulpy eruption of overripe fruit. Faces explode, heads snapping off careening bodies, limbs flying through the air, waves of guts erupting in a black wave across the gulley.

The massive horse slips on all the greasy matter now collecting beneath it.

For one terrible moment, the animal literally skates on the slime. Its front legs scurrying in place, churning wildly, it begins to slide sideways. Lilly feels the center of gravity shift, the entire metal buggy spinning out of control. Her ears ringing, her heart in her throat, she can barely hear Tommy Dupree's scream as the horse-cart begins to tip. The entire universe pitches on its axis.

The carriage slams down on its side, throwing Lilly on top of Tommy.

Lilly doesn't even see the other two horses behind them trying to stop until it's too late. Miles and his animal slide across the bottom of the gulley, lose their balance, and slam into the rear of the carriage, toppling over and sprawling to the ground in a slimy heap. The horse-cart shudders, throwing Lilly and Tommy against the sidewall. The contraption slides another ten feet.

Jinx and her horse career into the wreckage, slamming into the back of the carriage.

A moment later, her head spinning, her ears deafened, Lilly tries to get her bearings inside the fallen conveyance. She can see through the haze of dust that Miles Littleton is pinned beneath his horse. He struggles to pull himself free as Jinx crawls toward him, favoring her right leg. It looks as though she injured herself in the fall.

Lilly starts to call out when she hears another sound that stops her cold.

From the threshold of the forest, less than fifty yards away, oozing out between crooked live oaks and columns of pines, comes another wave of ragged figures. Like an oily, black tide issuing forth from the woods, they emerge in droves, snarling and dragging toward the humans.

EIGHT

"What now, Cap?" The man with the binoculars speaks with a jacked-up cadence, like a record playing a couple of revolutions per minute too fast. A hand-rolled cigarette dangles from one corner of his mouth, bobbing and dropping ashes as he talks. "Gonna let the pus balls take 'em out?"

"Lemme see." Bryce snatches the binoculars away from his second in command and peers out his open window at the action down in the meadow.

In the pale sunlight slanting down through the high boughs of the neighboring forest, Bryce can see the army of dead closing in on the Woodbury assholes, the outcome inevitable. The brown-haired chick—the tough one, the one who seems to be in charge—is helping the teenage boy and black lady out of the carriage. Then the chick spins, hauls off and fires at the incoming pus bags. Just like that. She takes down three of them without blinking, then turns back to the buggy and by God she fucking single-handedly shoves the carriage back onto its wheels. All this while the herd is closing in on her, and she's pretty much dead meat, and why bother, but she won't give up, this chick. She is one badass motherfucker, and Bryce can't figure out what to do with her.

Meanwhile, the other chick—the dykie one—is pulling one of the horses off the black guy.

Theodore "Beau" Bryce—former sergeant with the 101st Airborne

Division, twice deployed in Afghanistan—fiddles with the huge sig-net ring on his right hand as he continues to spectate and ponder what to do with these shitheads. It's a nervous habit he acquired after his discharge while teaching recruits at Fort Benning. As he speculates on some intractable problem or some recalcitrant buck private, he will compulsively thumb the bottom of that massive gold ring with its enormous ruby stone and Latin phrase across the band: STAMUS IN STATIONE PRO TE (we stand on guard for thee). Now he turns it and rubs it and turns it some more as he ponders how to deal with these half-assed rescuers.

A tall, lean, crew-cut man of indeterminate age, Bryce wears dusty body armor over his faded fatigues and has a craggy face that bears the remnants of every battle he ever fought. He's been shadowing these Woodbury cocksuckers for practically twenty-four hours now and he's starting to get cranky as he sits behind the wheel of his heavily armored Humvee. The vehicle is parked and idling on a sce-nic turnoff about a quarter mile east of the meadow in question, the rest of Bryce's group awaiting orders on their dirt bikes and in their vehicles farther down the winding two-lane. Ironically, the spot on which Bryce now sits once went by the name Lover's Leap or some shit like that—it's all on a sign by the guardrail. Bryce has very little time for such nonsense now that the plague has taken his family, his friends, most of his fellow veterans, and basically everybody he ever knew.

"Should we—*what*—intervene?" Daniels, the skinny, bald scare-crow of a man in the shotgun seat, keeps compulsively sucking on his skunky cigarette as he looks wide-eyed at his superior. "That's the good doctor's favorite word, isn't it? Intervene? Whaddaya think, Captain?"

The man behind the wheel doesn't reply or correct Daniels's idiocy—Bryce was never an officer, he worked for a fucking living—he just keeps looking through the open window with the field glasses, pursing his lips as he deliberates. He has to get back soon, or the old man will chew his ass for hours. The smart play would probably be to head back to HQ immediately, just let the maggots feast on these pricks. But something stops Bryce. Is it morbid curiosity? Is it the brown-haired chick? Maybe it's just boredom. "How many of those testing kits we got left?"

Daniels shakes his head at him. "Not a single one, Cap, we're out of 'em."

"What are you talking about?" The older man launches a searing glare at his subordinate. "We had two dozen of those things when we deployed this time."

Daniels shrugs. "They go fast, especially when you're going house to house."

"Goddamn it, I'm not bringing anybody else back with us on this run. We're outta room."

"What about Hopkins's van?"

"That piece of shit isn't even remotely secure. I'm not taking any chances."

"So let's just leave 'em. Who gives a fuck? They're toast, Cap. Problem solved."

"Yeah? You think?" He looks back through the binoculars. "I'm not so sure." He watches the action down in the meadow, his voice going low and cold. "This chick is resourceful. I'm telling you."

Through the lenses of his field glasses, Bryce can see the horses getting devoured. The commotion of the feeding frenzy has apparently provided enough of a diversion to give the brown-haired chick time to lead her people away from the throng of biters. And for a moment, with a sadistic kind of fascination, Bryce follows the small group of living as they dash alongside their leader, who is now hurtling toward the nearest grove of ancient, twisted oak trees. This chick is something else. Without much forethought, without hesitation, she chooses the largest, knottiest oak and helps her compatriots climb its cankered trunk. One by one they shimmy up the petrified monolith to safety—at least *momentary* safety—each of them awkwardly clinging now to a different gnarled offshoot. The chick-in-charge is the last to climb up the trunk, which she does with nimble facility, making Bryce speculate that she was once a tomboy.

He returns his gaze to the horses, or what's left of them, which sends a pang of revulsion through his gut. Bryce grew up in Virginia, the grandson of a horse breeder, and he learned to give the animals the respect they deserve. His grandpa was responsible for nearly two dozen blue-ribbon hunter-jumpers, a Grand Prix team member for twenty consecutive years. Bryce used to be a groom for many of his grandpa's clients, and spent the majority of his childhood—right up until the year he left for basic training—in one reeking stable after another, brushing and wrapping and cleaning and combing show horses. Now he flinches with sympathetic anguish as he watches the frenzy reach its peak down in the meadow.

From this distance, the dead appear as fleshy wasps swarming a scarlet flowerbed, draining every last drop of nectar from the writhing, shrieking horses. Blood swirls in rivulets out from under the flock, running in waves across the bare ground, as the sacrificial victims finally go still. This seems to send the throngs of walkers into deeper orgasmic convulsions of gluttony, their faces rooting down into the steaming innards of the horses' flanks and bellies, the furry flesh splayed and torn open now by countless sets of teeth digging in until Bryce literally has to look away. He has seen the most horrible carnage imaginable in the war zone. But *this*—somehow this eats at his soul more than most of the terrible sights he's seen. A pained breath escapes him as the nausea rises up past his windpipe and into his throat.

He scans the binoculars back across the middle distance to the forest of crooked live oaks.

In the binoculars' circular field of vision, Bryce can see the Woodbury contingent huddling precariously now on the boughs of a giant mother oak. Some of them hold tightly to the snaking branches with desperate horror-struck expressions on their faces as they witness the final stages of the feeding frenzy. In the late-afternoon light, their eyes blazing with awe and disgust, they look like owls.

Bryce finds himself once again focusing the telescopic lenses on the woman with the tight auburn ponytail, the intense eyes, the look that's all business, and the flannel shirt, ripped jeans, and jackboots that make her come off like some kind of lost Sandinista or guerrilla warrior in some forgotten banana republic. He steadies the binos and studies her behavior. Maybe he does it for later data retrieval—*know thine enemy*, that sort of thing—or maybe he's smitten with her. He can see her gaping now, her teeth clenched in thinly veiled anguish, mortified by the spectacle of her horses being devoured. Some of the others in her party look away. But not this tough little chickadee. She just stares and stares as her prize equestrian stock goes down the bloody drain. She looks as though she's about to scream but, of course, she holds it all in like a good soldier. Bryce knows that look well—that clenched, constipated scowl. He has exhibited it himself at times, when he's lost men on the battlefield, or lost friends to the biters.

Daniels's voice penetrates Bryce's ruminations. "What's the verdict, Cap?"

Bryce looks up at his second in command as though coming out of a dream. "What?"

"What's the verdict? Do we leave them for the skels or what?"

Bryce shakes his head. "No . . . they've come this far to get those kids back. I respect that. Here's what we're gonna do." He looks back into his binoculars. "Get Boyle and them on the blower, tell them to go ahead and take the kids back to the ranch. Tell them the rest of us are gonna wait here until dark, and then we'll see who's left standing out of this group. We'll take the leftovers quick and clean, test them when we get back to headquarters." He looks at Daniels. "You got that, Daniels?"

Daniels gives a nod. "Copy that."

"Good. And do me a favor . . . calm the fuck down." Bryce looks back into the binoculars and continues pondering the hard-ass girl with the ponytail. "We may be here awhile."

Dusk comes early that night, the summer giving way to autumn, the days getting shorter, some of the trees already starting to turn from deep green to faded teal to pale yellow. Shadows lengthen. The sky goes indigo blue and the temperature plummets. In the waning daylight, the rural hinterlands look different now than they did before the outbreak—darker, thornier, almost Amazonian. The topography of the land isn't the only thing that the plague has transformed. The very trees themselves have sprouted deformities, blight-riddled leaves and malformed limbs like the shriveled extremities of terminal patients exposed to massive amounts of radiation. Old-growth forests have twined and tangled together with the voracious speed of metastasizing cells. Even the massive, contorted, antediluvian monster on whose central trunk Lilly and her posse now perch themselves like stranded birds seems to have grown riot in the plague years, its knotted limbs forming insane networks of sinewy musculature. Some of the huge tributaries of the trunk have literally dipped so low over the decades that they now grow in and out of the ground like great leprous eels diving for sustenance.

Every few moments, Lilly gazes up through the chimney of branches to remind herself that the sky is still there, albeit now as dark as a funeral shroud, stippled with early stars. The constant, incessant, nerve-jangling drone of walker voices coming up from the ground forty feet below them has set Lilly's teeth on edge, and the density of the darkness is only making matters worse. The swarm has stalled. In the gloomy light, the meadow to the south teems with so many of the dead, it looks as though a moving carpet of shadows has unfurled across the land. The stench grips the air around the trees, mingling with the sappy odors of bark and moss and decay.

"I know it ain't much," Norma Sutters is saying in a hoarse, exhausted voice, her portly body awkwardly wedged in the V-shaped crotch between two trunks. The racket from below nearly drowns her voice. Her sweater reeks of walker bile and spoor, her duct-tape-wrapped ankles and Reebok tennis shoes dangling over the edge of the concavity, swinging like the legs of a small child. "Got some red licorice I managed to hold on to. Anybody wants some, you're welcome to it."

Nobody says anything. Jinx sits nearby on the horizontal elbow of the trunk, silently chewing a leathery hank of beef jerky, morosely gazing through squinted eyes at the length and breadth of the horde.

The loss of the horses has hit Jinx Tyrell hard. She has that look now that Lilly has seen from time to time on the faces of survivors—a raw, glassy, dazed stare—which usually precedes acts of intense violence. Next to her, Miles Littleton balances on a limb, struggling to open a can of Spam with his pocketknife, saying nothing, his expression pained and surly as he breathes through his mouth. Tommy Dupree is the only one standing. He holds a dangling spiral of vines as though gripping a hand-strap on a train at rush hour, waiting to be conveyed home. He glances at Lilly. He waits for her to say something.

Lilly takes a sip of water from her army canteen, wipes her mouth, and says, "From now on, we gotta conserve everything . . . water, food, bullets, first aid, everything . . . we can get outta this mess, I believe we can, but we have to pace ourselves. Horses are gone, that's a bad hit, but it's a given now, and we can overcome it."

She feels her heart beating too hard. It gets like this sometimes, like a broken bearing in an engine, misfiring, pinging. Up until now, she has controlled the panic reflex by thinking about the children, about getting them back through any means necessary. But she's losing her focus now. She remembers being seasick once on a ferry that she took with her father across the Tennessee River outside Chattanooga. She remembers her father, Everett, admonishing her to keep her eyes on the horizon. Always on the horizon. At the moment, unfortunately, the horizon has vanished behind the dark silhouettes of tree limbs and the tendrils of Spanish moss swaying like curtains in the night breeze.

Lilly fixes her gaze on the makeshift structure that has practically fused to the tree fifty feet away from them, its ancient planking faded and silvered by hard weather and rot. The old tree house looks to have once provided children with a secret fortress out here in the sticks, a place in which to escape the yoke of school and parents, a hideout where cigarettes could be smoked, beers could be chugged, and girlie magazines could be perused. The twenty-foot-wide shack lashed to the spreading trunk system sits out in the shadows, a cruel joke on the loss of innocence, the fragility of life, and the vagaries of the apocalypse. Some of the unevenly spaced windows have been boarded up, now looking like tiny burlesques of grown-up desolation. The sight of the thing makes Lilly's heart heavy. She had a tree house in her backyard for most of her childhood—it was the place she learned about boys, smoked her first joint, and regularly tippled stolen bottles of crème de menthe. Now this abomination silhouetted against the shadows twenty yards away makes her gut clench with anguish.

"You ask me," Norma Sutters grumbles almost under her breath, looking down but clearly directing her words at Lilly, "I don't know how we're gonna overcome a damn thing on *foot*, traipsing through this damn herd."

"Would you give it a fucking rest!" Jinx raises her voice at the older woman, the volume of it making everyone jerk. "You just have to keep on ragging!"

Tommy closes his eyes. "Not this again, please, please, please—"

"Hey!" Lilly raises a hand, scolding them in a loud stage whisper. *"Keep it down!"* She can feel the reanimated army beneath them shifting at the sounds of their voices like fish in an aquarium sensing food being dropped on the surface of the water. "Jinx, it's okay. She's just venting. I don't blame her."

"I ain't raggin' on nobody!" Norma counters in a wounded bark.

Jinx burns her gaze into the portly woman. "I got a news flash for ya! Lilly just saved your fucking ass, so show a little gratitude!"

"STOP IT!" Tommy Dupree twitches on his perch as though electrocuted by the argument. He nearly falls off the tree as he covers his ears. "STOP IT!—STOP IT!—STOP IT!—*STOP IT!!*"

"Okay, that's enough, everybody, cool down," Lilly says softly as she pushes her way across the gap and puts her arm around Tommy. She holds him tightly in her arms, cradling his damp, feverish head and whispering, "We're gonna get outta here, I promise you, we're going to be okay. We're gonna find your brother and sister."

For a single, surreal instant, there's a pause as though the very air around them has inhaled a giant breath, and Lilly hears the noise first. She looks up. "Hold it!" she whispers. "Wait a second. Hold on.

Listen . . . listen." The breeze clatters through the branches around them. Lilly wonders if the stress is making her hear things. Maybe she imagined it. She could have sworn she just heard a creak—an unnatural noise—coming from somewhere on a parallel plane with them, from somewhere in the shadows of the tree. It could have been a branch swaying in the wind but to Lilly's ears it sounded too sharp and abrupt for that kind of phenomenon.

"What is it?" Jinx wants to know, nervously looking down and scanning the restless horde. Thank God walkers don't climb trees.

Lilly shrugs. "I don't know, I thought I heard something coming from the—"

The noise reaches her ears again, louder this time, a sudden creaking followed by a thud—the sound so abrupt it makes Lilly bite her tongue—and she looks up. Her hand naturally goes to the holster on her hip. Her fingers grasp the Ruger's grip. But she stops herself. Her gaze locks onto something in the shadows of the tree. The others frantically look down below for the answer. Lilly can't breathe.

She stares at the tree house. She tries to form words but can only manage an anguished, terrified sigh as the creaking noises give way to the snap of wood. Mesmerized, paralyzed, thunderstruck, she watches the boarded door of the tree house burst open.

The others look up then, eyes going wide and bright with fear.

What emerges from that broken-down little fort defies logic, description, or categorization.

NINE

On a strictly forensic level, one would have to call the creatures that burst from the doorway of that forlorn little tree house *deceased children*. But in the murk of impending night, behind the drifting motes of cottonwood and fireflies, the figures that pour out of that derelict fort appear to have originated in a nightmare. No bigger than chimpanzees, their flesh the color and consistency of black mold, they share the fixed grins of the decomposed as they scuttle, some of them on emaciated hands and knees, down the main forking trunk. Some are still clad in desecrated OshKosk overalls or filthy baseball caps fused to their oozing scalps. Each rictus of green, rotten teeth appears too large for its tiny cranium, each eye socket too deep and iridescent for the width of its skull. Each dead child moves with the rusty, stubborn jerking motions of a broken puppet.

At the same time, every living human on that tree other than Miles Littleton rises, begins to back away, awkwardly inching down the length of that main horizontal trunk. Everyone but Miles instinctively reaches for a weapon, and everybody—except for Miles—seems to instantly grasp the enormity of the situation. They have so little ammunition, it would be useless to fire. At a glance, there seem to be at least a dozen of these cadaver kids now trundling like rabid tree monkeys toward them, jaws working, their husky snarling noises raised an octave as though coming from pull-string dolls.

Over the space of that single, protracted, excruciating instant, Lilly speculates that these are the lost children orphaned by the plague, the castaways who returned to the one place that gave them comfort in their latchkey existences, the place in which they were willing to not only starve to death but turn as a ragtag family. But at precisely the same time that Lilly imagines these things, she also sees that Miles Littleton is about to employ his own force of will to bring about the end of a different kind of predicament.

"MILES! FOR FUCK'S SAKE!—WHAT ARE YOU—MILES!! *MILES, NO!!*"

The pitch and tenor and volume of Lilly's voice not only paralyzes the others but also draws even more of the horde. Down at ground level, each and every walker within a hundred yards of the massive mother oak now languidly shifts direction and starts to swarm and press in and crowd the area, looking for the source of the human voices. Lilly ignores the hellish chorus of growls and indescribable odors wafting up to her. She sees that she has one chance to stop the young car thief from whatever heroic plan he has banging around right now in his traumatized mind.

She turns and shuffles back down the thick span of trunk when all at once she trips on a cavity, falls, and lands on her shoulder. Her balance goes haywire. She hugs the trunk, nearly slipping off, hanging there, digging in her fingernails. The impact has knocked the breath out of her. She looks up, her vision blurring, dizziness threatening to send her plummeting. She manages to see through watery eyes a dreamlike scenario unfolding before her.

Miles Littleton has stepped into the path of the tiny monsters as they approach, and he starts waving his hands as though guiding a plane in for a landing. He calls out, "Come and get me, you little motherfuckers! That's right. COME AND GET ME!"

Lilly fumbles for her Ruger, thinking she'll get one last shot off and perhaps stop this madness, but it's already too late.

The first dead child reaches the young car thief just as he glances over his shoulder and makes eye contact one last time with Lilly.

It's all there on Miles Littleton's face—a broken home, life on the street, a decade of drug addiction, his pride in his skills as a thief, his struggle to overcome his fate, his unshakable belief in God, and maybe even his secret longing for a mother, a family, a noble cause. Crouched only inches away from him, close enough to smell the acrid stench of the dead children swarming him, Lilly Caul realizes right then that she had never really studied the young man's face for more than a fleeting instant . . . until now. Now, she gets one last close-up glimpse of those long-lashed eyes, that vaguely feminine mouth, the straggly goatee, high cheekbones, and street wisdom flashing at her as the monsters pile up on him. One of them bites into his leg, another rooting into his kidney, another going for his neck. Miles has the strangest smile on his face now as he gives Lilly one last look. An almost beatific expression passes over his face that contradicts the terrible sounds coming from all around him, not the least of which is Norma Sutters's shriek. The portly woman is trying to intercede, trying to save her surrogate son, but Jinx—of all people—is holding her back. Miles grins and blood oozes from the corners of his mouth as baby piranha teeth pierce his abdomen and internal organs. Lilly screams as Miles finally twists around and then vaults into the air as though performing an awkward stage dive into oblivion.

Lilly reaches out for the young man as though it's within her power to stop the event from unfolding, pull him back, travel back in time, yank the episode to a stop, rewind it and prevent the young thief from performing this ridiculous act. But now, at least half a dozen dead kids cling to Miles as he plunges toward a weak point in the trunk system—a long, overhanging bough. He lands on the end of the limb and instantly breaks through—the rest of the small cadavers going with him as he plunges to his death—making the entire skeletal system of the tree vibrate and shudder.

Lilly watches on her hands and knees, still clinging to that center trunk, unaware that she has started to cry. The tears streak down her face in scalding, salty tracks. Her vision glazes over as she tries to focus on the gauzy outlines of the shadows below. The sound of Miles landing on the swarm at ground level is strangely muted, dampened by the cushion of countless dead. Norma's shriek goes on unabated, a terrible counterpoint to the rising choir of growls and wet snarling vocalizations reverberating up from below. Lilly wipes her eyes and fights the urge to vomit and sees the horde shifting down there in the darkness yet again, another countercurrent of shambling shadows pushing in toward the unexpected introduction of warm-blooded human meat to their ranks. Lilly tries to move, tries to react, tries to call out, scream, do *something* . . . but for a moment, all she can do is remain glued to that trunk and gape.

Then, a fraction of a second later, she realizes what's happening down below.

Jinx climbs down the massive central trunk first, followed by Norma, then Tommy, and finally Lilly. They each know all too well that the window of opportunity will only be open for precious seconds—the herd currently preoccupied with devouring Miles Littleton. The survivors descend, one by one, as quickly as humanly possible, skinning their knees, banging over cankers and cavities, and silently hyperventilating as they drop themselves into the clearing around the base of the mother oak.

For the moment—mercifully, miraculously—a single acre of bare ground as hard and smooth as a dance floor stretches before them, devoid of any biters, enrobed in the chill mists of night.

Now, keeping their heads down, moving single file through the shadows, they scurry across that hard-packed earth, setting their sites on the adjacent woods about a hundred yards away. If they can make it to the tree line before the rest of the horde catches wind of their hasty exit, they might just be able to escape. Lilly can sense the outer edges of the herd in her peripheral vision, between fifty and a hundred yards on either flank, a haphazard wave of walking dead suddenly noticing more humans in their midst, locking their metallic gazes on Lilly and her crew, which makes Lilly's pulse pound even harder as she hastens along, urging the others with hand signals to hurry the fuck up.

Not a single one of them dares to look back at the grisly feeding frenzy transpiring on the other side of the mother oak. By this point, Miles Littleton has been drawn and quartered by the gnashing wood chipper of countless rotting teeth. The ground is sodden with his blood. The odors and noises rise up into the night sky and dissipate in the wind.

Lilly feels the weight of her sorrow tugging on her as she closes in on the palisades of white pines less than fifty yards away now. The tears sting her eyes, astringent and raw in the wind. The landscape blurs. Her vision tunnels as she approaches the deeper shadows of the woods. Almost there. Forty yards now. Thirty.

She runs so hard, her tears so profuse now, she doesn't see the men on motorcycles waiting patiently on the gravel road a quarter mile to the west, their assault rifles propped on their hips like those of cavalrymen. Nor does she see the military vehicles on the opposite side of the meadow, idling in the darkness, lights off, the silhouettes of roughnecks inside the cabs smoking cigarettes, watching, waiting. It's too dark to see the ambush until the first flash.

On the back of one of the Humvees, an RPG suddenly spits fire, a strobe light flickering silver in the darkness above the treetops.

Lilly sees the rocket-propelled grenade strike a deadfall log fifty feet dead ahead of her, glimpsing this in her watery vision a split second *before* she hears the thunderous boom of the launcher. Wood pulp and shards of leaves and dirt erupt in all directions. Lilly goes sprawling to the ground. Ears ringing once again, breath knocked from her lungs, blood boiling with adrenaline, she tries to rise back up, go for her gun, get her bearings. Her body responds slowly, the sharp pain in her side weighing her down.

She sees huge halogen lamps snapping on with the loud pop of arc welders at key junctures up on the ridge and along the gravel access road to the east. Shafts of harsh silver light sweep across the dark meadow, penetrating the haze of dust and particulate. The walkers are still busy with Miles, the peripheral ranks still slowly approaching. Lilly glances over her shoulder and sees her people crouching down, looking for cover, Jinx going for a weapon.

An amplified voice makes Lilly jump, the source and direction from which it's coming undetermined at this point. *"Folks, I'm going to have to ask you to keep your hands where we can see them, and please refrain from drawing any weapons or we're going to be forced to go ahead and take you out, and nobody wants that."*

Lilly goes stone-still. Her heart thuds in her chest. Crouched there, blinded by the glare of the searchlights, she squints into the supernova closest to the sound of the bullhorn. The wind stirs the leaves and the treetops, the stench of the dead wafting, making Lilly's stomach clench. She can sense Jinx, Tommy, and Norma behind her, each of them paralyzed, the wheels of their brains frantically turning, grasping for a response, a way out of this mess. But Lilly has other ideas. She has latched onto the sound of this disturbingly casual, officious voice as a panther might latch onto the bleat of a lamb.

"What we need y'all to do now, if you don't mind, is we'd like you to go ahead and throw any weapon you might have on your person to the ground. And if possible, it would be really, really great if you could do this slowly. With no sudden moves, as they say."

Lilly rises to her feet and carefully pulls her Ruger from its holster.

"What the fuck are we doing?!" Jinx demands to know, her voice coming in a low, tense whisper from the beams of light behind Lilly.

"Just do what he says." Lilly throws her pistol on the ground. "This is the only way we're gonna find the kids."

"Fuck!"

Squinting into the brilliant white beams of spotlights, Lilly can see the others slowly rising to their feet, pulling weapons, tossing them. Norma's Bulldog lands with a hollow thud; Jinx's knives thump on the ground, one by one, as she clears her belt of its steel.

The leading edge of the herd has closed the distance on either flank to about fifty yards. Some of the corpses are getting so close now that Lilly can see what they were in their former lives—mail carriers, farmers, laborers, farmers' wives, white-collar drones—most of them weathered to a mildew-gray color. Only their eyes and mouths glisten with discharge, bile, and drool.

"That's outstanding, folks, we really appreciate that, we really do. Now we'd like to go ahead and ask you to form a single-file line starting with the lady with the ponytail. You'll be noticing a van backing toward you from the west, which will be your escort."

Lilly hears the whine of a large panel van running in reverse, closing in on them, coming through the fog bank of carbon monoxide to the west. Despite the fact that every molecule of her being is now screaming for her to get out of here, run, now, and under no circumstances get into that fucking van, she knows deep down that this is exactly how they're going to get their children back, so she assumes the lead position by showing her hands, nodding, and walking toward the sound of the engine.

"I can't fucking believe we're doing this." Jinx speaks under her breath as she turns and puts her hands on top of her head, falling in line behind Lilly. The walkers have closed the distance to thirty yards.

"Take it easy, trust me, we'll be okay, just don't panic."

"These people are fucking savages. We're just going to surrender?"

Norma speaks up, her hands raised and showing sweat spots on the fabric under her arms. "How do we know they ain't gonna just kill us like the rest of them poor folks? What good is that gonna do?"

Tommy stands next to Norma, nodding nervously but saying nothing.

"Okay, enough!" Lilly clenches her jaw, hands raised, eyes wet as she whispers. "Everybody—*trust me*. They could have smoked us a million times already. Just trust me and follow my lead, let me do the talking."

By this point, the van has emerged from the fog. It pulls up in front of Lilly, skidding to a stop on the bare ground. A few of the walkers have strayed a little too close for comfort. The van's passenger door swings open, and a heavyset man in camouflage leans out with an HK machine pistol. The blasts come in a succession of metallic snapping noises, the tops of walker heads bursting in plumes of pink mist that shimmer and vanish in the spotlight beams.

Then the amplified voice returns, sounding to Lilly like the folksy voice of an airline pilot inviting passengers to feel free to move about the cabin.

"And folks, please remember, there's no reason to be alarmed, and there's no reason for any harm to come to any of you, especially if you're all willing to cooperate. All we ask is that you go ahead and get inside the van."

The van's rear doors squeak open and a younger, skinnier man is standing inside the cargo bay waiting for them. Dressed in olive-drab army fatigues, a headset, and a Mohawk hairdo, he grins convivially with gold-capped teeth like a concierge in a fleabag hotel.

For just an instant, Lilly hesitates. The herd closes in. The wind bullwhips trash and the stench of dead flesh across the light-struck haze. Lilly takes a deep breath, looks at the others, and then gives a reassuring nod.

She climbs on board.

The others follow—one at a time, each one reluctantly breathing in a girding breath before crossing the threshold of the cargo bay. The door closes behind them with a bang as the vehicle pulls away to parts unknown.

PART 3

Nightshade

The stuff of nightmares is their plain bread. They butter it with pain. They set their clocks by deathwatch beetles, and thrive the centuries.

—Ray Bradbury

TEN

Georgia State Road 314 wends its way through the darkness of the outskirts, past the empty husks of latchkey communities now sitting in mothballs, the dollhouse cul-de-sacs of Fayetteville and Kenwood littered with wreckage and sun-faded personal effects strewn across the intersections like so much useless spindrift. Visible in the flash of passing headlights, bullet holes and blood smears pock the exteriors of every other building, as common now as fallen leaves. Bryce chooses the less traveled two-lane over Interstate 41 for many reasons. The main thoroughfares are all but impassable nowadays due to overgrowth and the decaying wreckage clogging every turn, every exit ramp, every culvert and overpass. Plus, there's a certain discretion in returning to town via one of the less traveled roads. These days, the tribes watch each other, and when Bryce has subjects on board, he wants to keep as low a profile as possible.

"You ever wonder about it?" Daniels's voice seems to come from miles away, distorted by the night winds through the Humvee's vent. Bryce barely registers it as he steers the behemoth past the ruins that used to be Hartsfield-Jackson Atlanta International Airport. In the darkness, the once great transportation hub now lies in heaps of burned debris and boarded terminals festering in the void of night. The runways crawl with the shadowy silhouettes of roamers. The central tower has collapsed into itself, and the scorched carcasses of aircraft scatter the scarred tarmacs as if an angry giant grew weary of playing with them. This is the back door into Atlanta, the service entrance. Bryce once again glances at the side mirror at the caravan—both twin and single headlamps—following him into the city.

Right now he can see the double high-beams of the large, battered panel van driven by a former grunt and munitions expert, Sonny Hopkins, in the middle of the pack. Bryce imagines that hard-ass chick from Woodbury in the back of that cargo bay at this very moment, plotting her countermeasures, stewing in her rage, biding her time. The civilians in Afghanistan were like that—quiet, unobtrusive, savage in their vendetta against outsiders policing their land.

Bryce throws a glance at Daniels. "What was that?"

"I said, do you ever think about it?"

"Think about what?"

Slumped in the shotgun seat, the smoke from his hand-rolled skunk-weed curling up and vanishing in the green glow of the dash lights, the younger man stares out the window at the passing nightscape. "Hold on a second, hold that thought." He digs in a pocket and finds another EpiPen. The device is a small, glassine tube auto-loaded with a premeasured dose of the mood enhancer known on the street as Nightshade. Most of the former soldiers in Bryce's crew became accustomed to using auto-injectors back in the Iraq War to counteract Saddam's chemical agents. Now Daniels presses the tip against a bleeding heart tattoo on his bicep and blasts himself with another ten milligrams of courage. He drops the spent pen on the floor mat and settles back, exhaling the supercharged breath that follows a dose of the stuff. For a moment, he smells ammonia and his brain spins like the tumblers on a slot machine. Finally he says, "What I mean is, do you ever, like, think about what we're doing?"

Bryce keeps the vehicle at a steady forty-five miles an hour. With the added impact of the makeshift cow catcher mounted to the front grill—a conglomeration of concertina wire, rebar, and a section from an old bulldozer scoop—the speed is fast enough to mow down any stray walkers who wander across the beams of their headlights.

"What do you mean, 'what we're doing'? You talking about this? The smash and grabs?"

The younger man shrugs. "Yeah, exactly. I mean, do you ever wonder about it?"

"What do you mean, whether it's right or wrong?"

Another shrug. "Yeah . . . I guess."

"There's no such thing anymore."

Daniels looks at the commander. "What are you saying? There's no such thing as right or wrong?"

"Not anymore." Bryce smiles to himself. "It's an anachronism nowadays . . . like fresh milk, Wi-Fi, and the sports page."

The younger man sits back, rubs his face, thinks about it, feels the drug working on his central nervous system, flushing his inhibitions and fears like toilet water swirling waste down a drain. "I don't know. I guess you're right. It's just the . . ."

Bryce lets the silence lie there for a moment. "The kids we took? The fact that we found kids this time?"

A shrug. "I don't know. Don't listen to me, I'm a fucking pogue."

"Go ahead, Daniels. Say what you want to say. Speak your piece."

"I just remember that second tour, we were actually making a difference. At least it seemed like we were. Building clinics and shit. There was that school we built for the folks in Helmand Province, remember?"

Now it's Bryce's turn to shrug. "That was a different world."

In the dim green light of the dash, Daniels looks like he's still processing something. "I guess you're right." He sighs. "I'm sure Doc Nalls knows what he's doing."

"Let's fucking hope so."

They drive in silence for a few minutes. Bryce notices the horizon to the east beginning to go from inky black to ashy gray, the dawn just behind it. He looks at his watch. It's almost five. They'll be back home before six. "How's that 'Shade doing? You feeling better?"

Daniels nods and smiles. "Feeling better all the time."

"You still want to have that deep discussion about right and wrong?"

Daniels looks at Bryce. In the green glow, the younger man's toothy grin looks cadaverous. "Fuck right and wrong."

Long after dawn breaks over the top of Atlanta's desiccated skyline, the deep canyons between the buildings stay shrouded in shadow. Bryce keeps his lights on as he leads the convoy past mountains of burning wreckage and around pockets of walkers so thick the creatures move elbow to elbow down alleys and walkways. The heart of the city has gone from bad to worse over the last year. The air chokes with death-scent, the smell so thick it seems to cling to the low clouds scudded across the sky. The narrow side streets teem with the undead, most of the buildings lost to the walkers. Many of the ground-level entrances have been breached and now hang open and blowing with trash and the dead shuffling aimlessly, shambling in and out of vestibules as though moving on muscle memory, shopping for some bargain they will never find. Bryce hates this town.

He turns right on Highland and leads the caravan toward headquarters when the crackle of Daniels's radio fills the Humvee's interior.

"Yo! Daniels, you copy?" The voice squawks from the tinny speaker. "It's Hopkins . . . over?"

The younger man grabs the walkie-talkie and thumbs the button. "Copy that. Go ahead, Hopkins."

"It's probably nothing, but it's something I thought you and Bryce might want to know."

"Copy that, go on."

Through the speaker: "It's really quiet back there. Has been for miles."

Daniels looks at Bryce and thumbs the switch. "Soames is back there with them, right?"

"Yeah but his headset went down, lost contact around Carsonville."

"It'll be fine, Hopkins, don't worry about it."

"I don't know. They were all yelling and shit, arguing with Soames, and then . . . nothing. *Quiet as fucking church mice. I don't trust these douche bags. They ain't going gently into that good night, if you catch my meaning."*

Bryce sees the corner of Highland and Parkway Drive in the early rays of the sun a block away. In the ribbons of morning fog, the sunbeams slant through the haze and illuminate a ragged contingent of dead milling about the leprous pavement of the intersection. An overturned MARTA bus, as scarred and scorched as the petrified remains of a dinosaur, lies in the background against cement barriers enclosing the former medical center parking lot. Bryce looks at Daniels. "Gimme the bitch box," he says.

Daniels hands it over. Bryce thumbs the Send button. "Hopkins, just take a deep breath and don't do anything stupid . . . we're almost home." Bryce tosses the radio on the seat and lets out an exasperated sigh. "Goddamn, I'll be glad when this one is over."

He yanks the wheel at Highland, mows down a couple of moving corpses, and then drives down the ramp into the shadows of the parking complex.

Lilly feels the undercarriage cobble over speed bumps. She braces herself against the corrugated metal wall and tries to think straight. Her cheek stings from getting slapped, her spine throbbing with agony. The cargo bay has a single dome light, hectic with mosquitoes, shining down on a filthy iron floor littered with candy wrappers, packing straps, and bloodstains. The air smells of urine and mold. Spent shell casings and used EpiPens roll around the cargo bay with each turn, each shift in gravity. And now, Lilly presumes that the vehicle is booming down a ramp into some underground garage or warehouse, the g-forces tugging Lilly and the others forward as they descend at a forty-five-degree angle. Her wrists burning from the cable ties shackling her hands behind her back, her flesh slimy with sweat, her ass aching from the rough ride into town, she tries to take steadying breaths. Her brain swims with panic. In the dimly lit, windowless chamber, she can see the inevitable taking shape.

Tommy Dupree, also hogtied, sits on the opposite side of the enclosure, his feverish gaze locked on Jinx in the rear corner. Norma also has her eyes glued to Jinx. Even their captor, the emaciated redneck with the Mohawk—currently crouching against the front firewall with his AR-15 between his knees—watches Jinx now with the intense curiosity and wide eyes of a little boy contemplating a new kid at school. Lilly feels the air vibrating with latent violence, a crackling, prickling tableau that she now realizes she can do nothing to stop.

"Is there a problem?" Mohawk chews gum furiously as he regards the woman. "Is this like the silent treatment I'm getting now?"

Offering no response, Jinx meets the redneck's gaze with tremendous calm. Her slender, lean body is folded like a praying mantis in the same corner into which Mohawk shoved her almost an hour ago.

The first thirty minutes of the journey, Jinx had sat there, hands tied behind her back, patiently working the stainless-steel throwing blade that she had hidden inside the lining of her leather vest into her bound hands. Lilly had been the first to see what Jinx was doing. Masking the delicate business of transferring the knife from the hem of the garment into the palm of her right hand, Jinx had launched into a series of high-pitched insults and threats directed toward Mohawk specifically and Bryce's entire unit in general. Lilly had happily joined in. When the others realized what was going on, they also started whining about being taken captive against their wills and treated like chattel, and who did these fucking people think they were? The argument had escalated. Mohawk started screaming back at them and finally got up, lunged toward Lilly, and slapped her.

The slap had occurred about midway through the journey—right around the time Bryce had been circling Hartsfield—and the shock of it had stricken everybody silent. At this point, Jinx had successfully gotten the knife's handle into her right hand and had commenced sawing the blade's edge against the cable tie binding her hands. The next thirty minutes had been spent gently yet steadily sawing, sawing, sawing, while everybody stared awkwardly at the grime-spotted floor. The silence had driven the redneck to distraction.

Now he rises up to his full height in the narrow chamber, the body odor and cordite smells radiating off him, the plumage of his orange Mohawk practically brushing the ceiling. The Nightshade in his system fizzes behind his eyes. "I don't think you understand how fair we're being with you guys, we could have just as easily taken you out back there. Why the attitude?"

Jinx looks down, almost serene in her Zen state, her cobra-calm before the storm. "I don't have a clue as to what the fuck you're talking about."

"What did you just say to me?" The gangly redneck takes a step closer and raises the assault rifle's muzzle. He glares down at Jinx. The van shudders for a moment, turning a tight corner in some unseen subterranean parking complex. The redneck staggers, almost loses his balance. He glowers. "Can you please answer me? I don't hear so good. What the fuck did you just say to me?"

Jinx looks up at him. "I said I don't have a fucking clue as to what you're babbling about." She proffers an icy smile. "But maybe that's your thing—all babble and no bite. Maybe you're one of those guys, talks a lot to cover up the fact his dick is so tiny."

The air pressure inside the van seems to suddenly contract, the silence broken only by the faint vibrations and muffled squeal of the tires as the van follows the caravan around tight turns. Mohawk stares at Jinx for a moment, utterly dumbfounded by this brazen woman with the shorn scalp and innumerable tattoos. In fact, for the longest moment, the man just stares, as though the very existence of this insolent, snotty Amazon does not compute.

At last, the man named Soames shrugs. He shows his stained teeth, and he lowers the weapon, and he chuckles as though getting the joke for the first time. The van jerks again as it comes to a halt. Voices echo outside, bouncing around the walls of some cavernous parking level. Mohawk doesn't seem to notice. His grin remains. "I get it, really, I do, I get where you're coming from with your—"

The speed with which Jinx rises up on her knees and drives the tip of that oval blade into the redneck's ear makes Lilly jump. The man convulses backward, his eyes rolling back in his skull, his hands frozen ineffectually around the stock of the assault rifle. Jinx lets go of the blade. The man continues staggering backward, the knife sticking halfway out his auditory canal, until he slams into the opposite wall next to Lilly. Blood fountains down from his head as he slides to the floor like a sulking child.

He dies sitting down, drenched in blood and cerebrospinal fluid, as the rear door bolts rattle suddenly across the enclosure. The sudden noise makes all heads jerk toward the rear of the van. Each captive—including Lilly—stares, paralyzed with indecision. They have mere seconds to launch whatever counterattack they have left in them. In three . . . two . . . *one* . . .

In that terrible moment before the van's rear doors squeal open, many things transpire in that reeking chamber—many of these things unspoken, communicated in quick gestures among the captives— starting with Jinx going for Mohawk's assault rifle. She wrenches it out of the dead man's palsied hands, which have frozen around the weapon's stock. Then she pulls the throwing blade out of the man's ear canal. It makes a sick, wet, smooching noise as it comes out, spilling another pint of fluid onto the floor.

Jinx lunges across the space just as the rear doors are starting to rattle open.

In quick flicks of the blade, Jinx cuts the bonds around Lilly's wrists first, then Norma's, and finally Tommy's. The doors swing open and the one named Hopkins is standing outside with an odd expression on his face—part amusement, part shock, part awe. This kind of thing just never happens. In this environment, captives are either too sick, too exhausted, too malnourished, or too drugged to do anything even remotely like fighting back. He flinches backward instinctively as he reaches for his HK auto pistol and lets out a yelp, accompanied by a single word: "WHOA!"

Jinx doesn't allow the man's hand to reach the gun on his belt.

She fires two quick bursts of 62-grain, jacketed, steel-core projectiles into the general vicinity of the man's head. Most of the rounds are direct hits, sending two enormous chunks of the man's brain out the back of his skull in florets of pink tissue and puffs of blood-mist. The man careens backward as though yanked with invisible cables, landing on his back, spread-eagle, bleeding out ten feet from the van's rear bumper. Lilly sees the HK still holstered on the man's belt, and Jinx sees it as well, but the footsteps coming fast across the adjacent lot take precedence.

From their vantage point, they see that they're parked in a sublevel of some vast, airless, deserted parking complex. About the size of a football field, the cavernous space has no power, a low ceiling dripping with muck and cobwebs, a few scattered vehicles either overturned or completely totaled, and piles of garbage drifted against three out of the four walls. All of these observations register to Lilly in the space of an instant, the sound of hurried footsteps closing in.

The last thing Lilly sees before the shooting starts is an ambulance sitting on blocks to her left, the wheels and trim and most of its accessories cannibalized. It sits in front of a huge sliding-glass door punctured with bullet holes and a million fractures. A sign above the lintel says EMER ENCY ENTRA CE.

Right then, Lilly realizes where they are. She's been here before. She's sure of it now. But she has no time to reminisce about succumbing to a ruptured appendix during her senior class trip all those years ago, and getting dropped off here by her drunken best friend Megan Lafferty, because right at this moment the two gunmen have arrived with muzzles up and ready to rock. They come around the corner of the rear doors, a big one in a leather biker jacket and a smaller one in army camo pants, fishing vest, and bandolier.

Camo Pants raises his M1 and screams, his voice echoing as it bounces around the cement crypt of a parking lot: "DROP THE WEAPONS NOW! DOWN ON YOUR FUCKING KNEES! NOW! OR WE WILL BLOW YOU THE FUCK AWAY!!"

Two things happen very quickly behind the rear doors of the panel van. Lilly glances over her shoulder at the other two members of her team, who are now standing directly behind her, coiled like springs, ready for action. In that heated instant, she sees something powerful on both their faces—Tommy's earnest chin jutting proudly, Norma's lips pursed with determination—and Lilly knows that they are ready now for anything. The second event that unfolds is Jinx crouching down and taking cover against the door frame, and then firing off another salvo from Mohawk's assault rifle, catching Camo Pants in his ribs.

The man in the leather jacket dives for cover behind the closest wreck as Camo Pants lets out a grunt and spins with the impact of the bullets, his blood spurting, his face going taut with pain. He drops his M1 and his legs give out, sending him to the pavement. His gun skids across the cement. He tries to crawl out of the line of fire but Jinx squeezes off a single shot from the van's rear doorway and puts a round into the back of the man's head.

Then, without skipping a beat, Jinx gives Lilly a hard look right before throwing her the assault rifle. "Here ya go, cover me!"

"The fuck are you doing?!"

"Just do what I say! Cover me and—!"

Right then a burst of automatic fire booms in the enclosed space, cutting off Jinx's words, the noise deafening. Jinx and Lilly jerk behind the door frame for cover, the others going belly down in the cargo bay. Leather Jacket fires a second time, the bullets chewing through the metal of the van's doors, sparking left and right, sending hot spittle against the side of Lilly's face. Jinx returns fire. Her gun roars and sprays the pavement in front of the wreck behind which Leather Jacket now hunkers.

"Listen to me!" Behind the cover of the door, Jinx grabs Lilly and shakes her. "I gotta get to the machine pistol on that stiff!"

Lilly wriggles free of her grasp. "NO! That's not the way we do this—*we go together.*"

"Okay, all right . . . but we need to do this now. We need to get the fuck out of here before the rest of them join in!"

Lilly glances over her shoulder. "Okay . . . everybody . . . we're going to make a break for those stairs on the far side of the lot! Stay behind me! Stay close! Jinx is going for that—"

The air lights up again. Lilly covers her head. Bullets gobble the bumper, taillights exploding, hot strings of tiny explosions puckering the metal above the doors. The salvo goes on seemingly forever. There might be more gunmen firing at them now, it's hard to tell in the thunderous, echoing chaos. Lilly can hear Jinx yelling.

The gunfire ceases.

"They start in with that RPG, we're dead meat!" Jinx grabs Lilly's sleeve and hauls her to her feet. "C'mon! We gotta go now!"

Lilly gives a quick nod. "Okay." She looks at the others. "Stay close." She nods at Jinx. "I'll lay down the rest of the rounds in the magazine but you gotta hurry!"

Jinx nods. "Okay. Good. Ready. On three . . . one, two, *three!*"

Sergeant Theodore "Beau" Bryce watches things go awry from the corner of the lot, sitting behind the driver's seat of his idling Humvee, shaking his head in disgust and nervously rubbing his gold signet ring as he sees the first figure lurch out the back of the van. It's the badass girl in the ponytail—surprise, surprise—now unleashing hellfire on Bryce's men, who are currently huddled like pussies behind a wrecked SUV with limited ammunition and no balls, and it makes Bryce want to scream.

He grabs his bullhorn, the batteries getting low now, the speaker crackling as he rolls down his window, sticks the horn out, and presses the button: *"Okay, folks, c'mon, this is not necessary . . . if we could just stay cool and . . . and . . . okay I'm going to have to ask you not to turn this into a thing . . . if you could just do me a huge favor and drop your weapons . . . I promise nobody will get—"*

Ponytail sprays a volley across the wreckage, the blasts flickering and booming in the claustrophobic space, sending blossoms of sparks up into the hazy, acrid air. Behind her, the other subjects shuffle quickly along on her heels. Somebody needs to shut this thing down before it gets any further out of hand. Bryce starts to say something else into the bullhorn but instead throws it on the seat in anger, letting out a grunt of annoyance.

Next to Bryce, Daniels is about to jump out of his skin, slamming a banana clip into his assault rifle and grousing, "I knew it . . . I knew it . . . I knew these fuckers were going to get creative."

"Calm down *ferchrissake*." Bryce reaches behind his seat and finds his trusty Remington 700—a weapon that has gone to the Middle East and back two times, serving as the most well-oiled killing machine in the history of the Scout Sniper platoon in Helmand Province. Bryce rarely uses the weapon for everyday skirmishes, but somehow this chick with the ponytail has gotten under his skin. He brings the rifle up to his lap and checks the breach.

"I'm going to nip these motherfuckers in the fucking buds!" Daniels has his piece locked and loaded, and he's starting to open his door when Bryce grabs the younger man's arm with vise-grip pressure.

"Stay put."

"What?! Cap, this is getting—"

"I'll take care of this." Bryce slams the cocking lever forward, injecting a long round into the chamber. He reaches for the door. "You stay inside this cab, try to avoid getting waxed."

Bryce steps out of the Humvee just as the telltale rattle of the HK fills the air, echoing off the hard walls and the cement crannies of the parking level. The air has gone hazy with blue smoke, smelling of scorched circuits and brimstone as Bryce's men scatter for cover. In the distance, the four subjects from Woodbury race toward the exit stairs embedded in the far corner of the lot, right next to the boarded elevator vestibule.

Flipping open the bipod legs on the end of the rifle, Bryce rests the weapon on the corner of the vehicle's hood. He looks through the scope and scans the crosshairs across the wasted pavement of the lot. His plan is to center them on Ponytail and take her ASAP. It's regretful but she's the one, has everybody up in arms, the ringleader. Take her down, eliminate the threat.

He finally centers Ponytail in the scope. At the moment, she's leading the boy and the black lady toward the stairs, and Bryce smoothly pans with her. The crosshairs of the scope find the target. His left hand gently caresses the underside of the forestock. He steadies the rig. Breathes out slowly. Body stone-still. He slowly starts to squeeze the trigger when the flash of the HK distracts him.

Through the scope, the silver strobe-light flicker behind Ponytail draws Bryce's attention to the other woman—the one with the tattoos and spiky hair—who is now spraying automatic fire across the warren of rusted-out wrecks where his men have taken cover. Sparks ping and ricochet in the haze. Some of the rounds find their targets, a few of Bryce's men going down in whirlwinds of pink mist.

The woman backs quickly toward the stairs, following closely behind her comrades while continuing to blast away. Some of the men return her fire, and they barely miss her, the rounds puffing in chunks off the pavement at her feet, but that doesn't seem to faze the woman. She keeps emptying the high-capacity clip until it starts clicking.

Bryce judges the distance and drop rate and fires a single shot at the woman's head.

ELEVEN

Jinx sees Lilly urging the others up the cement steps ahead of her—the three figures barely visible behind veils of gun smoke—when she gets hit. The wasp-sting of the sniper's bullet passes through the back corner of her skull, taking a small, ten-gram chunk of her cerebral cortex. Jinx lets out a gasp, staggers, and stumbles forward as if tripped by an invisible wire. Blinding, hallucinatory white light zaps across her field of vision as she drops the machine pistol and sprawls to the pavement. Her respiratory system instantly shuts down as though a switch has been thrown. She gasps for air and tries to signal to Lilly what's happened—tries to say something—but the catastrophic damage to her brain has already started her convulsing, the back of her scalp going icy cold and wet with blood, her arms and legs and every last voluntary movement practically useless now.

Not one to give up under *any* circumstances—even when it has dawned on her what's happened and what the implications of it are—Jinx starts to crawl. Virtually blind now, choking on her own blood, leaving a leech trail on the pavement of deep arterial crimson red, she struggles to see Lilly, to send the woman some kind of message to not worry and to keep going. Don't stop. Get the others out. Find those children and get them back safely.

In her final moments, which encompass all of twenty seconds or so, Jinx manages to register several things happening around her, glimpsed in the opaque, milky, failing vision of her ruined optic nerves. In the blanched white haze, she sees the surviving gunmen—amounting to only about half a dozen people positioned around the desolate parking garage—pause to either reload or await further orders or just take cover and watch. In this fleeting instant of stillness, Jinx hears the warbling, underwater sounds of Lilly screaming at her.

"I'M COMING, JINX!—STAY DOWN!—I'M COMING!—*DON'T MOVE!*"

The sound of Lilly Caul's powerful mezzo-soprano voice piercing the air draws Jinx's attention to the stairwell. Lilly comes out from behind the vestibule with the assault rifle raised, and that hard look on her face with which Jinx is all too familiar. The two women make eye contact one last time. Jinx manages to shake her head. This simple gesture seems to say a thousand words without saying anything. It's her final act of will, and it makes Lilly come to a sudden stop fifteen feet away, pausing behind a massive, graffiti-stained, load-bearing pillar.

Jinx gasps for air, her eyelids sinking, and she manages to raise a shivering, blood-soaked hand but doesn't complete the gesture.

Lilly will never know whether Jinx was about to wave goodbye, wave Lilly off, or blow a kiss. Lilly's eyes well up. Neither woman hears the second blast from the sniper's rifle. Nor does Jinx feel a thing when Theodore "Beau" Bryce—former sergeant major with the 101st Airborne Division of the United States Army—sends a second projectile directly into the back of her head.

For a moment, Lilly just stands there, gaping, breath seizing up in her lungs, tears searing her face as she tries to process this colossal loss. It is such an incomprehensible turn of events—it could be argued that Lilly was unaware how much Jinx actually meant to her—that Lilly now forgets where she is, forgets her mission, forgets Norma and Tommy, and forgets the dangers all around her. She can't move—even with the advent of Tommy's voice screaming, "Lilly! Lilly! Lilly!—LILLY, C'MON!"

The thing that wakes her up is the third blast from Bryce's Remington.

She jumps with a start at the blast kicking a bloom of sparks off the very pillar behind which she's hiding, and she jumps a second time at the booming report echoing off the mortar walls around her—the bullet moving faster than sound. The heat on the side of her face gets her heart pumping again. She spins toward the stairs.

More gunfire nips at her heels as she vaults across the gap toward the stairwell. She fires off a few wild rounds from the assault rifle as she lunges back into the shadows of the vestibule. She climbs the steps two at a time, her tears drying, her heart beating so furiously now it feels as though it might just pop through her sternum.

Tommy and Norma are waiting for her at the top of the staircase. They huddle inside a cement alcove situated on the corner of the ground-level lot. The adjacent tollbooth is boarded and gouged with bullet holes. Kudzu and brown vines have woven through every fence, every light stanchion, every sign. To their immediate right rises the circular ramp leading to the upper levels of the parking complex, and to their left, the tall buildings and barren architecture of the city loom—the awnings of the medical center, the neighboring residential blocks, the urban courtyards, and the glass canyons of offices. Lilly catches a waft of death-stench and senses in her peripheral vision a neighboring pack of walkers closing in, drawn to the commotion of gunfire. All of these observations she makes instantly, before saying a word to the two remaining members of her team.

"What happened?!" Tommy's voice cracks with terror. "Did Jinx—?"

Lilly doesn't answer, just shakes her head as she catches her breath and drops her ammo magazine. Metal clatters on the ground. She can hear the men down below coming out from their hiding places, voices yelling, footsteps shuffling now. They'll be here in a matter of seconds.

"Oh Lord have mercy," Norma Sutters murmurs, shaking her head and looking down.

"Fuck . . . fuck-*fuck*." Tommy clenches his fists, tries to put something into words that cannot be put into words. "What are we *doing*?"

"C'mon!" Lilly grabs Tommy's sleeve with one hand, clutching the assault rifle with the other. "There's no time, c'mon—c'mon!"

"NO!"

Tommy yanks his arm away, stands in one place, and shakes his head. "I'm not going."

Lilly looks at him, her neck prickling with panic. "What?—*what*?!"

"We gotta give ourselves up."

"Tommy—!"

"I don't want anybody else to die."

For a terrible beat, Lilly just stares at the boy, speechless, out of answers, out of wisdom. She shoves another magazine into the pocket and looks at Norma and sees that the older woman is still shaking her head, staring at the ground, looking as though she, too, might be ready to throw in the towel. Heavy boot-steps scuttle across pavement below them, men entering the vestibule, starting up the stairs, drawing closer and closer with each passing second.

Lilly grabs Tommy by the shoulders and gently shakes his gangly adolescent body. "Listen to me. Jinx gave her life so we could get away. Do you understand what I'm saying?"

"Bullshit!"

She shakes him again. "Tommy, listen, they will kill us. Believe me. We have to stay with the plan. We have one shot. Trust me, we have to get out of here right now. Jinx died for Barbara and those kids. Don't let her death be another meaningless tragedy."

The boy lets out an anguished sigh, his eyes welling up with tears. "Fuck it, fine . . . *whatever*."

Lilly turns and starts across the weathered macadam of the entrance ramp. "This way."

They don't get very far before Norma Sutters starts to limp and waver and lag behind Lilly and Tommy. They have crossed less than a quarter mile of urban real estate—circling around the front of the medical center, getting shot at a couple times, and giving wide berth to the gathering swarm of dead—and now they race down a side street. They reach the end of the street, and Lilly turns sharply down a narrow alley between two buildings.

The others reluctantly follow, Norma lagging back even more, gasping for breath, her dark skin glistening with sweat. The alley smells of charred timbers and the rotten-egg odors of sulfur and decay. The pavement is littered with human remains long ago turned to blackened skeletons in the unforgiving Atlanta microclimate. Lilly wades through the trash and the puddles of unidentifiable sludge. She has a fire escape ladder at the end of the alley in her sights. If they can evade Bryce's men long enough to get off the streets—and the ladder is a key to this—then they can proceed with the next stage of the plan.

The only problem now is Norma. She hobbles after them, holding her side, wheezing like a rusty engine slipping its cogs, her expression a heartbreaking mixture of exhaustion, grief, and hopelessness. When Lilly reaches the bottom rung of the ancient, wrought-iron ladder, Norma waves both hands as though finally surrendering on the battlefield to an unnamed enemy combatant. "You folks go on," she says, pausing about fifteen feet behind Tommy.

The boy whirls. *"What?!*—no, no, no, no, no. We have to stick together. Whaddaya talking about?"

Norma can hardly breathe. She bends over and puts her plump hands on her knees as though she's about to vomit. "I'm just holding y'all back."

"Stop it!" Lilly reaches up and tugs on the ladder's bottom rung, making the entire apparatus squeak noisily as she pulls it down. "We stick together. That's it. End of discussion."

"Maybe Jinx was right. I never should have come along in the first place." Norma swallows hard and breathes in pained gasps as though unable to get air into her lungs. "I'm gonna get us all killed." She starts backing away. "I'll be okay, I'll find y'all later."

"Norma, please—"

"I'll be okay," she reiterates with a nod, catching her breath and backing away. The look in her eyes says everything. It makes Lilly's stomach clench.

"Norma, stop. What are you doing? Don't do this." Lilly lowers the ladder the rest of the way. "Tommy, c'mon . . . up you go."

Tommy climbs the ladder to the first landing, pauses, and looks down.

Norma gives them a downtrodden wave. "I wish y'all Godspeed. I know you'll find them kids, and you'll get them back home safe and sound."

Lilly stares. "Norma, don't do this." A pang of terror stabs Lilly in the gut. She realizes that she not only expected this to happen but she has been dreading it ever since they left Woodbury. Norma Sutters has been—and continues to be—a voice of reason amidst the insanity of this suicidal rescue mission. But deep down, Lilly knows that she can't listen to reason. Operating on a deeper sort of animal instinct now, Lilly has thrown reason out the window.

Tommy wipes his eyes, looks down, and says, "Go ahead, leave, we don't need you! Get out of here! We don't want you anymore so go ahead and—"

"Tommy!" Lilly gazes up at the boy. "Stop it!" Lilly looks at Norma. "He doesn't mean it."

"That's aw'right." Norma keeps backing toward the mouth of the alley. She gives the boy a crestfallen smile, the look of a mother leaving a son at college. "You take care of Lilly, honey child." She gives him a patient, loving nod. "You're the man of the house now."

Then she turns and hobbles away, leaving Lilly raw and hollowed out inside.

It takes Lilly and the boy mere minutes to scale the remaining five stories of the iron ladder. When they reach the rooftop of the Chubb Insurance Group building, they're out of breath, sweaty, and jittery with nerves. The floor of the roof is a composite of gravel and tarpaper. The wind moans, gusting across the exposed clutter, whistling through weather-beaten metal chimney vents, medusa-like tangles of conduits, and air ducts the size of refrigerators. Dust devils of bird feathers and debris swirl up into the atmosphere like ghosts in the pale afternoon sunlight.

They hear the gunfire booming down in the glass canyons below, echoing up into the clouds. They hurry across the roof to the west ledge. They lean over the rusty metal flashing of the precipice and see the figures down below moving like pawns on a chessboard.

At first, gradually registering what is unfolding down there, Tommy lets out a moan—a strangled mixture of shame, guilt, rage, and bloodlust. His voice comes out in a low, almost feral groan: "We gotta do something." Almost involuntarily, he rises up and turns. "We have to help her!" He starts toward the other side of the roof when Lilly suddenly grabs him. He wriggles angrily in her grasp. "Let go—let go of me!"

She hisses her words at him, a whisper loud enough to be heard over the wind but soft enough to go undetected by those six stories down: "Keep it down! Tommy, look at me. There's nothing we can do."

"But we can't just let her—"

"We can't get down there quick enough, it'll be over before we get halfway down the ladder."

"*Fuck!*" Tommy goes back over to the ledge and gazes over the lip of the roof. He clenches his fists and breathes harder as he watches the chase unfold down in the labyrinth of side streets and alleyways. "*Fuck-fuck-fuck-fuck-fuck-fuck!*"

Down at ground level, unarmed, alone, and desperate, Norma Sutters races around the corner of Ralph McGill Boulevard and down Northeast Street as fast as her plump, arthritic legs will carry her. Even at this height and distance, it's clear that the woman is hurting, gasping for breath, drenched in sweat, pumping her arms as she runs, pumping them madly as though flailing at demons. Tommy wants to grab Lilly's assault rifle and lay down suppressing fire but instead he just watches and clenches his fists.

Half a block behind the woman, Bryce and his men follow, firing intermittently, gaining on her. The booming reports make Norma flinch as she runs, throwing off her gait, threatening to knock her off her feet. Bullets ricochet and spark off street signs and telephone poles next to her as she tears around another corner and heads east down Avenue E.

Almost instantly, it becomes apparent that she made a huge mistake. Her stride falters, and she nearly trips over her own feet as she sees the swarm of dead people ahead of her, blocking her path. They span the width of the hospital service entrance, several rows deep, like a disorganized army of pasty-faced junkies, staggering toward this unexpected morsel of living human flesh in their midst.

The portly woman skids to a stop. She looks over her shoulder and sees the paramilitary unit behind her racing around the corner of Northeast Street and Avenue E, boxing her in, trapping her, and firing off another volley of controlled blasts.

Norma ducks behind a ramshackle dumpster, bullets pinging and puckering the metal. Walkers close in, and Bryce and his men turn their attention to the swarm, unleashing a barrage on the dead.

Moldering skulls erupt, from the vantage point of the roof looking like strings of bloody firecrackers popping, water balloons bursting, blooms of pink tissue blossoming in a rotten garden. Emaciated figures fold one at a time, dropping in gruesome heaps. Tommy points at the fence behind the dumpster. "Look!" His voice is hoarse with terror, crumbling with emotion. "Look what she's doing!"

Lilly can see Norma Sutters on her hands and knees behind the dumpster. She has discovered a hole in the fence near a pile of refuse and discarded tires. Now she pushes it open with her bare hands. She crawls through it, struggles to her feet, and trundles as fast as she can across a deserted courtyard. She finds a narrow opening between two buildings and lurches through it.

"Oh shit," Tommy mutters, clutching the edge of the roof's metal flashing and gazing down at the far intersection of Highland Avenue and Northeast.

He can see that Norma has inadvertently stumbled into another trap. Surrounded by the massive ruins of overturned semitrailers and unidentifiable pileups long ago decimated by fire and turned into mountains of scorched rubble, she staggers to a stop, turns, frantically searches for a way out of the boxed-in corner. She drops to her hands and knees again and peers under the wreckage, and she sees another swarm coming from the south, and another one closing in from the east. From the north, Bryce and his men approach.

Lilly whispers, almost under her breath, "Goddamn, Norma, get the fuck out of there!"

Then the strangest thing happens. Norma rises back up to her feet, turns toward the oncoming soldiers, and brushes herself off as though about to face a firing squad. She juts her chin. She puts her hands on her hips. She cocks her head. And from such a high, distant vantage point, it's hard to be certain, but it looks as though she's about to bawl somebody out.

The sight of this gobsmacks Tommy. "What the hell is she doing? What the fuck—?"

Lilly sees the portly woman flinch again at a warning shot fired into the air by one of Bryce's men. The soldiers close in on her. The walkers close in. Norma is doomed, and she begins to almost involuntarily back away from the men approaching with their guns and grenade launchers. She doesn't see the manhole cover hanging loose and partially ajar ten feet behind her. But Lilly sees it, and soon Tommy does as well, and Tommy grips that metal ledge with vise-clamp intensity, his knuckles going white, as he softly murmurs, "No, no, no, no, no, no, no, no, no, no, no—!"

Neither Lilly nor Tommy can move or speak or do anything other than gape down at the street as Norma backs toward that defective manhole cover. The inevitable is about to happen and nobody can do anything about it. Norma raises her hands in surrender as the soldiers approach. Muzzles are raised and trained on the plump woman in the middle of the intersection, and Bryce calls out to her.

It's hard to hear what Bryce is saying from the windy precipice six stories up, but it's clear that the back of Norma's heels are inches from that fucking manhole. She keeps unconsciously backing up . . . and backing up . . . and backing up . . . until Tommy can't watch anymore.

Lilly gasps as the portly woman takes one last shuffling step backward and suddenly, without much ceremony or warning, accidentally steps on that loose manhole cover and plunges down into the dark cavity of shadows under Highland Avenue. From the rooftop, it would almost look like a magic act if it weren't for the back of Norma's head hitting the rim of pavement and blood spurting from her scalp, followed by the loud clang of that manhole cover flipping backward onto the pavement with the impact of Norma's body falling through. Then comes the resounding metallic *thunk.*

Norma's hasty, unexpected disappearing act takes Bryce and his men aback.

They stand with weapons raised for a moment as though not believing their own eyes. Bryce stays very still, staring, completely thunderstruck. At last, he holsters his pistol, turns to his men, and says something that Lilly assumes is filled with epithets and reprimands for being such poor shots that they couldn't pick off a single, middle-aged, overweight matron. Lilly feels her spine tingling, the rage and sorrow a potent cocktail, galvanizing her this time. All at once, she's vibrating like a tuning fork, no longer thinking about Norma, or about loss and grief and senseless death. All she's thinking about now is the plan . . .

. . . and watching Bryce's next move with the intensity of a hawk watching a field mouse.

It doesn't take Bryce and his men long to decide it's time to retreat. The sheer number of dead converging on the area due to all the noise and odors of human infiltration proves too much of a threat to ignore. Lilly watches all this from the roof of the Chubb building, her eyes narrowing to slits in the wind, her veins roiling with adrenaline. She can taste the vengeance on her tongue like metal. Her hands tingle. The pangs and bruises from the skirmish in the parking garage—exacerbated by the agonizing loss of Jinx and Norma—have all but succumbed to the buzzing sensation in her vertebrae, that invisible timepiece inside her solar plexus ticking . . . ticking . . . ticking.

Across the roof, Tommy Dupree is still processing Jinx's and Norma's demises. Sitting off by himself, Indian style, on the pebbly deck, he has his back turned to Lilly, his gaze cast down into his lap as though praying.

Lilly goes over to him, touches his shoulder. "C'mon, next part of the plan's in play!"

"What fucking plan?"

"Watch your language and c'mon, let's get moving before we lose them."

Something sparks behind his eyes. Lilly notices it. Maybe he's thinking about his brother and sister. He gets up and takes a deep breath. "Okay, I'm good. I'm ready." He bites his lip, his jaw set, his eyes glazed with anguish. "Let's do it."

They creep across the west edge of the roof, silently tracking the soldiers below. From this height, Bryce and his men look like a single-file line of insects with their dark carapaces of Kevlar and nylon and motorcycle helmets, their guns shouldered with muzzles sticking up like antennae. The sun has crested the tops of neighboring buildings, and Lilly takes care not to lean over the ledge too far for fear her shadow will cast down across the street and give her away.

At the corner of Northeast and Ralph McGill, the soldiers turn left and head west down the four-lane thoroughfare. They walk two abreast now, guns at the ready due to clusters of walkers closing in on them from either flank. From Lilly's vantage point, the dead look like scorched mannequins, reanimated through some dark magic, one blackened body indistinguishable from the next. Bryce orders two of his men to use silencers and small arms in order to pick off the front line of these roamers without drawing more of the herd from the excessive noise.

The sounds of .22-caliber blasts echo like balloons popping up the sides of the iron canyon.

Lilly is so mesmerized and fixated by the exodus down below that she doesn't realize she's about to run out of roof. She sees Bryce gesturing at his men as he marches along with his trademark John

Wayne stride, ordering some of his goons off to the north for some unknown reason. Then he grabs the two-way from his second in command and starts barking orders over the radio. More walkers close in on the soldiers. The wind kicks up again down in the tunnels between buildings, blowing trash and moaning. Lilly is watching all this with laser intensity when she hears Tommy's voice.

"Holy shit, look out!"

Lilly turns just in time to see that she has reached the end of the roof, and the next step she takes will be off the edge of the precipice. Tommy grabs her. Lilly's heart skips a beat as she lurches back away from the ledge. Dizziness courses over her. She nearly drops her assault rifle. The sudden vertigo makes her vision blur, the wind buffeting the side of the Chubb building.

"Fuck," she utters under her breath. "That was too fucking close."

"You got that right." Tommy stands back, shivering in the wind. His expression is heartrending. "We're gonna lose them. Aren't we?"

"No. No, we're *not* gonna lose them."

"We're never going to find Luke and Bethany, are we?"

Lilly turns to the boy and takes him by the shoulders, and once again she looks deep into his eyes and squeezes him gently, with tenderness rather than harshness. "Listen to me, I know you're broken up about our friends, what's happened. I am, too."

He nods and looks down. "I'm okay."

"No. Tommy, listen to me. We don't have the luxury to grieve right now."

"I know."

"We have a job to do."

He looks up at her. "I just want to find my brother and sister."

Lilly nods slowly but offers no reply. She notices something behind the young man's glittering, moist eyes—a familiar look that she's seen in the mirror many times—and it girds her, replenishes her, strengthens her resolve. She turns back to the precipice and gazes over the ledge at the street down below.

Bryce and his men have picked off another half dozen of the dead, and now the street behind them is starting to look like a battlefield, blood smears and human remains riddling the pavement between the piles of wreckage.

The soldiers make their way around another corner, now striding in that compulsory two-abreast formation down Parkway Drive. The once-landscaped road that wends its way around the west side of the Atlanta Medical Center now lies scarred and cratered with the aftermath of violence and human chaos.

Lilly sees Bryce heading toward the side entrance to the hospital. "We got these bastards," she mutters under her breath. She turns and looks at the boy. "We got 'em, Tommy."

TWELVE

Under optimum conditions, the jump from the top of the Chubb building to the uppermost deck of the medical center parking complex would give a Delta Force commando pause. No zip line, no safety net, nothing but crackled cement pavement on which to land, and no guarantee that the wind isn't going to blow you off course. By Lilly's calculations, the drop is about twenty feet. If she and Tommy are able to roll on impact—avoiding any broken bones or twisted ankles—they should be okay. But complicating matters is the fact that the gap between the two buildings is at least ten feet, so there's quite a bit of space to cross. "Let's not overthink it, let's just do it," Lilly advises, speaking more to herself than Tommy, as she backs away from the ledge, strapping the AR-15 securely to her shoulder. She gets a running start and she leaps, arms pinwheeling as she soars out across the windswept space between the buildings and then lands on the hard tarmac of the parking complex.

The impact drives her knees up into her chest and sends a lightning bolt of agony down her spine. She shoulder rolls, the weapon slipping and skidding across the pavement. She slams into a pillar, which knocks the air from her lungs and shoots Roman candles of light across her field of vision. For a moment, she can't breathe and gasps for air as she flops onto her back. She stares at the sky until she can breathe again. A moment later, Tommy jumps.

Blame it on his youth, or blame it on different body types, but the wiry young man takes the fall a lot better than Lilly. He lands squarely on his feet and staggers for a moment but never falls. He scuttles to a stop on the gritty pavement near the pillar and trots over to Lilly. "You okay?—You all right, Lilly?"

"Yeah . . . just great." She lets out a pained grunt. "Never better." Tommy offers her his hand and helps her up. Lilly brushes herself off and takes deep breaths. She looks around the deserted uppermost deck of the parking complex. She sees a few abandoned cars, their windows broken out, the hoods up, a few overturned wheelchairs. She checks her weapon. "C'mon, we gotta get outta sight."

She hurries toward the south side of the lot, Tommy following on her heels, both of them staying low, their gazes nervously scanning the upper floors of the hospital. The main edifice of the downtown campus is a relatively new building—eight stories high—housing the critical care wards, surgical suites, maternity, pediatrics, and in-patient rooms. Lilly remembers coming here once to visit her uncle Mike after his heart attack. She remembers the claustrophobic laby-rinth of corridors and the disinfectant smells. Now she sees that the building is a burned-out shell infested with windblown trash, scarred with bullet holes, and still smoldering on some floors from inexpli-cable fires or explosion. Many of the windows on the north side of the building are shuttered or covered on the inside by blinds or sheets. The upper floors have fared better in the plague years. A few of the rooms above the fifth floor still feature windows that are intact but it's too dark inside the glass to see what's going on. The medivac heli-copter still sits on its pad like a phantom from the hospital's glory days. Lilly sees no signs of life in any of the windows but she knows the men are in there somewhere. They have holed up in there among the storage rooms brimming with medical supplies, food, and drink-ing water. Even if the shelves have been ransacked, hospitals have generators, independent water supplies, working plumbing, hot water, showers.

Lilly searches for a fire escape ladder or some other mode of en-try from the outside rear courtyard. All she sees is a long-forgotten painter's scaffold dangling on twin cables, hanging down across the fifth floor. She takes a deep breath, turns, and surveys the immediate area of the parking deck. The only shelter is a small, freestanding, glass-encased elevator vestibule on the southwest corner of the lot. Most of the glass is grime-specked and webbed with hairline fractures but still intact for the most part. Lilly leads Tommy over to the enclosure.

"Gimme a hand with this door," she says, and the two of them force the powerless automatic door open with their bare hands.

Inside the vestibule, the air reeks of old urine and decay, and maybe walker stench as well, it's hard to tell. The twin elevator doors are stuck open about a foot and a half each, the darkness of the shaft behind each gap revealing a forest of ancient steel cables hanging down like vines. The cars must have stopped somewhere farther down when the power went out God only knows how long ago. Lilly looks around and sees a pile of drywall panels and rebar leaning against one corner of the vestibule.

"Help me with this stuff," she says to the boy. She leans her assault rifle against one wall. She turns to the pile. "We'll use it for cover."

They start wedging broken panels of particleboard against the cracked glass entrance doors. After a while, they have completely covered the glass and boarded themselves in. Now it'll be very difficult for anyone to see that the vestibule is occupied.

Unfortunately, it will be just as difficult for Lilly and Tommy to see any potential adversaries coming toward the vestibule from the outside.

Hours later, as the sun droops behind the cityscape and night closes in, they sit in the darkness of the enclosure, sharing Lilly's last stick of beef jerky. The stale, dry hank of mystery meat was mercifully left untouched in the pocket of her jeans, undiscovered by the thugs who had searched her earlier that day. Now Lilly and Tommy sit on the floor next to each other, passing the jerky back and forth, each gnawing another mouthful before handing it back, each dreading the fact that this is their last morsel of food.

"The fact is, we don't know for sure she's dead," Lilly is saying. "What I'm saying is, we didn't actually *see* her die. You know what I mean?"

Tommy nods feebly, unconvinced. "Yeah, sure, she might still be alive." A single tear gleams on his cheek. "You never know," he adds with little conviction.

Lilly studies the boy. "That's true. You never know. Good things can happen, too. It's not like everything that happens is bad."

He shrugs. "I don't know, Lilly. Lately, it *does* seem like everything that happens is bad. Like we're being punished for something."

Lilly looks at him. "I don't think that's—"

"I'm not talking about just you and me, I'm talking about all of us, we got cocky, and we messed up the world with, like, our pollution and war and greed and toxic waste and stuff, and now we're, like, being *punished*."

"Tommy—"

"I don't blame God for punishing us." He swallows as though trying to digest something far worse than beef jerky, something bitter and harsh and true. "I would punish us, too, if I had the chance. We're a bunch of dicks, you ask me. We deserve to go out like this."

The boy runs out of gas, and Lilly listens to the silence for a moment, thinking.

For Lilly, one of the strangest side effects of the plague is the hush that descends on the inner city of Atlanta at night. What was once a symphony of sirens, trucks banging around, horns, backfiring exhaust pipes, muffled music, car alarms, voices, shuffling footsteps, and myriad unexplained squeaks and thuds and scrapes and booms now presents itself as an eerie white noise of silence. Nowadays, the only sounds in the city at night are the drone of crickets and the occasional wave of distant moaning. Like tortured animals howling in agony, the swarms of dead will intermittently let their presence be known in warbling, echoing choruses of garbled, bloodthirsty snarling. From a distance, it sounds sometimes like a gargantuan, vast engine revving.

"I don't think it has anything to do with what we *deserve*," Lilly finally says. "I'm not sure the universe works like that, if you want to know the truth."

"Whaddaya mean?" Tommy looks askance at her, and all at once Lilly remembers Tommy's fundamentalist Christian parents, and how Tommy always told his little brother and sister Bible stories, and how the boy clings to religion in order to get through the long, dark nights. The boy's face is gaunt and bloodless in the shadows. "When you say 'universe,' you're talking about God?"

"I don't know. Yeah. I guess."

"Do you believe in God?"

"I don't know."

The boy's brow furrows. "How could you not know?"

Lilly sighs. "I don't know *what* I believe anymore. I believe in us."

"Would you still believe in us if we did bad things?"

She thinks about it. "Depends on the things. There's a new standard for bad now. You have to be specific."

"You want to kill these guys, don't ya?"

"Yes."

"But you want to get the kids back first? Is that the more important thing?"

"Yes it is."

"What if we don't get the kids back? What if they're not here?"

"Trust me, they're here."

"But if we don't find them, you're going to kill these guys anyway—right?"

"Probably, yeah."

"Why?"

Lilly thinks about this for a moment. In the darkness, she can see the boy licking his dry, chapped lips, staring at her, waiting intently for an answer. When he talks, his mouth makes dry smacking noises. They have no more water. They will survive maybe another couple of days without any, but that's about it. Finally, Lilly looks at the skinny young man and says with another shrug, "I don't know . . . because maybe it'll make me feel better."

She wipes her mouth, wads up the jerky wrapper, tosses it, rises to her feet, and grabs her assault rifle. "We got full darkness now. Let's move."

They smell the dead in profusion as they circle around the southeast corner of the tower. Creeping past the deserted loading dock, they stay low, keeping to the shadows. At one end of the dock, next to a cluttered workbench, Lilly sees a door—the top half of it frosted glass—which looks like it leads inside the ground floor.

They make their way up a short flight of steps and go over to the door.

The words AUTHORIZED PERSONNEL ONLY are stenciled across the milky glass. It's too dark inside to see anything through the glass, but the odor of dead flesh is stronger now, as intense as the bottom of a lime pit filled with entrails warming in the sun.

"Shit-shit-shit," Lilly mutters after trying the door and finding it locked. She looks around. Tommy waits for her to make a decision. Lilly sees a flashlight on the workbench. "Hand me that flashlight."

Tommy grabs the flashlight and hands it to her, and she thumbs it on. The narrow cone of light illuminates a hallway. Lilly presses her forehead to the frosted pane. She can see overturned chairs. She can see a corridor, blood streaks on the walls, fluorescent light fixtures flickering, a generator humming somewhere in the guts of the building. She can see movement.

Her skin crawls with goose bumps. Dark figures mill about the shadows of the hallway, so many that they brush against each other, elbow to elbow. Distorted by the dimpled glass, the details of their faces and clothing are amorphous and vague—appearing almost ghostly, dreamlike, nebulous—like shadow people.

"What is it?" Tommy's voice breaks the spell. "What do you see? Walkers?"

For a moment, Lilly is morbidly fascinated. There are too many to count. They infest the entire length of the corridor, wandering aimlessly in the flickering light like understudies in a silent film. Some of them seem to be former patients, now clad in desecrated smocks soaked in black blood and bile. Some have decayed to the point of mummification. Many seem to have wandered in from the outside. She watches the gauzy silhouettes as they react to the introduction of light. They start shambling toward the door.

"Very sly," Lilly mutters, essentially to herself. "Very clever."

"What?" Tommy clenches his fists, fidgeting. "What are you talking about?"

"It's just a hunch." She jerks back as monstrous faces brush up against the glass, jagged nails clawing, making horrible muffled scratching noises. "C'mon, give me a hand." She hurries back over to the workbench and grabs a few stray items—a screwdriver, a nine-volt battery, a box of nails, a coil of thick rope—and starts stuffing her pockets. She gives the screwdriver to Tommy. "Put this up your sleeve, backward, like this." She shows him. "Makes a pretty damn good weapon if you find yourself in close hand-to-hand with something that wants to kill you or eat you."

Tommy nods, swallowing hard. She can tell by his eyes that he'd rather not encounter something of that nature in hand-to-hand combat or otherwise.

"Okay, let's check one more thing." She starts toward the end of the loading dock. "Just want to be sure about something. Follow me."

Tommy does.

It takes them less than five minutes to retrace their steps around the north end of the building, then eastward, past the main campus, and down E Avenue toward the trauma center. They pass more boarded windows along the trauma center's street-level entrance.

Through the slats of one window, Lilly sees the ruins of a cafeteria crawling with countless dead. They lumber back and forth in the gloom, weaving between overturned steam tables and tile floors flooded with bodily fluids and rotten, maggot-infested food—all of which confirms Lilly's original suspicion.

The basement and ground-floor levels of the entire medical center are completely overrun.

"It's by design," she whispers to Tommy moments later, huddling inside a cement alcove at the corner of E Avenue and Northeast.

"What is?" His slender face twitches in the darkness as he hangs on every word.

"The ground levels, the basements, everything below the pedestrian walkways, it's all crawling with biters, and it's by design."

He nods. "Like, to keep people out?"

"Exactly. It's a defensive ploy like a moat or a fire line."

Lilly looks up at the glass-encased pedestrian walkway spanning E Avenue, connecting the main complex with the trauma center. Some of the glass panels have been boarded up, the panels dimpled with old bullet holes. Some of the glass is still intact, albeit thick with grime and weather. The monstrous shadows of walkers move to and fro behind the glass like exotic fish in an aquarium.

She sighs and says in a low, sober voice, "My guess is, it serves other purposes as well."

Tommy looks at her. "Like what?"

"For one, that stench probably does a pretty fair job of masking the smell of human occupants on the higher floors . . . keeps the hordes away from the building."

Tommy gives another nod. "Okay . . . so now what? What's the plan?"

Lilly licks her lips, pondering the elevated walkway and all the horrors sealed within it, when all at once she notices something she hadn't noticed before on the other side of the street. Above the pedestrian bridge, a few of the shuttered third-floor windows now glow from within with pale yellow light—either from oil lamps or incandescent bulbs—and the more Lilly stares at those windows, the more she registers the faintest flicker of movement up there.

She turns to the boy and says, "How do you feel about heights?"

The trickiest part is the first twenty feet. From the street-level façade of the trauma center to the top of the pedestrian bridge, there are no footholds, no handholds, no indentations in which to wedge a toe—just a smooth concrete wall leading up to the second-story ledge.

Fortunately, it turns out that Tommy Dupree is not only comfortable with heights, he also possesses the climbing ability of a large spider monkey. Lilly had suspected as much earlier the previous night when Tommy scaled that enormous live oak north of Haralson with lightning speed. But now she stands behind the cover of spindly shrubs next to the boarded trauma center entrance—neck craning upward—as she watches in complete awe.

The young man's nimble ascent takes mere seconds. He reaches the third-story ledge, hops onto the roof of the pedestrian bridge, pulls the coil of rope off his belt, ties it around his waist, and throws one end down to Lilly. She catches it, takes a deep breath, and starts slowly pulling herself up the side of the building.

As luck would have it, Lilly Caul has lost nearly thirty pounds since the early days of the outbreak. Of course, she was always thin, but the plague diet has turned her downright skeletal, not to mention lean and muscular from all the manual labor. Now she pulls herself up the wall with surprising agility.

She reaches the roof of the bridge and awkwardly rolls onto it. Her assault rifle nearly slips off her shoulder. She manages to hold on to it and rises to a crouching position, then pulls up the slack. A gust of wind suddenly buffets the bridge, and Lilly jerks.

"It's okay, I got you," Tommy says in a tight little whisper, winding the rope back around his waist. "Just do me a favor, and don't look down."

"Copy that." Instead, she glances up. She sees the painter's scaffold hanging down on its steel cables like a massive swing set. The wind makes the cables clang and ring against the wall. The sight of it sends chills through Lilly, makes her dizzy. "Let's get it over with . . . before I lose my nerve."

They start across the bridge. Moving single file, staying low, inching along, they cling to the roof as the night wind whistles through the glass and concrete canyon around them. They feel exposed, and they can hear the muffled, snarling drone of the undead in the glass walkway beneath them. They smell the death-reek.

As they approach the west side of the street, Lilly gives the boy a signal to stay down and stay quiet. She sees the light behind the shuttered third-floor window, and it makes her heart start to race. She carefully crouches beneath the window ledge and listens. Tommy kneels off to the right, practically holding his breath.

Muffled voices come from inside the window. Male. Two or perhaps three people. The venetian blinds are drawn tight. Adrenaline courses through Lilly's body. She tastes metal on the back of her tongue, the base of her neck humming with adrenaline as she carefully reaches down to her AR-15 and flicks the selector from Safe to Fire. Seven rounds remain in the magazine, one in the chamber. Eight rounds total. Carefully she peers through a narrow crack between two of the louvers.

She sees two soldiers sitting in a cluttered examination room that's been retrofitted as a barracks.

The observations flash through Lilly's brain: a pair of cots lined up along one wall of the dusty chamber, shelves brimming with bottles, canned goods, and supplies. A hot plate sits on a credenza and pornographic pictures are taped on the wall. Lilly recognizes one of the soldiers as Bryce's second in command, Daniels—the skinny, bald, emaciated meth-head—who now lies back on his cot with a dreamy smile on his face. He wears a wifebeater, camo pants, and jump boots, his withered arms sleeved with garish tattoos.

"Only thing that makes sense anymore is this shit," he comments in a languid voice to the second man, indicating the traces of unidentified drug left in an EpiPen on his side table. Daniels lets out a little intoxicated giggle. "Everything else is upside down."

"I heard that." The second soldier—his name unknown to Lilly—speaks in a thick drawl as he sits on a cot in his skivvies. A big lump of a man with huge sideburns, huge belly, and huge buck teeth, his gigantic hairy legs stick out of his boxer shorts like gnarled tree trunks. His 9mm Glock sits on a bedside table, a six-inch suppressor like a small black clarinet screwed onto its muzzle.

Lilly focuses her gaze with feral intensity on that pistol with its silencer attachment. She glances over her shoulder at the boy, takes a deep breath, and then motions for him to stay right there.

Then she turns back to the window, loosens the strap on her

AR-15, and starts tapping and scratching on the glass, careful to make the noise irregular and random.

"What the fuck?" Daniels looks up from his second injection of Nightshade, the tingle from the EpiPen prickling inside his elbow. He hears the noise coming from outside the window but doesn't really register it fully. It might be the wind or a fucking pigeon or some shit like that.

He looks down and sees a delicate strand of blood on his wrist, and feels the warmth chugging up his arm and into his cervical vertebrae like the world's greatest masseuse. Daniels usually needs two blasts of the stuff to maintain his equilibrium at night and get decent shut-eye.

"What the Sam-Fucking-Hell is that noise?" Markham rises and the cot seems to let out a squeaky exhalation of relief at the purging of his massive weight. The man stands at least six foot six in his bare feet. His huge pectorals look as though they could maybe use a Playtex Cross Your Heart Bra. He takes a step toward the window, his enormous feet making thunderous vibrations.

"I got it." Daniels waves him back. He tosses the spent EpiPen. "Probably one of them rats-with-wings we get in the gutters around here time to time."

Daniels goes over to the window, grabs the cord, and raises the blinds.

At first, the figure in the window does not compute: a slender woman with brown hair holding an assault rifle like a spear.

Daniels lets out a little impish giggle. The woman thrusts the barrel at the glass as hard as she can but the window holds. Daniels jerks back with a start. The window is made of safety glass and right now it merely cracks, doesn't break. Daniels giggles and giggles. He doesn't get the joke but still finds this whole thing hilarious. Who the hell is this chick, the fucking window washer?

"Who the fuck is that?" Markham's deep, phlegmy voice gets Daniels's attention.

Daniels turns and starts to say something when the second blow from the AR-15's muzzle breaks the window. Broken glass erupts. Diamond shards spray in all directions and a gust of noxious wind swirls into the room. Daniels rears back, nearly falling on his ass as the woman lurches into the barracks.

Markham turns and starts to go for his pistol when things begin to unfold very quickly.

The woman vaults across the room and simultaneously rams the butt of her rifle into the groin of the big man. Markham staggers, letting out a garbled cry as he slams back against the far wall, rattling the foundation and knocking a Barely Legal nude calendar off its nail. Daniels turns and fumbles for his HK, which lies just out of his reach on the end of his cot. The woman drops her assault rifle and lunges toward the Glock. At the same time, Markham dives for the pistol. Across the room, Daniels claws for the HK. Meanwhile, Markham and the woman get both their hands on the 9mm pistol at the exact same moment. By that point, Daniels has gotten his hands around the machine pistol, but it's too late. The woman has already managed to force the muzzle of the silencer up as she wrestles with the big man over domination of the pistol's trigger. Both their fingers are on the trigger pad now as they slam against the wall and struggle for the gun. The woman manages to squeeze off several wild shots in the general direction of the man across the room. The silencer pops, spitting sparks a half dozen times before the seventh and eighth blasts strike Daniels directly in the chest between his nipples, plowing through his heart.

The skinny soldier staggers backward, gasping wetly, dropping the machine pistol, struggling to breathe as he hemorrhages. He slides to the floor by the cot, letting out a death rattle, pink foam bubbling from his mouth, the off switch pinning his eyes open.

In the meantime, Markham has finally overpowered the ferocious chick. He wrenches the pistol away from her and throws her to the floor with the force of an overgrown child tossing aside a rag doll. The woman bangs the back of her skull on the tile, the impact knocking her silly. She tries to roll away but the big man has flopped down on her, sitting on her midsection. It feels to the woman like a Winnebago has landed on her.

She gasps for breath as Markham aims the pistol between her eyes, the muzzle inches away from her nose. He squeezes off a shot at point-blank range.

The gun clicks impotently, out of ammo. The big man angrily tosses the weapon aside. Lilly tries to wriggle free but he wraps his gigantic hands around her puny neck and starts to strangle her.

Lilly gasps for breath as the big guy tightens his grip and breathes his noxious breath into her face, which changes color as she starts to lose consciousness.

THIRTEEN

A ball of fire builds in Lilly's lungs as she struggles to breathe. Her vision blurs. The dim ambient light of oil lamps in the reeking barracks begins to fade, the darkness of oblivion closing in on her. All she can see now is the colossal head of her strangler—a monolithic planet orbiting Lilly's world—glowering down at her in all its cruel crystalline detail. She can see the man's acne scars on his livid cheeks, the nose hairs in his flaring nostrils, the green decay in between his yellow teeth, his liver-colored lips peeling back with psychotic rage. The final observation that Lilly makes before sinking into the void is the man jerking his head back suddenly and without warning. His eyes widen, and his mouth goes slack, and a stringer of drool loops down off his flaccid lower lip.

All at once Lilly can see the handle of the screwdriver that was given to Tommy Dupree now sticking out of the top of the man's skull, and she feels the man's huge hands suddenly loosen their hold on her neck.

Lilly gasps and coughs convulsively as the giant collapses to the floor next to her, revealing a smaller figure standing behind him.

"Oh fuck . . . shit . . . shit." Tommy Dupree stands dead still with his skinny arms at his sides, his fingers curled into claws, his eyes wide and bright with terror. He keeps murmuring to himself, "shit . . . shit . . . shit," while glancing down at the delicate little droplets of blood on his right wrist. Blowback from the impaling has spattered his entire sleeve.

Lilly tries to say something but is still too busy laboring to get air into her lungs. She pulls one leg from under the fallen behemoth. She rubs her neck, the tendons and cords panging with agony. She heaves for air. Wheezing and hacking, she manages to say, "Okay . . . Tommy . . . calm down."

"What did he think he was . . . ?" Tommy swallows hard, looking at the massive lump of a man on the floor, the screwdriver like a vestigial horn protruding from his head. "What did he . . . ?" Tommy stares at his hands with the expression of a person not completely awakened from a nightmare, the terror still clinging to him. He wipes the blood on his pants. "I had to do it . . . I had to because he would have—"

He pauses abruptly, a shudder passing through him, his tears welling up.

"It's okay, Tommy." Lilly gets her bearings, then rises on her unsteady legs. She goes to the boy and pulls him into her arms. She hugs him to her chest, feeling the shaking deep within him like a motor running. "You did the right thing, Tommy."

"I had to because he . . . he would have . . . he was going to kill you."

"I know . . . it's okay." She strokes the back of his head. It's dawning on her that perhaps the boy has never killed the living at such close range before, which is quite different from taking someone down through the distant perspective of a scope on a rifle. "Listen to me. You did well."

"He would have killed you." Tommy tries to stave off the tears by burying his face in the nape of Lilly's neck. "He would have done it."

"I know."

"He would have killed you."

"I know . . . believe me . . . that's about as close as I want to come." She gives him one last squeeze, tenderly stroking his hair. "Look at me now, Tommy." She holds him by the arms and speaks very clearly to him. "I need you to hear me. Look at me. I need you to listen closely. Are you listening, Tommy? Look at me."

He looks up at her through wet eyes. "I just wanted you to know I would never let anybody kill you."

"I understand that, I do, but right now I need you to listen to what I am saying."

His breath hitches with a sob. He's trying, bless his heart. He's trying so hard to be grown-up, to be dispassionate and cold and unemotional. "I just wanted you to know—"

Lilly slaps him. Not hard but brisk enough to cut through his tears. "That's enough now. Listen to me. I'm going to need you to stop talking. I'm going to need you to shake it off."

He nods. He wipes his face and nods again. "I'm good. I'm good."

"Shake it off."

He gives her another nod. "I'm good. I'm okay." Deep breath. "I'm good, Lilly."

"Okay, here's the deal. We don't have much time now. They're going to find these guys—it's just a matter of when. So I'm going to need you to help me get their bodies up in their bunks. It'll buy us a little time maybe. Who knows? Come on—first the big guy."

They lift the massive remains of Private First Class Glenn Markham onto the corner cot, covering him up to his neck in blankets. The screwdriver comes out of his head on a rivulet of blood. Lilly quickly wipes the excess with the end of the blanket.

It takes them another minute or two to drag Daniels across the floor and position him in the other bunk. They wipe the blood trail. Then Lilly looks around the room. "Look for any spare ammo, check that locker. See if there's another magazine for the Glock." She picks up the HK and shucks out the magazine, replenishing it with one from the Glock. It's a high-capacity version—thirty rounds when full—and now Lilly sees that it's a little over half-empty. She's about to say something when Tommy's voice interrupts her thoughts.

"Okay!"

Lilly whirls and sees that Tommy has found a bandolier with what looks like several dozen high-powered cartridges tucked into its loops. He looks up at her. His eyes have hardened, his jaw clenched as if he's ready now to do whatever it'll take to get his brother and sister back. "Does this help?" he asks.

The third-floor corridor stretches a hundred feet in either direction, deserted, dark, a few gurneys pushed up against the walls, the parquet tile floor old and overscrubbed. In some places, the beige tiles have been cleaned so many times they've turned gray. The air hangs heavy with disinfectant, ammonia, and something stale and food-like, maybe canned cream corn or dehydrated milk. Most of the numbered doors are shut. Muffled voices come from behind some of the distant ones, probably other soldiers medicating themselves with Nightshade.

Weighed down with heavy artillery, Lilly and Tommy move down the hallway without making a sound, staying close to the wall. Lilly has the AR-15 strapped against her back, the HK in her right hand. She also has a twelve-inch tactical knife that she found on Daniels now tucked into the shaft of her boot. Tommy has the Glock gripped tightly in both hands, the bandolier tight across his narrow chest, digging into his armpit. He awkwardly walks with the gun's muzzle forward, ready to rock, shaking slightly. Neither says a word as they approach the intersection of corridors at the end of the hall.

With a quick hand gesture, Lilly stops for a second and listens to muffled voices and footsteps coming from the floor above them. The sounds echo down a stairwell to their left. Another quick hand gesture, and they slip through a metal door and into the stairwell.

They climb the steps single file, guns at the ready. Lilly's heart thumps as they reach the top of the stairs and pause before going through the unmarked metal door. Lilly whispers in a hoarse voice, her traumatized vocal cords still sore and creaky, "Stay close, and follow my lead." She waits for a nod. "If bullets start to fly, stay behind me and stay low and look for a way out. Don't wait for me. Just get the hell out. If we get separated, we'll meet back at that rooftop. You got that?"

Tommy nods briskly, nervously. "What do we do when we find Bethany and them?"

"You follow my lead, and let me do the talking. I promise you I'll get you and the kids out of here alive. But you have to do exactly what I say. And if you have to draw down on anybody, don't hurry your shots. Take time to aim. I promise you, they'll take time to aim at you. You do the same. Put that front sight in the middle of that back sight. Squeeze the trigger in one fluid motion just like I taught you. Understand?"

He nods.

"Say it."

"I understand."

The first thing she notices about the fourth-floor corridor is the odor—a disturbing mélange of pine-scented death-reek and acrid chemicals. Then she notices hundreds—maybe even thousands—of little Renuzit bottles. They line the scabrous floor, one every few inches along the baseboards, some of them brand new with cheerful little pictures of pinecones and evergreen boughs, apples and cinnamon sticks. Lilly blinks, her eyes burning. She pauses and surveys the far end of the corridor. At the moment, the hallway is unoccupied—a long, wide expanse of ancient tile, flickering fluorescent tubes, and stainless-steel tables—but the sounds of voices and shuffling footsteps and generators hum inside many of the rooms.

Lilly slowly creeps toward the first open doorway, her back pressed against the plaster wall, Tommy right on her heels. She sees a sign hanging above the lintel that says RADIOLOGY. Gooseflesh pours down the backs of her arms and legs as she registers the garbled sound of walkers snarling and spitting, a human voice crackling out of a two-way radio, and the rattle of equipment. She motions at Tommy, and the two of them pause just outside the doorway.

Carefully peering around the doorjamb, Lilly gets her first glimpse of what seems to be a makeshift lab set up inside the cavernous radiology department. In the sputtering light of old fluorescents, amidst a labyrinth of shelves brimming with beakers and flasks and petri dishes and test tubes spinning on centrifuges, she sees the upper torsos and heads of the reanimated dead. They hang from stainless-steel hooks, their arms amputated, their heads lolling. Someone has sewn their mouths shut with thick surgical sutures. The severed heads continue to work their jaws like cows chewing cud despite their stitched and impeded lips. Their jugulars are connected to ports sprouting IV lines, which curl and twine down to large conical flasks and condensers and cannulas on the floor beneath them. The air vibrates with the whir of laboratory equipment and generators, as well as the smell of deodorized rot.

"Lilly—?"

The whispered breath of Tommy's voice sounds far away in Lilly's ears. For a moment, she's paralyzed, rapt, awed by the diabolical evidence of some sort of reorganization going on in the radiology room. She can see whiteboards along the back wall scrawled with feverish hieroglyph, hastily sketched formulas, chemical compounds filling every square inch of white space. She can see headless bodies lying on gurneys, their ragged neck openings vomiting spaghetti-like tangles of wires and tubes glistening with fluids in the fluorescent light. She can see far tables jammed with test tube racks and glass slides swathed with innumerable samples of tissue and blood and DNA from God only knows what source.

"LILLY!"

She finally tears her gaze from the room, pivots around, and looks at the boy. "What? *What is it?*"

"Listen." He nods toward the opposite end of the corridor, his eyes widening with alarm.

Lilly cocks her head and listens to a strange sound that seems to be warbling and emanating from some distant warren of corridors, mingling with the faint sound of footsteps, all of it coming this way. At first, it sounds like an exotic bird shrilling and squawking. And these are no ordinary footsteps. Hasty, rubbery, squeaky, they approach with the purpose and speed of a person on a mission.

"C'mon, this way!" Lilly grabs the boy by the collar and gently ushers him into the radiology department.

They choose a shadowy area behind the hanging specimens in which to hunker and wait. Crouching down in the fetid shadows, they hide behind an equipment locker—their fingers on triggers, poised to fire at a moment's notice—while they listen to the footsteps and the bird noises closing in.

Above them, the dripping upper torsos of the dead shudder and react to the introduction of humans to their personal space. Some of the heads twist around and search the darkness for the source of the human smells, their shoe-button eyes seeking fresh living meat, their jaws still hungrily clenching and working, their sutured lips straining to break free of the haphazard stitching. They make muffled moaning noises, their flesh filling the room with the reek of festering meat, and for some reason, it all strikes Lilly at that moment as more heartbreaking than horrifying.

Maybe the ghastly quality of dismembered pieces of the dead continuing to move and twitch—feeding off the nothingness—has lost its shock value. Now, in a way, it's more *prophetic* than terrifying. Like a burning bush. It's where everyone is headed. And Lilly finds it agonizing to watch but also mesmerizing . . . right up until the point she hears the footsteps and bird sounds approaching outside in the corridor.

A nurse swishes into the room with the casual briskness of a stock clerk searching for a part. A middle-aged woman with iron-gray hair done up in a haphazard bun, and a face as weathered and lined as parchment, she wears a white uniform that's shiny and pilled with age, and she carries a caterwauling baby in her arms. The infant looks to be only a few months old, its cherubic little face soiled and chapped, its body swaddled in an old blanket.

Crossing the room, the nurse absently bounces the baby on her hip in a futile effort to get it to quiet down. The baby runs out of air for a moment, then shrieks some more as the nurse casually walks up to a stainless-steel refrigerator. She elbows it open, reaches in, and pulls out a laboratory jar filled with unidentified pink fluid.

Then, just as abruptly as she entered, she turns and whisks back across the room and swishes out into the corridor, the baby squalling and ululating as they depart.

Lilly gives Tommy a nod. He nods back at her. Then Lilly rises to her feet and crosses the room with her HK in both hands, her gaze locked onto the corridor, her boots making very little noise on the parquet floor. Tommy stays close on her heels. Lilly reaches the door and hears the sobbing cries of the baby receding down the hall. Lilly takes a deep breath and peers around the jamb.

The nurse has reached the end of the corridor, and now she carries the infant through a glass door and up another narrow staircase. Lilly indicates to Tommy that he should follow her and do it quietly.

They slip out the door and start down the hallway, Lilly holding the machine pistol's muzzle out in front of her as steady as a ship's prow. Tommy does the same, both his hands keeping a sweaty grip on the Glock. They move silently, hastily, keeping close to the wall.

It takes them mere seconds to reach the stairs. They carefully open the door, slip into the well, and hurry up the echoing enclosure. The bleach-scented air makes Lilly's flesh crawl. She can hear the footsteps of the nurse fading away somewhere above her.

Lilly pauses on the landing at the top of the staircase, turning to Tommy.

"Trade with me," she says to him, handing him the machine pistol. "There's a certain way I want to do this, the less commotion the better."

Without a word, he hands over the Glock, a surprisingly heavy weapon with its six-inch silencer attachment weighing down the muzzle.

The fifth floor is the former home of obstetrics, the female wellness center, and the maternity ward. Now, at the far end of the main corridor, a spacious reception area sits empty and desolate, completely ransacked, some of the original furniture overturned in the corners. The cluttered counter of an abandoned nurse's station sits beside a huge bronze statue of a female patient holding a newborn. The tarnished, mossy green statuary stands in the center of a dry, out-of-order fountain. The carpet bears the stains of unidentified dark fluids and past struggles. The windows are covered with tinfoil and duct tape, a single bare bulb hanging down, casting a dim, jaundiced cone of light down across the worn nap of the floor.

A side hallway leads past a series of examination rooms, most of them unoccupied and locked up tight. The last room on the left has people in it. The telltale sounds of children whimpering echo out a half-ajar door, some of the voices familiar, some making muffled moaning noises, some hysterical and sobbing so hard they're out of breath. An adult female voice scolds one of the kids. The smell of talc and ammonia and dirty diapers gets thicker and thicker the closer Lilly and the boy get to the partially open door.

Lilly pauses just outside the room with the Glock gripped tightly, barrel pointing upward, safety off, a hot round in the chamber. Tommy presses his back against the wall mere inches behind her, swallowing hard, waiting for her signal. Lilly feels the heat of adrenaline lighting up her gut, spreading through her tendons, the AR-15 loosened on her back for easy access, the stock dangling across her right hip. She is in the moment. She is clear, her mind completely purged of distractions.

She raises her left hand, holding up three fingers. Tommy nods as she indicates the beginning of a countdown. She stares at Tommy, watching the boy go as still as a cat as she lowers her ring finger.

Two . . .

Not taking her eyes off the boy, breathing in and holding her breath, Lilly lowers her middle finger until only her index finger is raised.

One . . .

The entire universe seems to freeze as she makes a fist and pulls down.

The moment she lurches into the room, Lilly fires off a single noise-suppressed blast at the gray-haired nurse, who is fifteen feet away from Lilly's right flank (and in the process of turning toward a long rifle leaning against a coat rack in the corner). The report pops dry and metallic—like the clap of a screen door in the enclosed space of the examination room—sending a 115-grain 9mm hollow point into the woman's left thigh.

The impact spins the nurse in an awkward pirouette for a moment before knocking her to the floor and slamming her against the baseboard near the radiator. A garbled grunt escapes her lungs as she holds her leg, but Lilly knows as well as the nurse that the bullet cleared the femoral artery and simply passed through the meat of the woman's sturdy leg. Now the nurse writhes on the floor, holding her leg and trying to catch her breath and get her bearings. Lilly sees no reason to kill this woman . . . *yet*. The woman could be a captive herself. Who knows? Lilly doesn't have enough information yet. More importantly, the nurse might be a valuable asset to them.

Quickly, Lilly takes in the layout of the room practically in a single glance. High ceiling, fluorescent lights shining down on plaster walls and tile floor, screaming baby in a crib pushed up against one barred window, Norman Rockwell prints of family doctors, captive kids in the opposite corner with strips of fabric around their mouths, their eyes luminous with watery terror. No sign of Barbara Stern, and no time to worry about that right now.

Lilly's heart practically rises into her throat when she notices her sweet Bethany perched on a padded exam table, holding her brother in her arms. Little Lucas seems almost catatonic with fear. The sight of them squeezes Lilly's guts and makes her eyes water with a bizarre mixture of relief and kill-rage for the monsters who would snatch and brutalize these precious children. Thank God they're here, thank God they're still in one piece, thank God, thank God, thank God, thank God, thank God. Every molecule of Lilly's soul wants her to go to them right now, to breathe in the soapy fragrance of their hair, to hold their spindly little bodies . . . but she can't do that . . . she can't go to them . . . not yet.

Tommy softly shuts the door behind him in order to avoid drawing any unwanted attention to the noise, and Lilly lunges toward the rifle in the corner, kicking it out of the nurse's reach before the gray-haired woman can grab it. The nurse flops onto her back, still holding her leg and starting to scream: "BRYCE! DOCTOR! SOMEBODY GET—"

Her words get cut off by Lilly's hand slamming down on her mouth. "That's enough—quiet now, goddamn it—quiet the fuck down or you're gonna force me to—"

Lilly's own words are curtailed by a sudden and unexpected stabbing pain in her hand.

The nurse has bitten into the fleshy part of Lilly's palm—hard enough to draw blood—and Lilly involuntarily pulls her hand back and lets out a yowl. Blood stipples up across Lilly's face, stinging her eyes, and momentarily distracting her as the nurse claws at her.

Something primal bubbles up inside Lilly and all at once her vision tunnels and she grasps the nurse's head by its ears and slams it down on the floor.

On the first impact—the sound a sickening crunch—the nurse gasps. On the second impact, she chokes and struggles to breathe. On the third, her eyes roll back in her head. Lilly keeps slamming the woman's skull against the floor at least a half dozen more times until the nurse has gone completely limp and blood has begun to seep out from under the woman's head in a great billowing ruby-red sheet unfurling across the tiles. Lilly can see nothing but the blurry remains of a woman's face gone bloodless and still beneath her, the eyes frozen open, taking in nothing. In fact, Lilly is unaware of anything else in the room for several seconds . . . including the fact that Tommy has stepped in between Lilly and the children, blocking the children's view of the grisly proceedings.

"Lilly!"

She feels Tommy pulling her off the nurse. Like a switch being thrown, Lilly almost instantly snaps out of her rage reverie and blinks as though seeing clearly for the first time. She looks up. "Lock the door, Tommy. Now. Lock the door. And help me with the window."

Notwithstanding Lilly's vendetta directed at the kidnappers, and her cancerous rage, and her sparking synapses now telling her to shoot first and ask questions later, the plan has always been to make every attempt to rescue the children as quickly and efficiently as possible, and evacuate them from their confinement with a minimum of engagement with the enemy. But those options seem to be dwindling with each passing second as Tommy struggles to open the transom window above a storage locker positioned against the room's outer wall.

The other windows are lost causes with their impermeable bars and safety glass. Tommy stands precariously on one of the exam tables and discovers with great frustration and alarm that the transom window is also useless, welded shut from generations of dried, congealed paint.

"Are we gonna die?" Across the room, little Bethany presses up against Lilly, her mouth red and swollen from the gag, her eyes wet with agony. She keeps averting her gaze from the crumpled, blood-sodden remains of the nurse across the room, the woman's empty face marbled with blood, her head caved in like a deflated bladder. The little girl's voice is crumbly and hoarse from terror. On the other side of the room, the baby is sucking on a pacifier in its bassinet, quiet for the first time since Lilly arrived.

"No, sweetie, we're not gonna die." Lilly touches the girl's downy hair. "We're gonna get outta here now and go home. Okay?"

The girl doesn't reply. She is a sturdy child, approaching puberty, with dirty-blond pigtails and strong, intelligent brown eyes. She still wears her filthy little Duck Dynasty sweatshirt under a ratty denim jumper. Bethany has never allowed herself to be this scared, and the sight of her open display of fear has rattled Lilly a bit.

Bethany and Tommy's little brother Lucas clutches Lilly's other leg like some kind of marsupial offspring clinging to its mother. A freckled waif of six years with unruly hair, Lucas Dupree hasn't said a word since Lilly arrived. He has spoken only with his eyes, which continue to radiate utter horror.

"Okay, listen to me, everybody. Here's the deal." Lilly announces this to the kids in a sort of encouraging, camp-counselor-style tone of voice, giving Bethany Dupree a reassuring little squeeze. "Nobody's gonna die, we're all gonna get outta here, but we have to do it quickly, as quick as you've ever left a building. You understand what I'm saying? Yes, it's like a game, except that it's way more important than a game. You understand?"

Tommy's voice penetrates Lilly's train of thought from across the room: "It won't budge!"

"That's okay, Tommy. Get down, grab your gun, c'mon. You still got that rope?"

"This?" The boy climbs down, pulling the coil from his belt loops. The heavy-duty hemp rope is frayed and soiled from the ascent up the side of the building. He hands it over to her.

Lilly gathers the kids with exaggerated hand gestures, waving them into a semicircle around her, ushering the smallest ones against her hips. Most of them still semicatatonic with trauma, they press up against her like little pilot fish. Lilly turns to Bethany. "Go get the baby, sweetie."

"Why do I have to—"

"Don't argue, sweetheart, just do it—we're really in a hurry here."

Bethany goes and retrieves the infant, the baby still chewing its pacifier with relative calm. The child's cornflower-blue doe eyes seem to take in Lilly as a worshipper would take in a god.

Lilly turns to nine-year-old Jenny Coogan with her thick horn-rims decorated with nerdy masking tape wrapped around the center and her Japanese anime T-shirt. Jenny is the hipster of the bunch, and also one the strongest kids for her age. "Take this, honey, and don't let go no matter what." Jenny grips the rope with white-knuckle intensity. Lilly looks at the other kids and suddenly feels a wave of emotion pass through her, memories of little preschoolers like guppies following their nannies down the suburban sidewalks. "Everybody grab a handful of the rope, and hold on tight! Gonna move quickly toward the closest stairs, and don't stop no matter what. Even if you hear gunshots."

Nods from some of the older kids. The Slocum twins, dressed in their identical tattered pinafores and tiny Chuck Taylor sneakers, stand shoulder to shoulder like a Diane Arbus postcard. The freckled, ruddy-complexioned ten-year-old Tyler Coogan stands behind them, dutifully clutching the rope. He still wears his shopworn Braves cap as though it bestows superpowers to its owner. Lilly looks from child to child as she prepares to lead them to freedom.

These are all essentially children orphaned by the plague, and Lilly loves these kids with all her heart and soul. And for a brief moment, Lilly realizes she shares that distinction with them. Lilly, too, has been orphaned by the outbreak. She nods one last time, heavy with emotion and resolve, and reaches for the AR-15 strapped across her back.

She pulls the charging handle and releases the bolt, injecting a round into the chamber, and takes a deep breath before crossing the room to the door. Then she turns the knob and leads the group—with Tommy bringing up the rear, two-handing the machine pistol—out the door.

Unfortunately, nobody hears the heavy shuffle of combat boots charging down an adjacent staircase until it's too late to do anything about it.

FOURTEEN

Neither group realizes that each is stumbling into a head-on collision with the other until Lilly and Bryce make eye contact at practically the exact same moment, each of them rounding a corner at opposite sides of the reception area. Each instinctively fires off a single shot, both blasts going wide and high. Lilly's round chews a chunk of the lintel above the nurse's station, sending a spray of plaster dust into the air as thick as gauze. The other blast—a single blue flash from Bryce's stainless-steel .357 Magnum—shatters a glass cabinet still filled with long-out-of-date magazines one foot to Lilly's left. Crystalline dust sprays across Lilly's flank and sends her reeling in the opposite direction. Bryce and four other unidentified figures instantly duck down, most of them reaching for their guns. At the same moment, across the waiting area, Tommy shoves the children back against the wall like a crazed traffic guard, blocking them from the line of fire. Neck veins bulging, eyes bright with fury, the young man has the machine pistol in one hand—safety off, full auto—and he turns and lets out a strange war-cry that raises the hackles on Lilly's neck. It sounds like a hoarse, garbled bark—a mucusy howl—that makes all heads turn. Lilly answers it with her own cry: "Tommy NO-NO-NO!!"

Lilly's shriek comes one millisecond before the HK crackles, a barrage of automatic fire spraying the opposite wall where the others hunker down near the floor. One of the men—a middle-aged soldier in ratty green fatigues—takes one in the neck. He gasps and slams back against the nurse's station, dropping his gun, clutching his neck, choking out as the blood issues forth in a fountain of deep crimson arterial spray between the man's fingers. Pages of documents and paper registers and boxes of Kleenex and pens erupt across the counter of the station in blooms of white matter and shards of plastic detritus. Everybody hits the deck except Sergeant Beau Bryce. Lilly can see the graying, rawboned former soldier go down on one knee, assuming a shooting position, aligning the front sight of his massive stainless-steel revolver on Tommy, which prompts Lilly to raise the barrel of her AR-15 and prepare to take Bryce out—all this happening within the span of a single half second—when all at once a series of equal and opposite actions and reactions unfold, registering one at a time in Lilly's brain, bringing the gunfire to an unexpected and abrupt halt.

"BRYCE! HOLD YOUR FIRE! PLEASE! EVERYBODY! THERE IS NO REASON FOR THIS BARBARIC, RIDICULOUS GUNPLAY!"

The voice comes from one of the three surviving figures huddling down against the floor behind Bryce, their faces obscured behind the cover of the nurse's counter. The voice is feeble, scratchy, and ancient, but it seems to carry much weight with Bryce, who instantly averts the muzzle of the .357, letting out a tense breath. Then the source of the voice reveals itself as a man who looks to be somewhere between seventy and a hundred, awkwardly rising to his feet on wobbly knees, smoothing out the folds in his white lab coat, brushing off his baggy corduroy pants, and adjusting his eyeglasses. He has spidery silver hair, a cadaverous, wrinkled face, and thick, Coke-bottle glasses behind which his gray eyes are magnified into huge omniscient orbs. Lilly fixes her cobralike gaze on this older man as he raises his palsied arms as though surrendering.

All of this encompasses less than a minute, and in that length of time, Lilly hasn't moved from her position in the archway of the side hall, down on one knee, her assault rifle raised and ready, the back sight pressed to her eye, the magazine still filled with enough rounds to make every last one of these motherfuckers sorry they entered this vestibule. But before the old man can say another word—in fact, before anybody else in the waiting area can shift or say anything or shoot or even move—Lilly makes an instantaneous decision. It bubbles up out of her forebrain fully formed and galvanized with resolve. She realizes that this older man must be the ringleader of this circus, and from the way he's speaking to Bryce, it's clear he carries some kind of authority in the folds and stained pockets of that dull white lab jacket that drapes over his emaciated, stooped shoulders. All of which propels Lilly to her feet.

Before the old man can say another word, two things transpire in complete synchronous conjunction with each other: 1) Lilly leaps across the gap between her and the old man—a distance of about ten feet, maybe even less—at the same time, with one violent, fluid motion, dropping the rifle and pulling the twelve-inch tactical knife from the lining of her boot; and 2) Bryce pivots toward her with the barrel of his .357 raised, and he even starts to squeeze the trigger, when the old man in the lab coat cries out in his crumbling voice, slamming the brakes on the proceedings: "BRYCE, NO! HOLD YOUR FIRE! HOLD YOUR FIRE! PLEASE DO NOT SHOOT!"

Lilly presses the serrated edge of that brushed black steel knife against the wattled, turkey-like neck of the old man.

Time stands still in the dim, yellow light of that derelict reception area.

For the longest time, nobody says anything, and the silence seems to drip from an invisible faucet in that gloomy space, with its bullet-riddled nurses' station and tufts of paper littering the carpet now like cottonwood fluff—the fragments of happier days, the shards of once joyous moments documented on tearstained maternity forms. A dead man lies amidst the litter, soaking in his own juices. The children softly whimper. Tommy holds the machine pistol aloft, aiming it at Bryce, the weapon ready to roar at a moment's notice. Bryce seems oblivious to the boy's killing position. At the moment, the sergeant major is apparently interested solely in holding his enormous gleaming revolver on Lilly, his upper body coiled and poised to blow her away. Lilly can sense the barrel of the .357 aimed directly at a spot a few inches above her temple, and she can feel the old man trembling in her arms. She can hear his weak heartbeat racing—in fact, she can feel his faint pulse against the back of her thumb as she holds the business end of the knife against his jugular. She can smell his odors—stale Old Spice, bad breath, BO, and something unidentifiable like rubbing alcohol or ammonia—and she can sense his wheels turning. *What now? How do we proceed in the face of this interesting turn of events?*

"You've gotta be kidding me," Lilly finally says, breaking the spell with a voice dripping with contempt. She recognizes one of the men huddling behind the corner of the nurses' station, and she struggles to wrap her mind around what she's seeing. "You pathetic hypocrite . . . you have no shame."

The man to whom she refers—a tall, slender drink of water in a fedora—slowly rises up with his arms raised in surrender. Unarmed, dressed in his trademark Banana Republic outdoorsman garb and faux explorer khakis, Cooper Steeves looks as though he wants to crawl into a hole and die. His huge Adam's apple bobs as he swallows the humiliation and guilt. He purses his lips as though searching for the proper words but words prove elusive. "Wow . . . Lilly . . . you have no idea what you're dealing with here . . . trust me, this is not—"

"Trust you? *Trust you?*" She lets out a venomous, toxic chuckle. "That's rich."

"Madam, if I may explain." The voice of the old man resonates in her ear like a rusty hinge. "This Steeves fellow has done nothing more than help us find worthy subjects with a minimum of collateral damage."

"Please shut up." Lilly increases the knife's pressure on the old man's neck.

Bryce speaks up. "All due respect, may I add something at this juncture?" His voice is cold, calm, almost serene, as he holds the muzzle of the .357 Magnum inches away from Lilly's forehead. "We got a mutually-assured-destruction kind of thing going on here so why don't we all just go ahead and dial it down a little. What could it hurt to talk this out?"

"You're right." Lilly nods, her own voice as tranquil and hypnotic as the commander's. "We're all in each other's sites, sure, but I will end this old man with a single flick of my wrist if anybody tries anything. Even if you fire first, manage to get off a head shot, the body seizes up in death. You don't believe me, ask around. You shoot me, this old fuck bites it, and I'm getting the feeling that's a trump card around here, so do me a favor and shut your fucking mouth." She turns to the fourth figure still crouched down behind the nurses' counter. "But before you do that, tell your other goon to come out from under his rock, and tell him to drop his weapon."

Nobody says anything as a portly, middle-aged soldier in a Kevlar vest with a bandanna around his sweaty, bald head slowly rises and sheepishly comes around the corner of the counter with his M16 aimed at Tommy.

Lilly keeps her eyes on the barrel of Bryce's revolver, a tiny round black hole of doom sucking all matter into its gravitational field, unwavering, pointed at that same exact spot above her temple. She licks her lips. "I'm not seeing that rifle go down. Can somebody tell me why I'm not seeing this gentleman lay down his gun?"

"Lady, let me explain something to you." Bryce's voice is as steady as a tuning fork. A man of indeterminate age, he has that graying-at-temples, groomed, suntanned look of a general or a pro football coach. "In fact, I think it'll help everybody concerned if we all lay all the cards on the table, so to speak."

"Where's Barbara Stern?"

Bryce cocks his head. "Who the hell is Barbara Stern?"

"The lady, came in with the kids, where is she? Is she alive?"

The old man speaks, his voice like a purring cat in Lilly's ear. "She's very much alive. I assure you. May I ask your full name, Lilly?"

Lilly lets out a weary sigh. "You don't need to know my full name."

"May I finish?" Bryce keeps his tone measured, sanguine, even faintly deferential, as though he's a diplomat proposing a complex settlement. Lilly even notices a glimmer of something behind his gray eyes approaching respect, maybe even admiration.

"I'm listening." Lilly glances across the reception area at the little gaggle of captive children, their eyes blazing with terror, Tommy standing with his HK machine pistol in front of them like a royal guard, his chin rigid with that trademark jut, his gaze welded to Bryce's gleaming silver handgun.

"I understand your position here, believe me, I do," Bryce tells her, ever the helpful ambassador. "But the sad fact is, you harm this individual, then we'll have to go ahead and waste each and every one of your people, which is extremely unnecessary, and also regretful, I think you'll agree, especially with youngsters involved, but the thing is, it's a harsh environment we find ourselves in nowadays, and the consequences would be on you, so I'm not sure you really want to get into a situation where you're going around acting as though you—"

Tommy's voice pierces the air. "YOU SHOOT HER AND I PROMISE YOU I WILL SPRAY YOU WITH FUCKING—"

"Tommy!" Lilly doesn't flinch, doesn't budge, doesn't move her gaze one iota from the Magnum's muzzle. "Calm down! Nobody's shooting anybody right now. We're just having a little chat. Right, fellas? Just chewing the fat. Right? Nothing to get excited about."

"That's exactly correct, Lilly," the old man murmurs. "And if I may, I'd like to offer something else on which you might want to chew."

Lilly keeps the knife pressed against his throat and tells him to keep talking.

"My good woman, I don't think you quite grasp the importance of what we're doing in this facility, so in the interests of expediency, as well as the avoidance of further bloodshed, allow me to illuminate—"

"Excuse me," Lilly interrupts, the knife as steady as a chalk line across the old man's central artery. "Whatever it is, it does *not* justify mass murder, kidnapping children, and God knows what else."

"I understand your revulsion with our methods of procuring our subjects—"

" 'Procuring subjects'? Really. That's what we're calling it now?"

"Madam, what we call it is *closing in on a vaccine that will basically save mankind.*"

Lilly goes still, saying nothing at first, letting the words slowly register.

At first, the old man might as well have said "We're cloning giraffes and turning them into aardvarks." For a long moment, Lilly can't quite get traction on the entire concept of coming up with a vaccine for the plague. She initially thinks she misheard him. *Did he say "vaccine"? Or did he say "gasoline"?* But then, as she realizes the entire reception area has gone still and silent, awed by the simple words spoken with such casual certainty, she understands. "You're talking about a vaccine for the plague," she finally utters, practically under her breath, the pitch and timbre of her voice coarsening, lowering an octave. "For the walker plague."

"That's precisely what I'm talking about." The old man speaks in a soft, gravelly, sandpaper voice—a grandfather gently explaining to grandchildren the unfortunate need to drown kittens. "In today's day and age, people are less likely to volunteer for clinical trials. It's unfortunate but we cannot let this human impediment—understandable as it is—get in the way of our imminent breakthrough. If we cannot convince the subjects to come willingly, then we will take them by any means necessary. It's an unfortunate cost of progress."

Lilly feels her innards going cold and clammy like a slug has just crawled across the inside of her stomach. "Why the children?"

The old man takes a deep breath. "The younger the subject, the more pure the white blood cells. Postplague infants are now almost exclusively nourished with mother's milk. These innocent young things have immune systems beyond our comprehension. They're like nuclear reactors. Their leukocytes are smart bombs when dealing with unknown viruses, microbes, and foreign bacteria."

"Tell me the truth," Lilly demands, staring at the six-inch stainless-steel barrel belonging to Army Sergeant Beau Bryce. "And don't lie.

I'll know if you're lying and I'll open your jugular." She pauses. "Do your subjects survive your trials? Do they live?"

Another wheezing, pained breath gets inhaled by the old man with great dramatic flair. "Alas . . . some do and some don't. It is, once again, the cost of doing the research that will save these people's descendants." He wheezes painfully. Lilly begins to wonder whether this old wreck of a man is terminal himself. "Believe me, I wish things were more civilized, more humane," he goes on. "We try to keep our subjects comfortable with a series of central nervous system compounds that I have developed over the last couple of years using local flora as well as leftovers in the derelict pharmacies. I was on the cytocholine team with Pfizer in my previous life. My name, in case you're wondering, is Nalls. Dr. Raymond Nalls of Norfolk, Virginia."

A horrible revelation suddenly punches Lilly in the gut. She can barely get the words out. "You're testing the vaccine by letting your subjects get bit. Aren't you? That's your so-called clinical trial. Isn't it?" She waits but the old man remains silent. She presses the edge of the knife against his neck wattle, causing a thin tear of blood to track down the folds of his neck. "ISN'T IT?!"

Bryce moves closer, close enough to press the revolver's cold muzzle against Lilly's temple. "Back off or we're talking bloodbath right here in this waiting room."

"GET AWAY FROM HER!!" Tommy takes two steps toward the threesome, raising the HK to eye level, his arm trembling convulsively.

This gets the other soldier, the one in the bandanna and Kevlar, to aim his M16, with his finger poised on the trigger, directly at Tommy Dupree. The children let out whimpers and mewls, stutter-stepping backward, moving as one, each still clutching the rope. The air pressure in the waiting room seems to seize up, and the electrical polarities of fear and rage crackle behind Lilly's eyes, and she sees one possible future over the course of that single synapse firing in her brain: if she chooses to slit the old man's throat, the area would most certainly erupt in cross fire and cordite and smoke, the massive metal projectile from the .357 spiraling into her brain, the fountains of life-blood exploding all around her in clouds of pink mist as the lights flicker out, Lilly collapsing, darkness closing down like a shade.

"WAIT!"

She surveys the area, each combatant about to fire, when all eyes turn to her. She feels her heart racing so furiously inside her that her chest pangs with a deep, aching pain. Her pulse pops noisily in her ears, drying her mouth, as everybody waits. Lilly takes a deep breath and chooses her words carefully. She has a feeling that everything she's experienced in the plague years—perhaps in her entire life—has been leading up to this moment, and from this point on, everything will be measured either as Before This Moment or After This Moment.

She swallows hard and finally says very softly, "I'll make you a deal."

Ever so slightly the old man cocks his head. Lilly has spoken loud enough for Bryce and the others to hear her, but she has obviously directed this last statement at the old man, the kingpin, the ring-leader. His hirsute ear, tufted with dark, wiry hair, practically twitches. His voice sounds almost dreamy. "I'm sorry, could you repeat that?"

"I said I'll make you a deal—a one-time-only limited offer." Lilly feels a trickle of sweat tracing down the crevices of her collarbone, between her breasts, and down her tummy. It feels like a fire ant crawling across her skin. She looks at the side of the old man's face and tries unsuccessfully to read his expression.

Then she says in a low, sober voice, her words barely audible: "Me for the kids."

FIFTEEN

The old man tips his head slightly, his expression furrowing with incomprehension. "I'm sorry, forgive me . . . I'm not following. Did you say, 'Me for the kids'?"

"That's right. Let the kids go, and you can have me for whatever."

The old man chews the inside of his cheek as he thinks it over. "Forgive me for being impolite, but with the skirmish in the parking ramp as well as today's melee, you've killed at least a half dozen of my people. And I'm fairly certain we're going to find Mrs. Callum, the nurse, expired in that makeshift nursery. Is there some reason I should trust you now and take this as a serious proposal?"

Lilly nods, still pressing the knife into the folds of his neck. "I won't harm a hair on anybody else's head, you let those kids go. Stick tubes up my ass, dissect me like a frog, feed me to the biters. Whatever. Let the kids go. That's all I ask, and I'm yours."

The old man ponders for a moment, saying nothing, his teeth clenched in thought.

"You think Steeves here is a catch?" Lilly pours it on. "Seriously, I practically know every survivor from here to the Florida border. I'll help you get subjects, I'll tell you anything you need to know. Just let the kids go, and you got me. Nobody else from Woodbury will ever bother you."

Now the silence seems to crystallize around them as if the very air is suspended in aspic as the old man ponders this latest turn of events. The excruciating pause seems to stretch for an eternity as Lilly scans the faces of the children. They haven't yet processed this latest development. They still look thunderstruck and leery with their little pale white hands latched onto that rope, their imaginary lifeline, their coaxial connection to a gentler, kinder world where kindergarten teachers lead flocks of sticky-faced tykes to the school parking lot, where soccer moms await in SUVs with healthy snacks. Tommy Dupree keeps shaking his head but can't summon up any words. Bethany Dupree gazes at the floor with crestfallen, old-soul sadness, as though she expected something like this all along. A single tear clings to the tip of her nose, then drips to the floor.

Meanwhile, the old man arches his eyebrow and says to the bandanna man, "Lawrence, can you tell me if we have any of those primary reagents left in hematology?"

The man in the bandanna thinks about it, still aiming his M16 at the boy. "I believe we do, yes. There's still plenty of Anti-A, Anti-B . . . and I think there's even a tincture of Anti-A,B left."

The old man nods slowly, careful not to make any sudden movements that would alarm or spook the woman holding the knife. "All right, Lilly . . . I'll need to check one thing first, if I may . . . in order to intelligently execute this negotiation. Is that acceptable to you?"

Lilly shrugs. "Do what you gotta do."

They take a sample of Lilly's blood. It's not the most practical way to perform this procedure, by any means, but somehow they manage to do it quickly and efficiently with a minimum of fuss. The man in the bandanna does the honors, hurrying down an adjacent corridor while Lilly continues to hold the knife poised against the old man's neck. Within minutes, Bandanna Man has returned with a syringe kit, explaining what he needs to do, and Lilly tells him to take the blood from her leg. He does so and then hurries back into the labyrinth of side hallways to carry out his task, leaving a backwash of silence in his wake.

Completely vexed by the purpose of all this strange due diligence being performed on her, Lilly stands in awkward silence as they wait, the reception area still gripped in its deathly standoff, the knife's edge still pressed against the neck of the emaciated old man, the muzzle of the large-caliber revolver still aimed at Lilly's cranium. Except for the soft whimpering of the children, and the muffled buzz of an unseen generator, Lilly finds herself noticing disturbing little details about the reception area and the people in it. The single bare bulb that hangs down from the broken ceiling fixture intermittently flickers and fades in and out with the vacillating current, giving off a faintly hallucinatory effect to the area. Lilly notices a huge wart on the side of the old codger's ulcerated, livid nose, as well as a portion of a naked lady tattoo on Bryce's left forearm sticking out of his rolled-up sleeve. The odor of baby shit wafts across the waiting area as though commenting on the events of the day. Lilly's arm aches from the constant pressure of the knife on the old man's throat.

It's Cooper Steeves who first breaks the silence. He stands on the other side of the reception area, wringing his hands, his revolver still holstered. "Lilly, I'm sorry it's come to this, but I never wanted to—"

"Did anybody ask you to talk?" Lilly interrupts.

"They were going to take our people one way or the other, Lilly."

"Please shut your mouth."

"All right, that's enough." Bryce looks as though he's running out of patience. He taps his signet ring on the grip of his .357. "Let's turn the record over, okay, we've heard enough of this shit."

"May I make a suggestion?" the old man interjects, his voice dry and husky from the stress of having a knife pressed against his pulse point for so long. "This procedure could take ten or fifteen minutes, and the children look exhausted. May I suggest we all sit down?"

After a brief pause, Lilly says, "Why not?"

Across the waiting area, as though attending some kind of nightmarish daycare center, the children all flop down on the floor, most of them still holding the rope. Only Tommy and Bethany remain standing. The little girl has been fighting her tears since the standoff began, and now she simply stands with her hands on her hips, staring at the floor while tears roll off her face. She makes no sound. From across the waiting area, staring at her down-turned face, Lilly feels a pinch of emotion in her midsection. Is this the last time she'll ever see her kids? Is this why the little girl is crying so hard? Does she sense that this is the passing of some undefined era?

Lilly suddenly yanks the old man backward with her free hand, the knife still poised.

They simultaneously sit down side by side on one of the love seats next to a plastic ficus tree so furry with dust it looks as though it's made of cement. Bryce leans against the nurses' counter, lowering his .357 and letting out a sigh that sounds like he's grown bored with all the tedious dissembling and bargaining. Behind him, Cooper Steeves remains standing. Fidgeting like a boy who has just been sent to the principal's office, he looks as though he doesn't know what to do with his hands, refusing to make eye contact with the children. Despite his rakish attire, the guilt and humiliation radiate off him like a sour odor.

"Where are you from, Lilly?" Nalls asks with the casual deference of a man taking a census.

"What difference does it make?"

"Married?"

"Who gives a shit?"

The old man sighs, blowing air across his lips. "These are not trick questions, Lilly, just making idle conversation while we wait."

"What are you, my *date*?" Lilly wisecracks, then gives the side of that aging gray head a closer look. "I heard somebody call you the chemist. Is that what you did at Pfizer?"

"Precisely." He sits up straighter despite the tendril of blood on his shriveled neck. "I have found that chemistry is the basis of everything. Life, death, love, hate, happiness, sorrow, joy, and pain. Chemistry bonds the atomic particles of space and time. It is the thread that stitches together the universe, and chemistry, Lilly, is the thing that will ultimately get us out of this mess."

"That's all really heartwarming." Lilly says this more to herself than anybody else. "But what good does all this beautiful poetry do us if—"

The sound of hurried footsteps interrupts her train of thought, cutting off her words.

Bandanna Man comes around the corner of an adjacent hallway with a roll of narrow thermal paper curled in his hand, a readout from some sort of diagnostic apparatus. He has a strange look on his face, eyes wide with excitement, lips pressed tight with barely contained exhilaration. He approaches the old man with awe and reverence in his step.

Without moving his head, Nalls gives the man a loaded glance. "Well . . . ?"

The man in the bandanna just smiles and proffers the kind of nod one proffers when notified of a promotion or a tumor turning out to be benign.

The old man stares. "You're certain of it?"

Bandanna Man nods, his smile widening. "I ran the test twice." A big grin here. "Finally got one."

Nalls blinks. Then he gazes at Lilly as though looking at a white tiger. He turns to Bryce and says very softly, "Let the children go."

They give Lilly a few seconds to say goodbye. They let her do it at the top of the fifth-floor stairs at the end of the main corridor. Bryce and Bandanna Man watch from a few feet away, their guns at the ready, as the children take turns giving Lilly desperate, tear-sodden hugs, crying into the fabric of her flannel shirt.

"We can't just leave you here," Bethany Dupree sobs, hugging Lilly so tightly it feels to Lilly as though her internal organs are being compressed. "We h-have to stick together."

Kneeling, Lilly embraces the little girl, stroking the back of the child's hair. "You have to go, sweetheart. It'll be okay. I'll be fine. You and Tommy have to take care of the baby."

The girl gazes up at Lilly through enormous, wet, blue eyes. "But y-you said it yourself, we stick together, always . . . always s-stick together."

"I know . . . things change." Lilly holds her by the shoulders. "Look at me. You're strong. You have to go and protect your brother."

The girl sobs. The other children look down, some of them crying so hard now their little lungs are hitching and shuddering. The baby squalls. Tommy holds the infant, carefully bouncing it. Lilly rises to her feet and addresses the group. "You all have to be strong. Look for Norma. She's out there somewhere. Do what Tommy and Bethany say and you'll make it."

Tommy hands the shrieking baby over to Bethany. He looks at Lilly. "I'm not going."

Lilly feels the shell around her heart cracking. "You have to go."

Tommy's eyes well up but he continues to give her that macho chin-jut. "No fucking way, I'm not going. I'm staying with you."

"You have to go, Tommy. You're the only one who can get these kids back." She hugs him, his body rigid as he fights the tears. He knows he has to go, and Lilly knows he knows it. She holds him. "I love you."

Tommy loses it in her arms. He cries and cries into the crook of her neck, his sobs carrying up into the rafters of the gloomy corridor. The boy cries so hard that the two hardened men standing guard behind Lilly turn away. Even Bryce looks down at the floor.

Lilly tries to hold on to her wits, tries to control her emotions. She has to be strong for this beautiful boy. She hugs the wiry young man and whispers in his ear, "Try and find the train yard, stay close to the tracks, stay low and keep moving south." She swallows her sorrow and attempts a smile. "You're my son now, Tommy. I'm proud of you, and I will always love you. Always. Always."

The sorrow breaks through suddenly and courses through Lilly. She lets the tears come, and she weeps into Tommy's shoulder. She sobs so hard her throat goes sore and hoarse. Her tears soak the boy's shirt. She lets the storm move through her.

Then she gets her bearings back and gently disengages herself from the boy. She stands back and gives Tommy a nod. "It's time to go."

Lilly can't bear to watch the children leave. She turns away as Tommy and Bethany lead the gaggle of sniffling, shell-shocked kids through the emergency exit doors and down the stairwell. The ghostly echoes of the baby's caterwauling bounce around the cement enclosure.

Staring at the warped, decaying parquet tiles of the hospital corridor, Lilly hears the tiny shuffling footsteps reverberating in the stairwell, fading away as the kids make their reluctant descent down the iron steps. She feels dizzy. Her nose is running and she wipes the snot and salty tears from her face.

Within moments, the skittering footsteps fade to silence. A distant squeak somewhere in the maze of lower floors, followed by a metallic clang, signals the fact that the children have made their departure from the building. The sound is a death knell, a spike thrust through Lilly's heart. She swallows the anguish and grief. She tells herself right then—she makes a vow—that she will see her children again or she will die trying. She is thinking about this when she hears the baritone burr of Bryce's voice to her immediate left.

"All right . . . we good?"

Lilly looks up. "I wouldn't say that exactly."

"But we're done, right? Done with our little part of the bargain?"

Lilly shrugs. "Yeah, I guess you could say that."

"Good."

Lilly doesn't see the balled fist coming at her until it's too late to do anything about it: Bryce tags her squarely between the eyes with massive force, just above the bridge of the nose, a practiced roundhouse punch designed to send the recipient to the mat. The effect is similar to a cut-to-black in a movie, Lilly losing consciousness well before the moment when the floor rises up to meet the side of her head with an audible thud.

PART 4

Perchance To Dream

They will drink and stagger and go mad because of the sword that I will send among them.

—Jeremiah 25:15

SIXTEEN

. . . floating. . . .

. . . without form, without purpose, without memory, without identity, gliding over a patchwork quilt of ravaged land, farm fields blackened and scourged, streams and rivers running dirty crimson red, and the multitudes of ragged, naked, moldering souls wandering, aimless, maggots upon the earth . . .

. . . in the winds of the upper atmosphere she opens her mouth to scream and nothing comes out. . . .

. . . later . . .

. . . running, running . . .

. . . down a snaking blacktop road, across the threshold of a bridge, arms pinwheeling madly, breath chugging in tattered gasps, she races down the narrow planking, balance gone, side panging, vision blurring . . .

. . . she manages to glance over her shoulder and sees the horde on her tail, a thousand strong, squeezing into that narrow passage of a bridge, all those milky eyes locked onto her, palsied arms reaching for her, all those rotten lips working around slimy teeth, spurring her on, faster, faster toward the far side, toward freedom . . .

. . . without warning, all at once, the bridge collapses and she falls through the maw . . .

... gravity claiming her ...

... plummeting through space, shrieking a silent scream, plunging toward ...

... home ...

.. : at last ...

... she's home, in her little condo on Delaney Street, in her bedroom ...

At first, it doesn't occur to her that there's anything strange going on here—it's morning, it's a workday, the clock says 6:31 A.M., and the sound of Megan's ubiquitous hair dryer is crooning in the bathroom at the end of the hall. All is well.

She takes a deep breath, drags herself out of bed, and pads across the room to her closet.

She rifles through her outfits, looking for a clean outfit to wear to work. She chooses a macramé vest to wear over a nude-colored bra. Ripped jeans go on next, the cuffs rolled up over her high suede boots. She remembers there's a storewide meeting today among all departments, and she wants to represent her Handbags and Accessories Corner in style.

While she dresses, the room begins to bleed. Subtle at first, silent, just beyond the boundaries of her peripheral vision, the deep crimson fluid begins to seep from cracks and seams in the molding along the edges of the ceiling, tracking in slender rivulets like tears oozing down the surface of the cabbage rose wallpaper. She stares as the blood begins pooling on the carpet along the baseboard.

Stricken with shame, mortified, frantic that somebody will see the mess and blame her, she goes through her drawers for something with which to sop up the evidence. She finds her mother's funeral dress—the navy-blue shift, the one with the staples up the back. She grabs it, gets down on her hands and knees, and begins wiping up the blood. But it's futile. The dress is not even remotely absorbent, and the blood is like greasy paint.

Somebody left the TV on in the background, a droning anchorperson on the increasingly troubling reports of a new pandemic spreading across the earth. A strange commercial comes on. At first she merely hears a disembodied voice as she furiously wipes up the blood: *"I promise we shall do our very best to keep this process as pain-free as possible."*

Pain-free?

She glances over her shoulder. On the twelve-inch TV screen she sees a blurry image of an old man wearing a white sterile mask, his saggy, gray eyes staring into the camera. What kind of cockamamie soap opera is *this*? *General Hospital*? *The Young and the Institutionalized*? The man gazes out at us, the viewers, as he talks: *"You're going to feel a faint pinch, Lilly, and then a cold sensation in your arm, both of which are normal."*

The old man fiddles with something off screen, his mask obscuring most of his deeply lined, leathery features. His voice is disturbingly familiar to Lilly, and sends chills down her back as she hears her name spoken behind the mask. *"There, that's good, Lilly . . . perfect. Such a good patient. Each draw will take an hour or so, but such details should not concern you at this point."*

Lilly gets up, storms over to the dresser, and switches the TV off.

Then she's somewhere else. She's in a tunnel that stretches into the shadows ahead of her, a narrow channel of leprous stone and moldy timbers framing stalactites of calcium deposits and ancient cage lights dangling down, flickering and blinking at odd intervals. She moves cautiously. She feels the breath of monsters on her neck. She holds an ice cream cone that's melting. The sticky white liquid runs down her wrist, drips to the tunnel floor.

She stops. Her skin crawls. In the reflection of the melted ice cream she sees the ghostly, faded silhouette of the old man with his sterile mask—a doctor, she presumes—continuing to address her: *"I've taken the liberty of administering a twilight-inducing agent into your bloodstream, which will not only ease your pain, but will virtually make the passage of time seem irrelevant."* Lilly flinches, jerking away from the puddle with a start, dropping the soggy sugar cone, as the nasally voice behind the mask continues. *"You may even find it strangely pleasant, and you might dream. Your dreams may be vivid."*

A familiar voice rings out next to her. "Are you okay?"

"What?" She turns and looks into the droopy, hound-dog eyes of Bob Stookey. He stands next to her, his flesh as white as ivory. "I'm fine," she tells him. "Why?"

"You just jumped."

"I did?"

Bob frowns. "Did you take something? Did you drop that last tab of acid?"

Lilly backs away from him. He's supposed to be dead. Something bubbles up within Lilly, something inchoate and terrifying. She feels the tendons of the world stretching to the breaking point. Her vision blurs.

She stumbles deeper into the tunnel, and then she's somewhere else.

The girls' barracks back at the Kennesaw Sleepaway Camp—the place she spent her summers during her middle school years—is now deserted and run-down, many of the bunk beds overturned, the knotty pine walls green with mold, the floor littered with human bones. Lilly tries to get out through the door, but finds it locked. She looks out a window.

The landscape is decimated, a barren wasteland of bare trees and seared ground. It looks like the surface of a dead planet.

Lilly sits down in front of the window and waits for her dad to pick her up.

Weeks pass. Months. Years maybe. Lilly feels as though she has been sitting in front of that window for most of her life now. She feels as though the soles of her feet have grown into the floorboards like the stubborn roots of a tree. She can't move.

Then all at once she's somewhere else. She's back in Megan's condo, in the living room, on the couch, watching *The Young and the*

Restless on TV, when a volley of thunder rattles the foundation and shivers across the sky outside. She springs to her feet, races across the room, and slams out the front door. The green light and static electricity of a storm greets her, slashes her face with drizzle and wet winds.

The neighborhood swims in bleary, watercolor-streaked light. The huge dormer window rising off the condo's front roof-pitch has a wrought-iron weathervane on its crown that now spins wildly in the gusts. The tops of trees toss and rage as Lilly scurries across the courtyard to where her car was parked a moment ago but now is missing.

She hears the ghostly voice: *"Another day, another draw. And you continue to be so brave. You're doing so well, Lilly. I'm so proud of you. Just continue to relax and dream, and we'll take another 250 cc's of your remarkable blood."*

Her car sits at the end of the block, a boxy little onyx-black Volkswagen Jetta. She hurtles toward it, but abruptly comes to a halt on the edge of the yard, looking down at the puddle spreading across the gutter, the cold, needling rain hammering down on her.

She wipes her eyes, blinks, and stares at the oily surface of the puddle.

The phantom face, as pale as a milk cloud in coffee, partially obscured by that white cotton sterile mask, undulates as it addresses her: *"Do you know that you are the star donor here? Such beautiful veins you have. Today we'll harvest another 500 cc's of whole blood and even run some platelets on the side for good measure. There is no telling how many lives you will be saving, Lilly. You should be very, very proud, so very proud."*

The ghost takes his mask off and reveals the cadaverous, sunken cheeks and yellow smile of Doctor Raymond Nalls, formerly of Norfolk, Virginia. In his decaying, corroded smile Lilly can read an entire pandemic, the end of days, a world coming to a close—her memory flooding back as the lightning slashes down and strikes her between the shoulder blades.

Her eyelids snap open. Pupils dilate. The sharp scent of ammonia fills her nostrils. She can't swallow, can barely draw a breath. Something is weighing her down, something invisible crouching on her chest. All around her are impressions of dim light, pale surfaces, and rectangular patterns. She blinks and tries to move. Her body feels as though it's encased in cement. She blinks some more and realizes she's staring at a ceiling, the rectangular patterns revealing themselves to be ancient corkboard tiles, so old that their original color has faded from ivory to soot gray.

It's a while before she realizes she's lying supine on a gurney, engulfed in the stale reek of disinfectant and unidentifiable acrid chemicals. Her throat feels parched. She realizes she's so thirsty she can barely swallow. But right now she concentrates on moving. She finds that sitting up is too ambitious at this point. Moving her head might be the next best thing. But when she tries to turn her face to her immediate left, she is met with an alarming paralysis. It feels as though someone has driven a railroad spike down the center of her skull and into her spine.

All of which suddenly strikes her as hilarious. The thought of having a metal spear thrust down her core seems so ridiculous—in fact, comical—that she lets out a staccato burst of laughter that mingles with the strange noises that are slowly registering in her midbrain. If she could only find some water, maybe she could think. She's so thirsty, she can't think straight.

The noises intensify. She's been hearing the sounds ever since she came awake in this absurd room with its musty-sharp odors and stupid ceiling tiles. At first, the clamor seemed to exist in some remote universe light-years from here, irrelevant, white noise that has no purpose or bearing on her current situation. But gradually, the din has slowly registered before she's even been capable of identifying it, strumming some auditory nerve deep within her and sending warning signals to her brain. The distant cacophony comes from behind a door or wall, the muffled gunshots, screams, and crashing noises practically drowned by the unmistakable drone of walkers.

Walkers.

The word percolates up through her consciousness with startling power, filling her brain with half-formed images and memories that flicker and pop and make her giggle. But the snickering that comes out of her is brittle and hysterical in her own ears. There's nothing funny about the associations unfurling in her mind right now in the wake of that word. She remembers where she is, the plague, the struggle to survive, the loss of her father, Megan, Josh, Austin, the kids, and the world shutting down like a vast candle flame guttering out. Megan has been dead for almost three years. Then Lilly remembers the kidnapping. She remembers ending up in the ruins of the Atlanta Medical Center some time ago—days, weeks, months— and now she realizes she's still inside that crumbling edifice.

She manages to break through the paralysis and roll a few inches until she falls off the edge of the gurney.

She lands hard on the floor, an IV stick taped to her wrist tugging painfully at her, the air knocked out of her, a shooting star slashing through her vision. The room spins. She tries to sit up, tries to turn her head, tries to take in the rest of the room and figure out where the hell she is, but her body won't cooperate. The sensation—the way her entire being feels like a hollowed-out log—makes her laugh and laugh. She looks at the dried, blood-caked intravenous rig attached to her wrist, and she giggles and guffaws like it's all a big practical joke.

Then out of the corner of her eye she sees a water dispenser about ten feet away from her, nearly empty, a little left in the bottom. She crawls toward it. The inverted glass jug is shattered, but there's at least a half gallon of liquid remaining in the neck. She manages to claw at the tap, rising up enough to get her mouth around the nozzle. A few ounces of tepid water dribble out, and she swallows greedily, then collapses.

Lying there for a moment, spent, exhausted, staring at those ceiling tiles, nearly paralyzed, she hears the noises again coming from outside the room—choruses of watery, smacking noises, distant claps of gunfire, frantic voices shrieking. And even before she identifies the sources of these sounds, Lilly Caul intuits—despite her compromised condition—the dangers usually lurking behind such racket. This intuition sends waves of gooseflesh down her arms and legs. All of which seems doubly ironic and hilarious now that she realizes she's been dreaming or hallucinating the whole Marietta experience, and she's really not home, and the plague is real, and she's . . . she's . . . where is she?

She manages to roll onto her side and lift her head enough to take a closer look at the room.

At first, it appears to be someone's office or private quarters within the hospital proper. The painted cinder-block walls have bulletin boards plastered with handwritten notes, chemical equations and cryptic diagrams. Here and there hang framed lithographs of French impressionist paintings. She sees the bent IV stand lying on the tiles next to her, the puddle of her own blood, the empty Visqueen IV bag as crumpled and shriveled as a desiccated prune. She sees hypodermics and curled leaves of thermo-readouts and sticky patches littering the floor. She sees an antique Victrola against one wall with its hand-crank dangling off one side and its lid open, the sound of an old 78-rpm record spinning at the end of its grooves like a small animal hyperventilating: *Fuhssshhh-whap!—Fuhssshhh-whap!— Fuhssshhh-whap!* The noise of it, as well as the absurdity of it, makes her giggle again, her laughter so bone-deep that she clutches herself, holding her tummy as though it's about to burst.

She looks down and sees evidence written across her flesh that she's been in this room, probably drugged, probably comatose, for a long, long time. Countless needle marks riddle her arm above the intravenous port that still clings to her left wrist, the tube curling and spiraling across the floor. She's clad in a shopworn smock, barefoot, naked underneath. Her skin is the color of wallpaper paste, bluish and livid in places, and stretched taut across the angles of her bones and joints. She is so emaciated and malnourished that she looks like one of those photos of prisoners of war liberated from their dank cells, the simple fact of daylight tormenting them, making them cower—all of which makes her let out another burst of inappropriate, hysterical, humorless laughter.

Fuhssshhh-whap!—Fuhssshhh-whap!—Fuhssshhh-whap!

She makes another attempt to sit up and this time succeeds. Dizziness courses through her. She pulls the IV stick from her wrist, causing a sharp, stabbing pain in her arm. There is no blood left, however, the tube being completely drained. She giggles some more. Her heart races. The unholy choir of snarling and screams and gunshots outside her door rises and intensifies, the walker swarm getting closer. She turns her face away from the door and roars vomit.

The contents of her stomach spumes out of her, bright yellow, nothing but bile, splashing across the tiles, soaking empty glucose bags. She retches and heaves noisily until nothing but delicate strings of drool are looping from her lower lip, which elicits more dope-sick laughter. Her voice hoarse from the strain and dehydration, she laughs and moans at the same time. It sounds like the howl of a hyena. She drops to her side, still shuddering.

Fuhssshhh-whap!—Fuhssshhh-whap!—Fuhssshhh-whap!—Fuhssshhh-whap!—Fuhssshhh-whap!—Fuhssshhh-whap!

Her body goes still as she listens to the chaos approaching her door.

The door.

She looks up. Her head feels as though it weighs a hundred pounds. She can't see the door. Her body vibrates and her vision swims and doubles, her eyes dry and dilated, her heart thumping arrhythmically.

She's never been this stoned. Even in her wildest party-modes with Megan—even that night she forgot how many tabs of X she had taken, and walked around the Cavern Club with her skirt around her ankles—she had not gotten *this* high. She feels feverish and yet shivers with sick-chills. She sees brilliant white artifacts of light in the corners of her eyes as she searches for the door.

At last she sees it, a varnished slab of oak with a metal handle instead of a knob, shut tight and latched, about fifteen feet away. She starts crawling toward it.

It takes her several agonizing minutes to reach the door—or maybe it takes hours, it's hard to tell in her current condition—but when she finally gets there, she rises up on wobbling, uncertain legs, holding on to the door handle to steady herself. The door is locked, presumably from the outside. She lets out a sigh.

"Fffffuck . . . ffuck . . . fuck." The sound of her own voice is startling to her—a gravelly, toneless wheeze—the voice of someone who hasn't spoken in ages. Her words are slurred, the effect of whatever she's on causing her to sound inebriated. She turns and surveys the room one more time. She sees the clutter on a nearby desk, piles of spreadsheets and documents and computer printouts. She starts toward the desk. She trips over her own feet.

She falls on her face and lets out another hyena bark of inappropriate giggling. She struggles back to her feet. She staggers. She concentrates on putting one foot in front of the other. She shambles over to the desk and starts rifling through the documents.

Outside the door, a gunshot makes her jump as she discovers a note from a Dr. Raymond Nalls, PhD. It concerns something he calls "the setback of the recent reanimated tissue graft," and it's addressed to somebody named Colonel Wrightman, and it sends another surge of horrible recognition through Lilly like radio interference crackling in her brain, the recent memories of making her Faustian bargain with the old chemist coming back to her in one convulsive breath.

The chaos outside the door closes in as Lilly rifles through more of the documents.

She finds journal entries concerning EXPERIMENTAL SUBJECTS (L) and EXPERIMENTAL SUBJECTS (D), and she wonders what the letters mean for about half a second until she realizes with a shiver of disgust that the letters refer to "live" subjects versus "dead" subjects. But the thing that sinks a hook into her, and makes her go still with barely contained rage, is a series of notes that she happens across regarding the "children from the rural towns." The hastily scrawled note is written in the messy hand of an old practitioner accustomed to writing prescriptions only pharmacists can read:

It's unfortunate that most will perish over the course of the trials but fretting about such trivial matters as losing a few children is akin to an artist worrying about killing a few flax plants in order to make his linseed oil. We are engaged in a higher calling than saving the few snotty-nosed tykes whom we've harvested from the outlands. We are embarked on the grandest mission known to man, namely saving the world.

A burst of manic giggling spews out of Lilly as she tears the page from the notebook and tosses it across the room. She hears footsteps outside the door. She shoves the cluttered piles of documents off the desk, papers and printouts fluttering in all directions. She staggers toward the window, muttering angrily, drunkenly, "Thinks he's God, does he? Thinks he's going to—"

Behind her, the door bursts open, letting in a whirlwind of noise, flickering fluorescent light, and a formerly cloistered environment now turned inside out.

The old chemist lurches into the room, a pack of undead on his heels, the walkers swarming the narrow hallway behind him. The doctor's lab coat is soaked in blood, stained from hem to collar, his face shiny with perspiration, his eyes aglow with terror. He clutches a leather portfolio as if his life depends on it. Behind him, a rotting, reanimated corpse in a Kevlar vest, bandolier, and pasty white face lunges at him, clawing at the air.

The chemist slams the door on the walker's arm. Lilly rushes to the old man's side and helps press the door against the wriggling, clenching fingers of the walker. The flesh of the hand has molded, now looking like charred bark, and smells of the crypt. A signet ring with a red stone still adorns one of the hideous fingers. Lilly and the chemist both put their collective weight into the door, pressing it as hard as they can against the stubborn arm. Just for an instant Lilly peers through the narrow gap along the jamb and gets a fleeting glimpse of the walker's face.

The narrow, gaunt features of Sergeant Major Beau Bryce are nearly unrecognizable—bloodless and putrefied from early-stage decomposition—his cunning gray eyes now reduced to the dead white empty orbs of an amphibious creature risen from the swamp.

Without warning the hand hooks itself on Lilly's smock, and bunches the fabric, and starts tugging her forward. She pushes back harder and harder on the door. She screams and yells and barks garbled profanities that deteriorate into dope-sick giggles. The chemist puts his bony shoulder against the door and pushes as hard as he can, and finally, the collective pressure of the twosome bearing down on the door causes the tough cartilage and sinew of the dead arm to snap, dismembering the limb below the elbow.

The door bangs shut and Lilly rears backward, chortling hysterically now as she realizes the hand is still clutching her smock, burrowing into the fabric with alarming pressure considering the fact that the arm is no longer attached to a body. She bats at it as though it were an insect or a rat latched onto her clothing. The chemist tries to help her, clawing at the thing.

At last, Lilly tears the dead fingers from the fabric and tosses the appendage across the room. The thing bounces against the wall, fingers still splaying and clenching. It comes to rest on the tile floor, the thing going still, dying as a battery-operated toy might run out of power. Lilly stares at it for a moment, her laughter subsiding. She strokes the fabric of her smock with a sort of grim awe, the chills building within her, sending fresh waves of gooseflesh across the surface of her skin.

The old man puts an arm around her, uttering softly, "Are you all right?"

Lilly looks at him, says nothing, chuckles a little, and then slaps him. Hard. Backhands him across the face. The impact nearly knocks the feeble old chemist to the floor. He drops the portfolio and staggers for a moment, gasping, taken aback, rubbing his face. Then his eyes darken and he lunges at her.

The two of them grapple awkwardly, locked in a violent embrace, backing Lilly toward the wall.

She tries to go for his eyes. It's unplanned, spontaneous, feral in its savagery. Her nails are long and untrimmed, but unfortunately she can't cause much pain or damage before the old man gets his hands on her wrists. He shoves her against the wall. They slam into the plaster, the force of the impact knocking the wind out of Lilly. She gasps and spins away from the old man before he can hit her.

He accidentally slams his fist into the wall where her face was only milliseconds earlier. The sound of his knuckles cracking is a faint, sick, crunching noise, like celery snapping, and he immediately hunches over in agony, holding his hand. He lets out a muddled cry corrupted by the shock and pain, his voice sounding like a rusty hinge squeaking. He starts to say something when Lilly's knee rises up and slams into his chin.

The chemist staggers backward for a moment before tripping over his own feet and falling on his bony ass. Lilly kicks him in the ribs. He gasps and cries out again and rolls across the room. Lilly lets out a psychotic laugh as she follows him, kicking him again and again, eliciting torturous cries and garbled entreaties. "S-stop!—Are you insane?!" The old man slams into the wall, and covers his head. It sounds like he's crying but it comes out twisted like a warped recording of crying. "P-please—I'm begging you—please stop—you're going to kill me—and—and—this is—not in your best interest!"

Lilly pauses, breathing hard, the giggling subsiding one last time: nothing like a good beating to sober a person up. She stands over him, fists clenched, bare ass hanging out the back of her smock. Outside the door, the dead brush against the walls, the reek of rotting flesh so strong now that it has permeated the room. It smells like the bottom of a latrine in high summer. Lilly catches her breath. Her voice comes out flat and cold. "What possible good could it do me to keep your sorry ass around?"

The old man marshals his energy before answering, struggling to sit up against the wall. He manages to do so, his deeply lined face pinched with torturous pain, his liver-colored lips bleeding, his wheezing breaths ragged with misery. He wipes the blood from his mouth before speaking. "I don't blame you."

"How long have I been in here, drugged up, being drained like a cow?" She glares down at him with her hands on her hips. A loud thump against the outer door signals the swarm is building, intensifying. It makes the old man jump. The guttural chorus of moans and snarls echoes down the corridors. More walkers press in on the door.

The old chemist looks up at her through sagging, bloodshot, ancient eyes. "It's been . . . a month, perhaps."

A welding torch of rage blooms within her. "Give me a reason to let you keep breathing."

He looks at her, meeting her gaze, not looking away, not backing down. "Because I have the formulas, all the work we've done here." He points a crooked, palsied finger at the leather-bound portfolio lying on the floor across the room. "Don't let it be for nothing."

She doesn't say anything. She studies the leather case on the floor. It's a cheap nine-by-twelve-inch portfolio—maybe imitation leather—that has seen better days. The color of sun-bleached mud, shiny at the corners from wear, the seams splitting from being overstuffed with documents, the thing looks as though it's been through an industrial washer and dryer a million times. She stares at it, thinking, until the sound of glass breaking out in the hall shakes her out of her spell. The crashing noises rise above the drone of dead vocal cords, something collapsing.

The old man takes a deep breath. "Lilly, listen to me now. We were very close to a breakthrough before this facility fell. It happened so quickly, a few breaching the loading dock door and a few more on the inside getting bit. But the work must continue. Do you understand what I'm telling you?"

Still no response from Lilly. She's too busy thinking it over, listening to the rising tide of undead just outside their door.

"Do you know who we have to thank for our progress in recent weeks, Lilly?" The old man trembles with emotion. "We have *you* to thank. Your blood, Lilly—type O negative—the universal donor. Whether you like it or not, you are now inextricably linked to our research. Don't throw it all away. Join me, Lilly, and we'll get out of here together. What do you say?"

Still no answer.

She's thinking.

SEVENTEEN

They decide to barricade themselves in the room. They can hear the scuffling and the oily growling noises outside the room as they move a heavy shelving unit across the floor and up against the door. The horde has now flooded the fifth floor, the hospital completely given over to the dead. Lilly grabs a chair and wedges it against the shelves, lodging it underneath the door's handle. She can see the minute vibrations in the joints of the door as more and more dead push up against it.

"They can smell us." Lilly utters this on a dry, husky whisper as she backs away from the trembling door. Her legs are still weak and wobbly but they're improving. "We can't stay in here for long."

"We have no choice." Nalls backs away from the door, clutching his shopworn leather portfolio as if it were a life preserver.

Lilly looks around the room. The tiles are cold on her bare feet and she's still in that dizzy and dope-nauseous stage, but at least she can stand without keeling over. She needs to think. Her brain chugs, her bearings still slippery. She looks at the window, then looks at the old man. "What is this room? Where are we?"

The chemist smiles wistfully. "A little bit of home, actually, a place where I can think and work in peace." He looks at her. "I thought it would be safer for you to be in here. Some of the men, they . . ." He trails off and looks down at the floor. "I just thought it would be safer."

"What the fuck did you give me, kept me under so long and hallucinating like that?"

He sighs and clutches his portfolio. "It's a compound of my own design, used mostly to keep the troops docile and manageable at night."

"I don't care who designed it, just tell me what it is and how I get it out of my system."

"It's made from a plant, believe it or not. *Turnera diffusa* . . . better known as Damiana weed. Grows in profusion down here in the deeper South. I'm told it's called Nightshade on the street."

"So how long does it last?"

The old man purses his lips. "It has a long half-life, I will admit. But after an hour or so, most of its psychotropic properties will be diminished."

Lilly looks down at her withered arms, the constellations of red marks from the various IV sticks administered to her, signs of the relentless harvesting of her blood. Her head pounds. She can't get a full breath, and her body still feels like it weighs a ton. "How much blood did you take from me, anyway?"

"We were very careful, I assure you. We kept you nourished with glucose, electrolytes, nutrients, amino acids. There was never any—"

"How much *exactly*?"

The chemist looks down. "We took four pints over the course of . . . a month."

Her scalp crawls with dread. "Jesus Christ."

"I realize that sounds like a lot, but you've been monitored closely."

"Never mind. Doesn't matter. None of it fucking matters anymore."

"If I may be so bold as to disagree . . . respectfully . . . only *one* thing matters."

She looks at him. "And that would be?"

He taps the portfolio with a misshapen arthritic finger. "The vaccine."

She keeps her gaze fixed on his eyes. "How do I know there *is* one? How do I know there ever *will* be a vaccine?"

He swallows. "In these uncertain times, one must choose to trust or one is lost."

She lets out a sigh. "I'm not lost, I know exactly where I am."

He nods, and then his eyes soften, his jowls settling into an expression of sadness. "Young lady, I know I've been responsible for the deaths of innocent people. But we have an opportunity here—if we can get out of here with our skin intact, we can complete the trials. There's no guarantee the vaccine will work. But isn't it worth trying? I'm asking you to trust me. I have no right to ask this of you. But remember, I did hold up my end of the bargain with the children. I'm asking you, Lilly. Trust me. Please."

Lilly thinks it over, her head throbbing. She notices a full-length mirror across the room, next to an old antique armoire, and she sees her reflection, a pale rag doll clad in a threadbare hospital smock. She stands there for a moment, staring at her shriveled cadaver of a body . . . and then she notices her face. She hasn't yet seen a reflection of her face since her awakening. Now she gapes at the ghastly evidence. The face staring back at her has sunken cheeks, eyes rimmed in dark circles, ashy white skin, and dull, greasy hair that has grown so long and stringy that half of it dangles down the front of her, half hanging limply down the small of her back. Her guts clench, and it takes her a while to manage a response. "You couldn't have taken four pints of whole blood in a month," she says in a low, doom-laden voice. "I've donated enough times in my life to know you have to recover between donations."

The old man says nothing. He looks down and waits for her to solve the equation.

Lilly looks at the chemist. "Doc, look at me. How long have I been in this room?"

"It doesn't—"

"YES IT DOES MATTER! HOW. FUCKING. LONG."

The old man takes a deep breath and exhales in a long, crackling wheeze. "At the end of this month, you would be celebrating your six-month anniversary here at this fine institution."

For the longest moment, the old man is convinced that Lilly is about to attack him—probably with mortal consequences this time—and who would blame her? Raymond Nalls has played all his cards, has cashed in all his chips, and has reached the end of his role in this great and terrifying drama. Head drooping, eyes cast down at the floor, he waits for the woman to put him out of his misery. Will she strangle him? Will she beat him to death? Will she throw him out the door into the fray of the swarm?

He remembers the old adage that your life passes before you at the time of your death, and he wonders why he's not seeing bitter-sweet tableaus from his early days in Richmond on his father's farm, or his time at the University of Virginia medical school, falling in love with Violet Simms at the Debutant Ball, and starting their brood in Norfolk. He wonders why he's not seeing images of the plague, the early days of his journey in search of a facility, the struggle to develop an antidote. Shouldn't he be glimpsing flashes of hooking up with Bryce's militia as his caravan of ragtag medicos heads in a southwesterly direction—a couple of arduous miles each day—searching for the perfect medical center to begin the human trials? Nalls can't even remember when he was first stricken with the epiphany of how he would save the world . . . or how his soul got lost in the process. But now it's all crumbling before his very eyes.

An awkward moment passes as the woman continues to stare at the mirror, pondering her reflection, looking as though she might break down and cry at any moment. Nalls studies her for quite a long time. There's something about this woman that Nalls can't quite fathom. There's a strength underneath the surface of her casual, scruffy, bohemian manner. She has a certain gravitas that Nalls can't quite put his finger on but it's powerful nonetheless. Maybe she'll refrain from killing him, at least for the moment.

Nalls notices the woman shifting her gaze from the mirror to the door as the rising din of unholy hunger reverberates out in the hallway, vibrating the very foundation of the floor. Then the woman turns and glances at the window on the opposite wall of the room, shaded by wood-grain venetian blinds, rattling softly with each gust of wind outside. And Nalls immediately knows what she's thinking.

"If I may make a suggestion?" He asks this softly, tentatively, testing the unsettled waters of her anger.

She looks at him. "I'm listening."

He leads her over to the window and pulls back one side of the blinds.

Through the grimy glass, the skyline of postplague Atlanta is visible, stretching into the distance, the cathedrals of derelict skyscrapers, the spires of scorched, weathered towers as empty as the husks of dead beehives. Nalls waits for Lilly to notice the edge of the platform.

She looks down below and regards the maze-like patterns of streets now inundated with the dead. In the six months that Lilly has been in her induced coma, the walker population in the fallen city has increased tenfold. Now the very pavement is obscured by wall-to-wall hordes squeezing into every square foot of the urban landscape. They crowd sidewalks and press into vestibules and mill about aimlessly across storefronts and under bus stop shelters. Even from this height, the thick, oily meat-rot odor wafts on the wind, swirls and eddies like one vast monolithic entity. "What am I supposed to be looking at?" Lilly finally mutters.

"Very possibly the only way out of this facility." The chemist points at the edge of a wooden deck suspended by metal cables, swaying in the wind, thumping against the side of the building. Lilly stares at it for a moment, cocking her head as though not yet comprehending the purpose of the thing dangling there on its tethers. Only a portion of the object is within view from this angle. A filthy plastic bucket and a coil of rope are clearly visible, sitting on the corner of the platform where somebody left them years earlier.

The painter's scaffold.

Lilly swallows hard, then turns to Nalls and says, "Do you remember what you did with my clothes and my weapons?"

* * *

Minutes later, in a battered locker across the room, Nalls finds Lilly's personal belongings—which amount to her rucksack, tattered jeans, bra, a denim jacket, Doc Martens boots, and the same tactical knife she had held to the old man's neck six months ago in their standoff—and he brings them to her in a plastic bag. Meanwhile, she finds a roll of duct tape and a first-aid kit. The noises outside the door are constant now, the vibrations from the dead swarming the corridor, sending motes of dust sifting down from the lintel.

She needs to pack a water bottle—they'll die without it—but when she checks the dispenser across the room, she finds it empty. She throws an angry glance over her shoulder at the old man, who stands clutching his portfolio and looking sheepish and nervous. She keeps her voice steady, cool and collected. "What's the firearm situation?"

He frowns. "Meaning what? Bryce's little armory is on the first floor." A thud outside the door makes the old man jump. He swallows. "I highly doubt we'd be able to retrieve any of those weapons."

"Nothing in this room in the way of guns?"

"I don't recall—"

"Think!" She shoves the roll of tape into the rucksack. "Think, Doc!—*Think!*"

He looks around the room. Another thud from outside the door sends dust down from the top of the armoire. He licks his lips nervously.

"The clock's ticking, Doc. C'mon." Lilly sees the armoire trembling, the sound of the door rattling, the pressure straining the hinges. She shoots a look at Nalls. "More than twenty walkers can overturn a small truck." She nods at the barricaded door. "There must be hundreds now out in that hallway."

"All right . . . um . . . the top drawer possibly." He points at the desk.

She hurries over to the cluttered corner. Her legs are improving with each passing minute, her arms regaining some of their strength.

The dizziness has subsided somewhat. Her stomach turns and roils as she throws open the drawer. "Here we go," she says after uncovering the snub-nosed .38-caliber police special from a stack of forms, rubber bands, and ancient ballpoint pens. She holds it up, thumbs open the cylinder, and makes note of the six bullets tucked into the wheel. She snaps it shut. "It's not exactly a howitzer but it's better than nothing."

The old man looks down. "I almost forgot I had that. Kept it on hand for . . . personal reasons."

"What does that mean?" She fishes around the drawer for ammunition.

His voice softens. "In case I needed to . . . bring about an end to my own journey before . . . well . . . you know the rest."

She finds a small carton of .38-caliber rounds, so old the lettering has begun to fade. "Let's hope it doesn't come to that."

She sets the revolver and the box of ammo on the desktop and hurriedly dresses as the shifting and thudding noises intensify out in the hall and the door's hinges creak. The old man looks away chastely as Lilly quickly steps out of her smock, revealing her nude, malnourished body. Her ribs poke through her skin like tent poles, legs and armpits lush with hair from her months in drugged limbo. She shows no sign of modesty or embarrassment as she steps into her jeans, quickly yanking them on, and then hastily pulling on the rest of her clothes. She tapes her pant cuffs to her boots, winding several layers, as the door threatens to burst open at any minute. She stuffs her provisions into her satchel and straps it on, tightening its buckles so securely that a tornado couldn't blow the thing loose. She raises the collar of her jacket and winds tape around it, creating a thick layer of protection around the tender territory of her neck.

Then she kneels in front of the old man and tapes his trouser bottoms to his ankles, winding so much tape it starts to look as though he's wearing spats.

The chemist clears his throat, clutching the portfolio tighter. "Unfortunately, that window is double-paned reinforced safety glass." His voice is laden with doubt. He jerks at another thudding noise behind him, this one so loud it's accompanied by the sound of wood splitting. "It would take that howitzer you mentioned to break it open."

She finishes fortifying the sleeves of his bloody lab coat. "Maybe," she says, stuffing the tape back in her satchel. "Maybe not." She pulls the gun, spins the chamber, and thumbs back the hammer. "Stand clear, Doc."

Nalls backs toward the barricaded door. Clasping the portfolio, swallowing air, eyes shifting nervously, he watches Lilly yank the venetian blinds off their moorings. The louvers tumble to the floor with a loud crash, revealing the filthy glass. Diffuse light pours into the room from the ashen sky outside. Only inches from the door now, blinking, jerking at the muffled thuds behind him, the old man braces himself as Lilly aims point-blank at the glass.

"Here goes," she mutters, turning her face away and squeezing off a shot.

The booming report of the .38 pierces the air, making Nalls practically jump out of his skin. The blast chews a chunk out of the glass, sending a million hairline fractures like a halo around the hole. Wind whistles through the puncture but the window holds.

Behind Nalls, the armoire shifts on the floor, the door's hinges giving way.

"Fuck—FUCK!" Lilly shoves the gun into her belt and kicks the window—once, twice, three times. The glass cracks some more but still holds.

Across the room, Nalls points a palsied finger at the floor. "Perhaps if you try the—"

Behind him, the hinges hang by threads now, the door creaking open a few more inches, the armoire sliding across the tiles, the clamor and stench of the swarm filling the room. An arm thrusts into the office, dead fingers clawing at the air. Before Nalls can even jerk away, a second arm plunges in, reaching for him, the cold gray fingers hooking onto the back of his lab coat. He lets out a yowl.

Lilly sees this at the exact moment she also notices the object that Nalls had started to indicate a few seconds earlier—on the floor near the gurney, the overturned metal IV stand—and Lilly moves on pure instinct. In one painful, leaping stride, she lunges across the room and scoops up the stand. The metal apparatus is long, bulky, and awkward—with its tripod on one end and its bag hook on the other—but adrenaline now surges through Lilly, spurring her on, driving her across the room to where the old man wrestles with his coattails as more arms push into the room, a livid face behind one of them chomping with the fervor of a rabid dog. Nalls lets out a grunt of agony as he shrugs off his lab coat. The coat is ripped apart in one great, heaving rupture, leaving it in shreds in the clutches of dead fingers. The old man somehow manages to hold on to his portfolio as he staggers backward, momentarily dazed and insensate.

"GET BEHIND ME!"

Lilly's roar brings the chemist back to his senses. Now clad only in a yellowed undershirt, his gray chest hair blooming out the top of the collar, he grips the leather portfolio in his shriveled arms and does what he's told as a contingent of dead push their way into the office. Lilly shoves the old man toward the window. She turns and sees something huge coming toward her.

The first biter to shamble into the room is the same large male that she saw earlier outside the door, the one clad in the shredded Kevlar vest with the livid, veiny face of a cadaver and eyes as milky and opaque as old porcelain. The thing that was once Army Sergeant Beau Bryce now drags toward Lilly with alarming speed, the arm that once featured a large hand adorned with a signet ring now a ragged, bloodless stump. The thing makes a feral, wet noise as it reaches for Lilly with both its stump and surviving fingers.

Lilly drives the sharp end of the IV stand through the thing's nasal cavity.

Black fluid bubbles from the wound and runs down the shaft of the stand, the massive creature going limp. Lilly lets out a grunt of exertion as the monster sags on the end of the pole, still impaled on the makeshift harpoon. Lilly swings the dead weight toward the other creatures now pouring into the office, knocking over Louis XIV end tables and sending documents skittering across the floor.

The thing that was once Beau Bryce bowls over a half dozen smaller creatures, sending them tumbling.

Lilly yanks the stand from Bryce's skull, a fountain of greasy matter spewing like dirty sea foam. Lilly screams, "NALLS! GET READY!"

Across the room, near the double panes of grimy safety glass, the old chemist gets the message immediately and crouches down, covering his head with the portfolio. Lilly lunges toward the window, raising the six-foot-long metal stand as though it were a javelin. She drives it as hard as she can into the weak spot in the center of the window, the tip piercing the crater in the middle. The window holds miraculously, stubbornly, maddeningly. Behind her, the swarm pushes its way through the doorway and floods the former administrative office in a miasma of noise and stench, overturning furniture, banging into each other, lurching toward the humans on the opposite side of the room.

Lilly lets out a primal wail of effort as she levers the stand hard into the weak spot.

The glass collapses, a gust of wind blowing a nimbus of deadly, diamond-edged granules into the room, some of the particles spitting in Lilly's face before she has a chance to turn away. She shakes it off and grabs the old man by the nape of his undershirt. "C'mon!— You first!—C'mon now!—You can do it!—NOW—NOW-NOW-NOW!"

The chemist rises up, bats away some the sharper splinters of glass with his leather satchel, and hooks the strap around his hand. Then he awkwardly climbs outside into the wind and noise of the fifth-floor precipice.

Lilly wastes no time following him. Behind her, the swarm closes in. Only inches away from their clutches, she barely gets her leg up and over the windowsill before one of the monsters hooks a claw-like hand around her left ankle. She stiffens, then kicks out with her Doc Marten as hard as she can. Her steel-reinforced toe catches the owner of the hand square in the face, and Lilly feels something crunch beneath the welt of her jackboot.

She pulls herself free and shimmies the rest of the way out the window.

At that moment, for most of the creatures dragging across the room, the humans might as well have magically disappeared in a puff of smoke.

Climbing onto the scaffold turns out to be easier that Lilly thought—despite the fact that the platform hangs in front of the adjacent room to the south, not to mention the issue of the wind buffeting it constantly, every few moments banging it against the building. The base of the contraption stretches at least twenty feet lengthwise, as well as three feet deep, the overhang on the north side providing an easy hop from the office windowsill. Even the old man climbs onto the shelf with a minimum of fuss, still clutching his beloved leather-bound portfolio. Clambering aboard the wooden deck, Lilly is amazed that Nalls is barely winded. She never asked his age, but she can tell he's well into his seventies. For a man of that age to maneuver such a step impresses her. Of course, at that point, she never would have guessed that making it to the scaffold from the ledge of the office window would be the least of their problems. But she learns quickly—once she discovers the pulley system rigged to the sides of the platform—that lowering themselves to ground level may very well be their undoing.

"Wait—please—give me a second." The chemist holds his free hand up, shivering in the wind, his hunched back pressed against the building, his skinny legs in their shopworn trousers dangling seventy-five feet above the city streets. To Lilly, he looks like a gargoyle nearing the end of its tenure on the roof pitches of the hospital. The noise of the swarm flooding the office behind them wafts out the open window. The wind shudders through the tendons of the scaffold, bumping the rig against the brickwork and drowning the ambient noise of innumerable creatures below.

Lilly holds on to the cable to steady herself, kneeling on the deck. "Okay, okay . . . we'll rest for a second but just for a second."

She looks down. The dizziness courses through her. Her vision blurs, stomach roiling. She can see the morass of dead flooding the street grid, cancerous blood cells oozing down every artery of the city. She sees alcoves and parking lots and courtyards so thick with walkers that the pavement is obscured, as though a moving swamp of black death and ragged garb undulates across the public spaces. From this height, the abandoned vehicles and deserted buildings all look gray, blanched, and lifeless, like dead teeth scattered across the gaping bloody mouth of Atlanta.

All at once, Lilly hears a series of thumps from behind her—very close, maybe within inches—which makes her jump with a start, then whirl around just in time to see a familiar pale face pressed to the glass inside the window of the room closest to them.

Almost reflexively Lilly draws the .38, presses the barrel against the window glass, and starts to squeeze off a shot, when she stops and sucks in a shocked breath. The muzzle remains against the glass. Lilly eases off on the trigger. She can't breathe. She can only stare at the familiar visage behind the pane that is just now registering the barrel of the gun with an expression that Lilly hasn't witnessed on the face of any other walker. It has to be Lilly's imagination but it appears as though the dead woman behind the glass is recognizing the gun as not only an instrument of mortal danger but also, maybe, just maybe, a mode of deliverance. The dead woman's face goes slack as it slowly cocks to one side in a strange pantomime of being spellbound, rapt, mesmerized by the tiny black vortex inside the barrel of the revolver.

In her younger days, Barbara Stern had been a raving beauty, with a swimmer's physique and a lustrous flowing mane of blond hair. Lilly remembers seeing honeymoon pictures of her alongside her husband, David, and thinking that Barbara's younger incarnation—maiden name Erickson—was the spitting image of Cate Blanchett. But the years had widened the woman's hips and turned her flaxen locks into a matronly, fulsome, tightly curled mop of iron gray. She started favoring muumuus and Birkenstocks and looking like central casting for the archetypal earth mother—despite the fact that she and David had never produced any offspring. With the advent of the plague, the woman's face fell even further and developed deeper lines, but retained that generous, earthy warmth that made her such a steadfast guardian of Woodbury's children. Now, that once-generous face stares vacantly out at the barrel of Lilly's police special with catatonic, simian fascination. The formerly creamy complexion has sunken into itself and turned as pallid as bread dough, dried tautly around the angles of her skull like a Halloween mask.

The sorrow rams into Lilly, volcanic, seismic, practically taking her breath away. She trembles with sadness, the barrel wavering slightly as she shakes with grief, staring at that forlorn monster on the other side of the glass. For a moment, it seems as though the dead woman is gazing beyond the front sight of the gun and directly into Lilly's face. Lilly knows this is impossible. She knows it's wishful thinking on her part and yet . . . and *yet* . . . something behind those cataract-filmed eyes staring out at her wrenches her heart. The tears well up, track down her cheeks, and dry in the wind. The barrel of the gun trembles. Her voice is barely audible, even in her own ears. "W-what happened to us? H-how did we get to this point?"

Behind Lilly, the voice of the old man hardly registers over the wind and the pinging of metal cables. "She attempted the very thing you accomplished."

"What?" Lilly throws the word over her shoulder with the annoyed impatience of someone swatting away a fly. "What the fuck are you talking about?"

The old man looks down. "She begged us to take her in lieu of the children." He clears his throat. "She was being tested when you arrived." He swallows. "Later, she became your caretaker . . . while you were . . . indisposed."

Lilly presses the barrel against the glass a few centimeters above the bridge of the creature's nose. "I'm sorry, my friend . . . I'm so, so sorry." The trigger suddenly seems to be mired in cement. Lilly can't bring herself to put her former friend down. ". . . so sorry . . ." Lilly looks down. ". . . *vaya con dios, mi amiga* . . . "

Without looking, Lilly squeezes off a single shot that emits a small thunderclap, puncturing a penny-sized hole in the glass.

The impact of the bullet sends the being that once was a vital, matronly, loving wife whiplashing backward in a mist of pink matter. The creature folds to the floor, gravity claiming her, the stillness of death returning with the speed of a circuit closing.

Wiping her face, Lilly turns to the old man and starts to say something when the loud metallic snap of a cable—as resonant as a high-tension wire breaking—makes the universe tilt on its axis. Lilly gasps as the scaffold suddenly tips, sending the old man sliding and Lilly clawing for purchase on the ancient, weathered, worm-eaten wooden deck.

EIGHTEEN

In some miracle of physics, some innate spark of muscle memory from her brief stint as a freshman gymnast at Georgia Tech, Lilly manages to grasp the old man's belt before the chemist plummets fifty feet to his death, and thank God, the old codger is so emaciated he probably weighs less than a hundred pounds soaking wet. Lilly gets lucky a second time when the cable on the opposite side of the platform holds, and the scaffolding dangles there between the fifth and fourth floors, hanging in limbo, swinging wildly in the wind with Lilly clinging to the bottom edge.

Lilly gasps and cringes painfully, teeth clenched, her left arm tangled in cable as the apparatus bangs and skids along the side of the building, a giant awkward pendulum. Her left hand has a death grip on one of the stanchions. Her other hand, already greasy with sweat, keeps a vise-like grip around Nalls's belt. The old man hangs there, his spindly legs churning impotently in the air, breath wheezing out of him as he tries to make a sound, tries to yell, tries to shimmy upward without any kind of leverage. He has managed to hold on to his blessed portfolio with one hand. Down below, all the dead faces in the general vicinity tilt upward, drawn to the commotion with the robotic response of satellite dishes. The portfolio slips from the old man's grasp. Lilly hears the chemist cry out, and she sees the leather-bound object falling three and a half stories, landing on the awning across the hospital's east entrance. The portfolio bounces, then flips end over end off the awning, landing on the trash-strewn sidewalk. The impact barely registers a response from the battalions of dead milling about that cracked, weed-fringed walkway.

"Hang on! Hang on, Nalls!" Lilly's cry comes out thin and hoarse, barely discernible over the wind and the creaking of the suspension cables. "Stop wiggling!—We'll get it back!—Nalls, goddamn it, STOP WIGGLING!"

Right then, Lilly makes a split-second judgment call. She calculates the distance to the awning beneath them—a little over forty feet from the point at which their feet dangle—not enough to kill anybody, especially if they can avoid landing on hard pavement. She has no idea what's inside the awning, or if the ancient fabric will even slow their fall, but she has no better options, and she can feel her oily, sweaty grip on the old man's trousers slipping very gradually but very surely—only a matter of milliseconds before she drops him—so she times her move with the swinging of the massive rig as it pendulums up and then swings back down.

She drops the old man just as the apparatus swings back across the top of the awning.

Nalls plummets, flailing and convulsing, his rusty howl drowned by the winds. One nanosecond later, Lilly lets go and plunges through space. She lands on top of the old man, the awning collapsing with their collective weight. The folds of weathered canvas swallow them as they drop through a termite-infested trellis and into a trash heap. Landing on her side, Lilly gasps to get air into her lungs, the impact driving a spike of agony through her rib cage.

It takes a few seconds for them to reorient themselves to ground level.

Lilly sits up and pain stabs her side. She can't get a full breath, and her vision has gone haywire again. She sees the bleary outline of the old man next to her, hunched over, apparently in agony from the impact of her body. The massive stench of the hordes—aided and abetted by the methane radiating off three-year-old garbage—hangs over the collapsed awning like a pall. A few of the neighboring walkers have been crushed in the collapse, their contorted bodies lying amidst the trash heap, skulls caved in and leaking fluids. Lilly blinks and looks around. Blurry images on the periphery are closing in from all directions.

Then she sees the portfolio lying on the sidewalk about ten feet to the north of the hospital entrance.

Lilly manages to stand and wade through the wreckage toward the leather-bound case. She sees a pair of walkers coming toward her, approaching the spot at which the portfolio lies. The mob behind them has begun to coalesce and head this way. Lilly pulls the .38, forgetting that she only has four bullets left in the cylinder. She fires off a round at the oncoming walker, taking a chunk out of its skull, sending it to the pavement. She misses the second one. A third shot chews a divot from the thing's scalp, the creature folding to the sidewalk in a rotting blood-flood. She quickly grabs the portfolio.

"Lilly, look out!"

She hears the feeble cry of the old man at precisely the same moment that she sees the blur of another biter out of the corner of her eye, a tall, cadaverous female with a fright-wig of gray hair and a desecrated hospital smock, lurching at Lilly with exposed teeth working, chewing at the air. Lilly gets the revolver up at the very last minute and blows a channel through the creature's forehead.

It takes Lilly less than a minute to get back to the trash heap and grab the old man and drag him toward the boarded glass doors of the hospital. But by the time she realizes that the boarded entrance is impenetrable, and they're not going to be getting back inside the building anytime in the near future (and even if they did, the ground level is completely overrun and inhospitable), the death-reek and droning noise of thousands of walkers have surrounded them.

With one quick look over her shoulder, Lilly sees that they have very likely reached the end of their journey, and chances are, nobody will complete the project encased in that worn, dog-eared, imitation cowhide portfolio.

* * *

Whether it's human nature or simply the folly of some of the more stubborn members of our species, the refusal to give up—the aversion to letting go—may very well be encoded in our DNA. It's apparent in the unbreakable will a mother has to protect her children. It's present in the human instinct to survive in every situation, from the man in the wilderness finding his way home to the spermatozoa reaching the egg. And it's deeply embedded in Lilly Caul. Even now. In that wasted alcove. In front of that derelict entrance. In the shadow of that fallen medical center. She feels this unwillingness to surrender smoldering deep within her as she reaches back to the side of her satchel, feeling for the box of ammo, fumbling the carton out of a pocket.

Her hands shake as she tries to flip open the cylinder and feed another half dozen rounds into the chambers. Behind her, the old man babbles softly under his breath that it's over and all his work has been for naught and now the project will die along with him and God have mercy on them all. Lilly drops a bullet, curses herself, trembles, looks up and sees the tide of walkers—more than a thousand strong—converging on the entrance.

They come from everywhere all at once, a deluge, a mob of biblical proportions, drawn to the last-known humans in the area like metal shavings reacting to a magnet. They come from the desolate doorways and alleys and walk-downs and stairwells. They come from the ruins of public parks and derelict parking complexes. The city becomes a vast clown car vomiting endless ranks of the dead in all stages of decay and ghastly disintegration. Large, small, male, female, young, old, all colors and races and uniforms and walks of life, they close in, revealing more and more gruesome details, entrails hanging from some, the flesh of others dangling from old wounds and missing limbs and partial jaws, strips of skin hanging from some of them like rubber wattle, the sea of eyes a cruel constellation of shimmering coins all locked onto their prey against the boarded entrance.

Lilly shakily stuffs bullets into the cylinder of her .38 as if half a dozen rounds from a small sidearm could actually stanch this torrent. The odor is incomprehensible, a black shroud of degradation choking the air as the leading edge of the mob approaches. They drag through the garbage, stumbling drunkenly over obstructions as they reach blindly for the two humans huddling in the alcove.

Lilly takes the first biter down as it pounces, and a second one right behind it, the booming echoes of her revolver reverberating up off the underbelly of the clouds, washing the second line of creatures in pink fluids and tissue. By this point, the old man has dropped to his knees behind her and has started sobbing as he prays. His left arm is slightly contorted with more than one fracture, his bony elbow bulging. Lilly can hear his hushed moaning and garbled entreaties to God as she fires off another two rounds, hitting the third attacker, and missing the fourth.

Scores more push in behind the collapsing front line.

Lilly tries to squeeze off another shot when a tall female in a filthy robe, slippers, and exposed, mossy-green teeth lunges at her. Lilly drops the gun and catches the thing with both hands. The impact knocks Lilly backward off her feet, the monster falling on top of her, snapping-turtle teeth clacking inches away from Lilly's throat. Lilly shrieks obscenities and thrusts her thumbs into the thing's eye sockets and pierces through the gelatinous pupils into the soft meat of the frontal lobe.

The female collapses on top of her. Lilly pushes the dead thing off her and tries to get up. Two more creatures pounce—a pair of younger males, each clad in ragged mechanics coveralls—and Lilly kicks and claws and reaches for the tactical knife that's shoved down the lining of her boot. She gets her hand around the grip and is about to start stabbing when the bark of the .38 makes her jump. One of the former mechanics whiplashes backward, the bullet plowing through its brain and exiting on a gush of oily cerebrospinal fluids. The second blast takes the other one down.

Lilly twists around and sees the old chemist crouched against the boarded double doors, holding the smoking .38 with both hands, his deeply lined face wet with tears, his liver-colored lips trembling. He utters something in a broken voice that sounds like, "It's over, my friend . . . I'm sorry . . . it's over." He presses the barrel to his temple and squeezes the trigger, the impotent clicking noise signaling the empty cylinder, when several developments—each one very unexpected—unfold almost simultaneously.

The horde goes still. Lilly looks up. The half dozen or so closest creatures each pause in their frenzy to cock their heads sensor-like in the general direction of a new sound descending upon the area.

At first, in some tangential compartment of Lilly's brain, the sound registers as a helicopter, which is absurd since chopper fuel in this part of the world has long gone dry, and any working aircraft has long ago gone the way of Wi-Fi and the dodo bird. Lilly jerks at a crash coming from across the street. She throws a glance over her shoulder at the old man, who sits thunderstruck, the barrel still pressed to his temple. From the look on his face, it's clear that he too is taken completely aback by the rising sound of tires squealing on pavement, an engine roaring closer and closer, until finally the first walker body catapults into the air a hundred feet to the west.

Like a dream in which motion is suspended and the passage of time bends and warps, more and more ragged bodies heave up into the air from the throngs crowding the street. Some of them shoot straight up into the heavens as though launched from a cannon, others tumbling head over heels in a wide arc, their moldering limbs breaking off midair in vapor trails of pink mist, only to land on another part of the mob with watery thuds, compressing the standing-room-only horde.

Lilly rises to her feet. She backs away from the commotion until she stands next to the old man, who has also risen to his feet. They stand with their backs against the boarded doors and gape at the oncoming juggernaut.

The monsters circling them begin to turn, one by one, slowly, to drool and stare dumbly with their shark-like eyes at the oncoming miracle. From the rising drumming of tires thumping over curbs and obstructions to the intensifying roar of the engine, it soon becomes clear that the catapult is a vehicle and it's coming this way, cutting a swath through the mass of walkers straight toward Lilly and Nalls.

At last, in a cloud of carbon monoxide and arterial spray as profuse as a fire hydrant spewing into the air, the swarm closest to the entrance erupts. Body parts and tissue and whirlwinds of blood explode upward and outward in a particle bomb of decaying flesh. The last few victims are ground under the massive reinforced hood of a dusty, battered, well-traveled Humvee as it booms across the threshold of the entrance. Both Lilly and Nalls flinch and jerk out of the way as the huge military vehicle screeches to a stop right in front of them. Lilly brushes herself off, gets her breath back, swallows the coppery panic on her tongue, and stares at the cracked, tinted windshield on the driver's side of the Humvee. The side window rolls down on squeaking cogs. The driver sticks his head out, his face bloodless and gaunt. "Better hop in before they reorganize themselves."

For a moment, Lilly stares at the driver, the last person on earth she would have expected.

Then she snaps out of her daze and hurriedly ushers the old man into the cab.

"We're going in circles," Lilly cautions, squeezed between the driver and the old man in the massive cab as the vehicle weaves through the mazelike streets. She presses an ice scraper that she found under the seat against the old man's fractured arm and winds the remaining duct tape around it to form a makeshift splint. Nalls lets out an anguished breath, wincing with each twinge of pain.

Ahead of them, the iron-reinforced grill plows through slower-moving clusters of dead, sideswiping stagnant pockets of biters along the roadways, making the bomb-resistant chassis shudder and thump at irregular intervals. The wipers are on, squeegeeing blood instead of rain.

"Try Glenwood Avenue," Lilly suggests, turning to stare out the side window. "Maybe we can get out of town to the west, avoid I-20."

Hunched over the steering wheel, his breathing labored and wheezy, Cooper Steeves struggles to stay alert despite his deteriorating condition. The brim of his fedora is soaked in sweat. Multiple gunshots reveal themselves inside his bomber jacket, his shirt displaying a Rorschach pattern of deep-scarlet bloodstains. His face is so pale it looks almost gray in the dying light of the afternoon. He grips the wheel with white-knuckle effort. "I know a shortcut," he announces in a strangled voice. "Through Grant Park, m-maybe, maybe if the Cherokee entrance is passable."

Lilly nods, completing the jury-rigged splint, and gently laying the old man's arm across his lap. She throws a glance out the side window at the passing cityscape.

The desolation of southern Atlanta is heartbreaking. Not a single square block is free of the dead. The air has a chemical reek of sulfur, decay, and ammonia—*the way it must smell in hell,* Lilly silently muses. Most of the tall buildings—once upon a time forming a great skyline of modern architecture—now look ravaged by lightning, cleaved by glaciers, and lined in moss and mold. The burned-out shells of empty floors are windblown and sun-bleached, crawling with innumerable tattered, shadowy, shuffling silhouettes. A few moments ago, they passed Turner Field, and the devastation reminded Lilly of the sunken, ruined porticos of the Roman Empire, a modern wreck of a coliseum that would most likely never, ever play host again to anything but random wandering death.

"It was Bryce, in case you're wondering." The voice, barely audible above the singing of the engine and the hissing of wind, draws Lilly's attention back to the driver.

"Bryce shot you?"

A feeble nod from Steeves. "Best I can tell, it started when we got attacked by a group from the outside, not sure what they were after. Resources, guns. Whatever. But when everything fell apart, I tried to intercede and s-save some of the folks from Moreland. Haddie Kenworth, Joel . . . the young man with the tattoos." He pauses, his head lolling, his eyelids lowering to half-mast. Lilly grabs the wheel, which wakes him back up. He swallows hard and blinks. "Forgive me, sorry about that. I'm fine."

"What happened then, Cooper?"

"After the building was overrun, I stumbled on some car keys in the control group room. They were in Daniels's pocket . . . poor son of a bitch. They used him, by the way. After you . . . dealt with him. He turned, and they used him for m-months to harvest infected blood."

"Go on."

"I procured his keys and fought my way down to the motor pool in the sublevels. Took a while to figure out what vehicle these keys corresponded to. I almost made it. I was climbing into the Humvee when he caught me." Steeves pauses, launching into a coughing fit. Delicate little sprays of blood spittle spume out of him, spattering the steering column.

Lilly watches. "Bryce?"

Steeves gives a nod. "Shot me three times in the back before I managed to get the vehicle started. Barely got out of there alive. I'm no physician but I believe one of the bullets nicked my lung."

Lilly licks her lips and chooses her words. "Cooper, we'll get you—"

"No." He waves a bloody hand, not exactly dismissing her but instead alleviating her of niceties. "I won't be benefiting from medical attention. Too late for that. I'm resigned to it."

Lilly looks at him. "Cooper, I have to ask you. How could you have ever sided with these people—after what they did to the towns? Indiscriminately murdering almost three dozen people? How could you even trust—"

"To be fair," the old man interjects from the other side of the cab, his voice shaky and breathless with agony, "we never caused any harm to anyone unless they fought back."

"Are you serious?" Lilly shoots him a look. "Who's not going to push back? You people roar into town and take folks against their will, take their loved ones in the dark of night, take everything that matters. 'We're just gonna borrow your wife for a sec, your children—nothing to worry about.' Nobody knows your higher purpose, your noble cause. *Fuck* your noble cause. As far as we know, you're basically going to rape and kill us."

The old man stares into his lap, rubbing his arm and softly muttering, "Efforts were made, at first, to inform people of our agenda, but alas . . ."

"Alas?!" Lilly clenches her teeth, working hard to keep the rage under control. "Alas *what*?!"

Nalls shakes his head. "People are quick to f-fire upon strangers these days . . . no matter what the motives of the newcomers. We just simply did not get the opportunities to explain ourselves before the situations . . . escalated. But we never fired first."

"That's ridiculous," Steeves chimes in, his voice weakening yet still taut with outrage. "When they showed up in Moreland, I had to beg Daniels to tell me why . . . why you would take these risks, killing anybody who gets in your way. I had to cajole and pry the answers out of him. And that was with the barrel of a gun in my face!"

The old man looks down, his voice fading. "I will not apologize for our methods. They became . . . necessary. I won't deny they were harsh but they were necessary."

Lilly looks at the chemist. "How do you know the way it went down? You weren't even there!"

"I was at first," the old man says with another shudder of pain and regret. "But I'm not exactly the sergeant at arms I used to be." He lets out another sigh of agony. "The fact is . . . no amount of hand wringing will bring any of these people back. It's history now . . . part of the past. The only thing that matters now is what's in this portfolio . . . and what's up here." He points a trembling finger at his forehead. "Because the only thing that does truly matter now is the future . . . and whether or not we have one."

They drive in silence for a long moment, mulling that one over.

Steeves focuses on the cluttered road ahead of them, weaving a serpentine path between a series of overturned vehicles, sideswiping the rusty carcasses, and telling himself that he'll hand the wheel over if he starts to lose consciousness.

If he does lose consciousness, it will very likely be the last time he'll pass out before the inevitable claims him. He has fainted several times since tangling with Bryce. While trying to navigate the wreckage-strewn streets of the medical center's campus, looking for a clear escape route, he felt the atrial fibrillation of old heart surgeries. He knows enough about blood loss and catastrophic injury to know that a couple of ounces of peroxide and a few strips of blanket fabric wrapped around his sucking wounds are not going to stave off anything. He knows all too well that his internal bleeding is worsening, and he's slowly but surely slipping into hypovolemic shock.

He shivers as he drives, blinking and biting the inside of his cheek to stay awake. His extremities feel numb, almost frostbitten with encroaching paralysis. His ears ring, and he can feel his heart racing with a weak, out-of-rhythm pulse. His fingers tingle as if asleep. He's about to give up, pull over, and quietly let death come, when he says, "Caul, I have to be honest with you. I never really was that fond of you."

Lilly lets out an annoyed, breathy grunt. The grunt transforms into a dry, terse little chuckle, and the annoyance changes to amusement. Then she's laughing out loud. Her laughter is dark and sardonic, and neither of the other two men joins in, nor do they seem to even get the joke. Lilly wipes her eyes and just says, "Duly noted." Her laughter fades. "For the record, the feeling's mutual."

Steeves feels his head lolling forward; his skull seems to weigh a ton. "I always thought you were dangerous," he manages to add.

"That's good to know," Lilly Caul says with a shrug.

"Do you know why I thought you were dangerous?"

"Because I always refused to take any of your holier-than-thou shit?"

He shakes his head. "No. That's not the reason. That's not it at all."

"Well, don't keep me in suspense."

He flinches at a sharp pain in his chest, his heart seizing up. The cold spreads down his gut, through his tendons. His hands are slippery on the steering wheel with cold sweat, his vision blurring. The Humvee drifts.

Lilly looks at him. "Cooper? You okay? You still with us?"

Steeves blinks and puts every last ounce of energy into saying, "I always thought y-you were dangerous . . . because you give people hope."

Lilly stares, thinking about it. "Cooper?"

His eyes droop. His voice is as low and soft as a prayer. "And you n-never give up . . . *ever.*"

Lilly registers the words at the same time Cooper Steeves finally succumbs to massive blood loss and organ failure. He slumps forward against the steering wheel, his head lolling over the top of it, tiny rivulets of blood foaming from his mouth. Miraculously, by some random quirk of positioning, Steeves's deadweight pressing against the wheel, or the leverage of the dying man's boot on the accelerator, the Humvee continues hurtling down a side street at nearly thirty miles an hour, unabated, practically driving itself. Lilly is reaching for the wheel when she hears the old man's voice piercing the cab's interior.

"LILLY, LOOK OUT!"

She manages to yank the wheel just in time to avoid slamming into the concrete barrier of a bus stop. Its awning clips the roof of the Humvee, making a muffled scraping noise and sending shards of broken glass across the windshield. Steeves's limp form sags against Lilly as she tries to reach the brake pedal with her left leg.

They careen across the opposite side of the street and slam through a row of garbage cans brimming with three-year-old refuse.

Paper, detritus, and the petrified bones and crusts of ancient food explode across the Humvee's hood. The metal garbage cans skitter like bowling pins, making an awful racket that echoes down the labyrinth of narrow streets and reverberates up over the spires of hollowed-out high-rises. Lilly finally feels the edge of the brake pedal with her left boot and slams it to the floor, making the tires screech and sending the entire massive vehicle into a momentary sideways skid.

The Humvee comes to a rest after smashing into a broken fire hydrant in the shadow of a tall brick tenement building. The impact throws Lilly and the old man against the dash, knocking them momentarily senseless. They gasp almost in unison, slamming back into the seats, the air knocked out of them. They don't yet see the ragged figures emerging from the mouths of alleyways and the shadows of vestibules on either side of the street behind them.

NINETEEN

Lilly shakes off the pain and catches her breath and makes a quick survey of their situation. She notices the Humvee's reinforced grill has caved in on one side at the point of impact. The engine has died and steam rises from beneath the crumpled hood, the radiator most likely damaged. The dash has lit up with warning lights. The indicator that catches her eye is the fuel gauge. The needle is below E. She turns and quickly assesses the old man's condition and asks him, "Can you walk?"

He groans as he shifts his weight in the seat. He glances out his window at the big side mirror. He swallows the pain and says, "*Run* is more like it."

"What?"

He points at the mirror. "Our commotion has drawn the swarm."

"Fuck . . . I knew it." Lilly digs in her pocket and feels a few loose bullets from the carton of ammo that she tore open back outside the hospital. She has only a few left—three or four—and nothing in the cylinder. She looks at the old man. "You still have the .38, right?"

He nods and pulls it from the back of his belt. "A lot of good it'll do us without ammunition." He glances nervously back at the side mirror. "We need to make some executive decisions, they're getting closer."

Lilly is about to climb out of the cab when she hears the soft murmur of Cooper Steeves, very likely the last words he will ever utter. "... *never give up ... never ... ever ... ever. ...*"

She gapes at his ivory-white face as he goes very still, as still as a porcelain figurine. She reaches down to her boot for her knife.

The gesture is almost involuntary by this point—putting the punctuation at the end of a long sentence. She draws the knife and raises it. She pauses. Something about the man's face at rest calls out to her. Cooper Steeves—self-styled adventurer, insufferable know-it-all—has returned to his default self. In the tranquil, endless sleep of death, he is reduced to the face of an innocent, slumbering, guile-less little boy. Lilly can't bare to mar the illusion with the pointed end of the tactical knife.

"Lilly, please." The old man claws at the passenger door, frantic to get out. "If you're going to do it, do it now or you'll have to do *us* as well!"

She looks away and thrusts the knife into the man's skull above his ear—a single hard, sudden jab—as abrupt as a dentist pulling a tooth.

The blade goes in deep, the man's cerebral fluids gushing around the hilt. Lilly pulls it out decisively. Cooper Steeves flops back against the seat, the blood from the wound sluicing down his white, blood-less face in ribbons of deep crimson. The blood looks like a mask.

Lilly wipes the blade on Cooper's shirt, shoves the knife back into her boot, grabs her satchel, and quickly glances over her shoulder.

About fifty feet away from the Humvee's tail, a pack of several dozen creatures approaches in the washed-out sunlight. Two of the older ones—both male—are completely nude, their pectorals, bel-lies, and genitals dangling like marsupial pouches, their livid flesh bearing the gruesome suture tracks of autopsies. The others are from all walks of life, large and small, both eviscerated and intact. All of their faces are deeply furrowed with the trademark scowl of the hungry dead, their mouths working hectically, their rheumy eyes pinned open. The electric buzz of a feeding frenzy crackles from one face to another.

Lilly shoves the old man out of the open passenger door and then pushes her way out herself.

A moment later, the dead descend upon the Humvee and Steeves's remains, and the interior of the cab becomes a noisy abattoir as the lucky ones sink their teeth into the still-warm body.

To refer to the limping, lurching, half trot, half shuffle that Dr. Raymond Nalls employs in order to flee the swarm as "running" is a wild misnomer and exaggeration. This awkward locomotion is all he can manage for any extended period of time, and by the time they reach the end of Waldo Street, Lilly is seriously considering throwing the emaciated old codger over her shoulder and carrying him. They approach the intersection of Waldo and Glenwood, and Lilly decides to head west down Glenwood.

Bad decision. A wall of upright cadavers blocks their path—at least a hundred strong—spanning the wide street with scores of shark eyes as luminous as silver road reflectors in the dusk. The noise is incredible, the acrid stench hanging like a fog bank. Lilly scuttles to a sudden halt, the old man nearly crashing into her.

Without a word, without a sound, she grabs Nalls by the nape of his undershirt and pulls him back toward the intersection—back the way they have just come—so hard that the chemist is nearly pulled out of his shoes. If Lilly could just find a suitable building in which to hide—someplace that's still relatively sealed from the outside world—they might have a chance. But every broken-down address that they pass is either overrun or impassable.

They circle back north, toward Cabbagetown, toward the residential areas.

They take Wylie, a seemingly deserted access road that runs along the ruins of the Hulsey Train Yard. Mile after mile of derelict boxcars line the tracks now, many of them lying on their sides, most ransacked, all overgrown with opportunistic vines and kudzu as thick as shrouds. Above the tracks, the trestles drip with Spanish moss, and human remains litter the embankment as if an ancient battlefield has been left to the elements. Clouds of insects drift and dance like motes in the rays of the dying sun. Lilly and Nalls move as silently as possible under the shadows of the trestles, along the fossilized track, careful to make minimal noise.

Nalls slows to a limping shuffle, his breathing so labored and sickly that he sounds like a dying animal. Lilly walks ahead of him, every few moments glancing over her shoulder to make sure he hasn't collapsed. She carries the portfolio now, keeping it safely tucked inside her satchel. She has two bullets left. A pair of .38-caliber bullets to ward off a million cannibals. She carries the hope of the world—literally—on her shoulder now. She still believes they'll make it. Or at least she tells herself they will. She tells herself they *must* make it.

They hear another surge of vocalizations on the wind, another wave of death-stench wafting in, raising the hairs on the backs of their necks. Deeper shadows move across the warrens of side streets. Lilly sees another intersection ahead of them: Cherokee Avenue.

By this point, the sun has melted behind the horizon, and darkness has closed in like a predator sniffing at their heels. The alleys are plunged into dense darkness. The buildings are turned into silhouettes. Sounds begin to travel differently through the air. Lilly can hear their own footsteps now like pistol shots. She can smell rain on the wind, mingling with the rising odor of the dead. She can hear the far-off rattle of thunder—a storm moving into the area—the air pressure changing around them.

They reach Cherokee Avenue, turn north, and run directly into another megaswarm.

Lilly grabs the old man by the nape and tries to pull him away from the oncoming army of the dead, a thousand strong, moving shoulder to shoulder down Cherokee, a sea of pasty dead faces and shoe-button eyes, moving directly toward them. Lilly realizes that retreating in the direction they just came is out of the question. The other herd has boxed them in. She realizes this at the same moment the old man suddenly drops to his knees.

"The fuck are you *doing*?!" She tries to lift him back up. "Get up!"

"It's over, Lilly." He gazes out at the oncoming multitudes with eerie calm. "It's time to bow to the hands of fate."

"Shut the fuck up." She lifts him with both hands so violently he gasps. "C'mon. There's a place we just passed, might be able to get in—c'mon, goddamn it, get off your ass. Let's *go*!"

They reach the freestanding brick building one second before the walkers. Lilly yanks the old man down the narrow space along one side of the building—a passageway that could barely be called an alley—a loading dock at one end, a series of low windows hastily boarded with worm-eaten planking along one side. The last window has a board hanging by a thread, a gaping hole in the original pane. Lilly hurries toward it, still dragging the old man along, his Florsheims scraping behind her. She can hear the tidal wave of shuffling footsteps closing in behind them. She can smell the rot-stench rolling in with the strength of a storm front. She pauses under the window. She glances back over her shoulder. Shadows are unfurling toward them, the air prickling with decay and sulfur and latent violence. She reaches up and shoves in the broken pane, hears the muffled sound of glass hitting a floor. Then she helps the old man up and inside the darkness. She climbs in after him.

At first, they don't spend much time investigating the shadowy interior of the building or even identifying its original purpose. Lilly is too busy fortifying the windows and doors, making certain they're alone, and looking for any useful leftovers or provisions. Nalls is occupied by his fatigue and fractured arm. He sits on a steamer trunk and catches his breath while Lilly moves furniture around, shoving a heavy shelving unit against the broken window. The fading twilight seeps through the cracks of the barricades and into the cavernous room, illuminating unfinished walls and a high ceiling. The place is the home of dusty cobwebs, moldering wooden panels, and all shapes and sizes of cabinets and storage bins.

"Get over here, c'mon, help me with this," she orders the old man in a loud whisper, hyperaware of the gathering noise outside in the alley.

Nalls musters up a feeble surge of energy and joins her, pushing one side of a second massive metal cabinet across the dusty tile floor. The squeak of the legs on the parquet is excruciating and dangerous. Lilly senses the noise drawing more of the dead to the building. She can hear them outside, congregating in the passageway, brushing up against the boarded windows. The smell permeates: a thousand carcasses of rotting animals marinating in pond scum and swamp gas. It makes Lilly cough, and she holds her hand over her mouth as she searches the dimly lit room for a source of light.

She sees a workbench on the far wall, a few drawers, a pile of rags and oil-spotted documents. She wonders if this place was once an auto dealership or perhaps the back office of a garage of some sort. It's getting dark quickly. She notices two massive, garage-style doors on either side of the work area, now hastily boarded and reinforced, one of them draped with a tattered curtain. She notices cables and pulleys and catwalks up in the rafters of the ancient ceiling. Where the hell are they?

In one of the drawers, she finds a flashlight, and miraculously it still works—albeit dimly. "Look for water, we're going to need water, that I can guarantee you." She shines the yellow beam of light along the struts and exposed particleboard of the unfinished walls. "And we're going to need it soon."

The old man looks around. "What in God's name?" he murmurs, scanning the room, leaning against a trunk. He still breathes heavily from the journey across town, and his face is pale with exhaustion and pain.

Lilly tries a light switch. As expected, nothing happens. The place is as dead as that mob out in the alley. Lilly covers her mouth, the stench seeping in. More of the creatures have gathered outside, drawn to the commotion. There must be hundreds of them—thousands perhaps—brushing against the boarded windows. The foundation creaks and shifts with the sheer number of them. Lilly takes deep breaths as she goes through more of the drawers.

Behind her, the old man lets out a groan and lies down on top of the trunk.

In a drawer, Lilly finds inexplicable documents from the mid-nineties on, a thousand yards of velveteen fabric delivered on September 22, 2003, invoices for light filters, furniture, heavy-duty cable, replacement circuit breakers, xenon bulbs, sheets of plywood, rope, machine oil, and gunpowder. *Gunpowder?* Lilly looks more closely at one of the garage-style accordion doors. The frame is nailed in place, a few sheets of plywood haphazardly crisscrossing the egress—evidence of hasty attempts to batten down the hatches.

A noise creaks on the other side of the garage door, the telltale watery growl of a walker. Maybe more than one. Shuffling feet, guttural noises. Evidently the building is infested as well as puzzling in its purpose. Lilly doesn't notice the old man has begun to snore behind her. She rushes over to the fortified door and peers through a thin crack between the side rail and the plywood.

In the last rays of twilight, a larger room on the other side of the door is barely visible. About a half dozen shadowy figures are milling about a raised platform adjacent to the vertical door, and along the far edges of the space, scores of chairs are arranged schoolroom style. Lilly finally recognizes the place for what it is.

"We're backstage," she utters. Her voice is hushed, a mixture of awe and nostalgia for the days when people actually lived lives genteel enough to attend the theater. She gapes at the dead players lumbering aimlessly back and forth across a derelict stage, stiff-legged pawns on a chessboard grid that has lost all meaning. Were they actors? Were they theater people who got pinned down and turned? An unexpected fist of sorrow clenches Lilly's innards as she notices a dark, dusty sign made of tiny lightbulbs above an exit on the far wall of the theater: THE PENDRAGON SHAKESPEARE THEATER. Her eyes well up. "Backstage in a goddamn Shakespearian theater." She turns toward the old man. "How apropos. . . ."

She stops. She goes still. She sees that Nalls has fallen into a fitful slumber on a large steamer trunk near the window. Curled into a fetal position, he snores softly, eyeballs jittering beneath his lids.

Lilly exhales a sigh of relief. For a moment, she thought she had lost him. She realizes now that she needs the old codger for more than his vaccine. She needs a companion. She needs human company right now. "'To sleep, perchance to dream,'" she murmurs, thinking of *Hamlet*, thinking of *King Lear* as she gazes upon the slumbering old man.

Something catches her eye off to the right, a dark object sitting on the workbench next to Lilly's satchel: *the portfolio*. She goes over to it. Buzzing with curiosity, she picks it up, thumbs the clasp open, and takes a look at the contents. She stares. She frowns. The magnitude of what she's seeing doesn't immediately register.

She starts thumbing through the contents of the case, shaking her head, brow furrowed with confusion. What she expected to find were chemical equations, scientific notes, not *this*. She inspects the diagrams and hand-drawn illustrations, the odd little doodles, the footnotes to footnotes to footnotes, and the byzantine streams of thought. "What the fuck?" A few of the papers fall out, fluttering to the floor. She stares. "What. The. *Fuck*."

She kneels and takes a closer look. Some of the items are well-worn pages torn from spiral-bound notebooks, every square centimeter crammed with tiny, obsessive, feverish sketches that at first look normal if not a little chaotic—lots of arrows, labels, and concentric circles—all of them revolving around endless variations of the same motif: an angelic female figure with reddish-brown hair, ponytail, ripped jeans, and a halo. Mostly depicted in primitive, childish renderings, this eerily familiar-looking cartoon-woman is labeled on some of the pages as "donor zero," while at other points she's called "the panacea girl" or "the plague goddess."

A cold trickle of terror worms its way through Lilly's midsection as she notices that many of the pictures of the ponytailed goddess are labeled "L.C." or "Lilly C." In some of the more elaborate sketches, a second figure with a dirty face and yellow eyes (a walker, presumably) is drawn next to the woman in the ponytail. The two figures are connected by an umbilical of arrows, the arrows labeled with foreboding phrases such as "the final grafting process" or "the penultimate hybridization." Lilly stiffens. Her throat goes dry. She slowly rises, staring down at the madness and murmuring, "Oh no . . . no, no, no, no, no, no, no, no, no—"

"Oh yes, I'm afraid so."

The voice behind her is almost ghostly in her ringing ears. She whirls around just in time to see the scraps of plywood swinging toward her.

The board strikes her square on the forehead, sending a skyrocket of white light across her eyes and a sharp pain stabbing down through her skull as she staggers backward, tripping over her own feet.

She lands on the small of her back, the pain shooting up through the sprains and bruises of her battered joints. The old man stands over her, the board still gripped in his palsied hands and splint-laden arm like a Louisville Slugger. He has the strangest expression on his face, a mixture of defiance, amusement, and more than a little madness. "They say a catnap, even for a few minutes, can be rejuvenating for a person of advanced age."

Dazed and breathless, Lilly instinctively raises her hands to block the next blow, but the old man puts a surprising amount of force into the swing, especially for a person of his years. Maybe years ago, on the golf course, he was capable of magnificent, three-hundred-yard drives. Or perhaps he simply has been playing possum all along, concealing his reserves of strength. But whatever the source, that next blow tags the side of Lilly's face with the force of a battering ram and turns the lights off behind her eyes.

The last thing she sees before sinking back into the swamp of unconsciousness is the old man's yellow, tobacco-stained smile, the sound of his voice fading in her ears: "Good night, sweet princess."

TWENTY

Nalls stands there for a moment, assessing, pondering, taking shallow, asthmatic, hyperventilated breaths. His arm twinges but he ignores it. He drops the board and gazes down at the young woman in the ponytail lying amidst the shreds and litter of his portfolio, the contents of his genius. He feels a faint frisson of shame for lying to her about the advanced stages of the trials, but he had no choice in the matter. Otherwise she would not have taken him along with her, protected him, and kept him safe from the swarm. It is imperative that he be allowed to conduct this one final experiment—his combination magnum opus and swan song—before the course of events makes such critical research impossible.

He has very little time. He quickly turns and scuttles across the room to the workbench area. He starts going through the drawers, looking for a suitable apparatus with which to bind the woman. It must be stronger than mere rope, completely foolproof, or she will most certainly be able to finesse her way out of it. He also knows that his vigor is fleeting and temporary, a product more of adrenaline and epochal events than of health. The sickness will take him down soon. How soon, he doesn't know for sure. This is one of the frustrating conundrums of the microbial environment at play here. Incubation periods vary wildly. He rifles through the side drawers and finds nothing but old legal tablets, scripts, office supplies, and manila files brimming with meaningless ephemera. His head throbs with the fever, his vision swimming out of focus for a moment.

He pauses, knees turning rubbery, dizziness coursing through him as he holds on to the workbench with his left hand to keep from falling. His stomach lurches. Chills roll through him. He shivers. He's burning up but as long as he can still move and think, he can tend to the final parameters of the experiment.

Right then, a metallic object catches his eye on the other side of the room, shimmering dully in the gloomy beam of yellow light cutting through the dust. That single flashlight lying on the workbench is now the only source of illumination in the room, and those batteries are going down fast. He trundles quickly across the room.

The adjacent stage has a complex system of draping, as well as massive auxiliary curtains, all of which are controlled by a convoluted system of pulleys and counterweights high up in the rafters. Nalls takes a closer look at one of the cables dangling down in front of the lighting console. Judging from the positioning of the ancient metal stool in front of the console, a stagehand must have once perched here during performances and peered through the wings for his cue to move scenery, lift and lower curtains, and make timely lighting changes.

Nalls removes part of the block and tackle—a metal clamp used to grip cables and ropes for better leverage—and sticks it in his pocket. He remembers seeing a mountain climber on TV use such a device to ascend a slope. The chemist has the perfect use for it now. He gazes up. The next challenge will be the extraction of the largest steel cable. He looks over and sees a pair of pliers on the lighting console, and he grabs them. He now uses the sharp inner teeth— meant for stripping the jackets off electrical wire—to chew through one of the cables. In a matter of minutes, the cable snaps and Nalls pulls the rest of it free of its pulley system.

He returns to the spot where the woman still lies unconscious, arms and legs akimbo, her face already swollen and bearing the imprint of the board across her left temple. Nalls digs the tiny pencil-sized leather case from the back pocket of his trousers. Thankfully, he sees that the case hasn't been crushed. He believes that Lilly was—and remains—completely oblivious to the fact that he took the experimental drugs from the hospital.

Now he carefully opens the case and lays the vials labeled X-1, X-2, and X-3 on the floor in front of the woman. Nalls flinches at the onset of a coughing fit, and he coughs and wheezes for a moment, his skull pounding. He feels his forehead. His fever has become a furnace. He is certain that his temperature is going through the roof and guesses it has already reached the critical hundred and six degrees. Any higher, and the seizures and organ failure will begin, but he has much to do before that happens.

He screws the hypodermic needle onto its plunger and sticks the point through the tender skin under the elbow of his good arm, then slams the compound into his artery. He sucks in a breath as the cold spreads through him, a searing cold, the deep frozen maelstrom of liquid nitrogen or perhaps the lowest circle of hell.

His head tosses back in faux orgasmic response to the spread of the compound—an unprecedented event in medical history (if he may be so bold as to say so himself). The chemical invasion courses through every vein, every cell. He lets out a long sigh of victory— the exhalation of Alexander Graham Bell calling Watson, of the Wright Brothers leaving the ground, of Jonas Salk killing his first polio virus. It is the sigh of genius.

He trembles in the last stages of the disease, his sensory organs already starting to fail.

Time is of the essence. Timing is everything. He quickly gets to work on the woman.

Alas, it takes quite a bit of time to prepare her body for the experiment.

The slap wakes her. Perhaps *wake* is the wrong word. Something pops in her face. A bubble? A mousetrap snapping? She blinks and doesn't know where she is at first. She can barely make out blurry images moving directly in front of her. She tries to focus and figure out what happened to her. Did she pass out? Was she jumped?

She tries to move and realizes her hands are bound and tied behind her back. She blinks and blinks, and she realizes she's sitting up on scabrous floorboards against a wall in a dimly lit room, the old man sitting mere inches away from her, close enough for her to smell his sour, malodorous breath.

"Let me start by offering my sincerest apology for striking you like that."

With the creaky voice on which to train her gaze, Lilly Caul finally sees that Raymond Nalls is sitting cross-legged, Indian-style, on the floor directly in front of her. The old man is shiny with sweat, his flyaway white hair like a penumbra of smoke around his skull. His eyes burn with emotion, the bloodshot whites parboiled with fever. His rusty voice is surprisingly steady. "As I think I've made clear, I detest violence of any sort, even in the unfortunate environment in which we find ourselves."

Lilly tries to move but her head is pounding unmercifully, probably harboring a concussion from the impacts of the board, and rope digs into her wrists. She feels a pressure on her lower back, and hears a metallic jangle each time she strains against her bonds. Something cuts into her ribs. She looks down and sees that she is bound to the exposed wall with steel curtain cable. "What the f-fuck . . . ?"

"Take a minute, let it sink in," the old man urges helpfully.

Chills pour through Lilly as she gazes down and slowly follows the knotted cable around her midsection and realizes it crisscrosses her back and shoulders like a harness, the strands gathered through a metal clamp-like device, tightened down to piano-string tautness.

Outside the windows, a volley of distant thunder rattles the night.

The flicker of lightning spangles the room for a moment with silvery daylight, illuminating the backstage area of the Pendragon Theater: the sealed stage doors, the cobwebby rafters, the cables and pulleys hanging down, the huge flats of scenery—clouds, trees, castles, turrets, and giant clownish faces leering in two dimensions—leaning in heaps against the exposed wall boards.

Lilly sees the litter of insane notes and drawings strewn across the floor, and remembers getting walloped one second after seeing the abomination of madness inside that portfolio. She notices the old man has a similar armature of cable wound around his belly, across his shoulders, tightened and locked with a second clamp-like apparatus. Her mouth goes dry with panic. She starts straining with all her might, feeling the cold sweat break out on her skin. She strains and wriggles and angrily tosses her head. "M-mother-f-fuck!—What are you doing?—WHAT ARE YOU DOING?!"

The straining jiggles the old man, who grabs her by the shoulders as though offering solace. "Easy . . . easy there. We're going to get through this together. But it won't help to struggle. Trust me on this. It merely makes the device tighten."

Lilly lets out a shriek of rage. The raw, naked scream in the room makes the chemist wince and cover his ears with his hands. Lilly wrestles wildly with the bonds to no avail. She starts to well up with tears. The last thing she wants to do is cry but she can't stop the tears and snot from rolling down her face. The old man lowers his hands and watches with the look of a person at a wake or sitting shivah, waiting for a loved one to cry out their grief.

Over the next few seconds, Lilly makes several observations and deductions—even while fighting her tears—that could very well be of paramount importance to her survival. Lightning returns, flickering in the room, and Lilly sees streaks tracing across her field of vision. She feels strange, buoyant, like she just chugged a gallon of alcohol and the effects are mere seconds away, and she remembers the early stages of a Nightshade high. At least the pounding in her head has quieted down, the pain in her joints calming slightly. But not a single one of these realizations seems as critical as the faint sensation of her sweat-slick right wrist slipping ever so slightly within the knotted coils of rope binding her hands behind her back. At first, she's worried that she simply imagined it. While staring at the old man, defiantly refusing to look away, she discreetly tries a second time to slip rope farther toward her hand but the restraint holds tight. Her hands have no sensation left, the blood cut off. Lilly remembers studying the life of Houdini in high school, and reading about his technique of escaping the inescapable through a disciplined system of tensing and relaxing, tensing and relaxing, so she starts doing exactly that with the wrist restraint.

A moment later, her tears dry on her face. She swallows coppery blood in her mouth from biting her tongue and gets her thoughts together. She takes another moment before speaking. "Please, *please* . . . tell me what you're doing. You owe me that much."

The old man lets out a sigh. "In point of fact, I'm seeing through the penultimate stage of the human trials I started in earnest one year ago."

She stares at him. "There are no human trials, we both know that."

"Lilly—"

"You can stop the routine, your cover is blown. You're sick. Mentally ill. Deeply fucking deranged. You don't need to complete any trials, you need medication and a long stay in the funny farm."

He cocks his head at her as though sizing her up. "May I show you something without eliciting another outburst?"

She shrugs.

He reaches down to the hem of his soiled undershirt and pulls it up over his belly. Lilly stares. At first uncertain as to what she's supposed to be seeing, she notes the surprising girth of the man's gut. It hangs over his belt like a massive loaf of uncooked bread, hairy and stretch-marked. Nalls says in his feeble, croaking voice, "As you can see, my time is limited."

"What?" Lilly is confused. "What am I supposed to be looking f—"

She stops. She sees the marks. Below his left armpit, an inch outside his nipple, they are faintly visible in the dying beam of the flashlight, which still sits on the workbench across the room. "Alas . . . it's the scarlet letter of this age," Nalls comments sadly. "The two-way ticket, the return trip no one wants to take."

Lilly moves her mouth but can't summon any words. She feels the cable hugging her. It feels hot, as if the old man's fever is being conducted through the wire and penetrating her. "When did . . . ?"

He waves her question off. "It occurred in the corridor not long before you awakened."

She stares at the bite marks. Tiny sutures form little x's on each gouge. She can't get a full breath into her lungs. She utters, "How did you . . . ?"

"I stitched them up myself, a few were deep enough to involve an artery."

Lilly feels light-headed, wobbly, nauseous, like she's floating. The faint light coming from the workbench turns golden and warm in her line of sight. She can't think properly. She struggles against the restraints for a moment, almost involuntarily. The cable rattles against the wall. "Don't do this." She changes her tone with him, speaks evenly, softly, as though to a child. "Don't go out like this. Senseless. Heartless."

"Ahhh. To quote the bard . . ." He lowers his T-shirt, and coughs again between his words. " 'Therein lies the rub. For in that sleep of death what dreams may come.' " He smiles at her again, and for the first time, Lilly sees the extent of the madness crackling behind his eyes. "It makes a tremendous amount of sense, Lilly. Believe me. You will paint your name in blood on the roll call of history. Your essence is the essence of the Overmind, the Christhead, the road to the vaccine."

She notices a syringe on the floor not far from where they sit. "You gave me another dose of that drug, Nightshade, didn't you? Was that to keep me docile for the big finale?"

The old man breathes deeply as though weathering a surge of pain. He ignores her questions. "We did not have time to determine the genetic markers in your cells . . . but sometimes science is less a science than an art. One must employ intuition. I believe your blood will provide the missing ingredient for an antidote."

Lilly's head begins to spin, her stomach clenched with nausea, her vision streaking with optical fireworks. But at the same time, her brain registers another scintilla of slippage around her right wrist. "I don't understand."

"Yes, Lilly, I believe you do. I believe you understand perfectly."

"Listen to me. I'm sorry you're going to die but this is all a product of your sickness, your mental illness. I will stop you. I will put you down. I promise you, I will end you if you carry this through."

"On the contrary, you will join me." His smile makes the flesh on her neck bristle. "I will turn, and we will become one in a baptismal font, and the conjoining of our genetic material will yield the cure."

She feels the rage building within her, but it's dampened by the drug or compound or whatever the lunatic sitting across from her has administered. "You're a crazy old man who's lost his mind."

"Be that as it may—"

"YOU FUCKING LUNATIC, LET ME GO!" She struggles and writhes and yanks on the cables, making a racket that blends with another salvo of thunder. The rope around her greasy wrist holds tightly. In the flicker of lightning, she howls at the old chemist. "LET ME GO, GODDAMN IT!—LET ME GO!—LET ME GO YOU FUCK! LET ME GO! LET ME GO!!"

The lightning sputters away. The sound of rain now coming down in sheets outside drowns the noise of the swarm. In the darkness, the old man's face is reduced to a silhouette. "Join me, Lilly."

Her tears come again but this time she giggles stupidly through them—a desperate, frantic laughter. The batteries in the flashlight are almost gone. She shakes her head as if trying to rid herself of a cloud of gnats or mosquitos, hoping she can ward off the effects of the Nightshade through sheer will, through sobering rage. She gets her breath back and finally manages to say, "Please do me the courtesy of being honest . . . if I'm gonna die, please, just be honest with me."

The old man gives her a look, a faint expression of resentment. "I *am* being honest."

"There never were any breakthroughs, were there? You were chasing your tail, delusional, playing make-believe."

He purses his lips. The storm throbs outside as it approaches.

Lightning flickers, once again illuminating the pale, deeply lined face of a dying old man. "I will admit that we encountered . . . no pun intended . . . many *dead ends*. But I had always believed in the advent of a universal donor, and a very special combination of genetic materials introduced into the reanimated cells of those who had recently turned."

"But the thing is, you're insane . . . which is a major roadblock to any kind of progress or achievement, if you think about it. You realize that, don't you?"

"Copernicus . . . Columbus . . . Louis Pasteur . . . were *they* not thought to be insane?"

"Okay . . . you know what?" Once again Lilly feels the knot of rope around her right wrist give slightly. She works harder at it now. She tries to keep him talking. "You can dispense with the delusions of grandeur. It's falling on deaf ears. What I want to know is why you think this is going to lead to anything other than two people dying, reanimating, then sitting here and gnawing on each other for eternity?"

The old man nods. "I admit it's a primitive method of conjoining two samples. We attempted a few . . . *conjunctions* . . . while you were under . . . all to no avail." He coughs, wheezes, and takes a ragged breath. His eyes bug out with pain and yet he keeps speaking, keeps justifying his actions. "But I truly believe that the m-moment your DNA hits m-my *infected* system we will—"

He stops abruptly, interrupted by another cough, a bone-deep, congested bark. The coughing escalates into another convulsive fit.

Lilly can see the blood spewing from his mouth in delicate strands, spattering the collar of his undershirt. Across the room, the flashlight beam is so drained of power now, so feeble, that the backstage area is plunged into shadow. In the half-light, Lilly can see the old man gasping for breath, his droopy eyes rimmed in red.

The roar of the storm rises. It sounds as though it's directly overhead, the rain strafing down across the roof of the theater with the force of a Gatling gun. The drumming of thunder resolves into a brilliant display of lightning, the room exploding with artificial daylight for a few fleeting seconds as Nalls coughs and coughs. Soon he is choking. His face furrows with agony, then changes color and goes icy still. He tries to breathe but can only gasp for air in a creaking death-rattle.

A moment later, the old man expires in the flickering light like a character making their exit from a silent movie. In fleeting, flash-frame glimpses, he coughs up blood, hands clawing at his throat as he hemorrhages, convulsing, asphyxiated on his own bodily fluids.

Finally, his head lolls forward, his downturned face going as blank as stone. He looks like an emaciated nursing home patient who's gone to sleep in front of the TV. He twitches for a moment, residual nerve activity . . . then nothing but stillness.

Across the room, the flashlight has now faded to a pinhole of amber light inside its lens like a lizard's eye, and then even *that* smolders out, plunging Lilly and everything else into absolute darkness.

TWENTY-ONE

The incubation period between the time of death and the moment of autonomic resurrection varies wildly from subject to subject. Lilly remembers hearing stories of the recently deceased taking hours to reanimate. But with each documented case, an average transition length has emerged. The best estimates currently put the turn rate at around ten minutes. But right now, Lilly figures she has far less than that amount of time to somehow "Houdini" herself out of the wrist restraints, deal with the old man, and manage to escape the cable truss tethering her to oblivion. And the worst part—the part that is so overwhelming it's now threatening to paralyze her with inaction—is the fact that all this will have to transpire in total darkness.

She gives the immediate area a quick scan. The darkness is so opaque, so dense, so impenetrable, that it seems to have palpable weight, like some sort of soupy, inky liquid, or some kind of tide pool that has suddenly flooded the backstage area and now holds Lilly and the dead chemist in its black thrall. It is the darkness that eradicates size and shape and time and context. Lilly and the corpse to which she is attached might as well be microscopic. Or they could be the size of celestial bodies, planets gripped in each other's gravitational field. The darkness that engulfs them is the darkness of deep, deep space. It is the darkness in the back of a child's closet in the dead of night. It is the darkness inside a coffin long after burial, after the mourners have departed, and the grass has grown over the site. It is absolute and void of matter. It is impossible and inevitable.

All at once, another volley of thunder and lightning erupts outside.

The silver daylight—as bright as a camera strobe—illuminates the death scene for a single instant, and Lilly blinks, trying to take it all in. In one brilliantly lit tableau, she sees the dead body lashed to her via rusty cables, the ancient figure slumped before her, its head drooped across its chest, face downturned, shoulders as still as a statue. In the remaining nanoseconds of that silver flash, Lilly absorbs as much of the scene as possible: the metal clamp-like device locking the cable around each of them, the broken vials of drugs scattered across the floor, and even the far reaches of the room.

Then the light winks out, and darkness returns to the room like a flood tide.

Lilly blinks again, a strange retinal afterimage glowing on the backs of her eyes. Hypersensitive to the faintest illumination, her perception bolstered by the drugs spreading through her system, she can still see—even in total darkness—a milky photographic negative of the space around her, the old man's body, the restraints. She begins to let out bursts of inappropriate giggling, her mind swimming with both panic and fascination. She feels light-headed with adrenaline and yet delighted with this discovery—a way to extend the illumination of the lightning.

The glowing negative across her field of vision finally fades.

In the darkness, her brain splits into two halves. One half floats on a cushion of narcotic ennui, the other working like an engine to escape this inextricable trap. She increases the pressure of her right hand on the rope restraint, wriggling as hard as she can against the knotted, oily, sweat-slick rope binding her wrists together. She can feel the perspiration dripping off her fingertips. The rope has slipped a couple of additional centimeters but it still binds her, shackling her wrists so tightly that her shoulder blades ache. She can feel the presence of the dead chemist inches away from her.

How long has it been? Five minutes? Ten minutes? If it takes the average amount of incubation time for him to turn, she has mere minutes left, maybe more if he's on the high side of the bell curve, but it *could* happen earlier.

She wrestles and wriggles and worries her wrist back and forth within the restraint, the warm grease of her sweat now streaming down her forehead, dripping off her nose. She can feel sweat running across her forearm and dripping off her elbow. The pain intensifies, a burning sensation now in her wrist, and Lilly realizes that it's not sweat but blood that's flowing from her wrist. She senses the old man, still silent and motionless in front of her. She smells traces of his musky body odor as though the ghost of his living self still clings to him. He is a ticking time bomb. She giggles. Inside her, in that other part of her brain, she feels like screaming. She struggles to pull her wrist free.

Outside, thunder booms, and the rain furls and drones against the rooftops.

In some deeply buried compartment of Lilly's brain, she remembers the old childhood adage that during a storm you count from the moment the thunder fades to the first flicker of lightning, and that resulting number is the distance between you and the lightning bolt. She never really believed this wives' tale, or at least figured it was decidedly inexact, but some part of her took comfort in it. She remembers lying in bed as a kid, frantically counting, taking solace in the fact that the lightning bolt was usually miles away.

She feels her wrist slipping a few extra centimeters, lubricated by her blood. Not much farther now. She yanks and tugs and struggles until the pain shoots up her tendons and explodes in the rotator cuff portion of her shoulder. The pain is massive, a dagger thrust through her back, and she lets out a yelp.

Another salvo of thunder rumbles overhead, rattling the gantries and reverberating through the heavens.

Lilly grunts with effort, frantically twisting and yanking on the shackle, her hand slipping another centimeter, spurring her on as she counts in the after-echo of the thunder: *one . . . two . . . three . . . four . . . five . . . six . . . FLASH!* Lightning erupts outside the windows and above the transoms, filling the theater with another surge of magnesium-bright day.

The old man hasn't budged an inch, his lifeless body still sitting cross-legged on the floor, his shoulders still slumped, his eyes still tightly shut, his head still downturned, face as blank as a mannequin's. Lilly breathes a sigh of relief as the lightning flickers out. But it's only momentary relief. As the afterimage lingers on the backs of her eyes, she makes mental notes: the position of the pressure clamp, the razor-sharp frayed wire on the end of one of the cables, the distance between her and the old man's face, and then she increases the pressure on the wrist restraint.

By this point, the pain has worsened, turning into a numbing cold spreading through her. The Nightshade has fully kicked in. She has a serious buzz going, and she hallucinates microscopic artifacts in the dark—tiny streaks of colored light and little curlicues of impossible Day-Glo creatures swimming through the deep oceanic void. She can't help but giggle at such terrifying visions, which strike her as straight out of Nalls's notebooks.

At the same time, she works madly on the restraint, her wrist continuing to slip ever so slightly toward freedom. The grease of her blood is helping her, as is the numbness. Her brain works to find purchase in the dark, her scrambled thoughts bouncing off each other like pinballs.

Thunder crashes overhead, now closer than ever, shaking the foundation.

Lilly jumps. Her central nervous system crackles in a tug of war between the narcotic buzz of the Nightshade and the sheer terror of the ticking time bomb slumped cross-legged inches away from her.

Through her giggling, Lilly counts out the number of miles: "One . . . two . . . three . . . four . . ."

The strobe light flickers outside again and fills the room with artificial day.

The old man has raised his head.

Lilly screams.

The dead man's eyes pop open.

The next few seconds unfold in the druggy time-lapse slowness of a dream. In that momentary flicker, which lasts only a second or two, Lilly jerks back as the creature lets out a series of inhuman, wet vocalizations—part growl, part howl—its discolored lips already peeling away from the old, yellowed enamel of its teeth. Strings of drool loop out of its mouth. It smells of the slaughterhouse, and its head rotates as if receiving a signal from space as its reptilian eyes stay latched onto Lilly.

While all this is transpiring, Lilly finally—either through a sudden jolt of her adrenal glands or the greasy blood providing enough lubricant—manages to pull her right hand free of the knotted rope. Both hands are instantly liberated, and as the last of the lightning fades away, Lilly manages to grab the creature by the neck before it can bite her.

Total darkness returns, and Lilly applies every last ounce of her strength on the choke hold gripping that skinny, turkey-like wattle of a neck. The thing that was once a chemist emits a piercing, snarling cry that sounds like a strangled hyena, but continues to gnash its teeth. Right then, in the back of her chaotic thoughts, it occurs to Lilly that walkers don't breathe, so strangulation isn't a mortal threat, but right now it's keeping those yellow teeth away from the tender flesh above her jugular.

In the palpable dark, the afterimage of the hideous, livid, demonic face that was once Raymond Nalls lingers on the back of Lilly's retinal field. Unfazed, she keeps the vise-grip pressure on the thing's neck.

She can hear the creature's teeth—its incisors and molars—clacking like castanets, and she can feel the thing's wiry body writhing and wriggling in her grasp—an enormous, slimy thing pulled from the sea, fighting with the involuntary fervor of a barracuda on the deck of a boat struggling to escape the clutches of the net. Lilly lets out a piercing screech of rage and determination. She will *not* allow this thing to beat her.

By the time the next salvo of thunder and lightning explodes outside the theater, the cable around Lilly's midsection has loosened from all the violent struggling and strangling and writhing. Lilly feels the loops slip lower on her torso, the pressure now resting on her pelvic bone. The clamp has sprung open. It now lies at the bottom of the coil, on the floor between her legs. Still tangled up with the creature's truss, the loose coil will at least give Lilly more leeway.

In the brilliant, flickering firecrackers of light, Lilly's hands keep their white-knuckle hold on the skinny neck of the monster while the thing snarls and gnashes and wriggles with subhuman vigor.

The lightning flickers away.

In absolute darkness, Lilly takes deep girding breaths, preparing herself, telling herself to ignore the dopey high feeling and concentrate. Somewhere in the back of her mind, she realizes that she probably has just this one chance. She knows if she blows it, she's dead meat. The moment she takes her hands off this shuddering, writhing beast in the dark, she has about a second and a half to get the job done. Walkers are slow in an open field. Sure. They can't run, they can't climb, they can't maneuver through tricky obstacles. But up close and personal like this, especially in the dark, they can be ferocious and lethal.

This one will probably go for her throat. Lilly knows this from experience. She has seen lurkers surprise people and get to the tender flesh of their neck before the victim even has a chance to react. In fact, the speed with which the dead go for a pulse point such as the jugular is strictly innate, automatic, involuntary . . . like a wasp stinging its prey. Lilly feels the grease of her blood and sweat on her palms as she strangles the thing and wonders if this will be her undoing. You can't grab a weapon with any kind of speed or accuracy when your hands are as slick as this.

She pushes the doubt from her racing thoughts and silently prays for the lightning to return. She's losing her nerve, her focus, and her will. The drug is working on her, jumbling her thoughts into a chaotic mess. Her arms are killing her, her fingers numb around the thing's neck. It's slipping from her grasp—she can feel it.

She summons all her rage. Like a spot-welder, she focuses her anger and sorrow and dread onto this creature shuddering in her grasp, this denizen of the deep rising up to kill everything she holds dear. She summons all her emotions in order to destroy this natural enemy, this nameless, soulless *thing* that will happily steal her children, her life, her world. She thinks of this being in the darkness as Death. She will never surrender to it. She will never give in.

Lightning crackles outside.

The monster's eyes reflect the spark as Lilly makes her move.

TWENTY-TWO

At that moment, the radiant silver light fills the theater for a total of five discrete flashes—spaced fairly evenly, spanning a time period just shy of ten seconds—causing the action that unfolds to transpire in a dreamy, silent-movie-style motion that is neither slow nor fast but rather ethereal and otherworldly. And in that brief and eternal stretch of time, Lilly's hypersensitive brain—exacerbated by the hallucinatory drugs coursing through her—instinctively deconstructs those separate flashes into individual components of a longer narrative.

During flash number one, Lilly lets go of the creature as fast as she possibly can, moving her hand from the level of the monster's neck down to the loose clamp leaning against her thigh. Simultaneously, the creature's head jerks backward in reaction to the release of pressure around its cranial area. This latter movement is simply the law of physics at work, the coil of cables originally wound around the old man named Nalls now creaking and stretching with the weight of the whiplashing creature, its head snapping back violently.

The second flash is a transitional phase, Lilly's hand finding the sharp edge of the metal clamp, grasping it, and swinging it high and sideways toward the creature's skull. Lilly intends to strike the thing high above its temple hard enough to drive the edge of the metal device through the tough skin of the old man's scalp, through the periosteum, through the hard bone and marrow of the skull, through the dura mater, and finally into the critical spongy brain matter. The fact is, Lilly Caul has accomplished this task enough times with various weapons to understand the amount of pressure and force and speed with which to drive a sharp edge into the head of a walker to get results.

During the wide arcing swing of the clamp, the monster's head hasn't snapped fully back to its original position. It's still in mid-whiplash. All of which leads to an unexpected outcome during the next flash.

As lightning flash number three fills the theater with radiant faux daylight, the sharp edge of the clamp device collides with the creature's mandible just above its jawline. The force with which the thing strikes the monster's head—again, bolstered by the explosive cocktail of Nightshade, emotion, and adrenaline flowing through Lilly—completely rips through the bottom half of the creature's skull, tearing away an enormous portion of the original cranium. The entire jaw segment rips free, as well as the cheek and upper nasal passages, sending nearly half of the old man's face flying through the shadows on a kite tail of bloody tissue, bone fragments, teeth, and gums. The monster rears, half its face missing, the blood gushing and oozing down its sunken chest, one eyeball hanging by threads of optic nerves and blood vessels. Lilly holds fast to the clamp and slams backward against the wall, her scream a garbled cry of revulsion, rage, and terror. Right at that millisecond, the flickering dies away as quickly as it originally materialized.

In the ensuing dark, Lilly strikes again and again for another couple of brief moments.

On a cannon blast of thunder, lightning flares a fourth time, the storm right on top of the theater district, turning night to day, penetrating the cracks and gaps in the boarded windows, and illuminating the backstage area in sputtering silver radiance. By this point, Lilly's cable restraints have stretched to the point of slipping, dropping below the level of her pelvis, the monster across from her flailing stupidly, still a captive of its own steel harness. In the momentary flicker show, as bright as an operating-room light, the creature looks insect-like now, almost alien with only half its skull intact—no jaw, no teeth, no throat, no nose, a ruined eye socket—to the point that only the pulpy concavity of its lower submandibular ganglion is visible, its exposed carotid artery like a branch in need of pruning. In the brilliant light, it looks like a blood-sodden praying mantis. In fact, the sight of it tossing its partial head and straining the bounds of its coil is so disturbing, so surreal, so trippy to Lilly that she loses her focus for a moment and bursts out laughing.

The thing prods at her with its bloody brow ridge, and claws at her awkwardly, feckless and impotent now without its teeth, all of which makes Lilly laugh all the harder. She falls on her side, outwardly chortling with mirthless, frantic, hysterical laughter.

As the flickering light subsides and sputters away, she can hear her own laughter honking in her ears as though it belongs to someone else. It sounds to her inner self—the part of her that's not under the influence—like an old scratchy laugh track in some forgotten sitcom or game show. The more the creature flails at her with its crooked hands—hands that once belonged to a feeble old man, hands that once curled with palsy—the more ridiculous it looks. For one insane moment, it conjures images of pratfalls and spit takes and people slipping on bananas and stuffing their mouths with candy coming off conveyor belts. Lilly laughs harder as the creature futilely pokes at her with its dripping, bloody, praying mantis head. She easily bats it away with one massive slap, her head spinning, the dying light leaving streaks on her field of vision. Then the darkness returns, and the laughter dries up and leaves her with a desolate emptiness in the dark. Now all she can hear are the garbled, watery noises coming from the mutilated head of the walker inches away from her.

Lightning hit number five comes a moment later, revealing the fact that the monster has grown still. Lilly stares at it. Sitting upright—its mangled, deformed head with its eyeball hanging down on a pendulum of veins—it faces her as though waiting . . . waiting for deliverance. She blinks and continues to stare at it. The thing shudders at her—without a lower skull impossible to read—a growl, a cry, a moan? The room settles for a moment. Lilly can hear the throb of rain outside, incessant, sibilant, drowning the ubiquitous buzzing of the horde, now thousands strong, maybe more, drawn to the theater, sounding like bees swarming a hive. The drugs in Lilly's system act on her thoughts like rocket fuel for her brain. The thing across from her swipes at the air in front of her face, an ancient, claw-like hand missing her nose by a hair, as Lilly jerks back with a start.

Then she hears the low drone of the multitudes outside and gets an idea.

In the final few flickers of light, she wriggles out of the loose coils, extricating herself from the steel bondage as the pathetic creature on the floor prods at her and nudges her with its half face, the flood and fluids from its glottal opening still oozing. Lilly stands.

Dizziness crashes down on her, threatening to knock her over. In the last sparks of light, she sees the monster gaping up at her with its one intact eye, looking almost expectant, its other eye dangling. The front of it has soaked through with deep arterial red. Walkers don't exactly bleed. In the absence of circulatory functions, their blood leeches out of them with the slowness of sap extruding from a tree.

Inspiration strikes Lilly as she gazes down at it, and she smiles in spite of her repulsion.

The night swallows them.

Lilly feels her way through the darkness of the backstage area, leaving the mangled creature on the floor, trussed and bound in tangles of cable. As she moves through the dark, she takes deep breaths and fights the light-headed feeling. She is stricken with a diabolical idea. If she can only calm down and keep her wits about her and move quickly, she might be able to see it through. She takes one last deep breath as she approaches the workbench.

She pauses, getting her bearings. The storm has settled into a low, droning, white noise. The thunder has seemingly moved on, as though it has grown weary of the city and now has migrated out across the southern rural hills. Every few minutes, Lily can hear the distant rumbling like a vast stomach growling, and can see a few faint flickers of lightning somewhere far off in the farmland, barely illuminating the theater. She swallows dryly. It occurs to her that she's gone almost twelve hours without water. If she doesn't find some within a day or two, she could die. Which strikes her woozy brain as a stupid and ironic way to go out, especially after surviving all she has survived.

Now her eyes have adjusted enough to see the silhouette of the workbench in front of her.

She feels her way down to the stack of drawers, and blindly goes through them. She vaguely remembers seeing a sealed package of batteries but she's not sure. It might be her imagination. She feels around the contents of the drawer. In one of the last pale, feeble flashes of lightning, she finds a roll of black electrical tape, a stapler, and—lo and behold—a yellowed but still-sealed package of four Eveready AA batteries.

She cackles—still flying high on the Nightshade—as she fumbles with the flashlight. She gets the new batteries in it, switches it on, and sweeps the narrow beam of white light across the room. Along one wall, she sees the scenery flats, the massive marble columns made of Styrofoam, the huge balsa wood castle turrets, and the row of old armoires filled with wardrobe.

At the end of the armoires hangs a huge black coat. She goes over to it and takes a closer look. She wonders if it's from *Macbeth*. It could very easily have served as a witch's cowl—the kind worn by the three sisters in the play—which is one of the few memories of her single solitary theater class at Georgia Tech.

For some reason, right then, amidst her scattered thoughts, a line from the play bubbles up from her memory bank, unbidden, unexpected.

What are these
So withered and so wild in their attire,
That look not like th' inhabitants o' th' Earth

She pulls the coat off its hook, puts it on, and looks in the cracked, grime-specked, floor-length mirror leaning against the corner. In the beam of the flashlight, which now bounces off the mirror and reflects back at her, she looks like a child playing dress-up. The witch's coat is enormous on her. Another breathy, nervous laugh escapes her lungs.

She gives herself a nod.

This will work nicely.

She hopes.

An hour later, the dawn closes in and the rain lifts. The sky outside the Pendragon Theater on Cherokee Avenue turns an ashy shade of gray as the mob of ragged figures mills about the intersection of Cherokee and Platt, aimlessly wandering the adjacent alleys, their metallic gazes turning toward every errant noise from the rainwater ringing in the gutters to the caw of blackbirds ushering in the day as they soar over the petrified cityscape.

At first, the creak of the stage door at the end of the Platt Street alley draws little attention from the horde. The thing emerging from the theater drags out into the wan, gray morning with little ceremony, a pile of decomposing flesh draped in a theatrical cowl meant for an imaginary witch. It has spindly legs partially hidden by the gown. The smell it gives off is subtle—this one has died and turned only hours earlier—but it will soon join the others of its ilk in radiating tremendous rot.

The draped creature slowly turns and awkwardly shuffles toward the mouth of the alley. To a normal observer—i.e., a human—there might be something strange about this thing's stride, the way it carries itself. Unlike the myriad other denizens wandering the ruins—most of whom are now brushing past this newcomer, paying little attention to it—this robed creature seems to trundle slightly, as though it has *four* legs under its moth-eaten cowl. And the face also begs questioning. The dark visage that lurks in the shadowy depths of the oversized hood doesn't hold up under close scrutiny. Half of the creature's skull is missing and oozing fluids, and something moves slightly behind it, as though a nesting doll is hiding there.

Despite all these anomalous quirks, however, the thing in the witch's cowl passes through the throngs milling about the alley with little incident. Not a single member of the horde seems to notice any disparities as the newcomer reaches the street and turns down Cherokee Avenue.

If our theoretical human observer investigated even further, they might also note the way this monstrous thing is maneuvering itself—making willful turns, cocking its head toward noises, sidestepping obstructions and clusters of upright cadavers blocking its path—which completely sets it apart from the directionless nature of the other reanimated dead. This newcomer seems to have a purpose. It appears to have a destination that is beckoning to it somehow. In fact, it seems to be moving southward.

For a time, the hooded figure moves unabated through the swarm of dead, the witch's robe trailing after it like the train of a gown from some satanic ball. Every few moments, the sound of a cough comes from within the cape, which coaxes a ripple of turning heads and agitated growls among the horde. Something about this figure is starting to attract attention among the horde.

As the newcomer closes in on the massive culvert under Interstate 20—a graveyard of human remains that was once the home of countless plague refugees in squalid tent cities—the creature comes to an abrupt stop. From the way it tilts its hooded head upward, it seems to be gaping at something through its ruptured, mutilated eyes. Could it be looking at something along the trestle of the highway?

Agitated walkers surround the newcomer, sniffing it, their snarls and growls attracting more and more attention from the outer circles of the swarm. The coughing within the hooded robe intensifies.

At last, the thing inside the witch's cowl seems to convulse and give birth to the nesting doll—a living woman—who bursts out of the garment with a small-caliber pistol in her right hand.

The woman in the ponytail falls to the ground, vomit roaring out of her from the smell and the horrible slime of decomposing flesh on her skin, as the dead chemist, still clad in the costume, staggers backward, blindly and dumbly rearing his mutilated face. The closest members of the horde close in for the kill.

A single shot rings out, echoing down the cavities of the city as the woman fires on her attackers. She empties the remaining round into the closest walker, a nosy male in filthy overalls with a gaping hole in its midsection from which its entrails hang like strands of sausage in a store window. The male goes down in a gusher of oily, rotting fluids.

The woman pivots and finds an opening between two clusters of dead quickly collapsing in on her. She lowers her head and charges through the gap as fast as her wobbly legs will convey her, shoving one of them aside so hard the creature knocks down three others.

Within seconds, the woman in the ponytail has crossed a vacant lot and made her way up Oakland Avenue. All the while she keeps glancing over her shoulder at the enormous message spray painted in huge letters across the top of the interstate bridge.

LILLY IF YOU MAKE IT OUT ALIVE GO TO MEGAN'S

TWENTY-THREE

She gets lucky just north of Whitehall Street. Keeping under the radar of the horde, creeping silently through the garbage-strewn ditches and overgrown foliage of the train yards, she's been heading north for nearly an hour now. The sky has darkened and pressed down on the city, another storm on the wind, and Lilly has been worrying for a while now that she'll never make it all the way to the Georgia Tech student ghetto where Megan Lafferty used to rent her cozy little condo. Lilly assumes that it was Tommy Dupree who wrote that message across the top of the viaduct, but she has no idea how the hell he could have known about Megan, let alone where her former digs are. But what choice does Lilly have now? Hitchhiking back to Woodbury is out of the question, and there's a scarcity of taxis available downtown nowadays.

Out of options, out of ideas, out of ammo, she's just about ready to collapse when she sees in her peripheral vision both flanks of the train yard begin to rustle and teem with movement. She glances to the left and to the right and sees the yard filling up with walkers. The twin waves of the dead have snuck up on her like low rolling tsunamis from each direction—her throbbing concussion, the dizziness, and the lingering effects of the Nightshade dulling her senses and tunneling her vision—and she now realizes that she's trapped. If she retreats, she'll run into the third wave pushing up from the south. If she tries to make a run for it—heading north—she's screwed. The two regiments will collapse in on her and devour her.

She stumbles to a stop, and turns and turns, seeing no way out.

"Okay, now what?" She talks to herself in a voice that's cracking apart, her vocal cords in tatters. "What's the next move, genius?" She whirls and gazes at the oncoming throngs. "C'mon, you've been in worse jams than this." She sees hundreds of pairs of milky, fishy eyes reflecting the overcast sky—all locked onto her, floating toward her—the hunger so palpable it practically hums in her ears. "C'mon, c'mon, c'mon, *think*." She pulls the empty gun and holds it in her right hand—a security blanket, maybe a bludgeon—if she could only *wish* another six rounds into that cylinder. "C'mon, c'mon, c'mon."

As the vast sea of cadavers presses in, a stray thought flicks through her mind on a sparking synapse of terror. You can't go around them, you can't go through them, you can't go under them, you can't go over them. She sees something important in the near distance. "Go over them . . . fuck yes . . . go *over them*."

The distant ladder gleams a dull copper color: a series of iron rungs rising up the rear of a derelict caboose car.

The horde closes around her as she takes off in a dead run, the back of the caboose fifty yards away.

She fixes her gaze on it and lowers her head as she runs, the horde undulating and shifting languidly in response to her flight, some of them blocking her path, clawing at her. But by now she's built up enough of a head of steam that she bangs into the bolder ones as she approaches the rear of the train. The walkers go down like dominos.

She reaches the ladder and scuttles up the end of the caboose.

She starts down the length of an abandoned freight train that stretches for miles, literally hundreds of old boxcars with flat, corrugated rooftops left to rust and decay in the elements. Tangles of wild foliage and weeds have grown up between some of them, while others have sunken into the ground. Some of the couplers have come undone, and the gap between those requires Lilly to vault across spans of ten feet or more, which she happily does, jumping from boxcar to boxcar, gradually working her way north before the very eyes of the shambling horde.

The train tracks run alongside the Marietta Street artery, a major thoroughfare Lilly used to travel each night to get to her class at Georgia Tech, now as desolate as the River Styx. Much of the wreckage that blocks the street looks as though it has melted into the mossy, fetid surface of the pavement, the ironweed and vines cocooning it and turning it the color of bile. The lightning of the previous night has caught pockets of methane on fire, and now plumes of yellow flame dot the roadway. Megan's place on Delaney Street is still a good mile to a mile and a half away, but Lilly starts to believe that she's going to make it. The fossilized train seems to go on forever.

The walker population in this part of the city has grown since Lilly has been out of commission. Now the length and breadth of the swarm boggles the mind. In certain quarters, the dead number in the tens of thousands, the tops of their decaying skulls like stones floating on a sea of moldering remains, an ocean of moving corpses that seems to stretch as far as the Georgia Dome a half mile away. The air is so toxic and dank and thick with death-stench that an early-morning fog clings to the ground, shot through with black motes of ash and shiny pieces of particulate the texture of fish scales.

The sight of all this has a strange effect on Lilly as she leaps from boxcar to boxcar. It invigorates her, galvanizes her, makes her sniff back the fear as though snorting smelling salts. She pulls the rubber band off her ponytail and shakes her hair loose. The foul wind blows through it and makes her feel amazing. She feels more alive than ever—her aches and pains long forgotten now—and she quickens her pace.

"Fuck you all!" She gives the throngs a wave and then the middle finger salute. "Eat me!" She giggles in the wind as she runs. "EAT ME, MOTHERFUCKERS!" She chortles with laughter as she reaches the end of a long boxcar. "EEEEEEEEEAT ME!!" She leaps triumphantly through the air toward the roof of a battered passenger car ten feet away.

When she lands, the roof collapses with the impact of her weight.

She plunges through a cloud of dust and debris, and lands hard on the metal edge of a bench seat, the pain so sudden and enormous that she instantly blacks out.

Sometime later, the rattle of an automatic rifle stirs her. She twitches painfully at each noisy burst, waking with a start and feeling the searing, white-hot branding-iron of pain in her lower back.

She can barely breathe, lying crumpled in a fetal position on the shopworn leather bench in the middle of the Amtrak passenger car, but the sound of bullets strafing the side of the train gets her to look up and focus on her surroundings. The pale sun shines down directly above her, penetrating the massive, gaping hole in the roof through which she fell. Stalactites of fiberglass and metal hang down, and the air inside the car swims with specks of dust and ash. She turns her head—a move rife with pain—and sees human remains near the car's front pass-through door.

The engineer looks as though he's been dead for years, his skin the color of earthworms, the flesh of his skull stretched taut like a death mask. The shotgun is still gripped in his frozen hands, the muzzle aimed at his mouth, the top of his head blossomed open, the aftermath of his suicide marking the wall behind him as black as an inkblot. The sight of him—combined with the rising noise of gunfire—convinces Lilly to sit up. But when she tries, the pain explodes in her sacrum. She slips off the bench and hits the floor with a gasp.

Her back must have taken the brunt of the fall, one of her legs now as numb as deadwood. She crawls across the floor to the window, the agony like a hot poker stabbing up through her lower back.

It takes massive effort to pull herself up to the sill in order to see outside. When she finally accomplishes this and looks out, she sees a black, bullet-riddled Escalade backing toward her, an assault rifle blazing out one of the rear windows, the salvos picking off the closest walkers and making a path.

Lilly exhales painfully as the vehicle reaches the train car and skids to a stop. She can barely move. She has no idea if these are friends or foes but there's nothing she can do about it now. She's at their mercy. The Escalade's rear latch clicks, and the hatch jumps open.

"You're *sure* this is the one you saw her fall through," the young man inside the cargo bay is asking his comrade. He's a rough-hewn Mediterranean, olive skin, dark curly hair pulled up in a man bun, tats on his muscular arms. He holds an Uzi in one hand and a small first-aid kit in the other. "Wait! There she is!" He sees her through the window. "Well, hello there."

Lilly manages to slide the window open a few inches so that she can be heard. Her voice is hoarse and dry as a rasp. "Do I know you?"

"No, but you will soon enough." He gives her a good clean smile, and then notices the outer rings of the horde closing in on them. He puts down his gun and kit, and then reaches up to the train window. "C'mon . . . we need to get you out of there before we get mobbed. Can you climb?"

He gently extricates Lilly from the open window of the train car. Grunting painfully, wincing at the pain in her back, she slides herself through the open hatchway and into the rear of the Escalade, flopping down on the carpeted back deck just in time to avoid the unmanageable number of dead pressing in from all directions.

The SUV booms away in a dust devil of carbon monoxide and debris.

TWENTY-FOUR

Megan Lafferty's former home on Delaney Street with its big dormer window in front would never be depicted in *Architectural Digest* or win any Good Housekeeping awards for interior design, but it was always tidy, it was situated on a tree-lined boulevard, and it cleaned up well. In its heyday, the girls would pull out all the stops at Christmastime. Megan would climb up on the roof and hang multicolored bulbs and set out cardboard reindeer, and Lilly would string tiny white lights along the picket fence that lines the driveway. In the cold winter months, the odor of the landfill abutting their postage-stamp-sized backyard would be kept at bay, and the scent of pine and cinnamon would greet Lilly when she got home from school or work every night, stomping the mud off her boots in the vestibule. It was home for nearly three years while Lilly figured out who she wanted to be when she grew up, and it would always hold a prominent place in her heart. All of which is why she can barely look at the place as the Escalade tops the hill at the corner of Delaney and Sixth and the ruins come into view.

"Oh Jesus." Lilly grips the armrest, digging her fingernails into the upholstery. She can't bear to see the place like this, and yet, for some reason, she can't take her eyes off it.

The Escalade sideswipes a pack of walkers milling about the curb, then pulls onto the cracked, weed-whiskered pavement of the driveway. The vehicle shudders to a stop.

"You gonna be okay?" In the front passenger seat, the olive-skinned man with tattoos shoots a glance over his shoulder at her. His name is Musolino, a Portuguese day laborer from Louisville who lost his family early in the plague. Lilly can tell by the softness behind his eyes that he can probably be trusted. She has gotten to the point where she can see a lot simply by looking behind a person's eyes. It's an animal thing—like ferreting out a friend or foe by sniffing the pheromones. "We can meet them someplace else if this is too . . . whatever."

"No . . . it's okay. Just gimme a second." She gazes out the side window at the burned shell of a house, the roof gone, the dormer caved in, the building stripped of every accouterment, from its lamp-posts to its flower boxes to its garden hose. The place is so devastated by fire and looters that one can gaze straight through its first floor to the overgrown backyard. Huge shards of naked window frames and scorched support beams stick up in the air. The chimney has collapsed into itself and the interior has been decimated, scattered with broken tables, rain-sodden easy chairs, and overturned kitchen appliances. Lilly sees one of her wall hangings—a lithograph of Joni Mitchell from the early 1970s—impaled on a staircase newel post. "Are we early?"

The driver looks at his watch. "Not at all, they should be here any minute." An older man, balding, with horn-rimmed glasses, the driver goes by the name Boone. A few minutes ago, he explained to Lilly that he's the shrink of the group, a former social worker from Jacksonville, Florida, who ended up here in Atlanta after his former survival community in Panama City was overrun.

"Okay." Lilly takes a deep breath, bracing herself for the pain in her lower back to return. "I think I'll try and get out and wait inside."

Musolino throws his door open, flicking off the safety on his assault rifle. "We'll keep watch on the place, keep the walkers at bay." He opens Lilly's door. "Just be ready to take off if they swarm up on us again."

She gives him a nod as she climbs out. Pain flares in her sacrum as she puts weight on her left leg. She swallows hard, huffing and puffing with effort as she limps awkwardly up the drive to the gaping front door. The screen hangs on its hinges, and it detaches and clatters to the ground when Lilly tries to swing it aside.

The wind blows through the living room as Lilly crosses the threshold and looks around. She sees the old peach crates in which Megan kept her vinyl—Sabbath, Zeppelin, Metallica, Slipknot, Megadeth, Suicidal Tendencies—now reduced to kindling and splinters of black plastic strewn across the mossy floor. She sees the old grandfather clock Everett had willed to her, lying in pieces in the corner, the guts sprung and spilled. She sees a dozen or more picture frames broken and scattered across the floor. She kneels. She picks up an old, sun-blanched photograph of her father and her with fishing rods and a huge cooler between them as they sit beaming at the camera on the banks of the Chattahoochee River.

The emotions come on so suddenly, so unexpectedly, they practically knock her over. Tears fill her eyes. She wipes her face and brushes a fingertip across the face of her father. In the picture, the sun is setting behind him, dipping below his beat-up Ford Fairlane. God, Lilly loved that car. She learned to drive in it, and had her first romance in it at the Starline Drive-in. She's trying to remember the movie that was playing the night that Tommy Klein took her virginity when a voice from behind her snaps her out of her spell.

"Is that really you?"

She rises up, pivots around, and stares agape at the figure standing across the ruins of the living room. "Oh my God, I can't believe it," she utters and practically leaps across the room, nearly lifting Tommy Dupree out of his boots as she hugs him to her chest. "I can't believe it . . . can't believe it . . . I just can't believe it."

He grunts. "Easy does it . . . Jesus . . . you're gonna break my walkie-talkie."

She holds him at arm's length so she can get a good look at him. Six months and God knows what else have etched hard experience on his boyish face. Dressed in a chambray shirt with the sleeves cut off, black jeans all gouged and torn, and combat boots, he looks like a miniature version of Lilly. He has a huge Buck knife on one side of his belt, a stainless-steel pistol on the other. She smiles at him through her tears. "I'll be honest with you, I wasn't sure I would ever see you again."

He returns her smile. "I knew I'd see *you* again, I never doubted it, I just knew it."

"You're looking good, kiddo." She strokes his hair and notices how well nourished he looks, his skin a healthy ruddy color, his eyes clear, his body lean but no longer emaciated. He even smells good, like shampoo and deodorant. "What have you been doing with yourself?"

"We found a place, Lilly. Not far from here. It's unbelievable."

"First, tell me the kids are okay."

"They're better than okay. You'll see. They're all safe and sound, and doing great."

The sudden drumroll of automatic gunfire cutting down a few walkers across the front yard echoes and makes both Lilly and the boy jump. She lets out a breath and gazes at the two men guarding the front of the house. "How did you hook up with these guys?"

Tommy nods at the men. "Actually, I wouldn't be here, wasn't for them. That day we left the hospital, we got pinned down in the city looking for a safe place. We got surrounded, me and the kids. I thought we were dead meat for sure. But these guys saved us. They're good guys."

She looks at the boy. "How in God's name did you know about this place?"

He shrugs. "I know it sounds crazy but we found it in an old phone book, looked up Megan Lafferty. I knew you would get outta that place someday, I knew it. Some of our people, they tried to stage a raid on the hospital and rescue you but it went all to hell. That's why the place got infested. But even when the walkers took over, I knew you'd get out." Tommy pauses, clearing his throat. Lilly can see that he's fighting his own tears. "They told me I couldn't put the address of the store on the bridge—in the message I left for you—so I figured this was the next best thing. I knew you'd see it one day.

We sent search parties almost every day. When the walkers took over the hospital, one of our guys saw you with that old man. Then we lost you for a while." He wipes his eyes. "But we kept searching, kept coming to this place."

She cocks her head at him. "Store? You're hiding out in a store?"

He licks his lips, takes a deep breath, and then smiles, unable to find the words to describe his new home. At last, he merely says, "C'mon . . . I'll show you."

TWENTY-FIVE

Tommy leads them on horseback down Hemphill Street past the Georgia Tech student housing, modest cottages, and split-levels north of campus, an area now transformed into crumbling ruins and piles of cannibalized building materials. From the rear seats of the Escalade, Lilly can see that Tommy has not only gotten better at horsemanship over the last six months but has gotten even pluckier, tougher, more grown-up—if that's even possible. Now with hand signals and nimble turns, the fifteen-year-old leads the SUV east on Sixteenth Street. Soon the giant monolith appears over the tops of crooked pines.

Lilly leans forward and mutters under her breath, "Of course, *of course* . . . "

"Just wait," Musolino comments from the shotgun side as Boone slowly follows Tommy around the corner of Eighteenth Street and then down a gradual ramp. "You ain't seen *nothing* yet. This'll blow your mind."

Boone glances out his side mirror, looking for something behind them. "Trying to be discreet every time we come and go, trying to appear as though we're just passing by. You never know who's watching."

As they circle the gargantuan temple of modern retail, Lilly gazes up with more than a little awe at the trademark astro-blue and canary-yellow colors of the blocky five-story edifice. The neglect of the past few years shows on the surfaces—a patina of filth and weather clinging to the building like a malaise—but mostly the store is undamaged. The front façade on Sixteenth Street still has its familiar signage, each of its giant letters in one piece. Overturned shopping carts litter the alcoves and the parking lots are clogged with wreckage and wandering dead. Enormous hillocks of trash, spare parts, and scraps of lumber have drifted against the building, blocking the entrances, but Lilly wonders if these are defensive ploys. The place looks perfectly intact and perfectly inaccessible. She gapes at the windows. "Is there power?"

Boone and Musolino share a glance. Musolino smiles. "Them Swedes are thorough, you gotta give them that much."

Boone nods. "You want generators, we got generators . . . you want batteries, we got batteries."

"One thing, though." Musolino glances back at Lilly and gives her a look. "I hope you like Swedish meatballs."

They enter the building on foot, through the underground parking lot, after ditching the vehicle three blocks away and returning the horse to the makeshift stable hidden beneath the deserted Atlantic Square garage. They ascend a fire escape staircase to the first floor. For a brief instant, Lilly thinks of Dorothy in *The Wizard of Oz*, who steps outside her dreary farmhouse after the tumult of the tornado and finds herself crossing over into a Technicolor dreamworld.

Lilly takes her first step into the multihued wonderland of the first floor and practically loses her breath at the cornucopia spreading before her, untouched by the plague or looters, dusty perhaps, but still displayed in all its Day-Glo candy-colored shrink-wrapped glory: play sets, garden accessories, patio furniture, above-ground swimming pools, tents, sleeping bags, outdoor lighting, lawn mowers, tractors, ATVs, and shelf after shelf of smaller, unidentified seasonal products. The high ceiling is busy with girders and struts, and the color-coded moveable walls, floral-decorated childcare nooks, and cheerful international signage harken back to a simpler, gentler era of high-quality home furnishings at affordable prices.

"How could this still be here?" Lilly poses the question rhetorically to no one in particular. "How did this go unnoticed right in the middle of Atlanta?"

Tommy Dupree joins her, standing by her side, taking a deep breath before answering. "Trouble is, Lilly, it *did* get noticed. Lots of times."

"The boy's correct." Musolino approaches and stands behind Lilly, hands in his pockets, his voice lowering an octave, coarsening with sadness. "More than a few folks have died defending this place." He looks down. "Once in a great while we let new people in." He smiles. "Such as yourself."

Right then, Lilly notices other people in the room, keeping watch, guarding the place. A middle-aged man with an assault rifle strapped across his chest stands at the bottom of a frozen escalator. A thirty-something woman holding a double-barrel shotgun on her shoulder looks on from the alcove near the elevator. Others stand at key junctures, armed and ready to defend the castle. Suddenly, a sense of quiet martial law washes over Lilly. She gropes for words, overwhelmed by the place, dumbfounded by the mixed feelings of excitement, relief, and dread for what could easily come of this place if another group like Bryce's catches wind. She starts to put it into words when the room starts to spin, her vision blurs, and a gigantic stab of pain feels as though it's about to crack her head open.

She falls to her knees. She tries to speak and instead collapses.

Tommy and Musolino rush to her side, kneel by her, and feel her pulse. She doesn't pass out. But her head is so woozy from all the narcotics and pain and fatigue that all she can do is mutter, "I'm okay . . . I'm fine . . . just got a little light-headed, that's all."

"OH LORD HAVE MERCY THEY SAID IT WAS YOU!"

Lilly hears a familiar voice and twists around to see a portly individual rushing down the stationary steps of the escalator. Through her bleary vision, Lilly can barely make out the matronly figure in her do-rag and denim, jiggling all the way down the stairs to the first floor.

"Norma?"

Lilly collapses onto her back with a pained sigh, all the excitement taking its toll. In her daze, she sees the plump, cheerful, generous face of Norma Sutters floating above her, larger than life, like a parade float. "Oh thank the Lord, you made it!"

The plump woman reaches down and pulls Lilly into a tight embrace.

Lilly breathes in and savors the smell of chewing gum and the sweaty, musky scent of the woman. "Norma, thank God . . . I thought for sure we lost you."

"No such luck, girlfriend," Norma says with a sad little laugh. "Takes a lot more than that to take this old girl outta commission!"

"How did—?"

The sound of a familiar little squeal rings out from the top of the escalator, interrupting. Lilly recognizes the voice. She looks up at Norma, tears welling in her eyes. "Oh my God, is that—?"

Norma simply nods.

Lilly looks over her shoulder and sees the gaggle of children scuttling down the escalator steps. Bethany Dupree takes the lead, holding the baby in her arms. Her freckle-dusted face lit up with excitement, she wears a Beyoncé T-shirt under her OshKosh and rushes down the stairs clutching the infant, grinning from ear to ear. Lucas Dupree hurries along on her heels, struggling to keep up, his thatch of unruly chestnut hair still as cowlicked as ever. Behind him, jockeying for position, come the Slocum twins, followed by Jenny and Tyler Coogan, each of them aglow with excitement.

Rising to her feet, standing on wobbly knees, Lilly opens her arms and catches Bethany and the baby as they lurch into her arms on a nimbus of talcum and bubble gum.

The other kids arrive and slam into Lilly as though she were a backstop. Lilly wraps her arms around them for a sweaty, tearful group hug, which goes on for several euphoric moments, with Lilly trying futilely to hold in her emotions. Her tears track down her face, and she giggles, and for the first time in many days, her laughter is sober and joyous and real. She holds the children, and she softly speaks under her breath so that perhaps only Bethany can hear her. "Thank you, God . . . thank you."

The adults in the room—including Tommy—all begin to back away, giving a respectful amount of space for the homecoming.

That night, after getting medical attention in the nurse's department, and then having some of the freeze-dried fare found in the bowels of the cafeteria, Lilly personally puts the children to bed on the second floor, in the bedroom area of the home furnishings wing. Each child has personalized their own floor display, but tonight they all have an impromptu slumber party in Juvenile Furniture, where bunk beds are lined up two abreast, and interior decorators have accessorized each cubby hole with tasteful, fun, and nonthreatening posters of kittens and puppies and Ninja Turtles. Lilly reads them a story—*Where the Wild Things Are*—and leads them in prayer. Then she tucks each one in and leaves a desk lamp on. They fall fast asleep within minutes, far away from the cold wind and the unremitting drone of the dead.

Later, after many of the adults have retired to their own beds in their own corners of the home furnishings floor, Lilly has a drink with Norma and Tommy in the cafeteria near one of the tinted windows. They sample the Swedish glogg—a mixture of port wine, brandy, and spices—and they talk about the last six months. They each tell their stories, share the details of how they survived, mourn the loss of all their friends—Barbara, Jinx, Cooper, Miles—and most importantly, express their delight and gratitude for being together again. They go through an entire bottle of glogg, even allowing Tommy to tipple enough to get a decent buzz going. Lilly goes easy on the booze, still woozy from all the drugs and blood loss working through her system.

After a while, they realize it's time to get some sleep. They say their good nights, and Norma and Tommy promise Lilly that tomorrow will be a busy day. She'll meet all the inhabitants of the store, learn everybody's name, get oriented to the floor plan, learn the security protocols, get to know the provisions in the cafeteria, and visit all the departments from offices to textiles to organizational products to kitchens and appliances. Finally, Tommy staggers down the corridor to his bunk bed, leaving Norma and Lilly alone in the deserted cafeteria.

Lilly says good night and limps over to the window, gazing out at the dark city, the scattered fires here and there still glinting from lightning hits, and the low glow of methane giving off an almost medieval cast to the night. She can see the faint ocean of moving corpses like cancerous blood cells traversing the dark byways without purpose or destination. She hears Norma's voice speaking softly behind her.

"You okay?"

Lilly glances over her shoulder and sees the portly woman lingering, wringing her hands nervously. Lilly smiles and looks back out at the night. "I'm fine, Norma. Just gonna be a little restless until we get back to Woodbury."

The older woman comes closer, stands next to Lilly at the window, and lets out a sigh. "Honey, I don't mean to start something here but I don't think the boy made it clear what's going on."

Lilly looks at her. "Why do you say that? What's going on?"

Norma pauses, choosing her words carefully. "We're safe here, sweetie. Safe and we got food and fellowship . . . everything we need."

Lilly looks at her. "I don't get it. What are you saying to me?"

The big woman gives her a shrug. "I don't know, I guess I felt like we were done with Woodbury."

"What do you mean, you're just going to go ahead and leave David there?"

"David's a big boy, sweetie. David can take care of himself."

Lilly looks into her eyes. "Wait, you're telling me you're never going back to Woodbury?"

"Not while we got this place. And you shouldn't go back there either. It's not safe anymore. The towns are too dangerous now."

Lilly exhales a frustrated, anguished breath and goes back to the window to stare out at the primordial dark. She barely hears Norma's voice prodding her.

"You know I'm right, Lilly. These children don't want to go back there. They're terrified of the countryside. Don't drag them back there."

Lilly says nothing, just keeps staring out at the constellation of fires blemishing the dark, the shadowy tide of the dead constantly flowing.

"Promise me you'll think it over, honey. That's all I ask. Just give it some thought. Stay put for a while, give yourself a chance to heal."

Lilly doesn't respond. She can't think of anything to say. All she can do is continue gazing out at the night, the blackness of the dead city eternal, ceaseless, unremitting . . . silently calling to her.

extracts reading groups
competitions books new
discounts extracts extracts
competitions
books new events reading groups
events books extracts discounts
new titles reading groups
interviews
events extracts
discounts
events new
discounts extracts discounts
www.panmacmillan.com
extracts events reading groups
competitions books extracts new